MW01137164
SILVER LINING RANCH

LOVE'S SILVER LINING
Book 1 in the Silver Lining Ranch Series

Published by Julie Lessman, LLC

ASIN: B071K6ZQJH

Cover Design and Interior Format

LOVE'S SILVER LINING

SILVER LINING RANCH SERIES ~ BOOK ONE

JULIE LESSMAN

Acclaim for Julie Lessman

"Truly masterful plot twists ..."
—Romantic Times Book Reviews

"Readers who like heartwarming novels, such as those written by Debbie Macomber, are sure to enjoy this book."
—Booklist Online

"Julie is one of the best there is today at writing intensely passionate romance novels. Her ability to thread romance and longing, deception and forgiveness, and lots of humor are unparalleled by anyone else in the Christian market today."
—Rachel McRae of *LifeWay Stores*

"Julie Lessman's prose and character development is masterful."
—Church Libraries Magazine

AUTHOR ACCLAIM FOR JULIE LESSMAN

(authors listed alphabetically)

"With memorable characters and an effervescent plot that's as buoyant as it is entertaining, Dare to Love Again is Julie Lessman at her zestful best."
—Tamera Alexander, bestselling author of *A Lasting Impression* and *To Whisper Her Name*

"In a powerful and skillfully written novel, Lessman exposes raw human emotions, proving once again that it's through our greatest pain that God can lead us to our true heart, revealed and restored. Thoroughly enthralling!"
—Maggie Brendan, author of the *Heart of the West* and The Blue Willow Brides series

"Julie Lessman brings all her passion for romance rooted in her passion for God to A Heart Revealed. Emma Malloy is her finest heroine yet. These characters, with their own personal struggles and the ignited flame of an impossible love, fill the pages of this powerful, passionate, fast-paced romance."
—Mary Connealy, bestselling author of the *Lassoed in Texas, Montana Marriages, Trouble in Texas, and* Wild at Heart series

"What an interesting mix of characters. Rather than a single boy-meets-girl romance, Julie Lessman's latest novel takes readers on an emotional roller coaster with

several couples—some married, some yearning to be married—as they seek to embrace love, honor the Lord, and uncover a dark truth that's been hidden for a decade. Readers who long for passion in their love stories will find it in abundance here!"
—Liz Curtis Higgs, bestselling author of *Thorn in My Heart*

"Readers will not be able to part with these characters come 'The End."
—Laura Frantz, award-winning author of *Love's Reckoning*

"With an artist's brushstroke, Julie Lessman creates another masterpiece filled with family and love and passion. Love at Any Cost will not only soothe your soul, but it will make you laugh, stir your heart, and release a sigh of satisfaction when you turn the last page."
—MaryLu Tyndall, bestselling author of *Veil of Pearls*

SILVER LINING RANCH SERIES
CHARACTERS FOR
LOVE'S SILVER LINING

THE HEROINE:
Margaret Rose "Maggie" Mullaney: Newly graduated nurse from New York, suffragette, and
goddaughter/Aunt of secondary heroine, Libby O'Shea.

THE SECONDARY HEROINE:
Libby "Libby" Margaret O'Shea: Vassar teacher, suffragette, daughter of Maeve and Aiden O'Shea, and heroine from series prequel novel, For Love of Liberty.

THE HERO:
Brendan Zachery "Blaze" Donovan: Nephew of Finn McShane, older brother to Dash, Sheridan, and Shaylee, and foreman of Silver Lining Ranch.

THE SECONDARY HERO:
Griffin Alexander "Finn" McShane: Owner of the Silver Lining Ranch and Silver Mine, uncle to the hero, Blaze Donovan, and Sheridan, Shaylee, and Dash Donovan, and hero from series prequel novel, For Love of Liberty.

THE REST OF THE CAST:
Dashiell "Dash" Donovan: Brother to Blaze, Sheridan, and Shaylee, nephew of Finn McShane.

Sheridan Marie Donovan: Sister of Blaze, Dash, and Shaylee, niece of Finn McShane.

Shaylee Ann Donovan: Sister of Blaze, Dash, and Sheridan, niece of Finn McShane.
Jake (Sully) Sullivan: Blaze Donovan's best friend, close friend of

the family, and cowhand

Mrs. Poppy: A Pastor's widow and mentor to Finn McShane and Libby O'Shea.

Maeve O'Shea: Libby's mother.

Aiden O'Shea: Libby's father and banker in Virginia City.
Rachel Dixon: Blaze Donovan's girlfriend and saloon girl at the Ponderosa Saloon.

Chanel Monroe: Saloon girl at the Ponderosa Saloon.

Jo Beth Templeton: Finn's former girlfriend and daughter of Finn's political opponent, George Templeton.

Abigail Grace Mitchell: Nurse at St. Mary Louise Hospital and heroine's friend.

Andrea Jo Stephens: Nurse at St. Mary Louise Hospital and heroine's friend.

Gertie: The O'Shea's cook and maid.

Angus: Finn's cowhand cook.

Connie Michele Edwards: Friend of hero's sister, Sheridan Donovan.

Milo Parks: Finn McShane's best friend.

John Piper: Finn McShane's friend and political advocate, owner of Piper's Opera House.

Sister "Fred" Frederica: Administrator of St. Mary Louise Hospital.

Donald Raymond Turley, Sr.: Manager of The Gold Hill Hotel.

DEDICATION

To my dear friend and author extraordinaire, Mary Connealy—whose "Romantic Comedy with Cowboys" historical romance inspired me in this Western series.
Thanks, Mary, for always putting a smile on my face and a sigh on my lips.

And

To two of my dearest reader friends for whom I've named characters in my books—
Gabriella Dawn Smith and Casey Miranda Herringshaw—I am rejoicing that our God has blessed you both with Godly heroes of your own!

A threefold cord is not quickly broken.
—Ecclesiastes 4:9-12

CHAPTER ONE

Virginia City, Nevada,
May 1885

SWEET CHORUS OF ANGELS—PINCH ME! Palms to the windowsill, twenty-two-year-old Maggie Mullaney leaned out the back window of St. Mary Louise Hospital's hallway, drinking in the heady scent of freedom and pine. For the first time since she'd fled New York with Aunt Libby—and the sham marriage arranged by her stepfather—Maggie felt her ribcage expand in a sense of relief as wide and welcoming as the Sierra Nevada Mountains.

Breathing in the crisp, clean air of the Virginia Mountains that towered over Virginia City, she felt almost giddy, a sense of anticipation bubbling through her like the brook that gurgled below. *Imagine*—to practice nursing in one of the most renowned medical facilities in the country! Unleashing a contented sigh, she scanned the cloud-dappled sky with a heart of thanksgiving and a truly grateful smile. *Thank you, Lord, that I'll be serving the needs of mankind*—her smile crooked off-center—*instead of the needs of one man!*

"Psst … ma'am … uh, I could sure use your help."

A gasp caught in Maggie's throat as she lurched back inside the window, almost bumping her head at the sight of a bandaged cowboy peeking out of the stairwell. Her jaw dropped.

And not just any cowboy.

A *near-naked*, bandaged cowboy.

She swallowed hard, eyes circled in shock as she scanned from a well-worn Stetson down a bare, sculpted torso partially swathed in gauze.

A very muscular, *handsome*, near-naked cowboy.

Too stunned to avert her gaze, she was mortified to discover that her eyes had a mind of their own. Before she could look away, they scanned down a sheet awkwardly wrapped around slim hips, past bunched material to powerful legs attached to mammoth bare feet. Near faint, she jerked her gaze back up to a crooked smile that literally stuttered her pulse.

Cheeks pulsing with heat, she immediately slapped a hand to her eyes, quite certain that none of the patients she'd treated at the Bellvue School of Nursing ever looked like the specimen before her.

"Uh, I realize this is a shock, ma'am …," his low voice began, the barest hint of a smile lending a husky tease to his tone.

Shock? Maggie plastered another hand to her face, unable to dispel the image of brawn now branded in her brain. For the love of Florence Nightingale, this went well beyond shock to downright indecent!

"… but I'd be much obliged if you'd retrieve my clothes, boots, and holster from the nurses' station, so I can go home, ma'am, avoiding scaring anymore unsuspecting young ladies such as yourself."

Maggie squeezed her eyelids shut behind her hands, pretty sure one "unsuspecting young lady" was already scarred for life.

"Uh … miss?"

Swallowing the lump in her throat, Maggie inched a finger up to peek through her hand, mentally berating herself for allowing this man to unnerve her. For pity's sake, he was a patient and this *was* a hospital, and for the love of all that was compassionate and kind, *she* was a nurse. Or would be as soon as Sister Frederica finished her meeting with the staff and called her in for an interview.

He gave a sharp nod toward the nurses' station down the hall, and the action tumbled several sun-streaked curls onto his forehead while two deep dimples perfectly framed a little-boy grin. "Sister Fred tucked my things under the counter for safekeeping, but as I'm sure you can understand, I'm a mite embarrassed to parade down the hall like this …" Sapphire-blue eyes held her captive, their playful twinkle all but sapping the strength from her limbs. His easy smile coaxed, joining forces with a husky whisper that seemed to slide over her like melted butter. "So, if you wouldn't mind, pretty lady, I'd be forever in your debt …"

Maggie froze. *Pretty lady?* A shiver skated her spine while warning bells pealed wildly in her head, the sound of those two words severing the spell of the man before her faster than a physician's scalpel. The last person who had called her that had been David, her so-called fiancé, a society playboy with an insatiable eye for the ladies. A rogue she couldn't trust. Her eyes narrowed.

Not unlike the half-naked, bandaged cowboy smiling at her now.

With a forced square of shoulders, Maggie lifted her chin to focus only on the man's face, which was difficult enough given a perfectly chiseled jaw that sported a dangerous shadow of bristle. Quivering hands clasped at her waist, she managed a strained smile. "Why, I'll be happy to fetch your things, Mr. …."

"Donovan—Blaze Donovan, ma'am," he said with a flash of beautiful teeth that nearly buckled her at the knees. The blue eyes sheathed halfway to leisurely study her, lingering on her lips long enough to parch any moisture in her throat. "And you are …?"

"M-Maggie … uh, Mullaney," she stuttered, desperate

to get this man clothed and as far away from her as he could possibly get. She struggled to project a professional air, head tipped in assessment. "I assume you are a patient, Mr. Donovan, who has yet to be discharged?"

"No, I've been discharged," he said quickly, a flare of panic in those deadly blue eyes that caused her lips to twitch in a near smile. "Sister Fred said I could go home, but she has most of the nurses in a meeting right now, so I guess they plum forgot to bring me my things."

"I see." Nodding slowly, she pivoted to make her way down the hall. "Well, I believe I saw an elderly sister at the desk, so I'll be happy to check …"

"*No!*"

She screeched to a stop, her suspicions confirmed. With a slow turn of her head, she peered over her shoulder, the sheepish smile he gave her downright shameless. "I mean, no need to bother her, Miss Maggie," he said with a casual shrug of massive shoulders, rugged hands pinched as white as the sheet at his waist, "if you'll just discreetly snatch my clothes, boots, and gun, I'll be on my way."

She spun on her heel to face him with an arch of her brow. "You haven't been discharged yet, Mr. Donovan, have you?"

"Why, of course I have, ma'am," he said with an easy drawl she'd wager would have gotten him far more than his clothes from every nurse on the floor. "And I'd be fully clothed and walking out of here right now if the nurses were around, you have my word."

A smile twitched at the edge of her lips. *Oh, no doubt about that!*

Offering an almost shy duck of his head, he cuffed the back of his neck with a bulge of a bicep that slackened her mouth, masculinity oozing out of every pore of the man's half-naked body. "So, if you don't mind, ma'am, I surely would appreciate my clothes."

Maggie stared, in absolute awe of the raw magnetism

he seemed to possess, a draw obviously detrimental to all women given the wild racing of her own pulse. Shaking off the pull, she expelled a quiet sigh, peering up with a sympathy she truly felt in her heart. "As much as I'd like to, Mr. Donovan, I'm concerned for your well-being, so I really think it's best if you wait to talk to Sister Frederica."

The roguish air vanished in the hard clamp of his jaw. "Look, lady, I've been pushed and prodded in this sick-man's jail for over 48 hours now, and I'm going home whether you give me my things or not. So, I'm asking you to save us both a whole lot of humiliation and just give me my dad-burned clothes."

Maggie bit hard on her lip, desperate to thwart the grin that just ached to break free. But the sight of a near-naked, bandaged rogue with a tic in his temple was too good to resist, and with a sweep of her hand toward the end of the hall, she gave him a mischievous smile. "I assure you, Mr. Donovan, the humiliation will be all yours."

The blue eyes narrowed to slits of sapphire, and with a hard jerk of the sheet at his waist, he bolted past her, luring a giggle from her mouth when his bunched bedclothes whooshed by in a growl. "Thanks a lot, lady," he muttered, bare feet slapping against the wood hallway.

"Mr. Donovan, wait!" Feeling a wee bit guilty, Maggie gave chase, but the damage was already done the moment he stormed into the nurses' station. People gawked and stared in the crowded waiting room near the front door while he rifled through cabinet after cabinet, jolting a poor elderly sister out of a catnap on the counter.

"Where are my clothes?" he hissed, terrorizing the sweet old nun who darted away with far more speed than Maggie would have credited her, disappearing into the meeting room where Sister Frederica held court.

"Mr. Donovan, please!" Maggie rushed around the nurses' station, desperate to calm the man down. "You're making a scene."

He paused midway through gutting a drawer, the fire in his eyes singeing her to the spot while an entire waiting room looked on. "No, Miss Mullaney, *you're* the one who's made the scene by refusing a totally innocent request."

Her chin lashed up. "True innocence is generally fully clothed, Mr. Donovan," she said with a jut of her brow, determined that this swaddled Lothario would not pin any blame on her. "*And* possesses far more patience—not to mention clothing—than you appear to own at the moment."

Cauterizing her with a truly scorching look, he chose to ignore her while tearing through another two cabinets, linens and medical paraphernalia flying through the air.

"Brendan Zachery Donovan—*halt!*" Everything froze mid-air except the linens when Sister Frederica's booming voice paralyzed Maggie and every other living thing on the first floor.

He spun around to do battle like a patched-up Roman, but the sheet flaring around his straddled legs managed to steal a bit of his thunder. "Where-are-my-clothes?" he bit out, the sound as hard as the cut of his jaw.

"Safe and sound, Mr. Donovan," Sister Frederica said in an equally clipped tone, circling the counter with an amazing amount of grace given her wide girth. She slapped a large clipboard down on the counter to face him head-on, and Maggie stifled a grin when the sheet-clad Romeo took a step back. "Which is more than I can say for you, young man, if you don't get your carcass back to your room this instant."

He had the audacity to lean in, sheet cinched high. "Get this and get it good, Sister Fred. I am *not* going back to that cage, so unless you want me to continue making a spectacle of myself in your fine hospital here, I suggest you return my clothes to me right *now*."

Maggie pursed her lips to thwart a chuckle when Sister Frederica's intimidation ramped up with a fold of burly arms, her black habit expanding and contracting with a loud huff of air. "Don't you threaten me, young man. I wear a cornette headdress referred to as goose flaps in this town, so 'spectacles' hold no sway with me." Checking the watch pinned to her white bib, she invaded his space, the starched flaps of her white cornette jerking up along with her head to sear him with a fearsome glare. Despite merely coming to his mid-chest—or mid-gauze as it were—she poked a thick finger in obvious warning. "Now I promised your uncle you would get the rest and care you need to heal properly, so if you plan on leaving my watch, Mr. Donovan, I assure you most wholeheartedly—it will be *without* your clothes."

One of the nurses tittered, and the scoundrel wasted no time in homing in on the poor girl with a perilous smile, eyes and tone softening considerably. "Do you know where my clothes are, Cassie?" he asked quietly, his tender smile assuring her she was the only woman in the room.

Honeyed curls bobbed in consent, and his smile lit up like one of those mirrored lamps used in the operating rooms of Bellvue, eyes sparkling more than the cobalt poison bottles lining its shelves. Maggie smothered a grunt.

And just as toxic.

"Well, then, I'd sure love to take you out for a steak dinner tonight, Cass, at the Gold Hill Hotel if you like. All I need is for you to tell me where my clothes are, darlin', and I'll even get them myself."

Maggie watched in total fascination as the girl—a petite blonde with longing in her eyes—nearly swayed on her feet, eyes locked with Donovan's as if he were a snake charmer instead of a snake. Maggie suppressed a second grunt.

A misnomer if ever there was.

"Cassie?" he whispered, and the sound actually fluttered Maggie's own stomach, much to her dismay, so she knew poor Cassie had to be sucked under his spell. The girl wet her lips as if she could taste the steak in question—or the man offering it—then glanced at Sister Frederica to plead his case.

Before poor Cassie could even utter a word, Sister withered her with a scowl so potent, it eradicated every smile in the room. "Trust me, Cassandra, I am saving you a lot of heartbreak when I say …" Thunderous dark brows piled low into a threat. "The bedpans on floors three and four need attending, so I suggest you begin right now."

Thwack! Maggie startled when Donovan's fist bludgeoned the counter. "That is pure, unadulterated blackmail, Sister, and you know it!"

"Not at all, Mr. Donovan," Sister said in an unwavering tone, "there is nothing 'pure' about it, much like the bribe you offered that poor girl, I might add." She jutted her chins—all three of them—in challenge.

Beads of sweat glazed the man's brow as his desperate gaze darted from face to face, the fail-proof smile appearing about to crack. "A five-dollar gold piece to anyone who delivers my clothes, boots, and gun," he rasped, voice hoarse with desperation, "and an evening out I promise you will never forget."

"My, what an incredibly generous offer, Mr. Donovan," Sister said with a stony smile, one thick brow rising in question as she surveyed her staff. "Although I doubt a five-dollar gold piece can provide the ongoing security of a salary, despite the pleasure of your company." Everyone flinched when she clapped her hands loudly, shooing the rest of the nurses back to their jobs. "Back to work, ladies. I assure you Mr. Donovan will soon be back in your charge."

"The devil I will," he muttered, retying the sheet around his waist with a hard jerk of the corners. "Out of my way, Sister." Shoving past the perfectly calm nun, he stomped around the counter and strode straight for the front door, still ridiculously handsome in nothing more than gauze and lumpy cotton.

"And just where do you think you're going?" Sister Frederica demanded, bustling around the counter to keep up with the cowboy's long-legged stride. "You cannot leave here in that state of undress!"

"Watch me," he groused over his shoulder, ignoring an elderly woman who fainted dead out as he passed.

"You come back here right this instant, young man," she called, the loud boom of her voice apparently less effective the closer he got to the door. "Your dressings need to be changed twice daily and medication applied to avoid infection. And *you* need to rest."

"I don't have time to rest—I have work to do," he growled. Almost knocking a man down, he slammed through the front double doors to fly down the steps like a specter, his sheet—and any pride he may have had—blowing in the wind.

CHAPTER TWO

THE DOUBLE DOORS BANGED CLOSED, and Sister shook her head in apparent dismay, the flaps of her cornette in obvious agreement. She exhaled a noisy sigh. "A mule with second-degree burns," she muttered before issuing orders to one of the nuns to take smelling salts to the unconscious woman. She turned to make her way back to Maggie, who stood wide-eyed at the counter.

"Goodness, is he going to be all right?" Maggie asked, legitimate concern lacing her tone.

Sister's answering chuckle managed to escape from a mouth pursed in a tight-lipped scowl. Snatching her clipboard up, the nun made a beeline for her office, flicking impatient fingers behind her in a directive for Maggie to follow. "Well, the burns will eventually heal, Miss Mullaney, but I'm afraid the pig-headed obstinacy is here to stay."

She nodded to a row of wooden chairs parked in front of her desk and then closed the door as soon as Maggie took a seat. "Nonetheless, a good dose of humility via a traipse through town in a sheet will do that boy good." She dropped into her own chair with a groan, eyes lidded with heavy folds of skin that suddenly narrowed as if weighing her down. "A mite too cocky for his own good, Miss Mullaney, and in case you haven't noticed, a wee bit too handsome for it too. Seems to think he can charm anything in a skirt, so you best be on your guard."

Blood blasted Maggie's cheeks and her only defense was the thrust of her chin. "I assure you, Sister Frederica, that type of man holds absolutely no appeal to me whatsoever."

The edge of Sister's lip quirked, creating a rather endearing dimple to emerge in her overly generous cheek. "And I assure *you*, Miss Mullaney, that *that* type of man has stolen the affection of every female from here to Carson City. And that was *before* he risked his life to save one ofVirginia City's most celebrated citizens from a fire over a week ago." She lowered her head, piercing black eyes pinning Maggie to the chair. "Liberty O'Shea's father," she emphasized, "which is why I believe you're here in the first place?"

Maggie nodded, never more grateful for Liberty O'Shea, her mother's dearest friend, who had just rescued Maggie from a fate—and marriage—worse than death. "Yes, you see, Aunt Libby—" She paused, feeling the necessity to explain. "Well, she's not my aunt, of course, but I've always called her that because she's my godmother and was my mother's best friend. At any rate, she asked me to come with her after she received the awful telegram about her father's heart attack and her parent's house burning down. So, since I attended Bellvue School of Nursing, we both felt that St. Mary Louise Hospital might very well be the ideal place to apply for a job."

"Indeed." Sister squeaked back in her chair, meaty hands clasped over a formidable stomach. "I've already researched your credentials, Miss Mullaney, when Miss O'Shea telegrammed her request that I interview you, and her recommendation goes a long way in this town. So, I'm well aware you are more than qualified from a technical standpoint." She hesitated, lips compressed so much, they seemed to disappear altogether. "My concern would be more along the emotional risks involved, given your youth and naïveté."

Maggie blinked, somewhat taken aback at Sister's remark. "I don't understand, Sister. I'm twenty-two years old—that hardly qualifies as either young or naive."

"Perhaps not in New York, Miss Mullaney, but this is Virginia City, where there are over one hundred saloons, give or take a few, within a very small radius. That means a lot of what we see in this hospital has to do with a very rowdy and very lascivious male component." She lifted in her chair ever so slightly to assess Maggie's House of Worth coral silk dress, from its voluminous skirts to its tightly fitted bodice. Her gaze instantly flicked up to Maggie's chestnut hair, which she'd jumbled on top of her head in a cluster of ringlets and a sweep of soft bangs. A weary sigh escaped her lips. Sagging back in her chair, she studied Maggie through slatted eyes that held a trace of a twinkle. "I don't suppose you'd be willing to wear a sack?"

Relief coursed through Maggie's veins, assuring her she would do whatever it took to acquire this position. "Absolutely," she said without hesitation, "I would be more than willing to wear whatever you like, Sister, including a gunny sack."

Sister's mouth curled into a dry smile. "Over your head?"

Maggie stilled, all blood ceasing to flow until she realized Sister Frederica was joking. Her face flushed so hot, she was certain she resembled a saloon girl with rouge on her cheeks.

Wonderful. I should fit right in.

Sister hovered over her desk with a squeak of her chair, hands clasped and thick brows knit low as she bent to meet Maggie eye to eye. "Frankly, Miss Mullaney, I'm a wee bit worried you can't handle the element here. Suppose you tell me why I should hire an innocent like you, merely to expose you to one of the most sinful cities in this nation?"

With everything in her, Maggie strove to remain calm despite the awful hammering in her chest, knowing full well that the fate of her future lay in this woman's hands. Silently drawing in a deep swell of air, she met Sister's gaze head-on, a slow smile wending its way across her lips at the memory of a near-naked cowboy decorated in cotton and gauze. She arched a brow. "Because the arranged engagement I fled from, Sister, was to a man just like your bandaged cowboy and all womanizers of his ilk. Rest assured I have no interest in men like that or really any men at all at the moment." She sat straight up in the chair, shoulders back and lips firm, unflinching as she locked gazes with a woman she'd come to respect in mere minutes. "In fact, I find myself greatly inspired by women like Florence Nightingale and you, Sister, wondering if perhaps my calling isn't to remain single altogether."

Pride swelled in her chest as she thought of her godmother, Liberty O'Shea. Aunt Libby was a single woman who, up until her engagement to a professor at Vassar last month, had chosen service over servitude to a man, just like Maggie hoped to do. The thought lifted her chin with resolve as she gave the nun a bright smile. "And to be frank, Sister Frederica, I've been greatly influenced by brilliant career women like my Aunt Libby, in whose steps I hope to follow, opting for mercy to many rather than marriage to just one."

A smile flickered at the corners of Sister's mouth. "Which I assure you will be more than a challenge in a city where the number of men far exceed the number of women, my dear." She paused, her eyes narrowing in scrutiny. "Then may I assume that our 'near-naked cowboy' had no effect on you whatsoever?"

Some of Maggie's bravado faltered a bit when blood coursed into her cheeks, but she ignored it with an unyielding square of her shoulders. "I won't lie to you, Sister. Mr. Donovan does have a certain"—she swallowed hard—"charm, I suppose, but I quickly proved to myself and to him that I am immune."

"And how exactly did you do that, young lady?" Sister asked, forehead in a squint.

Maggie nibbled at the edge of her smile, the memory

warming her eyes to a twinkle. "Well, you see, he was hiding in the stairwell at the end of the hall when I went to look out the window, and the poor man tried every tactic in the book to coerce me into retrieving his clothes." She lifted a hand, ticking off Mr. Donovan's methods in a sing-song manner. "Flirting, teasing, begging, guilt, seduction ..."

"Pardon me?" Sister jutted a brow.

Maggie's smile took a twist. "He flexed a bicep," she explained with a dusting of heat in her cheeks, adamant that no cowboy—half-naked or otherwise—would ever get past her defenses.

The nun's low, throaty chuckle surprised her, and the satisfied grin on Sister's face immediately unraveled any knots in Maggie's stomach. "Well, young lady, you may be just what I'm looking for, then, as long as you can steer clear of handsome heartbreakers like our Mr. Donovan. But it won't be easy. There are a number of handsome rakes in this town who have proven to be a menace to the female society, and I assure you, our Mr. Donovan is right at the top."

"And why is that?" Maggie wanted to know. Yes, no doubt the rogue was one of the finest looking examples of manhood Maggie had ever seen, but it would take a whole lot more than a chiseled face and body to turn her head.

"Because, my dear, Brendan Donovan is not only handsome and charming to a fault, but he is also the foreman for his uncle's Silver Lining Ranch as well, which he has helped parlay into the largest, most profitable ranch in all of Nevada."

Maggie swallowed. *All right, a hardworking example of manhood on top of handsome and charming. But still, it wasn't enough.*

"And then, of course," Sister continued, an unmistakable look of affection flitting across the old nun's face, "he's utterly devoted to his family, a veritable hawk when it comes to watching over his two little sisters. And, I might add, a staunch mentor for his younger brother who works in a bar, much to his uncle's disdain."

"His mentor?" Maggie's smile tipped. "In drinking and womanizing, no doubt?"

Sister sighed. "Regrettably, you're correct about the womanizing, but the man has never touched a drop of alcohol as far as I know. Which is why he's so dangerous to the young ladies of Virginia City. Especially since he scaled a burning staircase to save little Frannie after rescuing both Liberty's mother and their housekeeper, who were asleep in their rooms."

"No!" Maggie could do nothing but gape, absently wondering if a cowboy could be canonized. "Please tell me the child wasn't hurt!"

Sister's mouth took a tilt. "A ferret, actually, and no, Maeve's beloved pet came through unscathed, which is more than I can say for Mr. Donovan. The poor man incurred several nasty nips from the ferret in addition to second-degree burns." The twitch of Sister's lips hinted at humor. "A *female* ferret, of course, lending credence to the saying, "Hell hath no fury like a woman scorned." She gave Maggie a wink. "Or in this case, a ferret mourned."

Maggie couldn't help it—she grinned.

Sister sighed. "No, there's no question about it. Brendan Donovan is a hero with a heart of gold," Sister continued with a shake of her head, "but with more stubbornness in his veins than silver in the Comstock." She bent in, smile dry. "Ironically, he's also one of my top volunteers at both our school and orphanage. Not only does he lend his carpentry skills when needed, but he is also a mentor for many of our young male orphans. He and several of his cowhands actually train a good many of them almost every Sunday at his ranch, teaching them how to ride and become future ranch hands for his uncle."

Another heavy sigh deflated the bib of her habit as she

pierced Maggie with a pointed look. "Regrettably, even a hero has flaws, my dear, and Mr. Donovan is no different because trust me—they don't call him 'Blaze' for nothing. He has a reputation for setting hearts on fire, and as the town's confirmed bachelor, I'm afraid he's left a lot of charred ruins in his wake."

Sister lumbered to her feet and extended a hand, which Maggie instantly took, the nun's warm and welcoming palm flooding her with a sense of safety and peace. "Which means, young lady, I am going to take a chance on you if you can safely avoid Mr. Donovan and any rogues like him, understood?"

"Oh, yes, ma'am," Maggie breathed, hardly able to believe she had landed her very first job!

"Good." Sister toddled around the desk and gave Maggie's arm an affectionate squeeze. "You start on Monday, Miss Mullaney, and your job will be to put those impressive skills to work on behalf of our poor wounded. And *my* job, my dear," she said with an outrageous wink that took Maggie completely by surprise, "is to keep *you* from being one."

CHAPTER THREE

"WHOOO-EEE! WHO KNEW YOU HAD such purty legs?"

Glaring at his brother, Blaze stormed past the barn on his uncle's Silver Lining Ranch, refusing to dignify Dash's remark with a response.

Not that he had much dignity in a sheet.

"Hey, Boss, your tail's a draggin'," his best friend, Jake, called from the corral, setting off a round of laughter from the other cowhands when Blaze yanked the trailing sheet up off the ground. Blaze ignored them all, from the cowboys perched atop the fence watching a rough rider break a cow pony, to his brother and best friend who now dogged his bare heels. Jaw stiff, he thundered up the wooden steps to the covered porch of Uncle Finn's sprawling log ranch house, stomping his feet as loudly as he could without boots.

With Jake and Dash following, Blaze strode into the two-story log house. The carved oak door—emblazoned with the ranch brand, Bar SLR—ricocheted off the wall with a loud bang, and Dash shook his head. "When you gonna learn not to tangle with Sister Fred, Blaze? Everybody knows she's more stubborn than you."

"Yeah?" Blaze jerked his sheet up as he took the steps of the polished log staircase two at a time. He paused on the landing that overlooked a gleaming hardwood entryway with a vibrant Navajo rug and thumped a fist to his chest, glaring down at his brother and Jake. "Well, she may run that blasted hospital, but she doesn't run me."

Nudging his hat back, Jake laughed, the sound rising to the vaulted ceiling along with the steam from Blaze's ears. "Except out of town," he said with a wide grin, pushing the door closed. "What, you couldn't bribe no pretty lady to smuggle your clothes and holster out under Sister Fred's nose?" An errant strand of black-brown hair tumbled over his forehead as he reseated his hat, his deep tan aided by olive skin from his Black Irish heritage. "You must've lost your touch."

"Along with his clothes," Dash said with a chuckle, leaning on the newel post as he grinned at his brother."

Blaze grunted, the memory of one pretty lady, in particular steeling his jaw. All this dad-burned humiliation could have been avoided if one Miss High-and-Mighty Maggie Mullaney had just done as he asked. But, no, she had to toe Sister Fred's proverbial line, completely ignoring the charm he'd put forth to win her favor. At first, he'd thought he'd had her, the soft blush in her cheeks and a daze in those golden-brown eyes as she tipped a head of the glossiest chestnut curls he'd ever seen. But then she'd snapped into Sister Fred mode so fast, he swore they were related. His mouth compressed. Except for that red silk dress that hugged a curvy form no nun or respectable woman should have. Why, he'd even been a bit smitten himself, lavishing her with a potent smile while he called her a pretty lady, a true compliment that would make most women swoon. He grunted again. Pretty lady, indeed.

Pretty mule-headed.

His uncle, Finn McShane, suddenly appeared in the archway of his study, hand on the brass knob of the door that had been closed, indicating Blaze had disrupted his work. "What the devil are you doing home so soon?"

A railroad-man-turned-rancher who'd made it big in Nevada's silver heyday, Finn McShane was one of the most respected men in Virginia City and Blaze's hero. Without him, Blaze and his younger brother and two little sisters would have been orphans in Cripple Creek, Colorado, likely starving to death after their pa was killed in a mining accident and their ma died in childbirth. Finn had brought them home to his Silver Lining cattle ranch, and Blaze would do just about anything for his uncle. *Except embrace his faith*, he supposed, one of the few rubs in their relationship.

His uncle stared him down, hip propped to the door jamb and arms in a loose fold. "Sister Fred said those burns needed close attention for another day or two."

Blaze hiked his sheet up several inches, along with his jaw. "She changed her mind."

The hint of a smile edged his uncle's mouth. "Well, it's a good look for you, Blaze," he said with a leisurely drawl, "especially since you're off work detail for the next two days."

True to his name, Blaze's temper flashed hot. "The devil I am! I already lost pert near a full week, Uncle Finn, and we still have miles of fencing to attend to on the south forty."

Mouth compressed, Finn ambled to the burnished ponderosa pine coat rack Blaze carved for him one Christmas, plucking his Stetson off a brass hook with his bandaged right hand. "I'm not above hiding your clothes like Sister Fred, son, so don't tempt me." Positioning his hat on dark sable hair barely sprinkled with silver, he peered up beneath the wide rim. Bourbon-brown eyes pinned Blaze to the landing with a smile as flat as Blaze's mood. He nodded toward his study. "Got a mountain of paperwork in there that needs attention, more than enough to keep you busy for a few days—"

Blaze slammed his fist on the knotty pine railing. "Blame it all, Uncle Finn, I need ex-ercise—"

"And *I* need help, Bren," Finn interrupted in a firm

tone, the use of Blaze's Christian name underscoring the authority of his statement. His uncle's pointed look, laced with both affection and sympathy, held more than a little warning. "You and I both lost time this week with injuries sustained from rescuing the O'Shea's …" He tried to flex his right hand, but the bandage was too thick and lumpy to allow much movement. His mouth quirked as he glanced back up. "And although you took the brunt of the heat, son, this blasted hand is slowing me down considerably with the books, so I sure could use some help. Especially since I'm off to see Aiden at the hospital to offer him and Maeve lodging till their home can be rebuilt." A grin tugged as he gave Blaze a wink. "But, don't worry—I'll sneak your boots and clothes out when Sister Fred's not looking."

Lips in a twist, Blaze huffed out a healthy dose of frustration, knowing full well he would do whatever his uncle asked. "The blamed woman probably doused 'em with holy water to mend my evil ways," he groused.

"One can only hope." Finn chuckled as he ambled over to the base of the steps to drape an arm over Dash's shoulder. "Foreman or no, Dash, if he steps one foot into a barn or pasture the next two days, you have my permission to hogtie him to a rocking chair on the front porch. With a quick tap of his nephew's shoulder, he peered up to the top landing, hand on the rough-hewn newel post while he shouted for Blaze's sister at the top of his lungs. "Sheridan Marie? Get your pretty hide down here, young lady."

Blaze's low groan was drowned out by the slam of a door followed by the clatter of boots in the upstairs hallway. Blaze's seventeen-year-old sister Sheridan appeared at the top of the steps in a pair of blue jeans and a pale blue blouse the exact shade of her eyes. "Yes, Uncle Finn?" Her gaze instantly lighted on Jake with a shy smile she'd reserved for Blaze's best friend since she'd been knee-high to a prairie dog. "Why, hello, Jake."

Jake smiled and tipped his hat, his dark eyes twinkling. "Half Pint."

Sheridan stood up as straight and tall as her slight five-foot-two height would allow, the square of her shoulders confirming she didn't appreciate Jake's refusal to see her as a woman. But with a twelve-year age difference, Blaze was grateful the only thing Jake saw when he looked at Sheridan was that lovesick little girl who used to follow him and Blaze around.

Finn expelled a weary sigh, and Blaze knew his uncle's concern over Sheridan's obsession with "falling in love" was equal to his own. It had always been so easy to put off her innocent longing for romance when she was no bigger than a mite, inviting them to her doll weddings every other week. But now that she was growing into a woman, Blaze was downright uncomfortable with the notion of any man sparkin' his sister.

Even a best friend.

Nudging his hat up a fraction of an inch, Finn offered Sheridan a patient smile, his affection for his niece obvious from his gentle tone. "Sweetheart, I'll need you to keep an eye on your brother so he doesn't leave the house while I'm visiting Mr. O'Shea at the hospital, all right?"

Blaze sagged over the railing with another groan, drawing a surprised gasp from his sister, who obviously hadn't seen him yet.

"Blaze?" She skittered down to the landing to give him a hug, voice soft with concern. "What are you doing home already? Sister Fred said it wouldn't be till Saturday." Her eyes grew when she finally noticed the sheet, fingers to her mouth to cover a grin. "Uh-oh … looks like Sister Fred's missing some linens …"

"And your brother a whole lot of sense," Finn said with a heavy sigh, "so I'll need you to tend to his dressing if you will, applying some aloe before replacing it with clean gauze. Then I'll ask Sister Fred for any additional supplies you might need."

"Ha! Like a length of rope to tie him down." Dash shot Sheridan a wink that earned him a giggle.

"Or to string him up if I hear he's stepped foot out of this house," Finn said with a thin-lipped smile while he sauntered toward the door.

"Uncle Finn—do you think Mr. and Mrs. O'Shea will accept your offer to move in with us?" Sheridan asked, eyes round with excitement over the prospect of another female in a house that harbored two brothers, an uncle, a male border collie, and one very crusty chuck-wagon cowboy named Angus who served as housekeeper and cook.

Blaze's heart cramped at the sound of hope in his sister's voice, well aware that both Sheridan and their thirteen-year-old sister Shaylee needed a woman's touch in their lives. Sheridan had been only four years old and Shaylee a newborn when their mother passed, so both had whooped out loud when Uncle Finn suggested inviting the O'Sheas to stay a while.

Uncle Finn huffed out a heavy blast of air. "Don't know, darlin'. Aiden's given me the cold shoulder for a long time now, and he was unconscious when I pulled him from the fire in his study, so I haven't had a chance to talk to him yet." A thin smile crooked the edge of his mouth. "And Sister Fred about tarred and feathered me when I tried to visit, and we all know there's no arguing with her."

Blaze grunted. "At least you left with your clothes on."

Grinning, Uncle Finn continued, his eyes softening as he gazed up at his niece. "But I'm hoping that saving his life will give me some favor with him, darlin', so we'll see."

"Good luck on that," Blaze said with a huff. "Sure didn't work for me with Sister Fred."

Boom! The front door flew open, missing Uncle Finn by mere inches when Blaze's thirteen-year-old tomboy sister Shaylee shot through. She skidded right into her uncle, who grabbed her by the scruff of her dusty plaid shirt. Freckled face smudged with dirt and boots and jeans splattered with mud, she sprang back in surprise, blue eyes spanning wide. "Holy Cats, what's going on here?"

"Cats are not holy, young lady," Uncle Finn said with an off-center smile, "and Angus's language won't be either if he sees you tracking mud across his clean floor." He led her back towards the door. "You know the rules, Doodlebug," he said, using the nickname he'd given her when she was small and loved to play with bugs, "around back and clean up first."

"So, who'd you whup this time, Doodle?" Dash asked with a lopsided grin, pride shining in his eyes for the little sister who could take on half the boys in the county and win.

"Horse-faced Milton Boyle," she said with a puff of her spindly chest, tossing an auburn braid over her shoulder.

Uncle Finn tweaked the back of Shaylee's neck. "We do *not* call people names, Shaylee Ann, no matter how obnoxious they may be."

"Except for Sister Fred," Blaze muttered under his breath.

"That's what I told Milton." Shaylee gave a pert lift of her chin. "Right after I whopped him for calling Dash a horse's behind."

"Me? Why?" Dash's dark brows tented in a show of hurt that made him look closer to Shaylee's age than twenty-seven.

"Excuse me, but all horse body parts aside …" Uncle Finn prodded Shaylee through the door with a firm hand to her back, eyeing her tracked mud with a wary eye. "You need to clean up both yourself and this mess, young lady, and then go put on some clean clothes."

"And Blaze just needs to put on any clothes," Jake said with a chuckle, shooting Blaze a grin as he and Dash moseyed toward the door.

Shaylee spun around, mouth and eyes gaping as she

finally saw her brother still draped in a sheet on the landing. "Gee whiz, Blaze, you're home already? And, flyin' batfish, you look like Lazarus in that sermon Pastor Tuttle gave last week."

Uncle Finn's mouth crooked as he ushered Shaylee out. "And just as dead if he steps foot out of this house today." He winked at Sheridan while he held the door for Dash and Jake as they filed through. "Sheridan sweetheart, you ride herd on that boy till I get back, you hear? And, Bren?" He nodded toward the study. "Get dressed and get busy with numbers, son," he said with a wicked grin, his laughter echoing in the foyer while he pulled the door closed. "Or I just might bring Sister Fred home for dinner to dress you down right."

CHAPTER FOUR

"MAMA, *PLEASE*—I'M BEGGING YOU—WON'T YOU and Papa consider staying with Aunt Marie and me in New York? Just until your house is rebuilt?" Stomach churning, thirty-nine-year-old Liberty O'Shea felt all of sixteen again as she pleaded with her mother across the dinner table in the dining room of The Gold Hill Hotel. Her heart bled with the need to provide love and support for Mama and Papa during this tragic time. But the moment she stepped foot in Virginia City, that familiar shroud of heaviness had descended as usual, reducing her to that frightened little girl.

The one her parents knew nothing about.

Swallowing hard to purge the nausea that always tainted her tongue when she visited Virginia City, Libby stiffened her jaw. *No, I will not let it win!* For heaven's sakes, she was an accomplished teacher at Vassar and an integral part of New York's suffrage movement, not a child reduced to panic every time she visited the hometown she'd fled over seventeen years ago. Mama and Papa needed her right now, and she was determined to be there for them!

No matter the memories.

Maeve O'Shea glanced up from her dinner, a crinkle in her brow. "Darling, there's nothing I'd rather do than stay with you and Marie, you know that. But there's no way Papa will ever agree, and I can't leave him alone after his heart attack."

Wringing the napkin in her lap, Libby's hopes sank along with her shoulders. She shot a glance at the concerned faces of her goddaughter, Maggie, and Mama's housekeeper, Gert, grateful for their support at a difficult time like this. She turned back to Mama and instantly felt a cramp in her chest over all her mother had gone through in the last week. For the first time, Libby noticed just how much Mama had aged in the last few years. In addition to snow-white hair that had once been as flame red as Libby's own, there was now an abundance of new wrinkles in a once creamy complexion.

"What does Papa plan to do?" Libby said quietly, knowing full well Papa would have his way as always, exercising the same iron-fisted control over the situation that he'd wielded over Libby her entire life.

Or tried to.

"Why, we're going to stay here at the Gold Hill until we can move back home, darling," Maeve O'Shea said, calmly sawing a piece of fried chicken with her knife. "Or perhaps Mrs. Cleary's boardinghouse would be homier." She directed a smile at Libby's goddaughter before taking a bite of her chicken. "Bertha Cleary is a bit of a gossip, Maggie, but she keeps a clean house, so I think we'll all be most comfortable there." A wrinkle appeared above her nose. "If she has room, that is."

Libby blinked. "Goodness, Mama, that could take six months or more!" she said, hardly able to believe her parents would consent to stay in a cramped hotel room after living in a sprawling ranch house for over twenty-five years. And the cost! She battled a sting of tears as she reached to graze her mother's hand, determined to be a tower of strength for this woman who had always been such a champion for her. "Mama, *please*—come back to New York with me. You can tell Papa it's just for a visit," she whispered, suddenly homesick for the closeness she and her mother had once shared. A closeness painfully interrupted when Papa sent

Libby away so many years ago to heal her heartache. "I'll even stay with you at Aunt Marie's instead of my room at Vassar. Then I can take care of you both."

Her mother patted Libby's hand. "Papa and I are perfectly able to take care of ourselves for the time being, darling, and besides, this is our home." Her mother's green eyes softened while a sad smile lined her lips. "Yours as well, at one time, if you recall."

Yes. Libby's lashes weighted closed as she slumped back in her chair. *And Finn's too.* Her appetite for the meat loaf on her plate was suddenly as diminished as her desire to stay in Virginia City. A former home that posed a triple threat to her state of mind: Finn's betrayal, Papa's dominance, and a painful memory she couldn't share. Which is exactly why this was the one place she'd avoided most of her life, visiting briefly only for Thanksgiving in the last seventeen years. In and out so fast, it had made her dizzy.

But better my head than my heart.

"Libby," her mother said softly, "think about it. You don't want to be saddled with an old grouch like your father, even for a short time. Heavens, it's bad enough I'm stuck with the man, darling, without adding to your grief too." The note of levity in her mother's tone matched a glint of tease in Maeve O'Shea's tender gaze, reminding Libby of the loving marriage her parents shared despite her father's propensity to control his daughter's life. It was the same type of marriage she had hoped for herself, before her heart had been crushed into a million pieces. Her mind flitted to Harold, her longstanding beau and Vassar professor whom she'd finally agreed to marry just last month. Not the loving match of her parents, perhaps, but a gentle, non-controlling man as consumed with women's rights as Libby, which made him the perfect match in marriage.

Agreeable to a fault.

"Besides," her mother continued with a gleam of trouble in her eyes, "I need you and that professor beau of yours to hurry up and get married so I can bounce grandbabies on my knee."

"Mother!" Heat scorched Libby's cheeks, as much from mention of making babies with Harold as memories of doing the same with Finn McShane during their brief sham of a marriage. A flash of heat swallowed her whole as she frantically flapped her napkin to cool off, the mere memory obviously as powerful as the attraction they once shared. Hand shaking, she dabbed the napkin to the back of her neck, dampness forming over the very notion of ever seeing him again, much less being in the same town. Which meant she needed to get back to the security of Harold as soon as possible.

Like, yesterday.

"Goodness, Mother—Harold and I are too old to have children," Libby finally managed, her voice far calmer than her pulse. She took great pains to steady her hand as she picked up her fork, her appetite as absent as she wanted to be. Sweet mother of mercy, what was her mother thinking? Harold was almost forty-five, and Libby barely a breath away from forty. Besides, she'd long since learned to satisfy her longing for motherhood by doting on sweet Maggie and the precious girls at the St. Patrick Female Orphan Asylum.

When she'd left Finn all those years ago, she'd filled her time—and her heart—with the teaching job Papa had helped her get at Vassar, then volunteering on behalf of women's rights, and finally, loving on the lost girls at St. Patrick's. Oh, how she longed to mend those sweet children's orphan hearts, but they had mended hers instead, striking a bond she hadn't expected. A kinship with little girls whose lives—or those of their mother's—had been compromised at the hand of a man. Every week Libby spent with them, her heart ached all the more over injustices many had endured. Injustices that far exceeded Libby's own, as painful as that memory might be. And so, they'd soon become her passion—along with women's rights—to somehow, someway, bring a little joy into their lives, hopefully to counter the pain of male oppression. A chill pebbled Libby's skin, reminding her how lucky she was to have escaped much of their plight, convincing her once and for all that babies were *not* in her future.

And neither was Finn McShane, God willing.

"Besides," Libby was quick to follow up, "Harold and I intend to devote ourselves to the cause of women's rights, not a family."

"Poppycock," her mother quipped. "Having babies is the greatest right a woman can have, young lady, and grandchildren is the second, isn't that right, Gert?"

Libby's former cook and housekeeper grunted, cheeks full of chicken. She swallowed hard, her skinny neck bobbing with the motion. "You betcha. Leastways, that's what my sister Oly always says."

Libby stifled a groan, hating to resort to bribery to hasten her departure from Virginia City, but what choice did she have? Her mother and father were homeless for the next six months at least. She needed them to agree to join her in New York for that duration and hopefully forever if she had her way. "Well, Mama, look at it this way," she said with a casual stab of her meatloaf. "The sooner you and Papa join me in New York, the sooner Harold and I can get married and give you those grandchildren." She popped the meatloaf in her mouth with a smile, hoping her mother would swallow the unlikelihood of Libby having children as easily as she swallowed her dinner.

Anxious to change the subject, Libby turned her attention to Maggie with a beam of approval. "Oh, and did I tell you that Sister Fred hired Maggie on the spot? She begins tomorrow."

Libby expelled a silent sigh of relief when her mother homed in on Maggie with a wide smile. "Maggie, that's wonderful! You're going to love Virginia City, young lady, and as soon as Mr. O'Shea and I have a home again, I insist you live with us."

"Goodness, Mrs. O'Shea," Maggie said, "I wouldn't want to impose—"

"Nonsense." Maeve took a sip of her coffee, green eyes so like Libby's own sparkling with delight. "Why, it will be like having a daughter at home again ..." She commenced to cutting more chicken. "Of course, I hope Sister Fred warned you that the caliber of patient you're likely to have can be a bit unruly."

"Oh, yes, ma'am, she did." Maggie patted a napkin to her lips. "And I'm afraid I've already experienced it firsthand."

Libby halted, a forkful of mashed potatoes halfway to her mouth. "Good heavens, Maggie, what do you mean?"

Laying the knife aside after buttering a bun, Maggie nibbled on the roll with a hint of mischief. "I had an altercation with a half-naked cowboy."

"What?" Libby's fork clanked to her plate while Mama and Gert only chuckled, Maggie's introduction to the crudities of Virginia City obviously part and parcel for the notoriously "Wild West."

Maggie's eyes sparkled, a bit of the "dickens" shining through that Libby had occasionally seen when Maggie was growing up. "A very impatient patient, I'm afraid, who wanted me to fetch his clothes, which Sister Fred apparently hid till he recovered more fully."

The blood immediately drained from Libby's face as she stared, grateful Maggie's mother couldn't see the vulgarities her best friend had exposed her daughter to. "How naked?" Libby whispered, the shock barely scraping past her lips.

A rush of color bloomed in Maggie's cheeks, reassuring Libby that her best friend's daughter remained unscathed by a town that could be a threat to a decent young woman. Her sweet goddaughter peeked up beneath a thick fringe of dark lashes, too much humor in her eyes to suit. "A bed sheet wrapped around his middle and gauze wrapped around his bare chest," she said shyly, "and when I refused, he stormed down the hall to terrorize poor Sister Berta and everyone else in the waiting room." Her lips squirmed with a near smile. "Until Sister Fred appeared, that is." The smile blossomed into a full-fledged grin as she thwarted a giggle with her palm. "When he bolted out of the hospital, bedsheet and all."

Libby's jaw dropped as both Gert and her mother laughed, quite sure she needed to hightail both Maggie and herself back to New York society and its more genteel ways.

"Did you catch his name?" Maeve asked with a grin that matched Gert's.

Cheeks bulging, Gert laughed as she chewed, her salt-and-pepper bun bouncing with the motion. "Maybe, maybe not, but I'll bet *he* caught some chiggers."

Another blush stole into Maggie's face. "Yes, his name was Blaze Donovan, and Sister Fred already warned me to stay away from him because apparently he's quite the rake."

Donovan? Libby caught her breath. The only Donovan she knew was—

"Well, that certainly sounds like Blaze Donovan," Maeve continued, as if half-naked men were everyday talk at dinner. "God bless his stubborn soul …"

"God *bless* him?" Jaw dangling, Libby stared at her mother, absolutely certain now that refined and educated women from New York had no business in Virginia City. "God *dress* him is more like it, Mama." She placed a hand on Maggie's arm, determined to do right by her best friend's daughter. "Maggie darling, I'm starting to wonder if your mother would approve of you living in a town like Virginia City—"

"Oh, for goodness' sake," Maeve said with a heft of her chin, a sure sign she was arming for battle. "Nurses see naked bodies all the time, Libby—"

"Yes, but parading down the street?" Libby leaned in, fingers gripped to the table.

"Only *half* naked, Aunt Libby," Maggie said softly, the concern in her tone proof that she wanted to stay. "He was wearing a sheet, after all."

"Precisely." Libby pushed her plate away with a heavy exhale. "A corrupt cowboy with no compunction or pride."

"Or clothes," Gert said with a chuckle

Her mother slanted in, sobriety dousing her laughter. "I'll have you know, young lady, that it was that same 'corrupt cowboy' that saved my life and Gert's, acquiring that very nakedness by braving a burning house to rescue dear Frannie." She arched a brow. "And, of course, it was his uncle who risked his own life to save your father's."

His Uncle. Libby's pulse thudded to a painful stop. The man who'd been her husband.

Before Papa had the marriage annulled.

"So, it's best to leave your high-and mighty opinions of Virginia City in New York where they belong, young lady," her mother said, ever persistent in her defense of the town that she loved, "and embrace both this town and its people."

Its people. Libby sank back in her chair, well aware that Mama was right. She still had family and friends here she loved despite her disdain for the town she once called home. Relinquishing with a weary sigh, she offered Mama a conciliatory smile. "You're right, Mama, and I'm sorry for being such a snob." She reached to squeeze her mother's hand, ashamed at the way she had turned her back on her family and her very roots. "And I promise you, I'll embrace both this town and its people as long as I'm here."

"That's my girl." Her mother patted her arm while Libby took a sip of her coffee, anxiety roiling in her stomach once again.

All but one.

CHAPTER FIVE

"SO, HOW'S OUR BOY TODAY, Sister Fred? Ready for visitors?" Finn ambled into the small lobby area of St. Mary Louise Hospital with hat in hand, offering a generous smile to the one woman he respected more than most men in Virginia City.

Sister Frederica glanced up from the nurse's counter, a clipboard in hand and a scowl on her face. "Alive at the moment," she quipped with a dry smile, "but dangerously close to Last Rites if he keeps his bellyaching up." Her mouth went as flat as her tone. "Keeps grousing to go home, but Doc McCoy says his blood pressure isn't cooperating." She scratched something on the clipboard and slammed it on the wooden counter, causing both Finn and the elderly sister behind her to jump. "And neither is Mr. O'Shea."

Finn inwardly winced, remembering all too well his ex-father-in-law's volatile temper in the brief three months Finn and Libby had been married. *Especially* the day he found out Pastor Poppy had accidentally married off his only daughter to the poor son of a man he hated. From that moment on, it had been war between Aiden and him, despite Finn's many attempts to make amends over the years.

"But," Sister Fred continued with a hike of her formidable chin, "I'm sick of coddling the old coot, if truth be told, and I'd like to see someone else try and calm him down."

A grin slid across Finn's face as he scratched the back of his neck. "Now you and I both know I'm the last one for that job, Sister Fred. I've always been the proverbial thorn in his side."

Her scowl gave way to a grin as wide as Finn's. She gave him a wink. "Yes, sir, I know, so I'm countin' on you to give it your best shot." She nodded toward the stairway. "Fourth floor, end of the hall. As far from the front door as possible to thwart escape and keep his caterwaulin' down."

"Thanks, Sister Fred—I owe you." Finn shot a grateful smile as he strode toward the narrow staircase down the hall.

Her chuckle followed. "Don't mention it, Mr. McShane, and I mean that literally. If Doc McCoy finds out I let his patient's nemesis in, he'll be screeching louder than O'Shea."

Offering a salute over his shoulder, Finn scaled the narrow steps two at a time, heart pumping when he finally reached the fourth-floor landing, but not all from exertion. Nope, he'd been praying for reconciliation with Aiden O'Shea for the last five years, ever since Pastor Poppy had talked Finn into forgiving Aiden for ruining his life. But the forgiveness had definitely been one-sided, and Finn wasn't all that sure that the feud would ever end—a feud that had robbed him of the only woman he'd ever really loved.

Thoughts of Libby struck hard as Finn approached the fourth-floor hallway, caught off-guard by an unexpected ache that he thought he'd purged long ago. Hand on the knob, he faltered, eyelids sinking at the memory of silky auburn hair that flamed as much as emerald eyes whenever Finn had stirred her temper. A smile shadowed his lips as he opened the door. A favorite pastime of his from the first day she'd arrived at the schoolhouse at the age of fourteen, the smartest girl he'd ever met.

And the most infuriating.

He'd harbored a secret crush all those years that had blossomed into love the summer after she'd arrived home from college. And when Pastor Poppy had pronounced them man and wife, the next three months had been the best of his life, even when they'd butted heads over her infernal women's rights. But her suffrage obsession aside, Finn couldn't deny the utter ecstasy of having Libby O'Shea as his wife. To him she was everything he had ever wanted—fire and femininity all wrapped up in the most beautiful, intelligent, and exciting package he'd ever seen. A woman who had been pure adrenaline to his soul.

In his blood.

In his life.

And in his bed.

"Confound it, woman, you touch me with that washcloth one more time, and you'll be wearing it."

Stepping into the hallway, Finn had no trouble finding Aiden. A young nurse bolted out of a room at the end of the hall, two circles of pink dusting her cheeks. A streak of swear words followed her as she hurried toward Finn with a wash pan in her hands and a towel over her arm, water splattered all over the bodice of her crisp, white uniform.

"Woke up on the wrong side of the bed, did he?" Finn asked with a nod toward Aiden's room.

The nurse offered a sympathetic smile. "I'm afraid Mr. O'Shea only has one side of the bed, sir, which is why Sister Fred relegated him to the fourth floor all by himself." Her mouth crooked. "Except for the poor nurses who draw the short straw."

Finn's smile was more of a grimace. "Short temper, short straw—not a lucky combination."

"No, sir," she said with a sigh, barreling toward the staircase door with an imp of a smile. "God be with you."

"Yeah, well, I'm counting on it," Finn muttered under his breath, steeling himself for the wrath of one of Virginia

City's richest and most powerful men. *And* the most stubborn.

Crash! A plate sailed into the hall along with several curses, shattering against the wall. "Where the devil are my clothes?"

Finn bit back a smile. Apparently Blaze and Aiden had something in common—the wrath of Sister Frederica. Finn peeked around the corner of Aiden's door with a wry smile. "You out of dishes, I hope?"

Aiden stared, his scowl clamping into a thin-lipped smile as he hunched on the side of the bed in a hospital gown, bare feet dangling. Short and stout, Libby's father carried the girth and authority of a man ten feet tall, traits that served him well as the president of Virginia City's largest bank. Silver hair usually neatly combed over a bald spot now stuck up all over his head, the perfect complement for a matching handlebar moustache gone awry. "It's about blasted time, McShane—I told that goose-flappin' woman I wanted to see you days ago. Where the devil have you been?"

Finn moseyed into the room, face immobile to mask his surprise over Aiden wanting to see him at all. "Sister Fred said Doc ordered no visitors till your blood pressure was under control."

"Aw, he's as loony as that goose-flap woman! My blood pressure is just fine." Grumbling, Aiden shuffled into the bed and hiked the sheet up to his chest, apparently uncomfortable holding court in his underwear. He nodded toward a chair against the wall. "Take a load off, McShane—you and I have some talkin' to do."

Tossing his hat on a credenza, Finn positioned the chair backwards at the end of the bed, straddling it with an off-kilter smile. "About time, O'Shea. Too bad it took saving your sorry backside for you to realize that."

Aiden cuffed the back of his head, ruddy color crawling up his neck as he cracked an off-center smile. "Yeah, well, next to the Grim Reaper, you suddenly don't look so bad."

Finn chuckled.

Aiden's eyes narrowed into a squint, white bushy brows slashing low as he gave a gruff clear of his throat. "Thank you," he said, voice raspy with something akin to humility. Splotches of color mottled his cheeks, evidence of how difficult this was for a man like him. "The way I've treated you all these years, Finn, I wouldn't have blamed you if you'd just left my stubborn, old hide to burn."

"Couldn't." Finn shifted, mouth hooking in an attempt to lighten an awkward moment. "Figured there was enough fire in your future, old man."

Aiden's rusty laugh bounced off the sallow walls of the small hospital room, the sound as foreign as the civility in his tone. He scratched the back of his bald head, further disrupting his disheveled hair as his smile faded into sobriety. "Regrettably, yes, but I aim to do something about that before it's too late." Meek blue eyes stared back, the lack of disdain Finn had always seen thawing them considerably from the ice-blue color that had always frosted Finn before. "Because you see, you not only saved my sorry life, Finn, you changed it forever." He grunted. "Or I should say the heart attack and fire did—flashing years of regret before my eyes." A lump jerked hard in his throat as his gaze met Finn's, his sorrowful sobriety convincing him that Aiden O'Shea was, indeed, a changed man. "But *you* gave me the chance to do it, Finn, and there's no way I can ever thank you for that. But I sure aim to try."

Finn smiled, gratitude to God for answering his prayers warming his chest more than a warm brick at the bottom of his bed. "You talking to me again is payment enough, Aiden."

"Yes, well, I aim to do a whole lot more than just talk." A fresh rush of blood mottled Aiden's cheeks as he gave an abrupt nod toward the hall. "Close the door, son, if you will."

Rising, Finn did as he asked, although he knew Aiden was the only patient on the floor. He settled back in his chair after turning it to face his former father-in-law this time, his curiosity piqued over what Aiden could possibly have to say other than "I'm sorry."

"Why haven't you ever married?" Shrewd eyes pierced Finn straight through, turning the tables to awkward.

Finn blinked, completely caught off-guard. Whatever he'd thought Aiden might say, that sure hadn't been it. The question immediately flashed an image of Libby in his mind, and for the briefest of moments, a twinge of the old anger toward Aiden flared in his gut.

"Never forget, son," Pastor Poppy had once told him, *"that bitterness is like handing your enemy a loaded gun to wound you all over again."*

The words now echoed loudly in Finn's brain, reminding him how dark and bitter his life had been the first few years after Libby left, leaving him an empty shell of a man. That is, until Pastor Poppy had filled him up with a faith that had saved his own sorry soul.

Shifting uncomfortably in the chair, Finn doused the old flames of fury with a silent prayer, forcing a casual shrug. "Marriage just wasn't for me, Aiden. Nobody knows that better than you."

"Horse puke!" Aiden shouted, shades of the old nemesis peeking through as narrowed eyes nailed him to the wall. "You're still in love with my daughter."

Finn shot to his feet so fast, the chair rattled on its legs. "*Was* in love with your daughter, O'Shea. And in case it's escaped your notice, I haven't seen hide nor hair of her in over seventeen years, so this is a devil of a way to say thank you for saving your neck."

"Sit down, McShane," Aiden ordered, raising the hackles Finn worked so hard to keep under wrap.

Jaw hard, Finn snatched his hat from the credenza, no intention of letting Aiden order him around *or* resurrect painful memories he'd worked so hard to forget. Striding to the door, he yanked it open, not even bothering to turn around. "Sorry, old man, but if you plan to take a stroll down Memory Lane, you'll have to do it on your own—"

"Libby's back."

Those two words stopped Finn cold, his back suddenly as rigid as the blasted wood door he was itching to slam. All at once, his anger slowly siphoned out as he lowered his head, eyelids sagging closed with a weight he hadn't anticipated. Of course, she was back—her father almost died and her parents had lost their home in a fire. He'd expected as much, but he hadn't expected to see her again *or* have his heart ripped out by the mere mention of her name.

"She's engaged to be married," Aiden said quietly, the regret in his tone not near a match for the keen disappointment that seared through Finn's chest.

"What's that got to do with me?" he said, unwilling to turn around lest Aiden see just how much he still cared.

"Everything. I don't want her to marry him."

A fury Finn didn't know he still possessed rose up like a phantom as he slowly angled Aiden's way, his fist knuckle-white on the knob. "Well, you have lots of experience handling situations like that, O'Shea," he bit out, his voice almost a hiss, "so have at it."

"Can't. She won't listen to me, Finn, but she'll listen to you."

Finn stared, eyes gaping as wide as his unhinged jaw. "That heart attack scramble your brain, old man? That stubborn daughter of yours wouldn't listen when I begged her to stay years ago nor even answer one of the hundreds of letters I sent, so I don't know why you think I would hold any sway."

"You're her husband—"

"*Was* her husband," he shouted, wondering what in the world he'd been thinking to even consider offering this cock-eyed family a home for the next six months. "She decided on that when she walked away and never looked back, old man, and you sealed it when you filed the annulment papers against my will."

"She didn't walk away," Aiden said quietly as he avoided Finn's eyes, voice so low Finn thought he'd misunderstood. "I sent her."

"What?" Finn's body went cold. "What do you mean you sent her?"

Chest expanding with a deep draw of air, Aiden finally faced Finn head-on, the remorse in his tone as thick as the tension in the air. "I mean I didn't give her a chance to cool down, Finn, after the fight you two had. I saw my chance, and I took it, hustling her out of town before she could change her mind. I convinced her you would tie her down, never allow her to pursue her infernal women's causes."

Finn could only stare in shock, the painful thud of his heart nearly ticking to a stop. "B-But … she never answered my letters, not one," he whispered.

A larger knot ducked in Aiden's throat. "She never got 'em, son. Her aunt had strict orders to see to that."

Rage like he'd never known broke through his stupor of stun, boiling up inside as he stormed to Aiden's bed. He fisted the old man's hospital gown like meat hooks, jerking him up so hard, Aiden dangled in the air. "You! You ruined my life, you snake-bellied polecat, and so help me, if you weren't laid up in a hospital bed, I'd put you in one." He hurled Aiden back onto the bed, bouncing him but good before he strode for the door, sorely tempted to turn back around and give him a piece of his fist. Hand on the knob, he wheeled to scorch him with a glare so full of fire, it singed his own sockets. "I should have let you burn, old man."

"But you couldn't," Aiden said in a rush, his breathing as labored as his words, "any more than you can walk away from Libby right now."

"No? Watch me!" He bludgeoned a thick finger in Aiden's direction, pretty sure he needed to leave before he tore the skunk limb to limb. "You and that daughter of yours are cut from the same cloth, old man—conniving and cold-hearted, the both of you. I want nothing to do with you or your blasted family ever again." Outrage pumping hot in his veins, Finn yanked on the door, body twitching to vent with an exit that would shimmy the roof.

"You can't walk away—" Aiden started to shout, but Finn had no desire to listen at all. Wrenching the door closed, it thundered in a deafening slam. But not before his blood turned to ice water over Aiden's final words.

"Legally, she's still your wife."

CHAPTER SIX

"GOOD HEAVENS, MR. MCSHANE, WHATEVER is going on?" Skirt flapping, the young nurse from earlier scurried down the hall towards Aiden's room, face as pale as her snow-white uniform.

Not that Finn's looked much better, he guessed. His blood had drained clear down to his toes, hard-pressed to make it back up to his brain, which teetered on the edge of comatose. At Aiden's final words, shock had paralyzed his entire body as he stood, hand still on the knob of his former father-in-law's closed door.

Correction: His current father-in-law.

The very thought ignited his anger all over again, and with a tight-lipped smile in her direction, Finn hurled the door open once again, banging it against the wall. "Sorry, ma'am, but the wind caused it."

Or the windbag.

Stepping back into the room, Finn drilled Aiden with a glare that could have torched both the bed and the man in it. "*What-did-you-say?*" he whispered, his words little more than a hiss.

"Mr. O'Shea, is everything all right?" The young nurse stood outside the door, her strained tone indicative that she thought her patient might be in danger.

Which wasn't far off the mark …

"I'd fetch a doctor, miss," Finn said with a stiff smile over his shoulder, "because Mr. O'Shea's about to have a setback." He backhanded the door closed in the woman's face and strode toward the bed, his stance so menacing, Aiden's jaw steeled in defense. "What do you *mean* she's still my wife?"

A hard smile shadowed Aiden's mouth as he dipped his head, peering up at Finn beneath bushy brows. "I *mean*, you mule-headed Irishman, Libby never signed the papers," Aiden emphasized, the seeds of a twinkle in his eyes, "which means she either forgot, overlooked it, or flat-out didn't want to."

Finn blinked, a slow smile easing across his face as the meaning of Aiden's words finally sank in. "You don't say," he whispered, gaze trailing out the window in a distant stare, liking the way this sounded a whole lot more than he should.

Libby McShane.

Or better yet …

Mrs. Griffin McShane.

"Yes, sir, I do, and although I would have been spitting fire seventeen years ago if I'd found out then, right about now I'm feeling mighty smug."

Finn's smile hooked into a near scowl as he drilled Aiden with a sliver of a look. "I wouldn't be feeling too blasted smug, O'Shea—you stole seventeen years from me with the love of my life, so what do you aim to do about it?"

A grin curled on Aiden's face as he settled back in the bed. "Plenty, McShane. Beginning with me and mine moving into your cozy ranch house."

Finn slacked a leg, hands parked low on his hips. "And just what is *that* supposed to accomplish?" he said in a lazy drawl, grateful Aiden was willing to stay at the ranch, something Finn hadn't believed he would do. He allowed his scowl to slide into a smirk. "Besides giving me a monumental pain in the neck."

Aiden cut loose with what sounded like a rusty bark, and Finn realized it was a cackle, the gleam in the man's eyes confirming his laughter. "It would give *me* the chance to insist Libby stays with us, too."

A wrinkle wedged at the bridge of Finn's nose as his eyes narrowed. "And what in tarnation makes you think Libby will stay at my ranch when she's only here for a short time and engaged to boot?"

"*Was* engaged," Aiden stressed with a fold of his hands on his ample stomach, his shrewd look explaining why he was one ofVirginia City's most respected businessmen. "Can't very well marry one man when she's already married to another."

Finn grunted and tossed his hat back on the credenza. "Wanna bet? The Libby I knew was cut from the same cloth as her father—stubborn to a fault. She'll just sign those stupid papers and get the annulment herself."

"Not if she doesn't have those 'stupid papers' ..." Aiden's sentence tapered off, the wicked glint in his eye making Finn glad that for once, they were on the same side.

Sliding into the chair, Finn hunched forward with hands clasped, striving for a casual air that belied the sprint of his pulse. "So, what do you have in mind, O'Shea?" he said, not daring to believe he could ever have Libby again.

Aiden's smile was devious. "How long do you think it will take to rebuild my ranch house?"

Finn cocked his head. "I don't know—six months, maybe, depending on how many laborers you hire. Why?"

"You reckon that's enough time to convince my girl you're the one she wants?" A sparkle lit in Aiden's eyes.

Enough time? Mulling it over, Finn thought of the fire-haired spitfire who'd drawn blood with a china teapot before she'd left. His smile went flat. As Virginia City's most eligible bachelor, he had no doubt he could convince most widows and unmarried females in the county, just based on the cakes, pies, and casseroles that came his way. But Libby O'Shea McShane?

Humph. A lifetime might not be enough.

"Because several months ago Libby requested I send the legal documents to her after her professor proposed ..."

Her professor? A nerve twittered in Finn's temple in time with the one in his jaw.

"Which is how I discovered she not only didn't sign them, but apparently I never mailed them to the Archbishop either. Just plum forgot after Maeve begged me to wait until Libby was good and settled in with her Aunt Marie in New York. So, I did, and that was that."

Finn grinned. "God bless Maeve. I always liked that woman."

A grunt erupted from Aiden's square jaw. "Yes, well, she always liked you, too, which is why I had such a devil of a time convincing Libby that moving to New York was in her best interests."

"Couldn't have been too difficult," Finn muttered, mouth taking a slant. "She never once tried to contact me or see me whenever she visited you, which I assumed she did."

"Not much, I'm afraid." Aiden leaned back on his pillow, regret shading his face once again. "Just flitted in and out once a year at Thanksgiving, always insisting we have holidays at Marie's. And since Maeve jumped at any chance to visit her sister and family back in New York, it just became a habit, I'm afraid." His gaze wandered out the window, the remorse etched into his face something Finn had never expected to see. "Especially since we had no grandchildren to keep us here," he whispered, as if he, too, regretted the loss of children Finn had always hoped to have.

"So ..." Finn interrupted Aiden's reverie, not willing to waste another moment after seventeen long years apart from the woman he loved. "What's your plan, O'Shea, because I guarantee that daughter of yours won't let a piece of paper stand in her way."

Aiden jolted, returning his attention to Finn once again. "Oh ... yes, right." He sat up straight, eyes thinning in thought. "Well, I'll just inform Libby that the terms for receiving her paperwork will be moving in with us at your ranch for the six months it'll take to rebuild our home."

"And if she refuses?" Finn cocked his head, unconvinced.

"She won't. It took me over a year to get the paperwork that far, so she'd have at least that on her own, plus she wouldn't have the clout of Monsignor Murray behind her request."

"That won't stop her," Finn said, quite certain that time was on Libby's side *and* "her professor's."

Aiden all but preened. "No, but money will."

Finn stared, eyes in a squint. "What do you mean, 'money will'? I heard she was a teacher at some fancy girls' school in New York—doesn't she support herself?"

Husky laughter bounced off the walls. "Yes, Libby teaches at Vassar—"

"Vassar?!" Finn bolted straight up in the chair, a swear word teetering on the tip of his tongue. "No wonder I couldn't track her down! I'd heard it was at The Convent of the Sacred Heart, whose Mother Superior," he said with a dangerous glint in his eye, "threatened a restraining order if I didn't stay away and stop sending letters."

A ruddy shade of red crawled up the old man's neck while Aiden laughed, the sound awkward as he scratched the back of his head. "Yes, a little rumor I started to keep you off-track I'm afraid, Finn, so I apologize once more." He shifted in the bed, all business again. "But whether The Convent of the Sacred Heart or Vassar, the salary is minimal at best, so it hardly pays the bills for her comfortable lifestyle. Nor does it subsidize her passion—her blessed suffrage involvement. Which means I'm holding all the cards in this game of high stakes, McShane, so if she refuses, I'll simply pull all my funds."

Finn shook his head, well aware that Aiden O'Shea was both a card—and business—sharp who would win anyway he could, regardless of blood relation. Leaning back in his chair, Finn was tempted to prop his feet on the bed. "I just assumed she supported herself," he said quietly, gaze trailing out the window while the final argument he and Libby had ever had replayed in his brain.

"Over-my-dead-body," he'd shouted the day she left, nose to nose with the woman who'd riled his blood in more ways than one.

"*That* can be arranged," she'd screamed right back, stomping out of his life so fast, she'd left a cold wind in her wake.

And a dead marriage.

Something cramped in his chest and he finally understood that he bore part of the blame for the demise of their relationship. They had both been so blasted young and everything had happened *so* blasted fast that neither had the time to learn what marriage was really all about. No time to figure out that true love was a give-and-take process that, if nurtured by faith, eventually mellowed into giving one's all.

Unconditional love. Something Finn had become painfully aware of when his sister died and left him with four kids to care for, nieces and nephews who had mostly healed his heart. *Mostly.* Finn released a silent sigh of regret, remembering all too clearly how the heat of attraction between Libby and him—and there had been plenty—had erupted into the heat of their anger, both so dad-gum pigheaded that when the smoke finally cleared, their marriage had gone down in flames.

Along with my heart.

A gruff clear of a throat interrupted his painful reverie, and Finn was suddenly aware that Aiden was staring at him as if Finn had gone soft in the head. And obviously he had if he was considering a cock-eyed venture like winning Libby back. Firming his jaw, he studied Aiden through razor-thin eyes. "Why are you doing this?" he asked, hardly able to believe that his former foe was now his partner in crime.

"Why?" It was Aiden's turn to ponder his remorse as he gouged the bridge of his nose, a wash of ruddy color rising up his throat. "Well, son, I have a number of reasons, but the main one is because my miserable life passed before me in that fire, a flash of conviction that leveled far more than my home, I assure you." He finally peered up with a rare humility despite the tight press of his lips. "It scorched my pride along with my house, Finn, showing me what a fool I'd been over the years, especially holding a grudge against you."

Finn eased back in his chair, head cocked and arms folded. "Mind if I ask why on the grudge, sir? Never could figure it out."

A large knot hitched in Aiden's thick throat as he looked away. "I blamed it on your pa, of course, after he made that spectacle at my bank, claiming I cheated him." He grunted, gaze trailing into a hard stare. "Cost me a fair amount of business that year, he did, but at least I managed to win most of it back after he—"

Aiden hesitated as he peered up at Finn. The hard line of Finn's jaw must have made him think twice about mentioning the betrayal and abandonment of Finn's father because Aiden looked away. His tone softened. "Well, that's neither here nor there. The real basis for my vendetta was my disdain for Irish Protestants, because of injustices I suffered at their hands in New York." His gaze sought Finn's once again, true remorse etched deep into his brow. "To my way of thinking, the last thing my Catholic daughter needed was a Protestant heathen, although Maeve has since convinced me that God is not a respecter of persons *or* denominations. So, I'm asking for your forgiveness, Finn, and the chance to make it right." Jaw compressed, he slowly extended a hand, dark eyes searing Finn with humble resolve.

Rising slowly, Finn shook Aiden's hand, a flicker of a smile playing at the edges of his mouth. "Forgave you long ago, Aiden, after Pastor Poppy hammered it into my hard head that I needed to—and I quote—'forgive that stubborn old coot' if I wanted blessing in my life."

Aiden chuckled, more color burning in his face as he scrubbed the back of his head with a sheepish smile. "God bless Pastor Poppy. The poor man was fit to be tied when he found out what I planned to do."

"Yeah, he was," Finn said as he resumed his seat. Gratitude swelled in his chest for the friend and mentor who'd not only married Libby and him, but provided years of comfort and counsel over the damage Aiden O'Shea had caused. Settling back in his chair with a relaxed fold of arms, Finn propped his legs on the end of Aiden's bed, studying his father-in-law through curious eyes. "You said you had a number of reasons …"

"Ah, yes," Aiden said, mirroring Finn's posture with an easy fold of burly arms. "Two other reasons. The first?" His chin rose in a rigid bent Finn remembered all too well. "Much as I hate to admit it, my daughter is as stubborn as her father, hell-bent on doing things her way. I've already seen the damage that has done in my life, and I don't want that to happen to her."

His gaze wandered a bit as his mouth gummed into a tight line. "She's not happy, no matter how much she claims to be, not with some namby-pamby professor cow-towing to her every whim." His gaze thinned as he looked up at Finn. "She needs a man who won't let her push him around. Somebody she can respect. Somebody like you, Finn, that she won't ride roughshod over." A heavy sigh blasted from Aiden's lips as he sank back against his pillow. "Back when you two got hitched, I was too blamed thick-headed to see you were perfect for her, but now I realize the error of my ways and I believe Libby will, too—eventually."

Finn issued a dubious grunt. "And how do you propose we do that? The woman has avoided me like the plague for seventeen years now. You and I both know she'll hightail it back to that job in New York and her namby-pamby fiancé as soon as she can."

"*Not* if she doesn't *have* a job in New York," Aiden said with a smug look, hands clasped on his stomach in gloating fashion. "Keep in mind that I was the one who got her that job in the first place. Pulled a few favors from an old school chum who's risen pretty high in the academic community, so I'm confident I can yank it just as well. And when Maeve's sister—who Libby lived with before Vassar gave her room and board—discovers that Maeve and I need Libby at home for a season to help us get past the trauma of the fire, my stubborn girl won't have a home either." He winked. "Conspiracy can be a wonderful thing, my boy, especially in the name of love."

Finn's mouth took a slant as he rubbed a scar on his forehead. "Well, I never stopped loving the woman, and that's a cold, hard fact, Aiden. But I sure didn't see a whole lot of that returned the day she clipped me with a flying teapot before walking out on our marriage." He cocked his head, assessing Aiden with more than a little skepticism. "What makes you think she has any feelings left for me after seventeen years?"

The gleam in Aiden's eyes worked its way into a gloat. "Because she's worked too blasted hard to stay away, that's why. A woman doesn't up and leave her parents with little more than covert fly-by-night visits here and there unless she's trying pretty darn hard to forget something *or* someone. Nor does she just up and forget to sign papers that will cut her loose from a man she doesn't love."

He shifted as if to get comfortable, the smirk on his face implying he held all the cards. "No siree, I'd lay odds that stubborn daughter of mine still has feelings for you, Finn. Now it's up to *you* to make 'em grow when she moves into your house along with me, Maeve, and Gert for the six months we're rebuilding."

A slow grin slid across Finn's face. "Is it now? Well, God willing and the creek don't rise, I just may be able to do that." He paused, eyes in a squint. "And your final reason?"

Aiden issued a grunt, adjusting the covers over his portly frame. "Not only am I just plumb sick and tired of hospital food," he said in a huff, the mock scowl on his face belied by the glint of tease in his eyes, "but the chef at the Gold Hill Hotel can't cook to save her soul."

CHAPTER SEVEN

"YOU'RE A BRAVE, BRAVE WOMAN, Maggie Mullaney." Ida Mae Rafferty, head cook for St. Mary Louise's prep kitchen, ladled stew into a bowl and plopped it down on a dining tray along with a crusty roll, cookie, and a cup of coffee. "Volunteering to take that crotchety old man his last supper." She gave a grunt that could rival any in the Ponderosa Saloon, her portly frame as intimidating as any man in that saloon. "Last supper, humph! Reckon even Jesus would balk at that." She wagged the ladle in Maggie's face, her scowl softening into a near smile. "Just make sure the last supper is his and not yours, missy!"

Maggie grinned. She repinned the nurses cap on her disheveled chignon that now sported wisps of stray curls from a morning of running meals and meds up and down four flights of stairs. "Oh, he's not so bad if you ignore the grouch in him," she said with a firm tug of her skirt-length pinafore apron before smoothing it down over her white cotton skirt. She carefully picked up the tray and headed for the kitchen door, tossing a return wink over her shoulder. "A tip I learned from Aunt Libby, who has valuable experience with her grump of a father."

Ida Mae grunted. "Aye, and God bless the woman's soul. I hear she's to be canonized."

Chuckling, Maggie made a beeline for the stairs, understanding her godmother's keen desire to move as far away from her father's tight rein of control as possible. Mr. O'Shea had not been an easy patient over the last few weeks, and Maggie could well imagine how dominant such a gentleman could be with a daughter. And yet, Maggie was more than a little surprised that she was sorry to see him go.

"Hope whatever you're toting there tastes better than the last slop you served, missy," he'd groused the second morning she'd brought his lunch. His cantankerous tone confirmed every snide adjective coined by the staff, from curt and crabby, to cross and crusty. So as the newest employee in the hospital, it was no surprise Maggie had been appointed as Mr. O'Shea's personal nurse throughout the rest of his stay.

She'd had to weather a fair amount of snarls and growls, certainly, before she'd finally detected the beat of a heart in Aiden O'Shea's chest. But after persistent smiles and even more persistent games of cards or chess, she'd also detected someone who deeply regretted the kind of person he'd been and wanted to change. The poor man just didn't know how.

Maggie's heart constricted, recalling the one conversation they'd had where he had all but bared his soul. Right then and there she'd made up her mind to medicate Aiden O'Shea with the one thing he needed more than anything: The love of God. A smile tiptoed across her lips. The only balm Maggie knew firsthand that could heal scars way beyond third-degree burns. Humming on her way down the hall, the savory aroma of stew reminded her she'd skipped lunch to play one last game of chess with the old crank.

"Excuse me, Miss, but can you direct me to Mr. O'Shea's room?"

Maggie froze, the sound of *that* voice chilling both her and the stew as she whirled around, sloshing coffee into Mr. O'Shea's saucer.

"You!" It was a rough whisper from the lips of the one man she'd hoped to never see again. Blaze Donovan's blue-green eyes narrowed as he nudged his Stetson up, unleashing a mop of errant golden-brown curls. "Figures you work here now—you fit right in with Sister Fred."

"I'll take that as a compliment, Mr. …?" She countered with a rise of her chin, completely peeved that this scalawag could parch her mouth dryer than the infamous bed sheet.

"Donovan, *Blaze Donovan*," he stressed in a clipped tone that flickered a nerve in his jaw, apparently testy that any woman would actually forget his name.

She gave a slow nod, her tone as sweet as the sugar cookie on Mr. O'Shea's tray. "Oh, yes, Mr. Donovan, I'm so sorry—I didn't recognize you without your sheet."

A rash of red crawled up his neck as that hypnotic gaze thinned to a blade of grass. "And I didn't recognize you without the fire in your cheeks."

Said fire promptly flamed, igniting her cheeks along with her temper. "Yes, well that tends to happen when near-naked men parade the halls swaddled in as much cotton as they have between their ears."

His jaw began to grind. "Look, lady, I came here for Mr. O'Shea, not for insults."

Maggie arched a brow, fighting the crack of a smile. "Yes, well, with Mr. O'Shea, I'm afraid it's one and the same, Mr. Donovan. I'm on my way up to the fourth floor to deliver his lunch right now, so if you'll just follow me …" Turning on her heel, Maggie hurried down the hall, a wee bit surprised when the rake beat her to the door to hold it open. "Thank you," she said, unable to keep the surprise from her voice.

"Even near-naked men have manners," he muttered, passing her to scale the steps two at a time, his comment kindling more warmth at the memory.

She was breathing hard by the time she reached the

fourth floor. Her face instantly pulsed with more heat when she spied him standing there with the door propped, arms casually crossed and a veiled smirk on his handsome face. "Thank you," she said again, annoyed when a musky citrus scent fluttered her stomach as she passed. Head high, she swished by with a death grip on the tray, limbs rattling as much as Mr. O'Shea's dishes.

"All righty now, Mr. O'Shea, here you go." She rushed into her patient's room, spurred on by the heavy sound of footsteps behind.

"About dad-burned time. A body can starve to death before anybody feeds 'em around here." Aiden O'Shea lumbered up to sit in his bed, handlebar moustache drooping more than usual. "About ready to gnaw on this infernal cast-iron bed."

"And good afternoon to you, too," Maggie said in a light, breezy tone, setting the tray down to adjust the grouch's pillow. "And I wouldn't be surprised if you *had* partaken of a little cast iron, sir, with all the nails you're spitting today."

"You'd be spitting nails, too, if you were holed up in this confounded goose-flappin' jail." Aiden snatched the spoon from the tray Maggie laid in his lap and started shoveling stew.

Maggie laughed and opened the curtains to Mr. O'Shea's windows, allowing sunshine to stream into the dark room before she returned to the other side of his bed. "Well no, I wouldn't mind that, actually, because *then* I could sell them to the mercantile on the side to make a little extra money. But, alas—I don't spit nails."

"Oh, I don't know about that, ma'am." Mr. Donovan strolled in with a one-sided smile, hat in hand while he moved to the other side of Aiden's bed. "Your tongue *is* mighty sharp and straight to the point. Howdy, Mr. O'Shea. This little lady giving you trouble?"

Spoon midway to his mouth, Aiden actually smiled, dropping Maggie's jaw so wide, she could have stored a box of those blasted nails inside. "Blaze, good to see you again, my boy! And call me Aiden, please. Any man who risked his life to save my wife, cook, and ferret deserves no less than a first-name basis."

"Thank you, sir," Blaze said with a ready handshake that Aiden pumped harder than a dry well in the desert.

Maggie blinked. *His boy?*

"Just dropped by to see how you're doing, sir. And to let you know we're looking forward to hosting you, Mrs. O'Shea, Gert, and your daughter at the Silver Lining Ranch." He slid Maggie a tight smile. "And Miss Mullaney, of course."

Maggie almost dropped the thermometer in her hand. "The Silver Lining Ranch?" She blinked at Mr. O'Shea. "Excuse me, sir, but I thought you were planning on staying at the Gold Hill Hotel until your house was rebuilt?"

Aiden chuckled as he tucked into his stew. "Not when Finn McShane and his strapping nephew here are willing to put Maeve, me, Libby, and you up at the finest, fanciest ranch house in all of Virginia City." He gave Maggie a wink, which prompted a second slack of her jaw. "Till I rebuild mine, that is."

"But … but … Aunt Libby told me we were all staying at the Gold Hill during the building process, sir, unless she could convince you to sell your land and move back to New York with her."

"Sell?" Aiden whirled to stare at her like she'd just spit in his stew, which given the news he'd just unloaded, she was mighty tempted to do. "Thunderation, woman, you're as daft as my daughter. I'm not selling and that's—"

Maggie shoved the thermometer in Aiden's mouth, cutting him off. "Aunt Libby and I are *not* moving to any fancy ranch house, Mr. O'Shea, so you can just put that in your pipe and smoke it."

Aiden whipped the thermometer out to glare, shaking it in her face. "For your information, missy, Sister Fred confiscated my pipe the first day, so you can just put *that* in your stew and stir it."

Maggie snatched the thermometer from his hand and laid it on his tray before confiscating both to remove his stew with a thrust of her chin. "No temperature, no stew," she said, holding his lunch as far away as she could. "The choice is yours, Mr. O'Shea."

"Is that so?" He flipped the sheet back and gingerly inched off the bed, his burns slowing him down considerably. "Well, then I'll just get dressed and bust out of this goose-flappin' prison with Blaze's help."

"Oh, yes, do that *please*, Mr. O'Shea," Maggie said with a chuckle as she and the tray headed toward the door. She turned halfway to award both men a bright smile. "In fact, Mr. Donovan is the perfect person to help you don your sheet since your clothes are locked in the closet down the hall. He's quite adept, you know." The smirk on Blaze's face withered along with the humor in his eyes as she turned on her heel. "Good day, gentlemen."

"Confound it, missy—you bring that stew back here right now! It's getting cold."

She tossed a glance over her shoulder, smile twitching. "Certainly, Mr. O'Shea. After I take your temperature."

A swear word sizzled the air as Aiden whirled to glare at Blaze. "Blue thunder, Donovan, don't just stand there—do something!"

"Yes, Mr. Donovan," she said with a challenge in her tone, "please do, but you'll want to grab a sheet first so your clothes aren't covered in stew."

Blaze took a step back with palms in the air and a flicker of a smile. "Sorry, sir, but I've tangled with this filly before, and I'm not hankerin' for another kick in the head."

Maggie arched a brow. "So, what's it going to be, Mr. O'Shea—cold stew or hot humiliation?"

"Humph, not sure I want to eat that stew after all. Probably poisoned it," he muttered with an abrupt swing of stubby legs back into the bed. "Bring that dad-burned temperature poke over here, missy, afore I croak from malnutrition."

"Nope, no poison in the stew, Mr. O'Shea," Maggie said with a satisfied smile, sweeping the tray back onto his lap with great fanfare before waving the thermometer an inch from his nose. "*This time*." She prodded the "poke" in his mouth with enough force to squeeze past the clamp of his lips. "But I can't vouch for the coffee, sir." She tapped her toe as she studied the watch pinned to her apron. "There's a pretty little plant on Ida Mae's windowsill that looks suspiciously like hemlock, which should give you"—her lashes flipped up to singe Mr. Donovan with a pointed look—"and anyone else pause for causing trouble."

Blaze afforded her a heated squint before turning his back to stare out the window. "Surprised you're still drawin' air, then," he said under his breath, his mumble almost inaudible.

Almost.

"I heard that, Mr. Donovan." She plucked the thermometer from Aiden's mouth and read it with an off-center smile. "At least I don't parade around in bed sheets, sir." She swabbed the thermometer with alcohol and shook it down. "Good, it's normal." Tucking it into her apron pocket, she proceeded to fluff his pillow. "Your temperature, that is. But your grumpy behavior?" She scrunched her nose while she took his pulse, halting the rise of his wrist as he clutched a roll in his hand. "Not so much." She dropped it, and his fisted roll hit the tray with a clunk. "Well, looks like Ida Mae's prayers have been answered, Mr. O'Shea, along with those of Sister Fred and every other nurse and nun in this building. "You're going home."

"And not a moment too soon with the likes of you pushing and prodding all day long, I can tell you that." His bushy brows bunched in a frown as he paused, coffee cup midway to his mouth. "Thunderation, you aren't going to be this bossy at the Silver Lining Ranch, I hope."

"Nope." Maggie recorded his vitals on the chart hanging at the end of his bed, ignoring the heat of Blaze Donovan's glare as he perched on the windowsill with arms in a tight fold. She glanced up at Aiden with a hike of her chin. "Because I won't be there, Mr. O'Shea, and neither will Aunt Libby."

"Care to lay odds on that, Miss Mullaney?" Blaze Donovan's drawl held just a touch of humor, as did the barest crook of his mouth.

"I don't gamble, Mr. Donovan," she said with a firm jut of her jaw. She quirked a brow at the smug, fully dressed cowboy, determined to keep the good-looking rogue on his side of the fence. "But my, my. A near-naked cowboy who does. What a surprise."

"Only on a sure thing, ma'am," he said softly, those penetrating blue-green eyes stirring both her and her temper.

She marched over to snap her patient's empty tray up, indifferent to the cup Aiden still held in his hand. "The only sure thing here, *Mr. Donovan*, is that Aunt Libby and I would rather be trussed up in tar and turkey feathers before setting foot on any ranch occupied by you and your uncle."

"A sight more unseemly than a bed sheet, ma'am, if I may be so bold." His voice edged toward husky.

Fire singed her cheeks, prompting a chuckle from Aiden. "Tar and turkey feathers notwithstanding, missy, you can tell that daughter of mine she'll be staying at Finn's ranch nonetheless, as will you, or else."

Maggie yanked the cup—unfortunately empty—from Aiden's hand and thumped it on the tray with a clatter before storming toward the door. Reining in her temper, she turned. "Or else what, Mr. O'Shea? You'll try to bully us like you try to bully everyone in this hospital?" She forced a tight smile. "I think your daughter will have something to say about that, sir."

Aiden actually chuckled as he brushed breadcrumbs from his striped nightshirt. "I have no doubt she will, for all the good it'll do."

Maggie bristled. "Wanna bet?"

"Uh, thought you didn't gamble, Miss Mullaney?" Blaze's half-lidded gaze couldn't hide the smoky tease in his eyes.

She didn't. But if she did, she'd lay odds the humor in his tone was purely to bait her.

When steers fly. Her lips quirked. *Or near-naked cowboys.*

"It's not a gamble, Mr. Donovan, but a certainty you can rely on." She whirled to leave, ignoring both men's chuckles. "Good day, gentlemen."

"Oh, Miss Mullaney ..."

She stopped long enough to toss a quick glance over her shoulder, the sound of Blaze Donovan's voice clearly laced with laughter. "If it's all the same to you, ma'am," he said with a lazy grin, actually having the audacity to shoot her a wink, "I'll just keep the tar warm."

CHAPTER EIGHT

"WHAT?" LIBBY SHOT OUT OF the velvet, tufted chair in the Victorian parlour of The Gold Hill Hotel, gaping at her father. "Absolutely not!"

Great balls of fire—Finn McShane was the last person she wanted to see! She clenched her shawl in her hands, fists as hard and white as the stones embedded in the fireplace where Papa stood, quite certain the smoke from the fire had injured his brain as well as his body. Maggie had mentioned Papa had threatened the absurd notion of Libby and Maggie staying at Finn McShane's ranch for a while, but Libby had only laughed, assuring her that a Nevada blizzard would blow through the devil's kitchen before *that* would ever happen.

With a deep inhale, she slowly relaxed her fingers, determined to maintain control over both her emotions and her life. After all, she was an educated and independent woman and needed to respond accordingly. She straightened her shoulders, grateful Maggie and Gert were still up in their rooms before dinner to honor Papa's request for a private conversation with his daughter.

But when his gaze locked on hers in silent threat, it catapulted her years back to her youth when stalemates with Papa were as common as air. The fire in his eyes suddenly sparked hers, and against her will, all hard-earned maturity fled as she notched her chin up with a jerk. "And you can't make me!"

"I can and I will, young lady," he said with a menacing look, the jut of his jaw as pronounced as her own despite the fatigue furrowing his pale face. Hand pinched white on the mantle, he puffed furiously on his pipe, the sweat gleaming on his brow a key indicator he wasn't fully recovered yet.

Guilt tempered her ire as she eased back down, knotting the shawl in her lap. "Papa, please—can't we talk about this later when you're feeling better? For goodness sake, Sister Fred just released you barely an hour ago."

Smoke billowed above him as he took another draw of his pipe, the maple and vanilla scent of his trademark tobacco melting the years away as quickly as her guilt melted her ire. His hand shook as he replaced his pipe on the cast-iron pipe rest on the mantle. "No, we can't talk about it later, missy, because I don't want to ruin my dinner." He yanked a handkerchief out of his pocket and mopped his face, wobbling enough on his feet to worry her. "Haven't had a dad-burned decent meal since they took me to that goose-flap farm over a week ago."

Mama rose to gently take Papa's arm, the crease of concern in her face identical to those Libby felt in her own. "Now, Aiden, you're getting yourself all worked up again, darling, so please sit down."

"Don't 'darlin'' me, Maeve. This headstrong daughter of yours is going to promise to comply with my wishes or there'll be perdition to pay." He waved his wife off. "Besides," he said with a tighter grip on the mantle, "I've been laid out like a corpse for a solid week now, and I want to stand, confound it."

Mama's tone stiffened along with her spine as she handed him his cane. "There's no need for language, Aiden O'Shea, and I am *not* going to live with a crab when good humor can heal both you and this situation quickly enough."

He snatched the cane from her hand and aimed it at Libby while her mother reclaimed her seat. "Tell that to your mule of a daughter, who's bucking me at every turn."

Libby was back on her feet, shawl slithering to the floor as she held up her ring finger, Harold's diamond glittering as much as her eyes, no doubt. "For heaven's sake, Papa, I'm a thirty-nine-year-old woman with a ring on my finger, a career in New York, and a fiancé awaiting my return. I'm a grown woman!"

"Then act like it!" he shouted, banging the cane on the floor. Her Mother started to rise once again, but Papa only cut her off with a raise of his palm. "No, Maeve, you sit right back down and listen to me"—he glowered at Libby with a look that always buckled her knees—"the both of you—*now!* Seventeen years ago, I made a huge error in judgment, and after cheating St. Peter out of an early retirement, I aim to make it right."

An error in judgment? Seventeen years ago? Shock stole Libby's tongue as her stomach took a tumble.

"Aiden, what are you trying to say?" her mother asked, teetering on the edge of a French provincial chair.

"I'm saying you were right, confound it—I should have never tried to annul Libby's marriage."

"*What?*" Libby sprang up so fast, she felt like a blasted marionette, body wobbling as much as the puppet her father obviously wanted her to be. "Well, it's certainly too late to worry about that now because I am engaged to be married!"

Her father stared her down. "*Were* engaged, young lady, because unless you join your mother and me at the Silver Lining Ranch for the next six months, there won't *be* a wedding."

Libby was so outraged she wished she were sitting down so she could jump back up. "I won't do it!" she shouted, hands plunked to the hips of her blue striped satin walking dress. "And if you persist with this ridiculous notion, I will pack my bags this instant and return to New York to marry Harold. Because in case you aren't aware, Papa, I *don't* need your permission."

Avoiding her gaze, Papa scratched the back of his neck as he retrieved his pipe from the mantle and took a lengthy draw. He blasted the smoke out again on the heels of a ragged cough. Some of his bluster floated away with the fog that slithered across the ceiling like a harbinger of gloom. "Not mine, perhaps, daughter," he said in a much quieter tone, "but most assuredly the Archbishop's."

She blinked as he swabbed his brow once again, his words not making a lick of sense. "Pardon me? What's *that* supposed to mean?" Her fury suddenly faded along with his, voice as wispy as the pale puffs of smoke encircling his head like a misplaced halo, drifting away.

Like my courage …

His gaze slowly rose to meet hers, moist with something she had never seen in her father before.

Regret.

Remorse.

Repentance.

"It means," he said, his weighty tone a portent of woe, "that Finn McShane is still your husband."

All she could do was gasp. Other than that, the only thing on her body that moved were her lids, which flickered several times while she stared, eyes dry sockets of shock.

No pulse.

No air.

No comprehension.

"W-what d-did you s-say?" she finally whispered.

Her mother hurried over to latch an arm to her waist. "Good heavens, Aiden, sit down this instant and tell us what on earth you are babbling about!" Her mother's arms were shaking as much as Libby's as the two of them sank onto the flame-stitch sofa, their faces as depleted of blood as Papa's.

Without further argument, Papa put his pipe back on the mantle and gingerly sat in his chair with a grimace, sweat now glistening on his cheeks as well as his forehead. "I'm talking about the annulment papers, Maeve—they were never filed."

"*What?*" Her mother's jaw dropped, the tremble in her voice matching that in Libby's stomach to a quiver. "You said you sent them in, for pity's sake."

"And I thought I did, Maeve, I swear." He fished a handkerchief out of his vest pocket to blot his face.

"Sweet suffering saints, Aiden O'Shea," Mama shouted, a rarity in and of itself. "How in the name of Providence could this happen?"

"How?" A faint spark of fire lit in her father's eyes as he squinted at his wife. "You blubbered and carried on if you recall, begging me to wait until Libby was good and settled with Marie in New York before I filed." His jaw cranked up to go chin to chin with hers. "And then you traipsed off to New York with Libby for six blasted months, woman, leaving me at the mercy of that chuck-wagon chippie while I'm wheezin' on my deathbed, no doubt poisoned to boot."

"It was barely a cold, you bull-headed Irishman, and Libby was so depressed after you bullied her into that annulment, I had no choice but to stay until she was better."

"Sure, coddle your daughter instead of caring for the man you vowed to love, honor, and obey—"

Mama bolted up, a rare trace of Irish steeling her jaw. "It was because of the 'love, honor, and obey' that you're even alive, Aiden O'Shea. If I hadn't left, it would have been 'love, honor, and *pray* for your sorry soul when I poisoned you myself!"

"Mama, Papa—stop, please!" Libby burst from her chair, her stupor giving way to alarm over her parents fighting, something even rarer than the apology she'd seen in Papa's eyes. "Can't we talk calmly and rationally, please?" She shot both of her parents a pleading look, barely able to believe she was the calm and sensible one for once.

"Rational? Your father?" Her mother issued an uncharacteristic grunt as she plopped back onto the sofa. "There was nothing rational about that annulment, Libby, but your mule of a father twisted my arm as well as yours, and I'm not sure I've ever quite forgiven him for that."

Eyes flaring in shock, Papa stared in silence, Adam's apple hitching hard in his throat. Without a word, he finally lumbered up from his chair and approached the sofa where they sat, a faint groan slipping from his lips as he dropped to his knees. "Maeve," he whispered, taking her reluctant hand in his, "I was a fool, darlin', and I'm askin' you to forgive me." His gaze swung to Libby with a sheen of moisture that mirrored her own. "Libby, I did you and Finn a grave injustice, and I don't know how you can ever forgive me, but I'm askin' you to, darlin', because I mean to make amends."

"Oh, Papa …." Libby launched into his arms, not sure what shocked her more—Papa's apology or the tears in his eyes, but either way, she slid to the floor to give him a violent hug. "Finn and I weren't right for each other, and I know that now, so I'm grateful you saved me from a life of utter domination." She pressed a soft kiss to his forehead, cupping his cheek with a tender smile. "Harold and I have waited this long; we can certainly wait a little longer while you send the papers in, so there's nothing to forgive."

He gave her back an awkward pat as he avoided her eyes, a ruddy shade of red creeping up the back of his neck. "Well now, you might want to reserve judgment on that just yet, darlin', at least till you hear me out." Squeezing her arm, he attempted to lumber to his feet, prompting both Libby and her mother to assist until they had him settled back into his chair, chest heaving from exertion.

Libby hurried to the mantle to fetch his pipe.

"You see, darlin' …" A harsh cough rasped from his throat. "You were so upset at the time that you failed to sign the papers."

She blinked, pipe in hand as she extended it to her father. "No problem, Papa. I can sign them now before you send them in."

"Well, that's just it, darlin'," he said as he peered up, the compassion in his eyes at odds with the hard clamp of his jaw. Her hand froze at the subtle twitch of his moustache, a nervous trait that always accompanied bad news. He reached for his pipe. "It won't be anytime soon."

CHAPTER NINE

"GOOD HEAVENS, WHAT ON EARTH could be taking so long?" Arms in a stiff fold, Maggie paced in Gert's tiny room, the growl of her stomach almost as loud as that of Maeve's ferret, Frannie, which lay on the cast-iron bed. The pet's menacing raccoon-ringed eyes followed Maggie nonstop, obviously as unhappy with her back-and-forth stride as Maggie was waiting to be called for dinner.

"A showdown between a donkey and a mule," Gert said with a grunt, her gangly body pert near longer than the bed as she leaned against the headboard with her boots on, polishing the ivory-stocked Remington pistol she kept in her apron. Cocking the hammer, she squinted into the barrel with a practiced eye, the bloomin' gun as clean as a whistle.

And just as empty as my stomach, Maggie silently bemoaned, in tandem with another Frannie growl.

Gert poked the ferret with the toe of her boot. "Hush up, Frannie. I put up with enough growlin' from that bully I work for; don't need you addin' to the mix." With a final rumble, Frannie plopped her chin on the bed, silently tracking Maggie's every move.

"But bullets to boots when the smoke clears, only one will be a standin', and it sure in the devil won't be Miss Libby." Pursed lips as skewed as the silver topknot on her head, she scooped up a handful of bullets and loaded the gun, making Maggie more than relieved she and the O'Shea's crusty cook got along.

Maggie paused mid-stroll, face in a scrunch. "What do you mean? Mrs. O'Shea said Mr. O'Shea just wanted to discuss Aunt Libby's future, to make sure it was secure."

The grunt that rolled from Gert's lips could have come from a gritty-eyed gunslinger as her silver brows slashed low. "That ol' bullhead wants to 'secure' her future all right, trussed up tighter than a piggin' string on a calf in a hogtying contest." She spun the gun chamber with precision and notched the safety before slipping it into the pocket of her cotton work dress.

"What?" Maggie could only stare, open-mouthed. "How?"

Gert paused for several seconds, eyes narrowed as if she wasn't sure she should say. She finally huffed out a sigh. "Might as well spill the beans since you'll find out soon enough anyway, even though Mrs. Maeve asked me to keep a lid on the pot till after 'the talk.'"

She leaned in, her smile as flat as her mood. "How? By forcing her to stay at Silver Lining Ranch for the next six months, that's how, with him, his saint of a wife, me, Frannie and"—she paused as if to underscore her point, a hint of compassion softening her gaze—"you."

"Me?" Maggie blinked, remembering all too well the confrontation with Aiden O'Shea in his hospital room.

And Blaze Donovan.

Maggie's mouth went dry at the notion of living under the same roof as that insufferably cocky—she swallowed hard—and regrettably handsome cowboy. Turning to adjust her skirt in the mirror, Maggie stiffened her shoulders, uttering a silent prayer that Aunt Libby wouldn't succumb to her father's threats. "Well, Mr. O'Shea may be stubborn, Gert, but the acorn doesn't fall far from the tree, you know." She whirled to face the housekeeper, the speed of her action causing Frannie to grumble. "Mama used to say Aunt Libby had a will forged in red hot steel and a temper to match, so I seriously doubt her father will be able to sway her."

Gert peered up beneath hooded eyes, her smile zagging sideways. "He will if he has her out on a limb and shakes it hard enough, missy, take my word for it." A scowl tainted her face as she crossed skinny arms across an even skinnier chest. "I'm mean as a rattlesnake, pert near unbeatable at poker, and carry a gun, but the mule manages to truss me up in a Frenchie getup to serve him his dinner, so you figure it out. Trust me, he's not just a card sharp with an ace up his sleeve—he's packin' the whole bloomin' deck—and the man cheats like the devil to boot."

Maggie's chin shot up, along with her ire. "That may be, but remember—God not only beat the devil, but he gave him the boot to a much warmer clime."

Gert cackled, the sound rather ominous when joined by Frannie's growl. "Well, that's real good, missy, because Mr. 'Pain-in-the-Posterior' likes to think he *is* God in these here parts."

And Mr. Donovan likes to think he's *God's gift, but so what?* Maggie squelched the urge to let out a Gert-style grunt. "Well, if I were a gambling woman—which I'm not—I'd lay my money on Aunt Libby."

The tiny bed rocked as Gert's laughter ricocheted off the walls of the tiny room, jostling Frannie along with it. "Well, if I were a drinkin' woman—which I am—I'd say you might want to start, missy, because I ain't ever known Aiden O'Shea to lose a fight."

Maggie crossed her arms, wondering if she should cross her fingers too. She steeled her jaw instead. "Wanna bet?"

Gert snorted. "Sounds like a gamble to me, young lady, but even if you're not a gamblin' woman …" Gert rested her head back on the curly cast-iron headboard as she grinned, a definite gleam in her eyes. "Odds are you darn well better be a prayin' one."

CHAPTER TEN

"WHAT?" LIBBY SNATCHED THE PIPE away from her father's reach, jaw dangling.

"Now, Libby, it's just for six months—"

"Six months!" she shouted, pretty darn sure she was burning inside more that Papa's infernal pipe. "Are you crazy?"

"No, daughter, just convicted. I assure you I've given it much thought and prayer since Finn saved my life—"

"But, Papa, he ruined mine, just like you're trying to do!"

"On the contrary," Papa said in a strained tone edged with steel, "I'm trying to save it, young lady." He leveled her with a tightly slatted look, eyelids weighted with fatigue. "You've always been headstrong, Liberty Margaret, but I hoped that someday you would settle down and become heart-strong as well."

Libby gasped along with her mother, his words piercing straight through the very heart he apparently thought to be weak. "And what is *that* supposed to mean?"

His gaze softened somewhat. "It means, darlin', that I fear in many ways, you've taken after your sorry excuse for a father, with a will—and a heart—as hard as your head."

"Aiden Michael O'Shea!" Her mother's tone was laden with shock. "How on earth can you say such a harsh thing to your daughter?"

"Because I fear it's true, Maeve, and deep down in your heart of hearts, you fear it too." His sorrowful gaze flicked from his wife to Libby, the sheen in his eyes a testament to his regret.

He reached for Libby's free hand, but she jerked away, too wounded to accept his affection. Throat tight with emotion, she pushed his pipe at him instead. "That is an utterly cruel thing to say, Papa, and totally untrue."

His sigh lingered in the air along with the scent of vanilla and maple. "Is it, darlin'? How many times a year do we see you?"

She battled a gulp, a knot of guilt constricting the muscles in her neck. "I come home every Thanksgiving, and you know it."

"Yes," he said with a slow nod, "for two days once a year like a thief in the night—in and out before anyone knows you're here."

"That's not fair!" she said, shame stealing her thunder. "You and Mama visit me in New York at least three times a year."

"Because you refuse to come to us."

"Because I have a job!" she defended, "and a fiancé who's entitled to my time."

"Ah, yes, your time." His lips pursed tight. "But not your hand, eh, darlin'?"

"Sweet saints above, Aiden, what is wrong with you?" Her mother expelled an exasperated sigh. "She and Harold are engaged, for heaven's sake!"

Papa peered up at Libby, eyes in a squint. "Of course they are, Maeve. Because after ten years of poor Harold pleading, Libby finally said yes. Not because it suits her heart, mind you, but her will."

"That's ridiculous," Mama said in a huff, settling back into the couch with a fold of her arms. "A woman doesn't up and marry a man she doesn't love unless she's forced to." She cocked a brow at her husband. "Like me. And *unlike* me, Libby is an independent woman, free to follow her heart."

"Only she isn't following her heart, Maeve, she's following her will." He slowly settled back in the chair as if exhausted, his breathing as shallow as hers. "*And* her fear. My gut tells me she isn't engaged because of love." His gaze shifted from his wife to his daughter. "It says she's engaged strictly for more freedom and control, isn't that right, Libby?"

Libby's body went to stone, her father's words a well-aimed arrow. Her lashes flickered closed to stem the rise of moisture beneath her lids. *No, I do love Harold*, she argued in her mind, but even she knew it wasn't the reason she'd finally said yes. Harold was a dear friend, and she loved him as such, but it was his recent appointment to Dean of the Faculty at Vassar that turned the key of Libby's will. As Harold's wife, she'd be able to quit her teaching post to volunteer full time at the National Woman Suffrage Association. And most importantly, she wouldn't have to rely on Papa's strict stipend to live and support her true love: women's rights.

The ultimate freedom.

Freedom from Papa's control.

And freedom from a controlling husband.

Finn McShane's image suddenly popped into her head, and although she hadn't seen the man in over 17 years, the thought of him still had the power to flutter her stomach. As always, anger surged at the control he still exercised over her heart, something she'd vowed she'd never allow another man to do. Yes, the three months they'd been married had been a dream come true and totally wonderful. *Until* he'd refused to allow her to begin a National Woman Suffrage Association chapter in Virginia City. *The nerve!* He'd known how much women's rights had meant to her and even admitted he'd admired her passion for it. But when push came to shove, he'd flat-out put his foot down, giving her an ultimatum:

"It's either your silly suffrage movement, Libby, or me, so take

your pick!"

And she had, furious the man she loved was strong-arming her just like her father had always done. Bullying and forcing their will over hers. A shiver scurried her spine.

Just like other men had …

Shaking off the nausea that started to rise, Libby recalled how Finn's threat had ended in a horrendous row where she'd hurled a china teapot at him before storming out the door.

"No wife of mine is going off half-cocked to stir up a hornet's nest in this town."

The memory caused two tears to dribble down her cheeks.

Because he never cared enough to put her needs—her passion—before his own.

And because he never came after her ...

For three heart-wrenching days, she'd cried her eyes out, but Finn never darkened her door, obviously waiting her out to exercise his control. So, when Papa hustled her out of town to visit Aunt Marie, she'd gone willingly, certain it would bring her husband to his senses.

Only it didn't. The only thing it brought was excruciating heartbreak when he never contacted her again.

"Libby?" her father repeated. "Isn't that right? Are you marrying Harold for love?" His eyes bore into hers. "Or for freedom and control?"

Her lips trembled as she handed him his pipe, wrestling with the urge to lie.

His answering sigh filled the silence in the room. "Don't bother denying it, darlin'. You forget Ryland Kendrick is an old classmate of mine who provides me with a wealth of information as interim Chancellor of Vassar. So, I know for a fact that Harold's appointment to Dean not only carries a far weightier salary than a mere professor"—his hesitation was long enough to underscore his point—"but mandates no fraternization with fellow teachers."

Her mother sat straight up on the couch, a deep wedge gouging the bridge of her nose. "Is that true, Libby? Are you marrying Harold for his money rather than love?"

"No!" she said too loudly, hurrying over to quell her mother's shock. She sat and took her hand, brows tented in a near plea. "I love Harold, Mama, I swear."

"Ah, yes, as ten years of friendship will attest," her father said while he sucked on his pipe.

Mama gripped her arms with an intensity that jolted. "But you are *in love* with him, Libby, aren't you? Like you once were with Finn? Because I raised you to be independent, darling, so you could be spared the awful injustice of an arranged marriage tainted by mandate or need."

"Why, thank you, my dear," Papa said with another lingering sigh, "for that rousing vote of confidence."

Mama tossed Papa a look pinched with annoyance. "Ours is the exception, Aiden, and you know it, but only because I'm a Christian woman who practices Biblical precepts."

"Humph ... a bit more practice might be in order," Papa mumbled.

"So, are you?" Mama pressed, dipping her head to drill Libby with a pointed look. "In love with Harold that way?"

Libby chewed on the edge of her lip, squirming over Mama's question.

"Of course not, Maeve," Papa bellowed, his temper apparently rising along with the smoke in the room. "Because she's still in love with Finn McShane."

"*What?*" Both Libby and Mama gaped, eyes bulging in shock.

Libby launched to her feet. "That is the most outrageous thing I have ever heard, Papa, and makes me wonder if the smoke didn't addle your brain."

"Libby!" Mama bolted up, staring Libby down. "Apologize this instant, young lady, because I'll not have you disrespecting your father." Her gaze thinned as it homed in on Papa with a tight purse of a smile. "That's my job."

Chest heaving, Libby attempted to tamp down her anger, flexing the knotted fists at her sides. "I'm sorry, Papa, but you couldn't be more wrong. I was the addle-brained one when I married Finn McShane, and I have no desire to ever revisit such folly."

"And yet you never signed the papers," Papa said quietly, the stillness of his tone as deafening as the pounding of her pulse. "And put Harold off for ten years."

Fingers gouging the side of her head, Libby began to pace, completely aware she hadn't signed the papers on purpose at the time. *But then she'd just assumed Papa had forged her name.* "Because I was young and foolish, Papa, and—"

"Desperately hurt Finn didn't come after you those first three days to take you back home …" he finished softly, and even the gentleness of his tone couldn't dull the slash of pain in her heart.

Halting mid-stride, she bowed her head with her back to her parents, hand quivering as it covered her eyes. *No, he didn't …* Which meant he was glad to be rid of her just like Papa had said …

"Libby." Her eyes shuttered closed at the sound of her mother's approach, moisture stinging beneath her lids when Mama slipped a tender arm to her waist. "Are you still in love with Finn?" she asked quietly.

No. Yes. A groan slipped from her lips. "Oh, I don't know, Mama, but either way it doesn't matter anymore because I'm going to marry Harold, case closed."

"Not if I can help it." Grunts and groans sounded as Papa obviously struggled to rise from the chair, prompting Mama to hurry over to assist.

Despite her frustration, Papa's labored breathing compelled Libby to peek over her shoulder in concern, and his stormy countenance did not bode well for his health. *Or hers.* "I have no intention of giving you those papers until you agree to my terms, young lady. Six months at Finn's ranch with Mama and me, take it or leave it."

Libby whirled around. "Well, then, I'll leave it!" she said, her ire once again going head-to-head with his own. "It didn't take too long to process those papers the first time, so I'll just file my own. Harold and I have waited this long, Papa, we can certainly wait a bit longer."

"Good luck with that, darlin'." Papa placed his pipe on the mantle, then faced her with a staunch tug of his suit-coat. "I had the favor of Monsignor O'Reilly on my side if you recall, who was kind enough to rush the paperwork through." He slowly buttoned his coat, pinning her with the same dogged look of determination she wore herself. "Which I understand can take up to a number of years." He paused for effect, chin rising along with hers. "*If* it's approved at all."

Libby's gaze darted to her mother, needle pricks of fear pebbling her skin. "Mama, *please*, can't you talk him out of this ridiculous demand?"

Her mother glanced from Libby to her husband and back, the sympathetic slope of her brows a sure indication she was about to side with Papa. "I would, darling, if I thought you really loved Harold—"

"Mama, I *do* love Harold, I promise!" she said with a plea in her tone, fear crawling in her stomach along with the nausea at the thought of staying in Virginia City at all, much less with Finn.

Her mother offered a tender smile as she moved to take Libby's hand. "Not like you loved Finn, sweetheart, and if Papa's suspicions—and now mine based on what Papa said—are true, then you've never really stopped, now have you? Besides," she said with a gentle hug, "You can use this six months to find out whose wife you really need to be because if Finn still cares for you too—"

"He does." Papa's tone was adamant.

"Then you owe it to Finn, Harold, *and* yourself," Mama continued with a patient smile, "to discover the truth and give Papa's request a chance."

"*Request?!*" Libby shouted, not giving a whit who in the hotel heard her. "'Threat' is more like it." She locked her arms across her chest in battle mode, refusing to be bullied by her father or any man *ever* again.

Especially the one who'd broken her heart in a sham of a marriage.

"Well, I won't do it, it's as simple as that," she said with a thrust of her jaw. "I have a job, a place to live at Vassar, and a fiancé who is more than willing to wait, so I'm sorry, Papa, but I will be leaving first thing in the morning."

"Well, I'm sorry, too, darlin'," Papa said with an absent scrub at the back of his head, "because about that job of yours ..."

His words snatched the air from her throat.

"As I mentioned before, Ryland and I are friends, so when I wired him you wouldn't be coming back for a while—"

"*What?*" Libby grew faint while nausea roiled in her belly.

"Yes," Papa said without a hitch, "we both concurred that you were best needed here for the time being. Especially since you'll be quitting after you marry Harold anyway, so he's replaced you for the time being."

Her pulse skidded to a stop. *Dear Lord, this can't be happening!* She swayed on her feet, lids weighting closed like they were made of lead.

No job.

No home.

No marriage.

No freedom.

Her eyes flashed open in fury, determined that her bully of a father would *not* win. "Then I will search for another job," she said with a thread of defiance.

Her father nodded as if giving that some thought. "Yes, you could do that, I suppose, although jobs will be scarce since most learning institutions have already hired for the upcoming year. And then there's the absence of funds …"

She leveled her shoulders. "My salary will be missed, yes, but I should have enough until I can secure a new appointment. In fact, the new building for the St. Patrick Female Orphan Asylum where I've volunteered for years will be completed next year, and Sister Leona has hinted at possibly needing additional staff."

Papa looked up beneath beetled brows. "I was speaking of your allowance, daughter, the one I will cease sending if you refuse to comply with my wishes."

Sleet slithered her veins. "You wouldn't," she whispered, her voice little more than a croak. *Not her allowance …* The breath in her lungs grew heavy and thick, clogging her throat. Long before Libby had secured her teaching position at Vassar, Mama had won the war over Papa's reluctance to subsidize Libby's income. An income that not only provided a comfortable living for their daughter, but supported Libby's passion for women's rights as well.

"Of course I would," Papa said in his matter-of-fact tone, one hand knuckled white on the back of the chair. "If I believed this was in your best interest, and I clearly do." His gaze softened the slightest bit. "Then if you still want to leave to marry that fop of a professor—"

"Dean of Faculty," Libby stressed in a tight tone.

A hint of a smile twitched beneath Papa's moustache. "Pardon me—if you still want to marry that fop of a dean after the six months, you'll not only retain your allowance, but I will use my influence once again to secure a final annulment."

Six excruciating months with the man who had broken her heart! Panic climbed up her throat like bile, all but choking her air. Her watery gaze slashed to Mama, the plea in her tone as clear as the moisture in her eyes. "Mama, *please*—don't let him do this."

"Libby," Mama whispered, an answering sheen of tears

glimmering as she moved to stand by Papa. He quickly latched an arm to her shoulder while Mama swiped at her sodden face. "We love you desperately, darling, and would do anything for you, you know that. But this time I believe Papa is right. It may be God's will for you to do everything to salvage your marriage."

"I have no marriage!" she yelled as she stomped back to the sofa, desperate to flee her father's control, even if it was only for a brief while. "And it's *not* God's will." She snatched up her shawl and slung it around her shoulders. "It's Papa's." She stormed to the front door.

"Libby, where are you going?" Alarm edged Mama's voice as she took a step forward. "It's time for dinner."

"I don't need dinner," she shouted, hand on the knob. "I need fresh air—lots and lots of fresh air." Lashing the door open, she barreled out.

Right into a mountain of a man who smelled like leather, lime, and mint. Bouncing off a granite chest, she gasped while a whoosh of familiar air sucked right into her lungs.

And God help her—it was *anything* but "fresh."

CHAPTER ELEVEN

WHAT IN THE BLUE BLAZES . . . ? Finn froze, "blazes" an appropriate word for the heat surging through his body the moment he realized the woman he loved was plastered against his chest. He grabbed to steady her when she ricocheted off and sorely wished someone could "steady" him as well. Not to mention cool his blood down when the familiar scent of lilacs ignited plenty of blazes throughout his body. And God help him, they were anything but "blue."

More like red, red *hot.*

Glad he'd always been fast on his feet, Finn ignored the sprint of his pulse as his lips slid into a slow smile. "Why, hello, Libby," he said in a husky tone edged with tease that he'd always reserved just for her. Taking advantage of her momentary paralysis, he allowed his gaze to travel the length of her before rising again to settle on her open mouth. "You're looking well."

Well? A grunt would have escaped if he wasn't so intent on maintaining control with an easy manner, but it sure in the blazes wasn't easy. Libby O'Shea had always been a fine-looking girl, but now she was a full-grown woman gently ripened by age. Generous curves only accentuated a soft beauty that was more defined with a sprinkling of nearly invisible laugh lines around her mouth and eyes. The girlish fullness of her once dewy face had matured into sculpted porcelain dusted with rice powder and, no doubt, a hint of beet juice to give her lips and cheeks that glorious blush. All perfectly complemented, of course, by deep copper curls pinned high on her head. A profusion of dark lashes flickered in surprise, framing green eyes that had always held him spellbound—the color of moss in a mountain brook during the spring.

Nope, make that *winter*, he decided when she swiftly pushed him away. *With an icy,* icy *brook.*

"H-Hello, F-Finn," she whispered, taking another step back, obviously to regain composure with a clamp of her arms. The lashes slowly lifted to pin him with an emerald gaze so distant, she may as well have been in New York. "You're looking well, too," she said quickly, taking another step back as her gaze dropped to his newly shined boots.

"I've missed you, Libby," he whispered, words rushing from his tongue as quickly as the longing that channeled through his bloodstream. He knew he shouldn't have said it, but somehow seeing her again—that tentative chew of lush lips he still dreamed about and the stiff barrier of arms to her waist—made it feel like she had never left. Never stayed away.

Never broken his heart.

Like that stupid teapot, into a hundred pieces.

Her head slowly lifted, eyes wary. "I suppose you're here to see my father?" she asked, completely ignoring his statement. "Because I'm sorry, but we're just sitting down to dinn—"

"Finn, my boy—right on time!"

Finn glanced past Libby while she whirled around, the look on Aiden's face a whole lot warmer than the one on his daughter's. He doffed his Stetson. "Evenin' Aiden, Maeve."

"What d-do you mean, 'right on t-time'?" Libby stuttered. "You didn't invite him to dinner, did you?" she said in a harsh whisper, as if she didn't want Finn to hear.

"No, of course not," Aiden said with a chuckle, making

his way into the foyer with Maeve on his arm.

"Oh, thank goodness." Libby's shoulders actually sank in relief.

"He invited *us*," his father said, bypassing Libby altogether to extend a hand to Finn. "Sure appreciate your hospitality, Finn. We're all checked out and ready to go. Our bags are lined up right there against that wall."

Libby spun around to where Aiden pointed, nearly toppling into Finn's chest once again, which prompted him to latch another hand to her arm. *Which* she quickly removed. "Please stop manhandling me," she whispered, coaxing a smile to his lips when he remembered just how much fun he'd had manhandling a spitfire like her.

Inside of marriage and out.

"Libby, behave," her mother said, hurrying over to give Finn a hug that warmed him to the bone. "Finn, I don't know how I'll ever be able to thank you for your kind hospitality, but I fully intend to try." She pulled back to pin him with a determined look, hands braced to his arms. "I understand your nieces lost their tutor this year, so rest assured that Libby and I will be happy to provide all the education they need."

"What?" Libby gaped, those amazing green eyes nearly eclipsed by white.

Maeve patted Libby's cheek. "It's the least we can do, darling, with Finn providing lodging for us."

Libby spun to face Finn with a strained smile. "Thank you, Finn, for your kind hospitality to my parents, but Maggie and I will be staying here." With a swish of her skirt, she side-stepped her mother like the poor woman was related to Finn.

"Mr. O'Shea!" Donald Raymond Turley, Sr. strode into the foyer in a three-piece sack suit too small for his portly frame, vest buttons pulled tightly across his ample belly as he waved a paper in his hand. "It's been our pleasure to serve you, sir, and we shall miss you and your family here at The Gold Hill Hotel." He handed the paper over with a broad smile before acknowledging Finn with a pleased nod. "Your receipt, sir, paid in full. Evenin', Finn."

"Evenin', Don," Finn said with a slight tip of his hat.

Libby's frantic gaze darted from her father to the hotel proprietor's. "Mr. Turley, just so you know, Miss Mullaney and I will be retaining our room."

Donald paused, the smile fading on his face as he nervously adjusted his vest. "I'm sorry, Miss O'Shea, but I'm afraid that's not possible," he said with a hard duck of his throat, gaze shifting to her father and back. "You see, we're completely sold out."

"But how can that be? Miss Mullaney and I haven't even checked out yet!"

Don managed an impressive show of teeth despite the gleam of sweat on his brow. "Oh, no problem, Miss O'Shea. Your father has already handled all the checkout details, so you're free to go."

Finn squelched a smile when Aiden smacked his cane on the hardwood floor with a loud thwack. "So, stop dawdling and go pack your bags, young lady, then rustle everybody else down so we can get a move on—I'm hungry."

"Oh, we'll pack all right, Papa," Libby said, "but we won't be going to Mr. McShane's." She turned to march to the stairs, shoulders firm and head high. "Maggie and I will just check into another hotel."

"Uh … that might be a bit difficult, darlin'," Aiden said with a sheepish scratch of his jaw. "Hear tell all accommodations are full up, isn't that so, Mr. Turley?"

"I'm afraid so, Miss O'Shea," Don said with a straight face, and Finn could only shake his head. How he wished he'd had Aiden O'Shea on his side seventeen years ago when Finn had battled with his daughter time and time again.

Libby pivoted on the first step, shock expanding her features. "I don't believe it." Her gaze swiveled to her mother.

"Mama, are you going to let him blackmail me like this?"

Maeve hurried over to give her daughter a quick hug. "Don't think of it as blackmail, darling," her mother said with a tender smile, "think of it as a father exercising his love for his daughter, all right? Now run along, sweetheart, and hurry everyone else down so we can get some food in Papa's stomach."

Finn took a step forward, hat in hand. His gaze flicked from Maeve to her daughter with the semblance of a smile. "Maeve, I'd be happy to take Aiden and you and everyone else who's ready to the ranch now and come back for Libby later if she likes."

"Perfect," Aiden said with another thump of his cane. "Libby, send Gert and the blasted ferret down along with that bossy nurse if she's ready, then Finn will be back for you later."

"If I'm still here," Libby said with a staunch thrust of her chin.

"Oh, you'll be here, darlin'." Aiden snatched his bowler off the rack by the door and placed it on his head with several firm taps. "Here tell the benches in the town square are a mite uncomfortable and noisy when the saloons let out."

Libby spun on her heel and yanked her skirt up as she stormed up the steps.

"Oh, and take your time, Liberty Bell," Finn called, unable to resist employing the nickname Libby hated to rile some sparks in those glittering green eyes. "I'm more than willing to wait." Strolling over to the baggage, Finn hefted two valises and a hatbox in his hands as he gave Maeve and Aiden a wink. "After all, I've had seventeen years of practice."

CHAPTER TWELVE

"SO, MAGGIE—DO YOU RIDE?"

Maggie looked up from her nearly full plate in Finn McShane's elegantly rustic dining room, vaguely aware her host had asked her a question. She blinked several times, lids flickering as much as the candles in the carved wooden candelabras, barely able to sort out her thoughts quickly enough to respond. Her mind—and her plate—were too full of unique things she'd never experienced before.

From squirrel stew and fried salt pork with gravy, to potato cakes and vinegar pie, she was totally agog over the bounty before her. *Especially* the warm and welcoming interplay of personalities around a table abuzz with chatter and chuckles. Totally mesmerized by the easy banter, she'd watched Finn rib Blaze and his brother Dash about besting them at target practice, two brothers who seemed more like Finn's sons than nephews. Which made perfect sense, Maggie supposed, since Finn had told them on the ride to the ranch that he'd unofficially adopted his nieces and nephews after his sister passed.

The two brothers appeared to be as opposite as Sister Fred and the girls at the Ponderosa Saloon. Fluid and easy with his smiles and compliments, Dash had dark sable hair and pale-blue eyes to Blaze's sun-streaked brown and turquoise blue. Where Blaze was tall and muscled, Dash was tall and lean, and yet a striking resemblance was more than obvious. Both had the same angular face dotted with deep dimples and the same full, wide lips, albeit Dash's curved up in laughter and tease throughout the dinner while Blaze's curved down.

At least when he looks at me.

Expelling a silent sigh, Maggie had turned her attention across the way, to where Mr. and Mrs. O'Shea laughed with Finn's nieces. Seventeen-year-old Sheridan was a petite golden-haired imp who boasted the same mischievous twinkle in her blue eyes as Dash, exuding a sweet sass that couldn't quite hide an air of innocence carefully nurtured, no doubt, by an overly protective uncle and two big brothers.

Her little sister Shaylee sat beside her, her freckled face, chestnut braids, and tomboy air making her seem far younger than the thirteen years she claimed. As fine-boned and petite as her older sister, Shaylee appeared as rough-and-tumble as Sheridan was feminine. Her exuberance for animals, bugs, and dirt stood in stark contrast to her sister's burgeoning womanhood, obviously preferring dusty overalls to Sheridan's pretty calico and ribbons. Where Sheridan seemed to revel in being a girl, Maggie got the distinct impression that Shaylee did not, perhaps due to the lack of female influence in her life until now. Although cute as a button, the young girl boasted the same pointed chin as her oldest brother, hinting at the streak of stubbornness Maggie had encountered in Blaze.

A cackle to Maggie's left indicated that even Gert was enjoying a rare laugh over Finn's jesting, although scowls usually reserved for Aiden now seemed to be aimed at Finn's cook, Angus McDougal. Wiry and witty, Angus had started out as a miner in Finn's silver mine on the west quadrant of The Silver Lining Ranch. *Until* Finn discovered he'd also been a chuck-wagon cook.

Once the mine prospered, Finn wasted no time turning Angus loose in his new, fancy kitchen. And now, Angus had boasted with a gap-toothed grin, he was as much a part of the family as Finn's border collie, Scout, now curled up at Finn's feet with Frannie snug in the middle. A contented sigh drifted from Maggie's lips.

A hodge-podge family that warmed her to the core.

The moment the buckboard had rumbled past the log and stone entrance of the Silver Lining Ranch, Maggie was certain the whites of her eyes would be dust-dry by bedtime. Backdropped by majestic mountains dusted with snow, the dirt driveway was edged by a pretty log fence while it meandered through a vibrant meadow of wildflowers and stately ponderosa pines. Out of its midst rose the largest two-story log house Maggie had ever seen, tucked against the base of gently sloping hills. Beyond miles of wood-slatted fence dotted with cattle rose a profusion of pines from which the Sierra Nevada mountains soared to the sky, a majestic sentinel for Finn's pastoral home.

Beautifully landscaped with wild roses and a variety of flowering cactus, the house took prominence over an enormous barn recessed on the far right and a long, narrow log building on the left, referred to by Finn as the bunkhouse and mess hall. The sounds of a harmonica drifted on the breeze while cowhands milled about, most perched on a fence to watch a rodeo of sorts, Finn said, where round-up contests were held to pass the time.

But when Finn had ushered them up the steps of the endless, log-hewn wrap-around porch through the mammoth oak door with its intricate carving of Bar SLR, Maggie had been speechless. The magnificent hardwood entryway with its vibrant Navajo rug, exquisite paintings, and unique pottery had literally stolen her breath away. And now, amidst the laughter and love of this truly unconventional family, it would seem her tongue had been stolen as well.

"Maggie?" Finn's voice jolted her out of her reverie.

Startling, she sheepishly looked his way, suddenly aware

everyone else had finished their dinner. Her gaze snagged on Blaze, and heat pulsed in her cheeks when those blue eyes pinned her with a hint of a smirk. He lounged back in his thick log chair, muscled arm casually draped over its back post. The bold masculinity in his gaze was so potent, she quickly averted her eyes, pulse pounding along with her heart. "Please forgive me, Finn, for indulging in a wee bit of wool-gathering, but I honestly have never seen anything like this before."

"Like what?" Shaylee asked with a scrunch of freckles, her chestnut braid as disheveled as the dusty overalls she wore.

"Oh, you know," Maggie began, offering a tiny shrug. "So much noise and food and fun at the dinner table. You see, I don't have any brothers or sisters, so dinners were always a somber affair."

"Holy frog spit—that sounds awful!" Shaylee said, face in a pucker as if she smelled something bad.

"Shaylee—" Warning edged Finn's tone.

Maggie whirled to flash a smile his way. "No, it *was* awful, Finn," she said with a giggle, suddenly feeling younger than Shaylee as she shared her grin with the rest of the table. "My stepfather was an associate judge on the New York Court of Appeals and demanded complete silence at meals, often glaring if my silverware dared to clink. It was so quiet, in fact, you could actually hear the clock tick in time with my stepfather slurping his soup."

"Oh my goodness, that *is* awful," Mrs. O'Shea said with a sparkle in her eyes over the rim of her tea cup, "and here I thought Aiden was a horror at dinner."

Laughter rounded the table as Aiden seared his wife with a mock glare. "Only since you and that quack of a doctor force me to drink tea rather than coffee. *And* whenever your daughter is around, in case you haven't noticed." He nodded his thanks when Angus rose to retrieve the teapot from the sideboard, pouring more hot water for Aiden's tea. "As you will all soon discover, I might add," he said with a droll smile, "when she—*and* the sparks—arrive."

Maggie laughed and tackled more stew. "Well I welcome any and all sparks at the dinner table because it's sure better then dining in a morgue."

Grinning, Sheridan leaned in with arms propped on the table, the lace trim on her blue calico dress puckering enough to reveal that Finn's niece was definitely growing up. "Holy buckets of yawn, Maggie, I'd die of boredom!"

"Almost did." Maggie spooned her final bite of stew with a proud heft of her chin, a mischievous smile tugging at her lips. "Till I suddenly developed a whole lot of colds—hacking, sneezing, and blowing my nose something awful." She gave Sheridan a wink. "You can't imagine how quickly 'The Judge' excused me to go to my room. *Where*"—her brows did a little dance—"either Mama or our cook, Elsie, would deliver a plate of fried chicken or whatever else we were having with all the trimmings."

"Gee Whillikers—did your mother have to be quiet too?" Shaylee's brows tented in sympathy on a face smudged with dirt she'd obviously missed when Finn asked her to wash up before dinner.

The smile on Maggie's face stiffened as she reached for her coffee, taking a quick sip to dispel the tight feeling in her throat. "Yes, that is until she passed when I was nineteen, she said quietly, determined to ward off the threat of tears that always arose whenever she thought of her mother.

"Our condolences, Maggie—we didn't know." Finn's voice was gentle enough to stoke the moisture in her eyes, much to Maggie's regret. His tone was laced with compassion. "With losing my sister and the kids' mother at such an early age, we certainly understand how difficult that can be."

"Yes, of course you would," she said with a smile that felt as wooden as the table now littered with dirty dishes, "but things work out because your nieces and nephews had you, and I had Aunt Libby." Her gaze flitted from the girls to Blaze and Dash and then finally to Finn, suddenly aware they had all lost someone they loved, another kinship with this unlikely family.

"Oh, I can't wait to meet Aunt Libby!" Shaylee gushed.

Maggie smiled. "Well, she's not really my aunt, of course, she's my godmother. But I like to call her that because as my mother's best friend, she stepped in as mother, big sister, and dear friend all in one."

"Well, she's definitely *our* aunt," Sheridan said with a smile, blonde hair trailing her shoulders, "and I can't wait to meet her too. When are you picking her up, Uncle Finn?"

"She's *your* aunt?" Maggie paused, the last spoonful of stew hovering before her mouth. She glanced around the table with a crease in her brow. "Aunt Libby's related to you?"

Glancing at his pocket watch, Finn pushed away from the table. "Right now, Sheridan, as a matter of fact." His gaze settled on Maggie with a smile. "The girls just like to call her that because they've always wanted an aunt."

"But she *is* our aunt," Shaylee insisted, "or at least she used to be because I saw your wedding picture hidden in your closet, Uncle Finn!"

Maggie gasped while the spoon clattered onto her plate, splattering stew on her crisp, white shirtwaist. Gaping at Finn, she dipped her napkin into her water glass to blot at the stains, barely aware of what she was doing. "You and Libby were *married*?" she said in a near squeak, mind dizzy at the thought. She'd known there was bad blood between her godmother and Finn McShane, but her aunt had never told her why. But marriage! *Sweet mother of Job—why hadn't Aunt Libby told her?* She blinked. *And why hadn't Mama?*

Sucking air through a clenched smile, Finn awkwardly cuffed his neck. "Yeah, well, it's a mite complicated, Maggie, but suffice it to say it was a long time ago and an annulment was involved. Now I need to go fetch the lady in question, so maybe Mr. O'Shea can explain it to you."

"Humph!" Aiden cut loose with a grunt. "Can't explain it to myself much less anybody else."

Laughing, Finn lifted his jacket off the back of his chair, slipping it on. "Or Libby can fill you in since you two will be sharing a room."

Shaylee squinted up at her uncle. "What's an annulment, Uncle Finn? And isn't Aunt Libby supposed to sleep in your room?"

A ruddy shade of red singed the back of Finn's neck as he pushed in his chair. "An annulment means two people are no longer legally married, Shay, and like I said, it's a mite complicated. But suffice it to say that I'm sure your aunt would be more comfortable rooming with Maggie for now. But I'll tell you what," he said with an overly bright smile, obviously wanting to move the conversation on, "I'm mighty glad I built six bedrooms upstairs. Sure comes in handy when five extra people move in, even if we do have to double up and send Angus to the bunkhouse."

"By jingo, it'll be like old times," Angus said with a chuckle, rising to gather up the dirty dishes while he gave Maggie a wink, "especially if I can hone my poker skills on a few of the new hands."

"Poker?" Gert's brows bunched low over black eyes that suddenly held a glint of interest. "You any good?"

"Good?" Dash tossed his napkin on the table and stood, nudging his chair in with a crooked smile. "He's a bona fide cardsharp, Gert, who's fleeced everybody in this family, so you best steer clear."

Gert's lips pursed in a thin smile before she shot Angus a narrow look. "Trust me, Mr. Dash, ain't nothing I'd rather do than steer clear, but I'm cursed with a weakness for poker."

"Pshaw, I can cure that right quick, missy," Angus said,

butting his way through the swinging door into the kitchen with a wink, the stack of dirty dishes in his hands clear up to his nose. "Once I hog-tie you and your money a couple dozen times." The door swung closed behind him before Gert could even respond.

Scrambling to her feet, Gert swiped up the rest of the dirty dishes, the scowl on her face not boding well for Angus. "This here house ain't big enough for the both of us," she muttered.

"Sure it is, Gert," Dash said with a slap on Blaze's shoulder. "My nose-to-the grindstone big brother here and I barely see eye to eye on black and white without butting heads, so if we can do it, you and ol' Angus can."

"Only if I do all the cookin' and *he* does all the dishes," she said with a gum of her lips, piling the last of the dirty plates and utensils high on her way to the kitchen. She paused at the door to deliver a rare wink laced with a smirk. "*Which* one quick game of poker should fix right now, so wish me luck." The kitchen door swung closed, unleashing more giggles and grins around the table.

Shaking his head, Blaze flicked his brother's hand off his shoulder and rose, his patient smile veering left. "We got along *before* we shared a room, little brother," he said while he pushed in his chair. "If my room starts looking like yours, you'll be sleeping in the barn." His lips quirked while he shot Shaylee a wink. "Where he belongs."

Dash chuckled as he ambled to the door, turning to flash his dimples. "Not necessarily a bad thing when you consider how you snore. Might be a tad quieter and definitely smell a whole lot better than you after a hard day on the range."

"Earned by doing a man's work, *baby* brother," Blaze said with a lazy smile, strolling over to loop an arm over Dash's shoulder, "not working at the Ponderosa, where the heaviest thing you lift is a mug of beer."

"*Countless* mugs of beer," Dash said with a wink at Maggie, "in a profitable establishment that will one day be mine."

"All things are lawful, but all are not profitable, Dash—1 Corinthians 10:23," Finn said with an affectionate clutch of Dash's shoulder, the easy smile on his face at odds with the hint of concern in his eyes.

"Uh-oh. Uncle Finn is spouting Scripture, so that's my cue to go to work." Dash offered a salute. "Good night, everyone, and I'm mighty glad you're all here. It's my night to close, Uncle Finn, so don't wait up."

"I'll have a stall ready for you," Blaze called as Dash slipped out the front door.

"Speaking of the barn …" Finn glanced at Maggie while she tackled her pie. "Back to my original question, Maggie—do you ride?"

"Horses?" Maggie said with a hard swallow, nearly choking on her vinegar pie. The smooth custard finally slid down her throat after she glugged a quick drink of water.

Blaze's patient smile took a twist. "Unless you're fond of walking, Miss Mullaney? In which case, you'll want to rise well before dawn to get to work."

Maggie gulped, the thought of riding a horse stuttering her heart as much as Blaze Donovan stuttered her pulse—two things she desperately wanted to avoid. She hadn't given any thought to needing a ride to the hospital each morning, but she supposed she would, seeing that the Silver Lining Ranch was well past the outskirts of town. She peeked up at Finn, the vinegar pie in her stomach suddenly living up to its name. "No, I'm afraid I've never ridden a horse before." she whispered.

"No problem," Finn assured her with a kind smile. "Blaze is a great teacher."

CHAPTER THIRTEEN

"*WHAT??*" BLAZE'S AND MAGGIE'S VOICES rose in unison, the only accord Blaze figured the two would ever share. Both of their heads jerked in Finn's direction, the shock in their tones mirroring the horror on their faces.

"Sure." Finn strolled into the foyer to snatch his Stetson off the coat rack before returning to stand beneath the dining room's wooden beamed archway. "Blaze can drive you to the hospital each day until you feel comfortable enough to ride on your own." He positioned his hat on his head just so. "Or you can take one of the buckboards, Maggie, but either way, you'll need instruction."

Blaze cleared his throat. "Uh, maybe it would be best if Dash teaches her, Uncle Finn. Or maybe one of the girls?" He tried to temper his desperation, the idea of spending time with Miss Goody Two-Shoes doing nothing for his mood. He stared at his uncle, hands buried deep in his pockets. "I mean, with branding starting up this week, I'll be rising before the sun as it is just to get things done."

"Yes, please, Dash or the girls would be fine," Maggie echoed, her face leeching as white as that blasted sheet he wore the first time he'd met her.

Huffing out a heavy sigh, Finn propped hands on his hips, drilling both Maggie and Blaze with a steely look of authority neither were likely to defy. "Sorry, Maggie, but Blaze needs to be the one to teach you because there's a tension between you two tighter than the reins on a buckin' bronc, and I aim to nip it in the bud right now. The last thing I need when Miss O'Shea walks through that door is more hostility in my happy home."

"It's Mrs. McShane," Aiden said in a matter-of-fact voice while he casually sipped his tea.

"What?" Blaze stared at his uncle, not sure he'd heard correctly. "What's he talking about, Uncle Finn?"

"I *mean* your uncle and my daughter are still married," Aiden explained with a satisfied smile, raising his teacup in a toast. "One of the few wrong things I did right, apparently."

A low groan left Finn's lips as he ran a hand down his face. "Thanks a lot, Aiden. I was hoping to save that bit of news for another day."

"Why?" Aiden asked, leaning back with one arm draped over his chair. "The way I see it, you're going to need all the help you can get corralling that stubborn girl of mine, so you may as well elicit your family."

"What the devil is he talking about, Uncle Finn?" Blaze demanded, his features so tight, they could have been carved from the blasted bedrock of the Sierras. "You told us the marriage was annulled seventeen years ago."

Finn expelled another weary breath. "Yes, I did, but it seems I was mistaken." He nodded toward Aiden. "The papers were never signed and submitted, according to Mr. O'Shea, so it appears his daughter and I are still hitched."

"Oh my stars," Maggie whispered, hand splayed to her chest. Sagging back in her chair, she gaped at Finn. "Does Aunt Libby know?"

Finn's mouth tamped into a thin line. "Yes, which is why I need everyone to help make this transition as smooth as possible. God's given me a second chance with the only woman I've ever loved, and come hell or high water, fire or flood, I aim to make her mine."

Aiden cleared his throat. "Yes, well, that high water

should come in mighty handy, my boy, once the sparks begin to fly and all hell breaks loose."

A grin slid across Finn's face as he tipped his hat. "The sparks are one of the things I'm looking forward to the most, Aiden." He winked. "As long as they light a fire under your girl, that is, because right now she'd just as soon shoot as look at me."

"Yeah? Well, she's not alone," Blaze muttered under his breath, hardly able to believe that Uncle Finn wanted a woman back in his life who'd abandoned him, betrayed him, basically left him for dead. And a so-called Christian woman at that, one who supposedly espoused love and faith in God, but sure in the devil didn't show it. A twinge of bitterness fanned the flames of his anger. *Like my mother.* He headed for the foyer. "Excuse me, folks," he said without a glance back, but I need to check on the new foal."

It took everything in him not to slam the blasted door off its hinges, but it wasn't the guests who had lit a fire under him. No, it was Uncle Finn—the man he loved and respected more than any man alive.

Till now.

Storming down the porch steps, he barreled for the barn, ignoring his uncle's call from the porch. It was a blatant lack of respect he'd seldom shown his elder before, but Blaze's respect for Finn had hit a rock in the road, and it was rapidly becoming a boulder.

Starting with the day he'd learned Libby and her family would be living at the ranch for the next six months.

"What?" Blaze couldn't have been more stunned if a blasted steer had kicked him in the head. "Aunt Libby left you high and dry, broke your heart and ours too, and now you're going to bring her and her family into our house?" He'd stared at his uncle as if he were the one who'd gone plum loco from a hoof to the head.

"They're homeless, Blaze, and they need our help."

Blaze's jaw dropped a full inch. "They're richer than you

are, Uncle Finn, and can certainly afford a hotel. *Especially* if that confounded woman who forced me to parade around town in a blasted sheet is with 'em."

A smile had flickered on his uncle's mouth as he'd leaned back in the cowhide chair in his study, hands resting on the arms like a gunslinger biding his time. "I know your stubborn temper, Blaze, because you inherited it from me, remember? And somehow I doubt that sweet nurse put a gun to your head."

"No, Sister Fred put the gun to my head," Blaze had mumbled, pacing back and forth in front of the massive oak desk at which his uncle conducted most of his business, "but that dad-burned nurse sure in the devil loaded the bullets."

Uncle Finn had risen to circle his desk and latch a hand to Blaze's shoulder like the father he'd become. His tone was laden with the same kindness and caring that had won Blaze's respect as an angry boy who'd just lost his mother. "It's the right thing to do, Bren," he'd said quietly, because like I learned and taught you long ago, true liberty is doing the right thing."

Blaze hadn't liked the whole idea at the time, but he'd known his uncle was right. Doing the right thing had been the first lesson Uncle Finn taught him after he'd rescued Blaze and his siblings following the deaths of their parents. And it had always proven true over the years whether Blaze embraced his uncle's faith or not, so he'd bitten his tongue that day in the study, reining in his temper.

Until just now, when Uncle Finn had tripped it again.

"God's given me a second chance with the only woman I've ever loved, and come hell or high water, fire or flood, I aim to make her mine."

"Blaze, hold up!" His uncle's voice carried across the yard, but Blaze just kept on walking, knuckles white and mood black as he blatantly ignored the man who'd become a father.

"I said, hold up, boy—*now!*" His uncle's harsh tone, a rarity in itself, halted Blaze dead in his tracks.

Blaze bowed his head with a low groan, aware that he'd obviously torched Uncle Finn's temper, something he rarely saw. He slowly turned to face the wrath of God. Which wasn't too far off given the fire blazing in his uncle's eyes and the tic pulsing in his jaw as he thundered up to go nose to nose with Blaze. "You work for me, boy, and don't you forget that," Finn said, his uncle's six-foot-three looming over Blaze's six-foot-two with far more than height. "When I call, you best listen, or you'll be collecting a paycheck somewhere else—is that clear?"

"Yes, sir." Blaze huffed out his frustration, facial muscles as stony as his uncle's.

"And another thing—the next time you disrespect our company like you just did, storming off like a bull toward a red barn, you can just keep on walking. Because I will not tolerate rudeness in my home. Is that understood?"

Blaze shifted, hands clenched at his sides. "Yes, sir."

"Good." Finn nodded toward the barn. "Now get your sorry hide in there to check on that foal so we don't have to add lies to your bad manners." Without another word he strode to the barn, leaving Blaze to follow. Halting in front of the stall where the new foal lay in a bed of hay beside its mother, Uncle Finn leaned his forearms on the fencing to study both mare and newborn while Blaze did the same. "You know, Blaze, you're a man fully grown," he said quietly, his tone that of an uncle now instead of an employer, "and I couldn't be prouder if you were my own son. But being a man doesn't guarantee always saying or doing the right thing, something I learned the hard way." He paused, his voice suddenly thick with affection. "As you did, son, with both your pa and your mother."

His mother.

Uncle Finn's little sister.

And the one person Blaze blamed for all the tragedy in

his life.

"She should've never married him in the first place," Blaze had once overheard Uncle Finn say to Angus, "and Ma and I tried to tell her that, but Peg was in love and as stubborn as they come. A woman of faith marrying a man who had none, but she thought she could change him."

Change him.

Blaze had felt the burn of his anger over the truth of his uncle's words because he knew it was true. His mother *had* done everything in her power to "change" Blaze's father, but she'd only succeeded in pushing him away, something Blaze had never forgiven her for. His father had been a kind man Blaze had respected and loved, providing for his family the best that he could. But it had never been enough for a woman who demanded submission to her God. As the oldest sibling, Blaze watched his mother harp and nag, finally driving his father to drink and gamble. The man he'd once respected became a drunk who put the almighty bottle before his family, and Blaze resented him for that. But not as much as the woman who drove him there. "A heathen destined for hell if he didn't change," she would threaten, and so he did. He "changed" his address, disappearing for months at a time to work in mines far enough away to escape condemnation. But at least he always sent money home whenever he could, lush or no.

His mother had taught Blaze and Dash how to pray, and so Blaze had, over and over, begging God to help his parents get along so that Pa would want to stay. But his mother made sure he never did, a "respectable woman" grinding her "infidel" husband into the dust until he left forever, killed in a mining accident just months before Shaylee was born. The burden of providing for the family fell to Blaze at the age of thirteen, a task difficult enough until his mother died giving birth, leaving them orphans … and leaving Blaze full of fury.

Until Uncle Finn took them in.

Pushing the unwelcome memories aside, Blaze kept his gaze fixed on the foal, feeling a kinship with it for all the hard lessons of life he had yet to learn. But despite the anger roiling in his own gut, Blaze knew there was no one he'd rather learn from than Uncle Finn. He was the one person who actually seemed to live his faith, not tap dance on top of it like everyone else he knew. No, his uncle's faith seemed to breathe from every pore, as naturally as air in and out of his lungs, and although Blaze refused to embrace it himself, he couldn't deny he respected it. *And* the uncle who professed it, a tried-and-true source of wisdom and strength in Blaze's life.

"Much as I hate to admit it, son, your Aunt Libby's departure seventeen years ago made me a very wealthy man. And I'm not just talking about the success of the silver mine or the joy of family with you and your brother and sisters." He turned, the potency of his gaze boring into Blaze's profile along with his soul. "I'm talking about the lesson God taught me when he set me free from jail."

Blaze turned his head enough to peer at his uncle out of the corner of his eyes. "You were in jail?"

A chuckle parted from Finn's lips as he reclaimed his position over the stall fencing. "Oh, yeah, as bitter and black an imprisonment as this man has ever known." He tapped a finger to his head as he slid Blaze a tempered smile. "Up here. Bitter at Libby, bitter at her family, and most of all, bitter at the God who'd promised me a hope and future."

A peaceful sigh drifted from his lips as he returned his attention to the mare nuzzling her foal, as calm as the faint smile on his face. "The Good Book says, 'all things work together for good to them that love God and are called according to *His* purpose,' so when Libby left, I took that seriously. Figured if I made her wait long enough, she'd come to her senses and be the wife I needed her to be."

His smile skewed. "Only she didn't, so I went after her,

thinking that at least she'd finally understand I wasn't a man to be controlled by a woman. But I couldn't find her, so I ended up being controlled by something far worse." His chest rose and fell as he glanced Blaze's way. "An anger and bitterness so pervasive, every breath I took was inside of the dark, cold jail of my mind."

He pushed away from the stall to face Blaze head-on, the compassion in his eyes a stark contrast to the fire that had been there only moments before. "I'd always believed Pastor Poppy's words that 'true liberty was doing the right thing,' but it wasn't until then that God taught me to live it. To battle the bitterness like I would a Mohave rattlesnake." One edge of his mouth tipped. "Staying far, far away. So I did—repented for my anger and bitterness and started praying for Libby and her family from afar, and you know what? Over time, every prayer eased my pain just a little more, and every blessing I wished on them turned the lock on that jail another hair or so. Until bit by bit, prayer by prayer, I was set free to be the man I wanted to be."

Uncle Finn laid a hand on Blaze's shoulder. "A happy one blessed with nephews and nieces who've become my loving family, and a ranch and silver mine that's the fulfillment of my dreams." He cracked a crooked smile as he checked his watch. "All but one. And she's waiting for me at the moment behind a bolted door, no doubt."

His uncle braced hands on both of Blaze's shoulders with a look of love so powerful, emotion thickened in Blaze's throat. "I love you, Blaze, too much to see you go down the path that I did before I found true freedom. So fix it, or I'll kick your carcass off this ranch so high, you'll think you're a bloomin' bird, got it?"

"Got it." Against Blaze's will, a smile gave way. "But I still think you're crazy."

Finn nudged his hat up. "That's a given, son, especially when it comes to Libby, but I guarantee it's a form of insanity you'll be afflicted with yourself all too soon."

Blaze grunted as he followed his uncle to his horse's stall. "Not if I can help it."

Uncle Finn's painted palomino, Lightning, nickered as Finn led him to the smaller buckboard. "Come on, boy, we're going for a ride," he said softly to his trusty mount, gently rubbing his neck, "because I'm going to need all the support I can get bringing this little filly home."

He tossed Blaze a glance while he hooked Lightning up. "And all of *your* support after I bring her home, too, Blaze." His uncle's vest rose and fell with a deep sigh as he rubbed Lightning's neck. "The truth is I've never stopped loving her, son. So I figure if God saw fit not to take her out of my heart after all the years I asked him to, *then* managed to get that crusty old father of hers to make amends, well … who am I to argue with the Almighty?" Eyes in a squint, he delivered a probing look. "Which means I'm asking you to do everything in your power to be courteous and pleasant to *all* of our guests while they're here, Bren, including your Aunt Libby."

"Courteous I can do," Blaze said as he helped his uncle finish up with Lightning, "but 'pleasant' is a mighty tall order." He slid a palm down Lightning's mane as he shot his uncle a sour smile. "Nonetheless, you have my word I *will* be courteous and will *try* to be pleasant to *all* of our guests while they are here." With a final pat of Lightning's neck, Blaze turned on his heel to head back to the foal, smile flat as he glanced over his shoulder. "But I sure in the devil don't have to like it."

CHAPTER FOURTEEN

"HEY, DON," FINN CALLED TO the hotel manager from the empty dining room table where he'd camped out for the last hour and a half. After five cups of coffee, he had enough nervous energy to fuel the blasted V&T Railroad. "Mind checking on her one more time?"

Glancing up from the front desk register in the foyer where he was closing out the books for the day, Donald Turley offered Finn a sympathetic smile. But the dip of bushy brows conveyed something else Finn wasn't used to.

Pity.

"One more time?" Don's roll of eyes might have been comical an hour ago when Finn's patience wasn't nearly as exhausted. Now it only confirmed the hotel manager was as fed up to the eyeballs with Libby's dad-burned lollygagging as Finn. "Maybe third time lucky, eh?" he said while his thickset body lumbered around the front desk to tackle the steps.

"Wait." Finn jumped up from the table to head into the foyer. "You *did* tell her she had to be out by nine, didn't you?" He glanced at the carved burl-wood clock behind the oak front desk as it inched a hair past 10:45.

The weary sigh that seeped from the hotel manager's lips seemed to sap the poor man's energy, his broad shoulders actually sagging as much as his whiskered jowls. "Of course I did, Finn—pert near every hour on the hour since her family checked out, including the two times you sent me. But she just keeps yelling through the door that she's 'indisposed' and not ready."

Venting with a noisy breath, Finn parked his hands low on his hips. "For pity's sake, Don, you're the blasted owner of this hotel—didn't you give her an ultimatum?"

"An ultimatum?" Hand to chest, Donald gaped, facial muscles as strained as the buttons on his overtaxed waistcoat. "To Liberty O'Shea?" His brows dug low. "For the love of mercy, Finn, I know you were only married to the woman for barely a blink, but even I remember that fiery temper of hers. An ultimatum?" He grunted. "Are you crazy?"

Apparently.

A once-familiar heat stirred in Finn, warming both his blood and his temper, something he hadn't experienced in many a year. His mouth tamped down. *Seventeen, to be exact.* "She's nothing more than a mite of a woman, Don, so you need to go up there right now and demand that she checks out or you'll call the sheriff."

"Humph." Donald tugged on his vest, the motion threatening to pop all of his buttons. "Already tried that before you arrived. But that confounded woman just carried on something fierce about feeling poorly, so Sheriff Polk just let her be, spouting something about you can't evict a sick woman."

"Wanna bet?" Finn leaned in to give Don a tinge of the temper few knew he had. After Libby deserted him, he'd worked hard at maintaining a reputation for a cool head and patient manner, mastering the temper he'd inherited from a hot-headed drunk of a father. But Libby O'Shea had always been the key to unlocking a storehouse of emotions in him, both good and bad, and he knew the time had finally come to confront them all.

Along with the woman who provoked them.

Shoving the brim of his hat up, Finn drilled Don with a deadly stare. "As manager, you need to demand once and for all that she vacate the premises, Don, and if she doesn't, you need to unlock that dad-burned door and bring her down."

Don stumbled back, all color siphoning right out of his ruddy cheeks. "Thunderation, Finn, you *are* crazy if you think I'm going to do that! Why, the lady could be undressed, and I am *not* that kind of man."

"No, but I am," Finn said in a near-growl, amazed all over again how a little bit of a thing like Libby O'Shea could light his fuse so darn quickly. As a staunch proponent for women's rights, the woman had always bucked every man she'd ever met, determined to get her way no matter the cost. And it had cost him plenty, and her family, too, and it was high time somebody saved his wife from herself. Forcing himself to calm down, he drew in a cleansing breath of air before slowly expelling it again, willing some of his frustration to diminish along with it.

He couldn't deny that when he married Libby, he'd fancied himself a likable Petrucio to Libby's Kate, a veritable *Taming of the Shrew* in true Shakespeare form, determined to make her the wife he needed her to be.

For I am born to tame you, Kate.

But after she'd left, God had tempered him greatly, revealing a mindset that had lost him the love of his life, badly bruising the only woman he had ever longed to cherish. So, this time he was determined to take great pains to "tame" her in a whole new way.

God's way.

Husbands, love your wives, just as Christ loved the church and gave Himself up for her.

And I will, Lord.

A slow smile inched its way across his face as his frustration channeled into the fire, passion, and challenge Libby O'Shea had always ignited in him.

As soon as I drag her out of that blasted room.

Reining in his temper, he extended his hand. "Give me

the key, Don."

Ol' Don distanced himself even further, his shock evident in the rush of blood that suddenly flooded his cheeks. "I can't do that, Finn. For the love of decency, man, the lady could be indisposed!"

"Well, if she isn't, she sure in the devil will be," Finn said, strolling around the front desk to pluck the master skeleton key off its peg. He strode toward the staircase with passion and purpose, ready to reclaim his wife one way or the other. "And any woman holed up in a hotel room half naked to thwart authority isn't a lady, my friend, so I'd reserve judgment on that one if I were you." He bounded up the steps two at a time, turning on the landing to shoot Don a strained smile. "Room three at the end of the hall, right?"

Sweating profusely, Don mopped his face with a handkerchief. "You're not gonna make a scene, are you? Because I'm full up tonight, and everyone's in bed."

Finn's smile was pure patience. "Don't plan to, Don, I promise. Unless I have to bang on every door to find her."

A shudder rippled through ol' Don as he dabbed the back of his neck. "Yes, room number three, but remember you promised, Finn."

"Yes, sir, *I* did," Finn said with a firm salute before tugging on the brim of his hat. "But that wildcat of a redhead barricaded down in that room?" He grinned as he gave Don a quick wink. "Good luck with that."

CHAPTER FIFTEEN

PEEKING AT THE ALARM CLOCK on her nightstand, Libby breathed a sigh of relief, finally allowing her body to sink into submission in the heavenly cloud of her feather-tick bed. The comforting bongs of the grandfather clock in the lobby boomed the hour of eleven, assuring her that Mr. Turley had likely given up and gone to bed. *Hopefully* locking Finn McShane out of his hotel as thoroughly as Libby had locked Mr. Turley out of her room.

She burrowed deeper beneath the covers to further contemplate about what she was going to do, something she'd been wrestling with all evening. Papa had boxed her in but good, ruffling her feathers more than she'd ruffled those in the blasted goose-down bed, tossing and turning. Great balls of fire, she needed that annulment to marry Harold so she could devote all of her time to her volunteer work, and unfortunately, she needed both Harold's *and* Papa's money to help fund it.

But not at the cost of six months under Papa's thumb … and Finn McShane's roof!

Rolling on her side, Libby punched and battered the down pillow several times, wishing she could do the same to Papa's diabolical plan to ruin her life. A chill rippled through her despite a mound of covers. *Because too many men had tried to ruin her life already.* Well, she wasn't going to give any man—be it Papa or Finn—another chance to push her around. At least not willingly, and if it took all night, she vowed to come up with a plan to circumvent Papa's. She nibbled the edge of her lip as the seeds of a smile tugged.

Or at least make him *wish* that she had.

She curled up, knees tucked to her chest, wondering if just possibly dear Mrs. Poppy might take her and Maggie in. Libby had heard that the town matriarch lived alone ever since her husband, Pastor Poppy, passed on a few years back, and the very thought caused a dull ache to throb in Libby's chest. The Poppy's had been like the grandparents she'd never had, the oldest, dearest people she knew. Her mouth hooked. Even *if* they bore most of the blame for her sham marriage to Finn.

Before she knew it, Libby's lips softened into a smile at the memory of Mrs. Poppy's prize-winning poppy-seed cake and the poppy-seed ice cream she'd served the night Finn and she had decided to court. The sweet, old woman had accidentally spilled a whole jar of particularly potent poppy seeds into her ice cream, quite surprised they added a "lovely little crunch." A soft giggle broke from Libby's lips as she lay in the moonlit room. A "lovely little crunch," indeed, which when coupled with an abundance of more poppy seeds in both the cake and tea she'd served, created a woozy evening none of them remembered the next day.

Until she woke up in Finn's bed.

In the Poppy's guest bedroom.

With a wedding ring on her hand.

Poor Mrs. Poppy had been beside herself when Papa showed up, ranting and raving that that the marriage would be annulled because Finn was nothing but a fortune-hunter.

Only Finn wasn't. He was the kindest, most gentle man she'd ever known. A wisp of a smile shadowed her lips as she swiped at the sudden moisture in her eyes. And then in one painful stutter of her heart, the memory of the day she'd left chased her smile away, reminding her of who

Finn McShane actually *was* beneath that so-called loving veneer: a bully who'd given her an ultimatum, obviously as controlling as her father.

In his dreams. Which, if she allowed her father to win this war, would become *her* nightmares! Jaw hardening along with her will, she flopped on her back, jerking the covers up to her neck as she stared at the ceiling. "When steers fly," she muttered. "Or mules, in the case of Finn McShane."

Tap. Tap. Tap.

Libby stifled a groan, ignoring the gentle knock on the door. *Go away, Mr. Turley.* She held her breath, hoping he would.

Knock. Knock. Knock.

Not responding, she squeezed her eyes shut as if that would make him disappear.

Boom. Boom. Boom.

"Mr. Turley, I'm in bed and nearly asleep," she called, yanking the covers over her head.

BANG! BANG! BANG! She shot up in the bed, temper suddenly exploding along with the stupid door. "I am in my nightgown, sir, so you can bang all night, but I am *not* opening that door!"

"Fine by me."

Libby froze to the sheets at the sound of *that* voice, goose bumps popping like measles while the turn of a key in the lock sucked all moisture from her throat. She caught her breath when the door squealed open, bucking up against the headboard so hard, it rattled along with her teeth. "W-What are y-you d-doing?" she hissed, covers clutched to her neck.

"Taking you home, Mrs. McShane," Finn said with a polite tip of his hat, his frame so tall and broad, he had to duck through the stupid door.

She gaped. "For the love of decency, I'm in my nightclothes!"

"Uh, no offense, Libs, but I've seen it before." A polite

smile hovered on those full lips as he quietly clicked the lock behind him, draining all the blood from her face. He leaned against the wood, hip cocked to the frame. "It's time to go, darlin'."

She wrapped the covers around her the best that she could, chin rising along with her temper. "I am not going anywhere with you, Finn *McShame*," she said, resorting to one of the many twists of his name she'd coined when they'd butted heads in school so many years ago. "So you can just march right back out that door."

A slow grin slid across his lips that annoyed her even further when it tumbled her stomach. Or maybe it was nausea.

One could only hope.

He nudged his hat up. "I've missed the nicknames, Libs, but I imagine I'll get a bellyful before all is said and done." Pushing off the doorframe, he stood to his full height, the grin fading into that equally irritating half-smile that always pitted his calm-and-collected against her flustered-and-fuming. "I'm taking you home, Libby, so we can do this easy or we can do it hard—the choice is yours."

"My home is in New York," she whispered loudly, "and since when did you ever give me a choice? Great balls of fire, I didn't even have a choice when I married you in the first place—had to be drugged to do it."

He idly scratched the back of his neck, that shameless twinkle causing more "nausea."

"You weren't drugged the next morning as I recall," he said softly, laughter crinkling at the corners of hazel eyes that had always cast a spell. "When you woke up in my bed"—he paused long enough for the fire in her cheeks to crawl clear up to the roots of her hair, then winked, his voice taking on a lazy drawl—"*buck* naked."

"Get out!" So much blood pulsed in her cheeks, she thought she might faint. Without a second thought, she hurled the brass and metal alarm clock at him with a grunt.

Catching it handily, he bobbled it in the air with a crooked smile. "Mite heavier than a teapot, for sure, but at least it won't shatter." He casually strolled over to set it back down, and she lunged to the far side of the bed, covers wadded to her chest. Hands on his hips, he nodded toward her arsenal of blankets. "Now, are you going to get dressed on your own, Liberty Bell, or am I going to have to do it for you?"

"Over my d-dead body!" she said in a hoarse stutter, hoping to scald him with a glare.

He shifted, eyes sobering and manner patient. "Maybe. But either way, Libby, you're coming with me. So, are you going to put some clothes on or should I do it for you?"

"No and no!" she said in another whispered shout, swiping a book from the nightstand to fire it as hard as she could.

Finn nabbed it easily, brows lifting as he held the book up. He shook his head with a tsk. "Flinging the Word of God around, Miss Bell?" He set it back down. "I doubt that's going to earn you any favor with the Almighty, ma'am." He moseyed on over to the bureau and opened a drawer, gathering up a chemise, skirt, and blouse before tossing them on the bed. "So, I'm going to ask you one more time, Libby, real nice and slow—you going to dress yourself or do you want me to do it?"

"You wouldn't dare!" she said in a near gasp, remembering all the times he'd given her an ultimatum—and won.

He folded his arms, mouth clamping into a tight smile. "Try me."

"Oooooo …!" Frustration surging, she crumpled the chemise up in a ball and pelted it straight in his face.

"Suit yourself," he said in an unruffled tone, moving around to her side of the bed with the chemise in hand.

"You are nothing but a bully, Finn McShane," she hissed, scurrying to the other side of the bed as quickly as she could wrapped in blankets like a rolled dumpling.

But apparently not quick enough given the fist that Finn latched onto her foot.

Bucking like a thorn-saddled mule, she tried to shake free with a kick, but he'd pinned her to the bed in a blink of those deadly hazel eyes. Eyes that *now* studied her with affection. "Holy saints above, I've missed you, Libby," he whispered as he hovered, the husky sound of her name on his lips disarming the blaze of her temper with a fire of a whole 'nother kind. Her tongue parched dry while her so-called nausea barnstormed her belly like a herd of hummingbirds. The hue of his eyes deepened to dark brown as he slowly leaned in, eyelids sheathing closed.

No! She was so stunned, she couldn't speak, and when he leaned in to nuzzle her mouth, his groan stole her protest altogether. She gasped, and those deadly lips took advantage with a kiss so deep, it collided with a weak moan of her own. "Libby, I love you," he rasped, "and God help me, I've never stopped."

Never stopped? His words instantly paralyzed her to the bed, dousing the heat of his kiss when she suddenly remembered the day of their awful fight. The day Griffin Alexander McShane bullied instead of loved, giving her no recourse but to storm right out of his life. The truth cramped in her chest.

And he let her.

CHAPTER SIXTEEN

"BULL BISCUITS!" SHE SHOUTED, FEAR and anger snapping her out of her stupor enough to thrust him away. Finn had always been able to disarm her with a kiss, but not this time. Eyes wild, she scrambled off the bed and darted to the bureau to snatch her hair comb, brandishing it like a weapon. "All you missed was bullying me around, Finn McShane, and I sure didn't come back here so you could start up all over again."

Easing off the bed, he cuffed the back of his neck with a teasing grin, eyes twinkling as he scanned her head to toe, taking in her waist-long hair tumbling down her nightgown. "No, ma'am, that's not all I missed ..."

"Ooooooo!" She snatched her robe off a hook on the back of the closet door and struggled to slip it on while she held out her comb, determined that Finn McShane would never weaken her with those deadly kisses again. Seventeen years ago, the attraction between them had been so strong, she'd all but melted at his touch, thinking he'd loved her. But it had just been another means of control over her life, and no amount of attraction was ever worth that. Not when she was so close to the independence she craved by becoming Harold's wife. Eyes blazing, she gouged the comb in the air. "You are a low-down skunk, Finn McShane, and I demand that you leave this instant."

The grin receded along with the sparkle in his eyes as his features dissolved into the serious mode she'd once loved, where sincerity and tenderness toyed with her emotions, dismantling her, deluding her.

Deceiving her.

Well, not this time, bucko.

"Look, Libby," he said quietly, the contrition in his tone more than convincing as he took his hat off, motioning it toward the bed. "I'm sorry for that, darlin', I really am, but confound it, Libs, you're my wife and I want to take you home."

Jerking the sash of her robe tight, she jabbed the comb at him once again. "First of all, *Mr. McShane,* I am not your darlin', your Libby, or your Libs anymore, and once this blackmail scheme of my father's is done, I won't be your wife either. So, you can just take those misguided notions right out that door, mister, because I am not going anywhere with you."

He calmly put his hat back on with a sober smile, a faint tic in his jaw the only indication that a carefully restrained temper hovered beneath the surface. "Well, I'm afraid that's where you're wrong, ma'am," he said as he bent to retrieve her chemise. He balled it up like she had and lightly tossed it at her, landing it on her shoulder. She scuttled out of his way when he strode to the closet to retrieve her valise. "I'll give you five minutes to get dressed and packed, Libby, and then I'm coming in to take you home." He placed the suitcase on the bed and without another word, stepped out into the hallway and closed the door.

She wasted no time flinging her comb down and darting to the door to quickly lock it, frantically looking around to see how she could possibly keep him out. Eyeing the bureau, she worried her lip, doubtful she could accomplish such a feat, but she had to try! At least to fight him tooth and nail, if not lock him out altogether. Her gaze then snagged on the bed, a sturdy mahogany frame that would be more difficult to move, but not impossible. Rushing to the far side of the bureau, she pushed with all her might, bare feet fused to the floor as she slowly inched it in front of the door, doing her best to stifle any grunts.

"Three minutes, Libs," his muffled voice called, so I suggest you get dressed or I'm taking you as is."

She glared at the door, feeling a lot like that high school girl Finn McShane always managed to rile, but it was no secret the man brought out the worst in her. She hurried to the far side of the bed and groaned as she worked to prod it away from the wall, finally butting her backside to the headboard to slowly maneuver it against the bureau. "There," she whispered, dusting her hands against each other. *At least that will buy me some time.*

Heart thudding, she darted to the window and threw up the sash, stomach turning over at the distance between her second-story room and the ground, the height making her dizzy. But she had no choice. Without another thought, she snatched both the sheet and the cover off the bed, doing her best to knot them together. She lowered them out the window, alarmed when they only reached three quarters of the way down.

"One minute," Finn called, and Libby was desperate.

Snatching up her chemise, blouse, and skirt she tied them to the top of her sheet, hands trembling more than her makeshift rope as it wavered in the breeze.

But she was almost there ...

"Time's up, Libby," Finn said, jiggling the doorknob.

Nooooo! Heart in her throat, she peered down at the ground, horrified to see her rope was still a good fifteen feet short.

The turn of the key stilled both her breathing and her pulse while Finn attempted to open the door. "Aw, Libs, are you serious?" he said, his husky chuckle stealing her air when her bed started creeping backwards along with the bureau. Panic struck when his head poked through with that crooked smile that used to make her dizzy.

She thrust her head back out the window, suddenly

encountering a "dizzy" of a whole 'nother kind at the distance she had to descend. *Please God, please God, please God* …, she silently prayed, wishing she hadn't let her relationship with God lapse as much as she had. But that, too, she blamed on the man on the other side of the door.

Screeeeeeeeeech.

Hyperventilating, she yanked her robe off, fingers fumbling as she knotted it onto the rope, praying she wouldn't break her silly leg with a ten-foot jump.

"Libby—don't you dare!" Finn shouted, hazel eyes all but singeing her as he thrust the door open as much as he could with 200 pounds of furniture in the way.

Hurry! The blood pounded in her ears as she clumsily attempted to tie the robe to the sash handle, the material almost too bulky.

"Libby, *no!*" Finn pushed through.

And Libby dropped the rope.

Terror-stricken, she bolted to the closet and slammed the door, heels dug in as she clung to the knob in the dark.

Screeeeeeeeeech.

Chest heaving, she held her breath. It sounded like the bureau was being shoved back in place, followed by the scrape of the bed across the plank-wood floor, finally hitting the wall with a thud. She clutched the knob all the more, body slanted diagonally to exert her full weight while she waited … and waited …

Nothing happened.

Allowing herself to breathe, she cocked her head to listen, trying to distinguish the faint movement she heard across the room. Leaning close to the door, she pressed her ear to the wood. *What on earth is he doing?*

A drawer slammed and she immediately jerked back, nearly horizontal as she re-gripped the knob for all she was worth. Which wasn't much at the moment given the sweat of her palms, growing slicker at the heavy thud of boots approaching the door.

His footfall stopped along with her breathing, and with eyes squeezed shut, she wrenched back as far as she could. *Please God, please God, please God …*

Whoosh! The door flew open, and Libby went flying back.

Oomph! Right on her backside.

All she could do was blink as Finn McShane's silhouette stood in the blazing light like a confounded angel of God, hand on the knob and hip cocked. "It's time to go, darlin'," he said in that infuriatingly patient tone, swooping her up before her protest could even clear the roof of her mouth. He dropped her on the bed without ceremony, right next to the open suitcase he'd haphazardly packed. "I suggest you pick something out to wear right now, Libs, and gather anything I missed from the closet and nightstand because I am taking you home. *With* or without your things."

Totally infuriated, she promptly upended the suitcase, dumping everything onto the floor. "Get it through your thick head right now, mister, I am … *not* … going anywhere with you!"

"No?" Sweeping her up, he clamped her firmly to his chest, restraining her movement with a steel grip. "Beg to differ, darlin'," he breathed in her ear, riling her all the more when he pressed a quick kiss to her neck on his way to the door, "but we *are* going home."

Ice water shot through her veins. *He wouldn't!* "But I'm not dressed!" she said in a near shriek, heart thumping chaotically when she realized he fully intended to carry her out near naked.

"Sorry, Libs, but you had your chance."

"No, *please*—I'll get dressed this time, I promise, so give me another chance."

He grunted. "You mean like you gave me after you left? Sorry, darlin', but I'm a little low on patience right now, and don't even get me started on trust." His iron grip loosened a hair when he attempted to open the door, and she jumped at her chance—*literally*.

Limbs lashing, she apparently stunned him when she lunged from his arms, bucking like a hot-pokered mule when he tried to grab her again. "I … am… not … going … with … you," she gritted out, kicking and battering for all she was worth.

Which wasn't much given her ragged breathing when he crushed her to his chest like a vise. "So help me, Libby, if you kick and scratch me one more time, I'm going to tie you up in a sheet," he hissed, his words as winded as hers. Pinning her all the more, he butted her bottom with his knee to reach for the knob, leaving her arms free for barely a second.

But it was more than enough.

One arm lunging free, she tried to whop him but good, but all she managed to do was knock his hat off his head.

"That's it," he shouted in that strained voice that indicated she'd breeched his temper, flinging her on the bed so hard, she bounced like a jackrabbit on springs, nightgown flapping in the breeze. Before her lungs could kick back in, he'd ripped the sheet out from under her to topple her to the edge of the bed. "I'll be hog-tied and hand-stuffed if you think I'm going to let you claw me like a cougar, woman." Chest heaving, he rolled her up in the sheet so tight, she felt like one of Gert's homemade sausages stuffed in pork casings.

"Finn, *no!*" she cried, her desperation obvious in the use of his name. "I'll get dressed—I swear!"

"Too late, darlin'." With a do-or-die look she remembered all too well, he proceeded to whip off his belt. She gasped when he wrapped it around her arms and torso so securely, it felt like a strait-jacket, a rather appropriate analogy considering he was making her crazy!

"You untie me this instant!" she demanded, flailing furiously to no avail while he tossed her over his shoulder like a rolled-up rug.

"Sorry, Libs." He snatched the cover from the bed and hurled it over her. "It's for your own safety and mine, Mrs. McShane, just till we get out of town."

Her heart climbed into her throat when he marched to the door. "I swear I will scream blue murder if you don't put me down!" she hissed. The blanket fell off when she flopped like an earthworm on a desert rock at high noon.

"Doubt it." He calmly plucked the blanket up and flipped it over his other shoulder, his serene tone in direct contrast to the frenetic pounding of her heart as she dangled all the way down the hall. "Unless you want every customer in this hotel to see you wrapped in a sheet and little more." Chuckling, he bounded down the steps, mortifying her when he ran a palm down the length of her body. "Especially when it doesn't appear you're wearing much underneath."

Blood instantly gorged her cheeks, nearly asphyxiating her when Mr. Turley gaped with saucer eyes at the base of the stairs. Mortified, Libby wanted to bury her face in Finn's shoulder, but had to settle on squeezing her eyes shut instead.

"Borrowing your blanket, Don," Finn said in a tone laced with humor, "but I'll return it later when I retrieve everything she so rudely threw out the window."

"No problem, Finn." Don shuffled back out of Finn's way. "But I'd be happy to pack up your things before you go, Miss O'Shea, if you like."

"Oh, Mr. Turley, yes, please—"

"Naw, Don," Finn said, cutting her off on the way to the door, "Miss O'Shea will be sharing a room with Miss Mullaney, so she may as well share her clothes too." Finn tossed a wink to Mr. Turley over his shoulder. "Gave her a chance to pack, but she wasn't so inclined at the time, so thanks anyway."

"Finn, *please*, I need my things!" Libby pleaded, but Finn just kept walking.

The hotelier scurried to open the front door. "Sure thing, Finn. You two have a wonderful evenin', now, you hear?"

Wonderful? Libby's lips gummed as tightly as the stupid sheet plastered to her body while Finn nonchalantly toted her through the lobby. *Not until I have my comb in hand …*

"Oh, and Miss O'Shea," Mr. Turley called as Finn hauled her outside, "do come again anytime, all right?"

Oh, I will. Libby issued a grunt as she bounced over Finn's shoulder.

And way sooner than you think.

CHAPTER SEVENTEEN

SOMEWHERE A HOOT OWL CALLED, and Maggie released a contented sigh. The soft trill of desert crickets blended with the gentle creak of the rocking chair on the wooden wraparound porch of Finn's house, nearly lulling her to sleep as she waited for Aunt Libby. She glanced at the watch pinned to her blouse, it's ivory face perfectly illuminated by the light of the desert moon overhead. Almost midnight, and no sign of her godmother yet!

Wrapping her shawl more tightly, Maggie was grateful that everyone else had long since gone to bed except for Dash, who plied liquor at the Ponderosa Saloon till the wee hours of the morning. And then Blaze, of course, who apparently plied women with his charm, at least according to his younger sisters who seemed to adore both older brothers despite their questionable ways.

Charm. Maggie's smile took a twist. As far as possessing any, Blaze Donovan had certainly fooled her. Other than the heart-melting smiles he'd given to lure her into retrieving his clothes on the day they had met, his so-called charm had been as cool as the desert night—brisk, bitter, and chilling to the bone.

As timing would have it, a cool breeze rustled her hair just as the thundering hooves of a lone rider reached her ears, the desert night somehow less cool now that Blaze Donovan was galloping down the drive, leaving a cloud of dust in his wake.

Along with a string of lovesick women, no doubt.

I should go up to bed, the thought occurred, avoiding Blaze Donovan far more appealing then butting heads with him again. But Maggie desperately wanted to be here to greet her godmother, especially given the coercive circumstances of her arrival, so cowardice was out of the question. Besides, if Mr. Donovan had been slated to teach Maggie to ride beginning tomorrow, it was probably best to clear the air tonight. Right?

Right. Maggie gulped as Blaze disappeared into the barn, evidently putting his horse up for the evening. "As long as I can steer clear," she muttered when he reappeared, Sister Fred's warning that first day suddenly echoing in her brain.

"Well, young lady, you may be just what I'm looking for then, as long as you can steer clear of heartbreakers like our Mr. Donovan. But it won't be easy."

Maggie grunted, the sound drowned out by the accelerated groan of her rocker as it picked up pace along with her pulse, both going at a fast clip. *Easy?* Well, keeping her letch of a fiancé at arm's length hadn't been "easy" either, but she'd managed, and she'd do it again with a Romeo like Blaze Donovan, too, six months under the same roof or no.

"Good evening, Mr. Donovan," Maggie said with a firm lift of her chin, her smile as polite as her tone. "It's a beautiful night."

"That's debatable." Blaze mounted the porch steps slowly, pausing at the top to study Maggie through hooded eyes that held the trace of a tease. "After all, you're not the one who's been tossed out of your bedroom for company, Miss Mullaney."

"No, but the company certainly appreciates it, Mr. Donovan, fresh sheets and all." She bit the edge of her lip, battling a telltale smile. "Although it likely means you're several sheets short in your wardrobe, I'm afraid."

His mouth compressed, but she thought she spied a sliver

of a smile. He nudged his hat up to give her a half-lidded stare. "You're never going to let me forget that, are you?"

"Nope." Maggie kept on rocking, lips curved as she observed the moon in the sky. "Too good of a memory." She glanced his way, pretty sure her eyes twinkled more than the stars overhead. "One rarely sees a stubborn cowboy cloaked in humility, you know."

He shuffled over to take the chair next to hers, commencing to rock in a slow and easy rhythm far more relaxed than her own. "I know what you mean," he said in a lazy drawl, the heat of his gaze burning into her profile. "I've yet to see a New York debutante cloaked in anything but jewels and fancy airs, hunting for a husband."

Heat burnished her cheeks as she peeked at him out of the corner of her eye. "I deserved that, I suppose, but I'm no longer a husband-seeking debutante, but a woman who has chosen to walk away from that lifestyle in order to serve others."

"Uh-huh ..." Voice soft, he drilled her with a look that made her blush. "Or *run* away, as the nurse chatter implies."

Maggie's chin rose. "We're all running away from something, Mr. Donovan, whether it's an unwanted lifestyle in New York or the fear of commitment right here in Virginia City." She arched a brow. "At least according to the aforesaid nurse chatter, which I wager is far more vociferous than any gossip I might arouse."

A rich chuckle drifted into the air, doing funny things to her stomach. "And you think *I'm* stubborn," he said with a scratch of his bristled jaw. He leaned his head on the back of his chair while he rocked. "Just goes to show you can't trust idle gossip."

"Or desperate cowboys draped in sheets?"

His mouth hooked. "Especially desperate cowboys draped in sheets." Extending a hand, he offered a sideways smile. "What do you say we start over, Miss Mullaney, fully clothed?"

Cheeks hot, she hesitated before carefully shaking his hand, his powerful grip sending skitters all the way down her arm. "I think that's wise," she said before quickly pulling away, swallowing hard to deflect the butterflies in her belly, "especially given that Aunt Libby and I will be living here for a while."

"Agreed." His large, work-roughened hands casually rested on the arms of his chair, fingers relaxed over the edge. "And since we'll be under the same roof like family for the next six months, maybe we should forego on the formality as well." He met her gaze head-on with a glint of challenge. "What do you say, Maggie?"

She nodded slowly. "I think that makes a lot of sense, Blaze, especially if we're going to be friends."

With a painfully slow perusal from the curls atop her head down her shawl-covered shirtwaist to her skirt and back, his eyes took on a hint of a sparkle she hadn't seen before. "That's generally not what most women are looking for, Maggie, so you think we can? Be friends, that is?"

The flirtation caught her off-guard, warming her face. "I certainly hope so," she said with a thrust of her jaw, determined to establish a friendship and nothing more. "The next six months could be pretty taxing without it." Ignoring his lazy grin, she forged on, tone serious. "So, is Blaze your given name?"

"No. My name is Brendan Zachary Donovan, but my brother used to call me BZ for short, which for some unknown reason, ended up as Blaze."

"'Some unknown reason?'" A grin tugged at the edge of her smile. "Well, *Blaze*, the way I hear it, you have a reputation for being a womanizer who sets hearts on fire, leaving charred ruins in your wake."

He tugged his hat down and grinned. "Naw, that's just sour grapes from some of the mothers in town because I prefer spending more time with the girls at the Ponderosa than with their daughters, so you can't believe everything you hear."

Maggie crooked a brow. "It was Sister Fred."

He scowled and scooped up an acorn, firing it into the yard with a grunt. "Yeah, well that explains it. The woman flat-out doesn't like me."

"Sure she does," Maggie said in a matter-of-fact tone, bundling up in her shawl. She snuck a teasing look his way. "She just doesn't want any *other* women liking you. Says you're a menace to the female society."

"Ha! That's the toad calling the frog jumpy if ever there was." He slid back in his chair to roost his head on the back, hands behind his neck and eyes closed while he crossed long denim-clad legs at the ankles. "More like the female society is a menace to me," he muttered.

Maggie shifted in her chair to assess him more closely. "And why is that?" she asked, curious as to the root of his notorious reputation.

"Why?" He glanced up as if he wanted to toss her over the front rail like the acorn. "Because respectable girls are just looking for a husband, that's why, and I have no intention of ever getting married. Already told Rachel and every other woman in this confounded town that I am *not* the marrying kind, so they best not get any ideas." He grunted. "Sweet mother of sanity, the last thing I need is to be shackled to a so-called good girl, who will just harp on me about God and church the rest of my days."

Maggie blinked, eyes spanning wide. "You don't believe in God?"

"Of course, I believe in God," he said with an even bigger scowl than before. "I just don't like Him a whole lot, that's all. Nor do I believe He has my best interests at heart. And I can tell you right now that my best interests don't lie in some church-going woman judging or pushing me around." He cut loose with a grunt. "Or trying to change me."

Maggie sucked in a breath, taken aback by the sharp

edge to his tone. "Goodness, sounds like you have a few sour grapes of your own."

His eyes narrowed beneath the brim of his Stetson. "Yeah? Well you'd have a few sour grapes, too, lady, if you were raised in a so-called Christian home where one parent lived a lie and the other flat-out abandoned you."

Maggie's heart cramped at the thread of pain she heard beneath Blaze's anger, the same thread that had tried to strangle her own faith after her mother had died. Drawing in a deep breath, she laid a gentle hand on his arm, shocking him enough to bring his rocker to a halt. "Actually, I did, Blaze," she said softly, her gaze gentle to convey the unlikely kinship she suddenly felt, "so I understand your pain and I'm truly sorry."

It was his turn to blink. "You?" His brows dug low as he commenced rocking. "How?"

Expelling a weary breath, she sagged back into her chair, the creaks and groans of her rocker suddenly in tune with his. "My father died when I was about three or so, so my memories are dim, but I do remember how much he loved my mother and me and that he was a godly man who prayed with me every night."

Blaze nodded. "Sheridan was four when our mother died, and it breaks my heart that neither she nor Shaylee have any woman in their lives they can relate too."

"That would definitely be harder, I think," Maggie said quietly, heart aching for Blaze's sisters, "than losing a father at a young age because mothers are so critical to a daughter's development."

A tic twittered in Blaze's jaw as he stared into the dark yard, fingers curling into fists over the arm of the chair. "It was, but Uncle Finn, Dash, and I have worked real hard to give them the family they need."

Maggie smiled. "That's more than obvious, Blaze, from the closeness your family shares and from the way the girls adore you, Dash, and Finn."

"Yeah." His facial muscles relaxed along with his hands.

"I would have been lost without my mother," Maggie continued. "We were very close." The muscles in her throat tensed. "Until she married my stepfather, that is, when I was barely thirteen." A once-familiar veneer glazed Maggie's voice, reminding her of the hurt that sometimes still reared its ugly head. "My mother tutored students in our flat to support us, but when I became very ill, it wasn't enough for our medical bills, so she was desperate. That's when she met my stepfather at church, whom she discouraged at the onset, but he eventually wore her down. On the outside, he appeared to be a fine, upstanding Christian man who was desperate to sweep Mother off her feet, you see." Maggie's lips compressed. "But in actuality, he was a cold, calculating magistrate equally desperate to sweep me out of their lives."

Maggie sighed, shoulders sagging with her exhale. "He promptly sent me to a boarding school, convincing my mother I needed polish if I was going to properly 'come out' in society, so she agreed at first. But then she missed me so much—and I her—that she begged my stepfather to allow me to return home and attend nursing school."

Leaning her head back, Maggie closed her eyes, remembering all the arguments that ensued between her mother and stepfather when they discovered The Judge's plan to marry Maggie off to the highest bidder. "My mother and I rekindled our close relationship during her final years even though I'd felt abandoned after she married The Judge. That's when she'd encouraged me to seek a marriage of faith rather than one of convenience as my stepfather wanted me to do. And with her help, I was able to thwart a number of my stepfather's truly horrendous matchmaking efforts."

"But when she died last year"—tears pricked before she could blink them away—"it almost felt like I'd been abandoned again ..." Melancholy stole into her voice as her shoulders lifted in a resigned shrug. "Which is why I fled both New York and a fiancé I didn't love."

"I'm truly sorry about your mother, Maggie," Blaze said quietly. He was silent for several seconds before he leaned forward to stare her down. "But you're engaged?"

"*Was* engaged," she emphasized with a pointed look. "I broke it off with David in a letter I sent the morning I left New York, so I am completely unattached and plan to stay that way."

A grunt tripped from Blaze's lips. "I thought respectable women weren't supposed to lie."

That lit some sparks in her eyes. "I'll have you know, sir, that I do not lie," she said in a clipped tone, hoping to strongly convey she was one "respectable woman" who had no interest in marriage *or* in the town's most eligible bachelor. "I have absolutely no desire to marry, Blaze Donovan, so between my aversion to womanizers *and* marriage and your aversion to women of faith and church, I'd say you're fairly safe."

"Only fairly?" His teeth flashed white in the moonlight.

"Yes." Maggie jerked her shawl closer to her body, thinking it would be far easier to wait for Aunt Libby up in their room than on this porch with this truly cocky cowboy. She hunkered down in the rocker, determined to stand her ground. Lips pursed, she slid him a gaze as thin as the smile that twitched on her lips. "You know—in case I throttle you?"

CHAPTER EIGHTEEN

"COLD?" FINN SHOT LIBBY A sideways glance, battling a chuckle as her sheet-clad body sat ramrod straight on the buckboard bench, as white and prickly as a White Persian Cat Cactus under the light of the moon. "I'm talking about your body, not your heart," he teased, remembering all the times he'd rib Libby out of a bad mood, one of the most effective means of disarming his beautiful wife during their three-month marriage.

After kisses.

Nothing moved but her gaze as she seared him with a nasty look out of the corner of her eyes, setting free the laughter he'd tried so hard to restrain.

"Come on, Libs, I was willing to make this easy on you, but admit it—your dad-burned temper got in the way as usual." He chuckled as he lightly snapped the reins.

Her profile notched up, and he hated how that made her all the more attractive. Confound it, the woman's blasted spunk and fire had always drawn him like a moth to flame. His mouth tipped up on one side.

Or a man to wildfire.

Where said man could be seriously burned. And Libby had burned him but good. Not only with her temper, but with her fire and spirit that had torched all interest in any other woman. Of course, three months of wedded bliss with that rare flash of fire sure didn't hurt either, convincing Finn she was the only one for him. And after years of head-butting in high school, Finn had finally convinced her he was the only one for her too. His humor abruptly evaporated like desert warmth in the cool of night. But that'd been way back when she loved him as much as he loved her. His jaw stiffened. Now she was in love with some namby-pamby professor she intended to marry.

Over my dead body.

A droll smile returned to his lips. Which, given the stone scowl on Libby's face at the moment, might be sooner than he thought. Fingers stiff with both resolve and cold, Finn realized the chill in the air didn't come entirely from the woman beside him, who hadn't moved or said a word since they'd left the hotel ten minutes prior. Which might mean she was frozen as stiff as she was stubborn. After all, all she had on under that thin sheet was—

"Whoa, boy." Body suddenly too warm to suit, Finn tugged on the reins, bringing Lightning to a halt a quarter of the way to the ranch in the middle of nowhere.

"Why did we stop?" Her head lashed his way to stare wide-eyed, reassuring Finn that any stiffness in her manner was more from stubbornness than cold.

"You're freezing," he said in a definitive tone, intending to undo his belt from her sheet like he'd done when they'd left town. But the dad-blamed woman had promptly taken off like a shot, pert near killing herself when she tripped on her way back to the hotel. So, Finn had had no choice but to truss her up again until they were a safe distance away.

He reached to unbuckle the belt, and she instantly lunged to the far edge of the seat, feet poised to kick.

He shook his head and grinned. Maybe "safe" wasn't the right word.

"Come on, Libby," he coaxed in a husky tone that had always worked wonders in their past, "your lips are blue and goose bumps are popping out on your sheet, so let me untie my belt so you can cover up with the blanket."

"This is nothing but unadulterated kidnapping, Finn McShane, and when my fiancé finds out, he'll wrap you up in a lawsuit so fast, you'll wish *you* were wearing a sheet on F Street instead."

"Not much of a case, Libs—a husband kidnapping his wife? Besides," he said, shaking his head while sucking air through a clenched smile, "when your professor finds out you've been married all along, I doubt there'll be any engagement."

"Ooooooooooooo!" She promptly stomped her foot, which was now as blue as her lips.

He grabbed the blanket puddled on the seat around her—the one that had shimmied off her shoulders when she'd tried to jump from the wagon right outside the city limits. "Look, Libby, you're a bloomin' icicle sitting there, and although I'm not any happier with you than you are with me at the moment, I sure don't want you to catch your death out here in the frigid desert air. So, let me take off the blasted belt so we can wrap you in this blanket, all right?"

Eyes skittish, she studied him with a cautious air. "If you touch anything but that belt, mister, you will be so sorry, do you hear?"

"I hear," he said while he gently unbuckled the belt, his somber gaze locked with hers as he quietly looped it back into his jeans. "And I'm already sorry, Libby. Sorry that the only woman I have ever loved despises me enough to risk pneumonia, falling out of a wagon, or jumping out of a window to break her silly leg."

"Ha!" She grappled with the sheet until her arms were free, swiftly wrapping the blanket around her body. "If you loved me, you wouldn't break into my room and hog-tie me like a steer, rolling me in a sheet and dragging me through a public lobby."

Finn leaned in, going eye to eye. "First of all, Libby O'Shea McShane, I didn't break in, I used a key after waiting two blasted hours for you to honor Don's request to check out."

"I wasn't ready." Her voice tapered off as she clutched the blanket to the neck of her lace-collared nightgown, jaw stiff as she stared straight ahead.

"Secondly, yes I hog-tied and rolled you in a sheet because frankly I was tired of wrestling with a wildcat who clawed till I was near bleeding."

Inside and out.

"And finally," he continued, pinning her with a pointed gaze, "I didn't drag you, I carried you, Miss Bell, through an *empty* public lobby because it was the only way to get your stubborn carcass in the bloomin' wagon and take you home. Where, I might add, your goddaughter and family are worried sick about where you are."

"It's not my home," she whispered, guilt obviously tempering her resistance.

He relented with a heavy sigh. "No, it's not, Mrs. McShane." He mauled the back of his neck. "But it will be for the next six months if you want to marry your professor, so I suggest you make the best of it, Libby, because that will make all of our lives a whole lot easier."

Resigned to the fact that he wasn't going to conquer Rome—or his mule-headed wife—in a day, Finn clicked his tongue. "Come on, boy—let's go home."

The wagon lurched forward, and Libby bobbed so much, Finn gripped to steady her before quickly letting go. "And for your information, Liberty Bell, I *do* love you and never stopped, which is why I never married anyone else, if you must know."

She turned his way, her sweet smile appearing way more innocent than it was. "Really? I just figured it was because every girl in this town finally woke up one day to realize you were a nightmare of a bully."

Finn grinned, the barest trace of tease in her tone giving him hope. "Nope, can't keep up with all the pies, casseroles, and dinner invitations as it is, from all the hopeful mothers and widows out there." He shot her a wink, pretty sure his next statement would ruffle her sheet but good. "Especially Jo Beth."

That porcelain profile hardened to granite as her chin jutted high. "Good—she deserves you," she said in a near snarl that made his grin grow. It was nice to know that the woman Finn stepped out with before he married Libby could still flare his wife's fuse. One of the things he'd always enjoyed about Libby was all the sizzle and spark their sparring brought out, lighting those green eyes on fire and setting that wild auburn hair aflame.

Among other things.

Like now, when even the desert breeze couldn't cool the heat she generated a mere three feet away. The memory of waking up with her in his bed after that unexpected honeymoon night filled him with a fierce longing, causing an ache in his chest over all they had missed. If not for Libby coming home from college that fateful summer and Mrs. Poppy's inadvertent poppy-seed overdose, Finn might very well be married to Jo Beth right now. A shudder traveled his spine, making him realize once and for all that Libby O'Shea was the only woman for him. And whether she knew it or not, he was the only man for her.

Now, Lord, he thought with a brisk flick of the reins.

Don't let it take six months to prove.

CHAPTER NINETEEN

IT WAS A REAL SHAME Maggie Mullaney was one of those "respectable" types because for some strange reason, there was a draw Blaze couldn't deny. A draw he seldom felt with other women that made him want to pitch all reservations and explore the possibilities.

Along with those lips.

He watched her now as she chattered on about her patients like a proud mother, and he swore her eyes sparkled more than the stars up above. They'd spent the last hour talking about everything under the moon, and the time had clipped by in such a blink, he would have sworn it was five minutes instead of sixty. Other than with his family, his best friend, Jake, and Rachel Dixon—his girl at the Ponderosa Saloon—Blaze couldn't remember enjoying a conversation more.

But what surprised him the most was the depth of conversation that made it feel like he'd known Maggie Mullaney all of his life. He was pretty sure he'd never shared with any other woman how painful his mother's passing had been as a boy of thirteen on the heels of his father's death in a mine. He'd been forced to grow up fast as the man of the house, responsible for his siblings long before his mother had passed. The experience had both helped and harmed him—instilling a deep devotion to his family, yes, but also a healthy distrust of marriage and the women who sought it.

"I have absolutely no desire to marry, Blaze Donovan, so between my aversion to womanizers and marriage and your aversion to women of faith and church, I'd say you're fairly safe."

Safe. Looking at Maggie Mullaney now in the moonlight—lush lips always kissed by a smile, chestnut hair that shined more than the moon, and a shapely body that shouldn't belong to a friend—somehow Blaze doubted his safety.

A thought that definitely enticed.

If it didn't scare him silly first.

"May I ask you a personal question?" she asked, and Blaze tore his gaze from the beautiful tilt of her mouth to meet those hazel eyes dead-on, rounded with an innocent curiosity that was *way* too attractive.

Battling an annoying urge to sample those perfect lips, he tugged his hat lower to deflect the desire pulsing through his bloodstream, gushing faster than the melted snow that flooded the creek in the spring. "Sure," he said with a tight smile, propping his hands behind his neck as he distanced himself with another lazy stretch in the chair. All at once he was downright disgusted that the more he talked with Maggie Mullaney, the more his body didn't want to, craving a communication of a whole 'nother means. His mouth tamped into a thin line. What the devil was wrong with him tonight anyway? For pity's sake, he'd just spent the evening with Rachel, so why was he hankering for another woman?

A respectable one at that?

A *God-fearing, church-going* respectable woman to boot.

Who could put a noose around his neck if he wasn't careful.

In reflex, he inched his rocker back a fair amount under the guise of angling her way, figuring the more space between them, the better. "Ask away, ma'am, he said in a casually polite tone he hoped would rein in feelings of friendship that were starting to feel a mite too friendly.

Maggie shifted to face him as well, head tilted in a wide-eyed curiosity that made her look more like Shaylee than a woman in her twenties. "You've mentioned someone named Rachel several times, Blaze. Do you mind if I ask who she is?"

He sucked in a slow, uneven breath, not exactly sure how to frame his relationship with Rachel. At least not to a lady like Maggie Mullaney. But then, maybe the bald-faced truth was just what he needed to quash this irksome attraction he felt. He already knew Maggie wasn't interested in marriage, or so she claimed. But once she found out how he spent his time at the Ponderosa Saloon, she'd surely judge him like the rest of those church-going types, putting an end to these unwanted feelings.

Cuffing the back of his neck, he peered up beneath the brim of his hat with a sheepish smile. "Well, you might say Rachel Dixon is my special girl. The only lady I commit to"—he paused, his gaze locked on hers with a wayward smile—"romantically, that is," he said softly, his direct look making his point crystal clear. "If you know what I mean."

A lump bobbed in her throat, the motion as awkward as this conversation. "I thought you said you didn't have any intention of getting married?"

"I don't," he said with an easy smile. "Rachel and I enjoy each other's company and a lot of the same things, that's all. You know—sarsaparilla, dancin', poker, billiards"—he paused to deliver a cheeky grin—"sparkin'."

Even in the moonlight, he could see the blush that bloomed in her cheeks, but she was saved by the sound of Uncle Finn's buckboard rolling down the drive. "They're here!" she said, voice hoarse as she jumped to her feet.

Unfortunately. Blaze lumbered up from the rocker, the arrival of a second religious female on the ranch souring his mood considerably. Especially one who'd turned her back on Uncle Finn, his brother, and him.

"Whoa, boy ..." Uncle Finn brought the buckboard to

a halt in front of the porch and Blaze ambled down the steps behind Maggie, who literally threw herself into Aunt Libby's arms the moment Finn lifted her down.

"Aunt Libby—I'm so glad you're here!" Maggie pulled back, head tipping the slightest bit as she surveyed the blanket haphazardly draping her godmother's shoulders. Her voice suddenly lowered to a hoarse whisper. "Are you … wearing your nightgown?" she said, and it was all Blaze could do to keep from grinning, the blush in his aunt's face as blatant as Maggie's.

Libby cinched the blanket more tightly, slipping Uncle Finn a thin-lidded glare. "I'm afraid Mr. McShane rushed me out of the hotel so quickly, I didn't have a chance to dress."

Uncle Finn's laughter rang out as he rounded Lightning, pausing to rub the Palomino's neck on the way. "It's not Christian to lie, Libby—you had plenty of chances to dress and you know it. You were just too much of a mule to take 'em."

"I'll get your luggage, Aunt Libby." Blaze moved toward the bed of the wagon when Finn's chuckle stopped him mid-stride.

"It's still at the hotel, Blaze, so if you could pick it up when you drive Maggie into town tomorrow, I'd be much obliged." He nodded toward Libby with a wink. "*And* return the blanket we stole."

"Brendan?" Ignoring Finn's comments, Aunt Libby squinted at Blaze in the moonlight as she moved in close. "Oh my goodness, is that really you?"

"Yes, ma'am," he said with a smile as stiff as the hug he returned when Libby gently embraced him.

Pulling away, she cupped a hand to his stubbled cheek, a mix of shock and wonder in her eyes tinged with an unmistakable hint of regret. "Heavens, where did the time go?" she whispered. "You're a man now—how old?"

"Twenty-nine," he said in a terse tone before shifting his

gaze to Finn, the awkwardness of the situation swiftly propelling him to his uncle's side. "Uncle Finn, I'll be happy to put Lightning up for you."

Finn clapped Blaze on the back. "Thanks, son. I'd like to get your aunt settled in, so I appreciate that." He strolled over to Aunt Libby and extended an arm to the house. "Don said you skipped dinner, Libby, so how 'bout I fix you a quick bite to eat?"

"I would appreciate that," his aunt said, so quietly Blaze could barely hear it. His uncle towered over her with a smile while she looked up, bundled in her blanket like a little girl.

Hopping into the buckboard, Blaze watched the interplay between them—a silhouette of a distant memory that tugged at his heart. Wonderful memories, he recalled, of a truly happy newlywed couple who'd visited long before his mother died. They'd stayed for only a week, but it had been one of the best of his life with lots of laughter and love, games and giggling, giving him hope that happy marriages could exist. Jaw hardening, he picked up the reins of the wagon, remembering how crushed he'd been when he'd discovered Libby had abandoned them all.

"I'll have the wagon ready at seven sharp, Maggie," Blaze said as he clucked his tongue for Lightning to go, offering a tip of his hat.

Following Uncle Finn and Aunt Libby into the house, Maggie turned on the top step with that sweet smile that stuttered Blaze's pulse more than he liked. "I'll be ready," she called with a wave, "good night."

He nodded his response as he guided Lightning toward the barn, thinking it certainly had been a "good" night for a while. At least till Aunt Libby arrived. He snapped the reins, prodding Finn's Palomino on with a scowl. *And* till he realized his annoying attraction to Maggie.

Because suddenly, it didn't feel so "good" anymore.

CHAPTER TWENTY

OH, MAMA, HOW I WISH you could see me now! Whip in her right hand and reins in her left, Maggie was downright giddy she'd picked up the knack for driving the buckboard in only a week! She smiled up at a sky as clear and blue as a robin's egg, pretty sure Mama did see her. She was, no doubt, smiling down as brightly as the blazing orb in the sky, so proud of the horse-skittish daughter who'd finally mastered her fears.

"So … what do you think?" Maggie said, turning to beam at Blaze while she absently snapped the whip on the horse's rump with unbridled excitement. "How am I doing so *fa*—?" The question veered into a high-pitched squeal when the wagon did the same, scraping against a boulder in a ditch that jostled so much, she dropped the reins.

"Uh, eyes on the road, Maggie," Blaze said with a low chuckle, snatching the reins up to redirect his horse before handing them back. "The barest tap of the whip is all you need, and never, *ever* let go of the reins, remember?"

"Oh, right. Sorry." Sucking in a deep draw of air, she refocused on the road that led into town, properly humbled. Blaze had carefully taught her everything she needed to know to drive the wagon to and from work for the last week now. First with Shaylee's docile quarter horse the first three days, which had gone fairly well given she was petrified of horses and her hands had quivered more than the reins. Then with Sheridan's paint the next three, where she'd improved considerably if one didn't count the turtle she'd run over. She'd been so horrified, she'd slapped hands to her eyes with a shriek, reins flopping on the floorboard while the paint moseyed off to nibble some yarrow. And then finally today, with Blaze's own horse by the name of Minx, who was obviously the most ornery. Her lips kinked.

Shocking.

Her bodice expanded and contracted with a wispy sigh. She supposed the humility was well deserved. She'd had way too much fun toying and teasing Blaze about being a "cocky cowboy" since they'd forged a friendship the night Aunt Libby arrived. But Maggie had gotten a little cocky herself, it seemed, her comfort level with Blaze a little *too* comfortable for humility. Her mouth pursed. *And for friendship?*

She swallowed a gulp.

No question Maggie had been hesitant about forging anything with a man who was every bit the heartbreaker Sister Fred claimed—handsome, charming, a hard worker, a lover of family, and *way* too easy to talk to. He had surprised her that first night with his unassuming candor and sincerity about both his past and his family. They were everything to him, and you could see it when he spoke—the liquid warmth in his eyes, the way his voice turned husky and thick.

His honesty had certainly disarmed her, but his intelligence and wit amazed her, enabling him to talk about any and everything from ranching and mining to politics and people. An avid reader, his Uncle Finn had insisted the same in his nieces and nephews, not only providing an entire library of literature in his study, but insisting both Blaze and Dash attend the University of Nevada. "You boys need to be educated to run both your lives and this ranch in the future," his uncle had told them, and although both boys resisted, their Uncle Finn had prevailed.

With Uncle Finn's best friend, Milo Parks, being the editor of *The Territorial Enterprise* and Uncle Finn's own aspirations to run for mayor in the next election, Blaze had a fertile grasp on anything political that Maggie wanted to discuss, even if the two didn't always agree.

"What do you mean you don't see the need for women to vote?" Maggie had demanded, stunned that such an intelligent man could be so ridiculously stupid.

Blaze had only grinned with a shake of his head, keeping tabs on her driving progress while he read his newspaper. "Come on, Maggie, women have no need to clutter their brains with politics—that's what their husbands and fathers are for. Besides"—he casually turned the page of the *Enterprise* with a lazy smile she suspected was meant only to rile—"men are the providers and clearly the most educated."

"I beg your pardon," she'd said with a drop of her jaw, promptly steering the horse off the road, "I'm a provider, I'll have you know, and educated too, for your information."

"Yeah, but you're the exception to the rule, Miss Mullaney, because you have no intention of ever getting married, remember? And let's face it—jobs and education for women only cause problems in a marriage." He turned another page with a grunt. "Aunt Libby is certainly proof of that."

Maggie's hand had instantly tightened on the whip, sorely tempted to use it on Blaze instead of the horse. "I would contend that it's your Uncle Finn who caused the problems, Mr. Donovan, with his blatant refusal to allow the wife he supposedly loved to practice her passion."

He had the nerve to toss her a wink. "That's because a woman's passion should be her husband, Miss Nightingale, not stirring up trouble for him."

A bee had chosen that inopportune moment to buzz

Maggie's face, causing her to squeal and scream as she frantically swatted it away. Blaze had laughed his fool head off when the confounded horse—a male, no doubt—had lurched forward in a dead run, rocking Maggie back in her seat with a shriek.

But as exasperating as Blaze could be, she quickly discovered that underneath the easy charm and devilish tease dwelled an honest and forthright man who'd simply been hurt—*a lot.* Oh, he was still a womanizer all right—you couldn't possess the looks and charm that Blaze Donovan did and not be—dazzling every woman he met with a mere smile or a tip of his hat. At least, according to several of the nurses who'd taken to congregating on the front steps of the hospital whenever Blaze dropped Maggie off. But he never acted on it, they told her with a collective sigh, opting to spend most of his social time at the Ponderosa Saloon.

Heartbreak all the same.

Especially for Rachel, Maggie was certain, the one woman Blaze did "act upon."

"You might say Rachel is my special girl."

In addition to the one that he "sparked," Maggie recalled, chancing a sideways peek as Blaze read an article to her from *The Territorial Enterprise.* When he'd told her that, she'd been utterly mortified until she learned Rachel's uncle owned the Ponderosa and was also one of Blaze's and Dash's good friends. Maggie swallowed hard. Surely an uncle wouldn't allow Blaze to take advantage of his niece that way. *Would he?* She quickly jerked her attention back to the road, hoping he didn't notice the blush that burned hot in her cheeks. Because sweet mother of Job, after more than seven solid hours alone with Blaze Donovan to and from work, Maggie already knew how deadly spending time with the man could be.

Sparkin' or no.

Her stomach flip-flopped when she noticed a wagon

rumbling their way, and chewing her lip, she attempted to steer closer to the edge, squealing when the wagon tipped.

"Easy does it, Flo …," Blaze said with a grin, utilizing one of the Florence Nightingale nicknames he'd coined when she'd met him in the barn the first morning in her uniform.

Claiming the reins once again, he coaxed Minx out of a rut with the same soothing voice of encouragement he used to teach Maggie to drive. "There's plenty of room for you and anybody else on the road, Maggie, so just relax." He was so close she could smell the faint scent of cedar from Angus's soap on his fresh-shaven jaw, causing her stomach to flip-flop for an entirely different reason. "Feet braced on the front board for stability like I showed you and reins firm between your index and third fingers, all right?"

"Yes," she said in a meek voice, feeling anything but stable—both in the wagon and in this newfound friendship with Blaze Donovan. Her breathing was shallow as they made their way down the main street toward the hospital, already bustling with people, wagons, and horses. "Uh, I'm not exactly sure where or how to park—"

Chuckling, he tapped her arm. "Move over, darlin'," he said patiently, butting so close, a bolt of shock rippled through her at both the intimacy of the endearment and the press of his thigh against hers when he took the reins. A shot of heat whirled in her belly while the air stalled in her lungs, seeping out in a fractured exhale when he finally pulled in front of the hospital. "Whoa, girl." At the gentle coax of his voice, more heat burnished Maggie's cheeks over a command that could have easily applied to her as well as to Minx.

He handed Maggie the reins while he hopped out and rounded the wagon. "Now, that wasn't so bad, was it?" Hands to her waist, he lifted her down before she could even blink. "At least not bad for your first few times behind a rig, Nurse Mullaney. But I'm afraid we'll need a few more lessons before I can turn you loose on your own."

Patting her nurse's cap to make sure it was still pinned in place, Maggie managed a tentative smile as she adjusted the pinafore apron of her uniform. "I think that goes without saying, Foreman Donovan, so thank you for your patience." She shaded her eyes from the sun as she peered up, feeling like a runt next to a man who seemed to tower over her like the mountains towered over the hospital. "But I suspect you are a far better teacher than I am a student when it comes to horses." She cast a repentant glance in Minx's direction.

"You'll be fine, Maggie." With a tip of his hat, he mounted the wagon, tossing her a lazy smile that sputtered her pulse. "I'll be in town today building new bookshelves for the school, so I'll pick you up right here at the end of your shift, all right?" He clucked his tongue with a flick of the reins, setting Minx in motion. "And remember—if you can handle Aiden O'Shea on your first day at the hospital, you can handle a horse and wagon, trust me."

Oddly enough, I do. She blinked, managing a listless wave as Blaze's wagon rumbled down the street. *It's me I'm worried about.* Because as much as she hated to admit it, her trust factor in—and attraction to—the former near-naked cowboy was disturbingly strong after spending time with him this last week.

Expelling a sigh way too weary for this early in the morning, Maggie turned to trudge up the steps to the hospital, mood pensive at best. For pity's sake, if Blaze Donovan could trigger these pesky feelings after so little time together, no matter how personal, what could he do living under the same roof day in and day out? Sister Fred had warned her, but with Maggie's aversion to both rogues and marriage, she honestly hadn't thought it would be this hard. Shoulders slumped, she mounted the hospital steps, Sister Fred's words echoing loudly in her brain.

"Which means I am going to take a chance on you, young lady, if you can safely avoid falling under the spell of Mr. Donovan or any rogues just like him, understood?"

She swallowed a gulp. Oh, she understood, all right—*all* too well. She was going to need a mountain of prayers the size of the Sierras to battle unwanted attraction to a man with whom she was determined to be *only* friends. After all, the stakes were just too high—three of them as a matter of fact. The first being, she simply could not jeopardize a fledgling friendship that just might be a means of bringing a lost man back to God.

"Of course I believe in God—I just don't like Him a whole lot, that's all."

Refortifying with a deep breath, she looked up at the impressive four-story brick structure of St. Mary Louise Hospital. *Nor* would she risk disappointing her superior in a job she truly loved. This was one of the most important hospitals in the country, boasting thirty-six rooms with hot and cold running water. Offering some of the best medical care in the West, it could service up to seventy patients with excellent food and top-notch medical personnel. Maggie's chest immediately swelled with pride as she slowly moved toward the entrance. Of which *she* was now an integral part.

The front door flew open when a mother ushered a herd of children out of the building with a baby in her arms. Maggie greeted them warmly, the sight of her little boy in an arm cast and a proud grin coaxing a smile to her lips. She gave the patient a wink as she held the door open, but the moment they passed, her thoughts returned to Blaze and the third thing at stake that worried her the most.

My heart.

"Trust me, my dear—they don't call him 'Blaze' for nothing. He has a reputation for setting hearts on fire, and as the town's confirmed bachelor, I'm afraid he leaves a lot of charred ruins in his wake."

Squaring her shoulders, she straightened her skirt with shaky hands, determined that the only thing that would go down in flames in this situation was her attraction to a man she had no intention of getting any closer to.

At least, not *that* way.

Chin high, she marched through the lobby to Sister Fred's office with a wave and a smile to the front desk, determined to cut these disturbing feelings off at the pass with the only lifeline she knew.

Prayer.

And Sister Fred was *just* the one who could throw her the rope that would pull her out of the sea of temptation onto dry land. After all, she thought with a firm knock on the hospital administrator's door, she'd already mastered one fear today, right?

"Come in."

Maggie pushed the door open with purpose, her smile tamped in resolve.

Might as well make it two.

CHAPTER TWENTY-ONE

DEAR MRS. CONWAY …

Achoo! Libby's handkerchief flew to her nose just in time. She sagged against the headboard with pen and notebook on the lap of her red plaid skirt, no longer grateful for the sniffles she'd caught on the ride home from The Gold Hill Hotel.

I am writing this letter on behalf of the National Woman Suffrage Association—

Sniff.

Yes, this bug had allowed her to avoid Finn by hiding out in her room all week, but she was *so* ready to be done with this nasty cold. A nasty cold, compliments of Finn McShane when he'd dragged her out into the frigid night air in a thin nightgown.

She sneezed again, causing the notebook and pen to shudder along with her, finally willing to admit she had no one to blame but herself. She knew full well that both her father and Finn were masters of control, two mules intent on pinning her beneath their thumbs. She'd never been able to fight either one of them and win, which is why her only option had been to flee. After all, she'd learned long ago she couldn't live in the same city with them, much less the same house. She blew her nose loudly.

Until now, apparently.

Tap. Tap. Tap. "Aunt Libby, may I come in?"

Libby glanced up from the bed where she was composing letters to potential donors, the only volunteer work she could do while holing away in the bedroom she shared with Maggie. "Of course, Maggie—come in!" Libby's mood instantly picked up, her deep affection for Maggie infusing her words with a warm welcome. "Goodness, this is your room as well as mine, sweetheart, so you don't have to knock."

Brows sloped in sympathy, Maggie quietly closed the door behind her. "Are you feeling any better?"

Heat braised Libby's cheeks, but not from the fever she claimed to have. Rustling her letter and notebook aside, she sank back against the headboard with a palm to her forehead. "A little, but not much, I'm afraid," she said with a heavy sigh, grateful it wasn't completely a lie. After all, she *wasn't* feeling any better. She was still prickly as a hedgehog in a cactus patch that she had to live in this house for the next six months. Because not only had Finn resurrected feelings she'd believed to be dead and gone, but now her nieces were making inroads as well, making her care.

A deadly situation.

Blue blazes, she couldn't afford to care! Her life was in New York with Harold, her students at Vassar, and the sweet girls at St. Patrick's, along with her volunteer work for the National Woman Suffrage Association. Not on a ranch with a man who only wanted to clip her wings and tie her down, adorable nieces notwithstanding. Libby's heart cramped. Precious nieces, for sure, who'd been doting on her for a solid week now, cheering her up with giggles and games that brought unexpected joy.

Reflecting on the girls, she nervously smoothed the shirtwaist and skirt she'd put on this morning, so very tired of wearing a nightgown day after day. Despite Libby's bedroom barricade, Sheridan and Shaylee brightened her days by bringing her meals, reading her books, and plying her with questions and chatter as if starved for a woman's voice. And she supposed they were, living on a ranch surrounded by men. Her heart wrenched, feeling the pull to be that voice. A frail sigh drifted from her lips. But she knew she couldn't be, as much as she was coming to care for them. She had long ago committed her life to being a voice for many women, not just two.

Many? Or just one?

The renegade thought caught Libby off-guard, depleting all moisture from her mouth as she battled her own conscience, rearing its ugly head to remind her of all she'd abandoned.

Her city.

Her family.

Her marriage.

"Oh, good, you ate your dinner!" Maggie's face lit up when she glanced at the tray of empty dishes on the night stand. "I've been really worried, Aunt Libby, since you've barely touched any of the trays I've brought up this week."

Avoiding Maggie's eyes, Libby reached for the extra fleece blanket Sheridan had lent her, focusing on covering her bare feet and skirt. She was far too embarrassed to tell Maggie about her three a.m. treks to the kitchen. But her father had forced her to dine with the family the second night, and the cozy revelry around the table had been too inviting for a woman who wanted to stay removed from Silver Lining Ranch. So, Libby had opted to hunker down in her room to nurse her cold the rest of the week. It had been the perfect excuse to bide her time till Maggie was allowed to drive the rig alone, finally able to drop Libby off at Mrs. Poppy's to visit.

Or "beg" might be a better word.

Because Papa might have her over a barrel, but it didn't mean she couldn't hide away in that blasted barrel till she could arrange lodging elsewhere. Yes, she would stay in Virginia City the entire six months—what choice did she have? But maybe—just maybe—Mrs. Poppy would allow her and Maggie to stay with her until then. She was almost certain she could convince Papa to agree, given the hardship two extra guests posed to Finn's household. Especially if Libby promised to visit the ranch on a regular basis.

True, sleeping in Mrs. Poppy's guestroom would be difficult, lying in the same bed in which she and Finn had lain that fateful night. Just the thought caused an ache in her chest, eyelids flickering closed at the memories of his tender kisses and love, intimacies that had long haunted her dreams with what might have been. But it was certainly better than lying awake in a bed down the hall from his, in a house that was once intended for her.

"Aunt Libby?"

Libby's lashes flipped up, the concern in Maggie's eyes inflicting a sharp stab of guilt. "Yes, sweetheart?"

"Are you all right?" Maggie moved toward the bed and placed a palm on Libby's forehead. "You looked like you were going to be sick for a moment there, but you feel cool."

"Yes, of course. Just a twinge of something that's on its way out, I hope."

Like me.

"Well, can I get you anything—water, tea, bromide?"

Libby massaged her temple. "No, Maggie, I'm fine. I think I'll just finish some letters and go to bed early again. Hopefully tomorrow will be a better day." She paused, weighting her words. "When is Blaze going to let you drive the wagon to work by yourself, do you know?"

Chewing on the edge of her lip, Maggie picked up the tray with a nervous smile. "Tomorrow, as a matter of fact, so I'm a wee bit nervous. I'm supposed to meet him in the barn right now so he can teach me how to harness and hitch the cart."

A silent sigh seeped from Libby's lips. "Would you … like some company then, on the way to town tomorrow?"

Maggie blinked before her lips curved into a grin. "Seriously? You think you'll be up to it? Because I would absolutely love that, Aunt Libby, but only if you're feeling well."

"Something tells me I might be," Libby said with a matched smile, "although it may be boredom whispering in my ear. But either way, I think it will do me good to get out the house."

Permanently.

"Besides," she continued, reaching for her papers and pen once again, "I've been longing to visit Mrs. Poppy, so I was hoping you might drop me off there on your way."

Maggie's eyes flared as she stilled, tray in hand. "You mean the pastor's wife you told me about? The one whose late husband married you and Finn?"

"Yes," Libby said with a soft smile, realizing how much she'd missed the dear woman. Her gaze trailed into a far-away stare. "In fact, I think she may be just the medicine I need."

"Oh, I'm so excited!" Maggie set the tray back down to give Libby a hug. She pulled away, two tiny ridges furrowing above her nose while she held Libby's arms. "But *only* if you're much better, all right?"

Libby gave a crisp salute. "Yes, ma'am." Her smile turned tender as she gently stroked Maggie's cheek, rib cage expanding in gratitude for this young woman who'd become the daughter of her heart. "I love you Maggie," she whispered with a glaze of tears, "and I will be leaving a piece of my heart behind when I return home."

"Maybe you won't have to." Maggie's eyes grew misty as well. She gave Libby another squeeze. "Who knows, Aunt Libby—maybe you'll end up liking it here and stay."

"Margaret Rose." Libby's voice tapered soft as she gently caressed Maggie's hands. "Harold is waiting for me in New York, sweetheart, and so are my girls at St. Patrick's. And then there's my commitment to the National Woman Suffrage Association, so I *have* to go home, sweetheart, because that's my journey." She wrinkled her nose in jest, hoping to temper her response. "Abruptly interrupted, I'm afraid, by this short and unsightly detour on the garden path of my life."

Maggie nibbled on the edge of her smile. "Not so short from where I'm standing, Aunt Libby," she said, obviously referring to Finn given the twinkle in her eyes. "And *definitely* not unsightly." She rose and picked up the tray, tipping her head in tease, but Libby didn't miss the hope in her goddaughter's eyes. "Finn really is a wonderful man. I really like him."

Libby arched a brow. "That's because he's not riding roughshod over *your* life, Margaret Rose Mullaney, reining you in on everything you want to do."

A giggle escaped Maggie's lips as she made her way to the door, butting the tray on her knee while she turned the knob. She shot Libby a grin. "If Mama were here, Aunt Libby, I have a feeling she might say that perhaps you *needed* to be reined in every so often, so who knows? Maybe Finn's the one for the job."

"Oh goodness, bite your tongue!" Libby chuckled, mention of her best friend bringing a sheen to her eyes. "Yes, your mother would most likely say that, being the maternal soul that she was." Her chin notched up despite the smile twitching on her lips. "But she supported me nonetheless, even allowing me to take *you* under my suffragist wing against The Judge's objections. Remember, darling—the name is '*Liberty*' O'Shea, which is no accident and definitely not just a first name. It's symbolic of what I hope to help attain for you and me and women everywhere."

"Yes, ma'am," Maggie said with a squirm of a smile, the wiggle of her brows confirming her tease. "But don't you mean Liberty McShane?"

A chill rippled Libby's spine that felt far warmer than it should. She swiftly countered with a firm shake of her head and a purse of a smile sealed with sass. "No, you little stinker, I don't. Not even a little."

CHAPTER TWENTY-TWO

"PERSONALLY, I THINK TOMORROW'S TOO soon for you to ride by yourself," Blaze said to Maggie, giving her that half-lidded scowl that told her he was teasing. *Almost.* He looped the driving halter over the bridle on a Shetland who looked like it was asleep.

"But I don't have a choice," he continued. A bolt of lightning struck a blasted fence post on the south forty, and I need every able-bodied man including Angus down there tomorrow to help round up the cattle."

"Gee whiz, Mr. Donovan, can we stay and help too? Please, *please?*" "Pee-wee" Randall Portell stared up at Blaze with brown eyes as big as the Shetland's, the twelve-year-old orphan's small stature earning him his nickname from the cowhands of the Silver Lining Ranch. Maggie couldn't help but smile, hard-pressed to say what glowed more in the boy's hopeful gaze—excitement or adoration.

Blaze tightened the girth to ensure it was snug before turning to address the boy's question, the wide-eyed expectancy of the other two orphans with him just as pleading. Giving a teasing tug to the brim of the cowboy hat Pee-wee had won in a horseback drill, Blaze slacked a leg, hands perched low on his hips. "Sorry, guys, but Sister Fred would have my head if I didn't deliver you back to the orphanage tonight."

A chorus of moans rose as Pee-wee screwed his eyes shut, head slung back in theatrics Maggie suspected were calculated to make Blaze feel badly. She bit back a smile.

They worked.

"Come on, fellas, have a heart," Blaze said, pinching the bridge of his nose. "You guys should be plum worn out from all the riding and roping we did today."

"But we're not!" Willie Turner begged, his demeanor as urgent as Pee-wee's. He lifted his hands in prayer mode, and it was all Maggie could do to keep a straight face. "We can bunk with the hands, Mr. Donovan, and be ready to go in the morning."

Blaze rolled his eyes. "Oh, yeah, Sister Fred would just *love* that."

"She won't care," Pee-wee argued, the three boys circling Blaze's resistance like vultures, ready to take him down. "She loves you, Mr. Donovan. All the nuns do."

It was Maggie's turn to roll her eyes, thinking Blaze Donovan was a bit too charming for his own good. *Except the day we met, that is.* A smile tickled her lips as she recalled his reaction to her denial to retrieve his clothes, madder than a wet hen. She bit her lip to keep a grin at bay.

In a wet sheet.

Blaze bent down to look each boy in the eyes, jaw sculpted tight. "Look, guys, I can't let you stay at the ranch tonight because Sister Fred would string me up." He paused, as if weighing his words. "But—"

The boys whooped and shouted so loud, Maggie winced along with Blaze, shaking her head when the little scamps jumped and punched their fists in the air.

Straightening, he glanced at Maggie and grinned, and sweet mother of mercy, her stomach instantly flopped along with the boys.

"But *what,* Mr. Donovan?" Jimmy Baxter asked, the other boys punctuating the question with more jumps and shrieks.

"But ..." He gave Maggie a wink, wreaking more havoc in her middle. "Miss Mullaney let it slip that she's never been fishing before, so I was planning on teaching her how *after* we took you back to town—"

"You were?" Maggie blinked, a slow smile of surprise curving on her lips as the boy's shrieks turned to groans.

"But I *suppose* we can wet a line on the way …," Blaze said in a rush, and the boys went wild with Pee-wee tossing his hat in the air while Willie gave the Shetland a kiss. Blaze aimed a stiff finger at all three boys, his tone stern despite the twitch of a smile. "But just for a while, then no complaints when we head home, understood?"

"Yes, sir!" All three boys shouted in unison.

Blaze tousled Pee-wee's hair before hitching a thumb towards the back of the wagon. "So, get in the wagon bed till we're ready to go, butts down all the way. After I help Miss Mullaney hitch up Snowflake, I'll get some more rods. But … no touching rods or tackle till I say so and no standing or hanging out of the bed, got it?"

"Got it," they parroted back, hopping into the wagon bed with more shrieks and laughter.

Blaze threw his hands up in the air as he looked at Maggie, smile askew. "Well, so much for the nice and quiet fishing expedition I planned." Wagging a finger in her face, he issued a warning tinged with a smile. "I'm going to teach you how to fish, Nurse Nightingale, but if I do, I don't want to hear any whining when you have to bait your own hook, you hear?"

Maggie stomped a boot where she stood, arms in a threatening fold despite the glint of humor in her eyes. "I do *not* whine, Blaze Donovan! Say that again, and you'll be wrestling with some lightning right here as well as the south forty."

His rich chuckle filled the horse barn with a sound she had come to love. "No, but you have been known to *demand*, Miss Flo, which is worse to my way of thinking." He attached the trace to the wagon, and Maggie was grateful he'd explained all parts of the harness before their second drive to town. He finished up with a wink, then ambled over to prod her toward the horse, his hands squarely on her shoulders from behind. "You already know how I feel about pushy women."

She teased with another stomp, adding a mock glare over her shoulder for good measure. "And I am *not* pushy either—"

He raised a palm. "Pardon me, Miss Particular—independent, then." He pinched the back of her neck, causing her to scrunch her shoulders with a giggle. "Which is pert near the same thing to my way of thinking. Now, young lady, once Snowflake is harnessed up and hitched, which"—he leaned over her shoulder to give her a stern eye—"is too big of a job for a runt like you …"

She jabbed his shin with the heel of her boot like they were siblings. *Only we aren't*, she quickly reminded herself.

He bellowed a fake groan, rubbing his ankle as he sidled next to the Shetland. "So, Clint volunteered to harness her up each morning and take care of the rig when you come home." His smile compressed at the mention of the one cowhand Sheridan said matched Blaze head-to-head, be it with guns, bronc busting, or the ladies. "Most likely because he's sweet on you, Nurse Mullaney, so I'd keep a wary eye on that one because he has a reputation."

"Oh, you mean like you?" She fluttered her lashes, fully aware he didn't particularly like it when she called him a Romeo. He always insisted he was a one-woman man despite his flirtatious nature with nurses, nuns, or other "respectable" women in town.

"But," he said with tight emphasis, clearly ignoring her comment, "you are responsible for checking all your straps before getting into the carriage, so make sure every buckle is buckled and your traces are flat and untwisted, all right? Then you want to make good and sure your reins are straight from the bit, over the back, and to your seat on the carriage."

He demonstrated and she repeated his every motion, almost letting out a squeal when he clamped hands to her waist and whirled her up into the wagon without notice. "Now, you'll want to sit in the center of the seat when you're alone, so go ahead and finish what I taught you, walking me through it."

Scooting to the middle of the seat, she sat up straight, then picked up both reins and the whip. "Whip in right hand and reins in left, firmly held between index and third fingers," she said with no little pride. "Then gentle contact with the horse's mouth so his ears flick back to listen like this." She gave a gentle tug, giggling when Snowflake did just that.

"Her," he corrected.

"Her," she repeated with a roll of her eyes. "When I'm ready to go, a gentle tap of the whip on the rear will suffice along with the verbal command to 'step up.' Then, with my hand light on the reins, I gently guide her where I want her to go, and when I need to stop, a soft tug will do, with the least amount of pressure."

"Good." He studied her through narrowed eyes, arms in a fold. "Why?"

"Because this teaches the horse to obey a soft touch, which will help me in the long run to keep him light in the bridle instead of wrestling with me."

"Her," he said again, butting his hip to the rig with a crooked smile. "Now, why do I get the feeling you've 'wrestled' with more 'hims' than 'hers'?"

"Because I *have*." Heat dusted her cheeks while the edge of her mouth tipped up.

Chuckling, he left to rustle up more rods and reels while she chatted with the boys, finally jumping up in the wagon beside her. He made himself comfortable with hands behind his neck while he stretched out, long legs to the floorboard with ankles crossed. "So … what do you do once you get to town?"

She sucked in a deep breath, feeling a lot like she had when she took her nursing exam. "I always make sure to leave a wide space when going around corners or passing other people or wagons. To stop, a gentle tug will do it along with a 'whoa, girl.' Then I tie the horse up at the hitching post behind the hospital till I'm ready to go home again, making sure to give *her* a carrot, water, and lots of love during my lunch hour."

The faintest of smiles shadowed his sober lips while the boys chattered like chippies in the wagon bed. "And finally, what should you never, *ever* do, Nurse Mullaney?"

Chin high, she gripped the reins all the more. "You never *ever* let go of your reins while in the rig or out until you've safely tied them to a hitching post." Chewing her lip, she chanced a sideways peek to see his response, and a thrill rippled through her at his smile of approval.

"Excellent," he said with a wink that unleashed another quiver of pleasure along with a touch of warmth to her cheeks. He tipped his hat down as if to take a rest, a sculpted jaw peppered with dark bristle the only thing she could see. "Now take me out the front gate to the main road."

She blinked. "You mean you're going to let *me* drive to the fishing hole?" she said in a near shriek that rivaled those of the boys'.

"Yep," he said in a lazy drawl, not even bothering to look up. "Consider it your final exam, Miss Mullaney. It'll be fun."

"Fun." She slid him a thin gaze. "Is there a decent road to travel?"

He nudged his hat up a hair to reveal shuttered eyes assessing with a secret smile. "Why, you scared, Flo?"

"Of course not!" She swallowed hard as she glanced down at her calico dress. "I'm just not sure I'm dressed appropriately for either fishing *or* bumping along a weedy field to access some remote fishing hole."

"It's on our land, Maggie, so I promise it's not all that

remote." He squinted up at the sky, where the sun was edging toward the horizon. "We have a couple of hours of daylight, and I guarantee you're going to love my favorite fishin' hole." His smile crooked. "Or at least the boys will. And don't worry, darlin', you're dressed just fine." He nodded toward the gate. "Now get a move on, woman," he said as he settled back once again, hat over his face. "Those fish sure won't catch themselves."

CHAPTER TWENTY-THREE

"OH MY GOODNESS, HAVE YOU read Mark Twain's latest—*Adventures of Huckleberry Finn*?" Maggie's breathless tone told Blaze that at the moment, she'd rather focus on literature than fishing. Bubbling more than the cool, crisp mountain stream that rippled and rushed against scattered boulders, she chattered on. The sound of her voice was in beautiful harmony with birdsong, the boys' laughter, and the gurgle of the brook as it swirled against the mossy shore.

"I absolutely loved it!" she gushed on, not even giving him a chance to answer. She literally glowed, competing with the desert sun as it made its lazy descent over a profusion of pines. Barely taking a breath, she told him everything she liked about it and everything she didn't, finally leaning forward as if she had a secret to tell. Shooting a quick glance to where the boys were fishing downstream, she pressed a hand to her mouth, her whisper laced with mischief. "But sweet Providence, some of the language is so coarse, I was sorely tempted to wear gloves in bed while I read it and turn the pages with a bar of soap."

He chuckled and cast his line, the mental picture making him grin. Perched atop a large boulder on a blanket with boots crossed and pole limp in her hand, she sparkled as much as Blaze's favorite fishin' creek, glittering with the promise of adventure and fun. Which was something Maggie Mullaney always delivered, he soon discovered.

Whether discussing literature, politics, or current events in the world at large or at the hospital, she was a wealth of chatter and opinion that provided endless hours of lively debate or agreement. Somehow the woman could even make cleaning bedpans sound exciting, and Blaze was never bored when she was around.

Grinning, he recast his line. "Uncle Finn bought a copy as soon as it released earlier this year," he said, "but I haven't had the chance to read it yet. But I sure enjoy his style." He slipped her an off-centered smile. "*Especially* his irreverence."

"Oh, now *there's* a shock!" she teased, bobbing her rod as if that would somehow hurry the fish. "I know Nevada sees him as a favorite son and all since he worked for *The Territorial Enterprise*, but honestly, the man does ruffle feathers with his scathing satire on traditional thought." Reeling her line in, she tossed him a playful grin. "Not unlike someone *else* I know."

"Keep that up, young lady, and you'll be baiting your own—"

Her high-pitched squeal interrupted when she jumped up, making him wince. "Sweet jubilation, my fourth catch!" she said while she reeled her fish in, presiding over that blasted boulder as if she were Queen of the Creek. Boots straddled and rod straight in the air like a scepter, she beamed while she held the line as far away as she could, allowing plenty of distance for the fair-sized largemouth bass that wiggled on her hook. "Oh my goodness, this is fun!"

"Yeah, fun," Blaze groused with a mock frown, but he was actually pleased as a prairie dog in a patch of petunias that Maggie was enjoying herself as much as the boys were. He liked showing her a good time, which wasn't hard to do because the woman put so much passion into everything she did. His gaze drifted to those full berry-colored lips, and he couldn't help but wonder what kind of passion she'd put into—

"Don't look now, mister, but I believe I'm winning ..." Her voice took on that adorable sing-song quality whenever she bested him at a challenge, which lately was more often than he liked. Although Maggie Mullaney was one of the sweetest, kindest human beings he'd ever met, when it came to a contest, he soon discovered she bordered on diabolical. Didn't matter if it was checkers in the parlour or pitching pennies on the porch—the girl had to win or it doused her good mood faster than a cloudburst on a campfire.

He shook his head with a wry smile. For a Christian lady who didn't like to gamble, she sure liked to wager on whatever she could. One edge of his mouth ticked up. But *not* for money. Nope. The woman was obsessed with butterscotch candies from Mort's Mercantile, and would pert near do anything to win them. Just like he would for peppermint drops.

Thus, this confounded fishing tournament he'd actually *expected* to win.

She waved the stupid fish in his face. "My, this one has a rather large mouth, doesn't it?"

"Yeah." He snatched it from her hook with a wry look. "And the fish does too." He squatted to attach the bass to their stringer beneath the cool water. Correction: *her* stringer since most of the fish on it were hers. His mouth went flat. "That's because I spend all my time baiting your blasted hooks," he mumbled, pride pinched that she was whipping his hide when he'd been the one to teach *her* how to fish.

"Or maybe I'm just naturally better at it because, goodness—I surely seem to be on fire." She fluttered those ridiculously long lashes as if fanning that blasted "fire," clucking her tongue in a show of sympathy that was anything but. "While you can't seem to catch a fish to save your soul."

Eyes locked on hers, he slowly rose to his full height, delivering a shuttered look as slim as his smile. "Well now, maybe you are better, darlin'," he said as he reached into his bait bucket for the longest, fattest worm he could find, "and probably better at baiting hooks too, so here you go." With a flick of his wrist, he pretended to fire it at the little brat.

He was pretty sure her shriek could be heard in the next county, drawing the boys' attention and scaring the fish away, no doubt. It bounced off the mountain peaks like a screaming banshee as she abandoned her pole to leap up and down, slapping invisible worms off of her body like her dress was on fire.

"Uh, Mags?" Bobbling the worm in his hand, he gave her a wicked smile. "The next time you malign my fishing skills, ma'am, you'll be wearing this one and plenty more." Retrieving her pole, he calmly baited her line with the offensive worm, eyelids lifting a hair to pin her with a pointed look. "And leave my soul out of it," he said with a faint smile.

"What soul?" A shudder traveled her body as she clutched her arms to her waist like a barrier, nose wrinkled in distaste. "Anyone who can scare the breath out of me like that has no soul. I despise worms," she announced with another shiver, gaze as thin as the line on her rod. "Especially the human kind."

"*Ah, ah, ah,* those worms have put you ahead of me in this competition, Miss Mullaney. But … not for long." He ambled over to the wagon and exchanged his fishing pole for his sure-fire fly-fishing rod rigged with the special lure he'd made himself out of feathers.

"What are you doing?" Maggie asked, a hint of alarm in her voice when he reached for his net.

"Teaching you another lesson." Strolling to the water's edge, he plopped down on a flat boulder and laid his rod and net aside to yank off his boots, brow arched as he delivered a challenge. "Sportsmanship. So, I suggest you get movin', darlin', 'cause you are not a gracious loser, and once I start, I'll be leaving you high and dry."

"What do you mean I'm not a gracious loser?!" she said, casting her line into the water with a little too much force. "I'm gracious about everything."

"No, you're not." He took his time to carefully roll his jeans with a wayward grin. "At least not losing. Although I will admit I've never seen a prettier pout than when I best you at checkers, and don't even get me started if I finish a book before you. There's no question that when it comes to manners and kindness, you are one of the sweetest gals I know, Maggie.

His gaze sharpened. "But let's face it, darlin'—if we're talking winning or losing, you're a regular Nurse Jekyll and Miss Hyde," he quipped, proud of himself for referencing the new Robert Louis Stevenson book they were both dying to read. "As well as a cocky winner, especially when you're 'on fire.'" He winked as he stood and hooked his net to his belt, finally wading into the water in his bare feet with fishing rod in hand. "But that's okay, because I'm gonna douse you like a wet blanket, woman."

Which wasn't far off. Because within minutes, Blaze had several nice-sized trout to add to the stringer while Maggie worked her line as furiously as she worked her bottom lip, her mood—and her chatter—clearly taking a dive. Reeling in and recasting, she glanced at the sky. "The sun has disappeared over the tree line, so maybe we should go," she said when he'd netted his fourth fish, the tiny crimp of worry above her nose almost making him feel bad.

But not quite.

"Oh, no you don't." He hooked his fourth trout on the stringer, the droop in her shoulders inflicting a wee bit of guilt, especially when he knew the best time to catch trout was in the evening. He grinned.

Right before dusk.

He rinsed his hands in the stream, then stood, tempering his smile while he wiped his palms on his pants. "Come on, Maggie, we've got at least thirty minutes of daylight left and we're nose to nose, so don't you want to know who wins? Besides," he said with a fluid cast of his line, unable to restrain his own cocky grin, "I'm all out of peppermint drops."

"I hate peppermint," she said in a mope, that lush lower lip pushed into a pout that made him chuckle. Especially when he knew she didn't. She huffed out a noisy sigh. "Almost as much as worms."

Mood obviously subdued, she focused on her line, mouth clamped as tight as her grip on the pole. Her prior chatter gave way to the soothing sounds of dusk—the faint roar of rapids upstream, the burble of the brook as it rippled over boulders and stones, the occasional squeal or splash when one of the boys caught a fish.

Somewhere a whip-poor-will sang its summer song accompanied by the boy's distant laughter and the crooning of crickets coming alive for the night. Maggie's silence was rare, but not uncomfortable. In fact, nothing about being with Maggie was uncomfortable. He glanced over, gaze tracing every generous curve down her body before he could stop himself, then scanning right back up to settle on the face of an angel framed by chestnut curls now tousled and free. He swallowed hard, mouth suddenly dry.

Well, almost nothing.

There was still the jump of his pulse whenever she smiled his way.

The slow thud of his heart whenever laughter lit in her eyes.

The way she invaded his sleep with a longing that didn't belong to a friend.

He turned away and flicked his line with a taut hand, thinking he was long overdue for some kissin' on Rachel. He'd spent the entire week with Maggie in the evenings, teaching her to drive the rig or ride the Shetland, horseshoes with the family, or group games in the parlour. He was usually at the Ponderosa two or three nights a week, but this week he hadn't been even once. His fingers suddenly itched for a pool cue and the crack of ivory, where secret smiles promised far more than words.

With an absentminded back cast, he snapped the line forward, settling the fly upstream from a flash of silver. The fish took the bait—like Maggie whenever Blaze offered a challenge—and he set the hook hard, reeling the catch in. "Well, well," he said with a wide grin as he scooped a nice-sized trout up in his net, "looks like I'm in for some peppermint candy."

"*Noooo!*" Maggie stomped her boot on the boulder. "The sun hasn't set yet," she said as she recast her line with a grim set of her jaw. "I can do this."

"Doubt it since the light is fading as fast as your chances. Just give it up, Maggie, and admit I won." He pulled the stringer from the water and held it up. "I'd say this is a pretty fair start to a mighty fine fish fry, if I say so myself." Retrieving his rod and net, he sauntered over to the wagon to stash the fish in a bucket of water, tossing a glance over his shoulder to check on the boys. "Ten more minutes, boys," he called, turning back to Maggie with a smirk he just couldn't resist. "Besides, this is your chance to teach the boys how to be a good loser."

"I *am* a good loser," she said with a jut of her lower lip, her pout so darn cute, he had to smother a chuckle lest he rile her even further.

He unloaded his tackle while Maggie followed suit, her mood dragging as much as the blanket she carried back to the wagon. "Well, that was fun, even if you *did* cheat," she said with a sour smile.

His jaw dropped. "Cheat? You're the one who had the time advantage, young lady, while I was baiting your hook over and over."

"Yes, but *you're* the one that used that fancy rod and reel with that stupid feather on the hook." She crossed her arms in a stiff fold.

"It's a fly," he corrected with a grin, thinking she may be a bad loser, but she sure was a cute one. "And it's not a 'stupid' one either—it won me a bag of my favorite candy, which is more than I can say for your stupid worm." He strolled over to the bank to wash up, lobbing a lazy smile over his shoulder meant to goad her all the more. "Hey, I forgot to grab the bar of soap from my tackle box, Mags, so you mind tossing it? I hate the stink of fish on my hands."

"Yeah, well I hate the stink of something too," she muttered, rattling around in his tackle box before he heard her sliding down the embankment. "And I'd sure like to toss something right about now as well, cocky cowboy, but it sure isn't soap. Here …"

The soap came flying at his head, and Blaze caught it mid-air from his crouched position, flashing some teeth. "I'm sure you would, darlin'," he said with a chuckle while he lathered up good, "but that wouldn't be good sportsmanship, Mags, now would it? So, let me clean up, and we'll shake hands over a close contest before we head home, all right? After all"—he scrubbed his hands in the creek before he shot a cocky grin over his shoulder—"with the night cooling down, that wet blanket could get mighty cold."

CHAPTER TWENTY-FOUR

"SAINTS ALIVE, AND YOU CALL *me* 'a cocky winner'!" Her good humor sorely taxed, Maggie loomed over Blaze while he washed and chuckled his fool head off over his silly "wet blanket" remark. The clean scent of Angus's homemade cedar soap drifted in the air while soap bubbles popped on the water faster than her hopes for a win. Heaven knows she didn't *want* to be such a poor loser, but merciful Providence, games and competitions were the only things she *could* win after Mama had married The Judge. The man ruled with an iron gavel inside of the courtroom and out, robbing her of so much more than just freedom.

"Education is wasted on women," The Judge would rant whenever Mama broached the subject of Maggie going to college. "It's men who have the keen minds and wills to win, the strength to succeed and the reason to do so. A woman's role in life is to please her husband and raise his offspring."

The memory of his words flattened Maggie's mouth as she locked arms over her chest, a shadow of a smile gracing her lips. Because despite all of The Judge's objections, she had won in the end when Mama disguised Maggie's nursing education as a "finishing school" to prepare her for her station in life as a wife and a mother.

"Not a lie, exactly," Mama had whispered later when they giggled together in Maggie's room, "since nursing school will put the 'finishing touches' on a life of your own choosing."

And chosen she had—to leave The Judge, his money, and a roving fiancé behind, accepting Aunt Libby's offer to flee to a place of freedom neither man would ever find. Her chest expanded with pride over the fact that she had finally won over two close-minded males who had only wanted to lord over her. Her lips kinked.

No, make that three …

She studied Blaze's broad back straining beneath his shirt as he scooped water to his face, momentarily halting the cocky whistling he'd resorted to after mocking her without mercy. "'Wet blanket,' indeed," she mumbled under her breath, shifting her stance with a huff while Blaze lapped up water like he'd been the one to haul the wagon instead of Snowflake. She fought off a roll of her eyes.

Ridicule obviously *works up a thirst.*

Her body suddenly stilled, mouth tipping up in a smile.

Well, then, let's slake it, shall we?

Almost giddy at the thought of retaliation, Maggie retreated a number of yards away, glancing the boys' way before turning and barreling toward Blaze with a war cry, the whites of his eyes expanding when he glanced over his shoulder.

Oomph! She plowed into him with the full force of her palms, launching his body face down into the mossy water.

Ker-splash!

"Oh, look," she said with a satisfied giggle when he slowly pushed up on his knees, "I guess my blanket's not the only thing that's all wet."

Blaze calmly rose and turned, his open-mouthed smile and arched brow conveying his shock. "I can't believe you did that," he said in full gaping mode, swiping a hand over his wet face. He shot a quick look in the boys' direction as if to make sure they hadn't seen his demise, then recovered his hat and slapped it hard against jeans that clung as tightly as moss to rocks.

Giggles bubbled up inside of Maggie like one of Mort's fountain sodas as she slowly backed away, inch by inch. "Well, you looked so thirsty," she said with an innocent lift of her shoulders, "I just thought I'd help."

"Did you now?" Snatching up his bar of soap, he casually sloshed to the bank, dripping like a sieve while his gaze bonded to hers.

Her pulse sputtered at the challenge in his eyes while he made his approach, his chambray shirt clinging to sculpted muscles like a second skin. She chewed on the edge of her smile, body poised for flight while a nervous chuckle tripped from her lips. "I figured this way we're both a little wet, right?" She extended a bright smile like an olive branch, shooting an anxious glance back at the wagon to decide if she could outrun a man in bare feet.

"Oh, not yet," he said with a tight smile, leisurely plunking his Stetson down on an unruly mop of wet curls.

Uh-oh. Run!

Whirling around, Maggie tore up the hill like the devil was on her heels, and she wasn't all that sure he wasn't, given the gleam of trouble in Blaze Donovan's eyes. "Blaze, I'm sorry," she shouted, heart hammering against her ribs as she took cover on the other side of the wagon. Hands latched to the bed, she gulped large swallows of air in between giggles, figuring if she couldn't win, then getting the best of Blaze was the next best thing. "And you have my word I will never do that again."

"No doubt about that, darlin'," he said with a lazy smile, his leisurely ascent up the hill far too ripe with resolve for her liking. "Especially after both of us are, in fact, 'a little wet.'"

Her smile dimmed as she grated her lip, gaze flicking to the darkening sky, where fading shades of rose gave way to a purple dusk. "It's late, and we need to get home." Her gaze darted to where the boys were still fishing. "Boys, it's time go," she shouted, hoping to deter Blaze with their presence before she turned to give him a repentant smile. "Come on, Blaze—can't you just accept my apology and we'll go on home?"

"Of course I accept your apology, Maggie, and yes, we'll head on home," he said, plucking a rag from the wagon bed to dry his hair. "But first, don't you think you owe me a congratulatory handshake? After all, we both know I won fair and square."

His gaze drilled into hers as he slowly rounded the rig, arm extended in truce. Scrambling up onto the seat for safety, she did the same, fingers quivering as she made the reach. Lightning struck with a thousand sparks when his large, work-roughened hand closed around hers, damp warmth seeping all the way in. She swallowed hard and nodded. "Yes, you won fair and square, Blaze, so congratulations. And I'm sorry I was such a poor loser."

"Why, thank you, Maggie," he said with a heft of a bristled jaw, a gleam of white teeth in a bronzed face still slick with water. "Apology accepted." Climbing up into the wagon, he stopped halfway, thick golden brows slashing low. "Wait—we forgot the blanket."

"No, it's right here," Maggie said, pointing to the coverlet she'd carefully folded and placed in the back bed.

"No, not that one," he said with a cheeky grin before latching onto her hand, completely catching her off-guard when he swept her across the seat. "The 'wet' one, darlin'," he said with a dangerous smile that bore no good will.

She squealed when his free arm encircled her from behind, unceremoniously dragging her from the rig and tossing her over his shoulder with a grunt. "Blaze, no, please!" she begged, kicking and thrashing for all she was worth, but the man was a steel trap as he strode back to the stream with her slung over his shoulder like a baby possum on its mother's back. Desperation grew—along with the whites of her eyes—the closer he got to the water, and with a wild jerk of her body, she tried to break free, pummeling his back for all she was worth. "Two bags of peppermint candies, I promise, and I'll never be a bad sport again."

"Sorry, Mags, but you said it yourself that I was a good teacher, and this is one lesson I need to drive home." His wicked chuckle said he was having *way* too much fun as he gave her waist a light pinch. "All wet, if need be." At the water's edge, he locked her legs with one hand while he gripped the small of her back with the other, as if ready to heave her into the water.

"No, Blaze, please! *Boys!*" She launched for his neck, clinging harder than the stupid breeching straps wrapped around the shaft of the wagon, screaming for the boys as if they could stop a six-foot-two mountain of a man from tossing her into the drink. "I'll do anything, Blaze, only don't throw me in the creek, please!"

He paused at the edge of the brook, face angled her way. "Anything?" A tease tiptoed around his voice.

"Anything—within reason." She stopped breathing while he apparently gave it some thought.

"All right, Nurse Mullaney." He relaxed his hold, and she waited for him to put her down. "*Two* bags of peppermint candy, then."

Her breath silently seeped out. "You drive a hard bargain, Mr. Donovan, but mercy comes at a high price, I suppose." She wriggled to get free, and he finally let her, his hands slowly guiding her down.

Too slowly.

Her heart drummed a traitorous beat as she slid to the ground, their bodies bonded all the way down. The dampness of his clothes bled warm into hers despite the cool of the night, kindling renegade thoughts as shallow and fast as her air. "We need to get back," she rasped, voice breathless as she tried to step away, wondering where in the devil the boys were.

"Maggie ..."The husky sound of her name on his tongue weakened the tendons at the back of her knees, and she tried to pull away, but he wouldn't let go. "The peppermint candy be dashed," he whispered, his voice suddenly as ragged as hers. He leaned so close, she could smell mint on his breath, warm against her lips as his mouth hovered over hers. "One kiss is all the payment I need."

"No!" She pushed him back, palms hard against his chest while she squeezed her eyes shut for fear those blue eyes would disarm her, dismantle the boundaries she'd worked so hard to maintain. "We need to go, Blaze, *now*—"

Her next breath snagged in her throat when he gently lifted her chin. "What are you afraid of?" he said softly.

"This!" she rasped, eyes blazing open with raw honesty. "Of ruining this friendship we have, which happens to mean a lot to me, Blaze Donovan."

A crooked smile tipped the edge of his mouth as his thumb caressed the curve of her jaw. "It means a lot to me, too, Maggie, but it might not ruin it, you know. Might just make it better."

She answered him with a grunt, straining his hold when she leaned away with a taut fold of arms.

"Besides, you said 'anything,'" he continued in that lazy drawl he always used for a tease. His gaze flicked to her lips and back, pooling heat at the base of her belly. "And I thought you were a woman of your word."

"I am, you insufferable rogue, but apparently you aren't a man of yours."

"Pardon?" He gave her a squint. "How you figure that?"

She arched a brow. "Rachel?" Chin high, she placed a hand over her heart as she mimicked his words in a gruff voice. "You might say Rachel is my special girl. The only lady I commit to"—she paused to flutter her lashes—"romantically, that is."

Hands dropping from her waist, he huffed out a groan while he mauled his face with his palms. "For criminy's sake, Maggie—Rachel is just a friend."

"Yeah, well I'm your friend, too, but I sure don't want to be *that* kind, mister, so you can just save your stolen kisses for her."

His palms dropped enough to see the deadly twinkle in his eyes. "What about being my girl—*that* hold any appeal?"

Her grunt could have belonged to one of the ranch hands. She held up forefinger and thumb in the shape of an "O" a mere inch from his nose while her mouth tipped in a slant. "Absolutely zeeee-ro," she enunciated clearly, "because I'm one of those 'respectable girls,' remember? The kind who will just harp on you about God and church the rest of your days'?"

He grinned. "Oh, yeah, forgot about that. Sorry, lost my head for a second."

"Well, you're going to lose a whole lot more than your head," she called over her shoulder as she marched toward the wagon, "if you ever get that gleam in your eye with me again."

"Yes, ma'am." Giving a sharp salute, he followed her up the hill, chuckling all the way. He paused to whistle for the boys with two fingers to his teeth, appearing satisfied when they started running back. He gave Maggie a wink. "But at least I got two bags of peppermint out of it."

"One." She mounted the wagon and sat, brow arched while she arranged her dress with great care. "Cocky cowboys with gleams in their eyes don't deserve more than that."

Hopping up on his side of the seat, he stared at her, jaw swagging low. "Yeah, well, respectable girls don't push men in the lake either," he said with a quick snatch of the reins.

"No," Maggie agreed, back straight as she folded her hands in her lap with a smug smile. "But the smart ones do."

CHAPTER TWENTY-FIVE

"WHERE'S LIBBY?" PULLING OUT HIS chair in the dining room, Finn sat down, scanning the table for the one face that had been missing all week. "I thought she was feeling better."

Maggie glanced up, brows pinched in concern. "She was, Finn, but I think she may have overdone it going out with me today, so she headed straight up when we got home."

Aiden grunted, which pretty much said it all for Finn too.

Unfolding her napkin, Maeve delivered a passive smile. "She told me she was hoping to visit Mrs. Poppy, but apparently the dear woman was out, so Libby spent the day shopping." Her mouth quirked. "Then took ill the moment she stepped in the house."

Aiden grunted again, stirring sugar into his hot tea.

"I feel just awful," Maggie said, eyes soft with regret, "for even pushing her to go out."

Finn shook his own napkin out and placed it on his lap, bowing his head to say grace while everyone did the same. When he finished, he reached for the rolls and plopped two on his plate before passing the basket to the left. "How did she seem today, Maggie?"

Maggie nodded her thanks to Sheridan for the fried potatoes and proceeded to scoop some on her plate, pausing briefly to give Finn's question some thought. "Wonderful, actually," she said with a smile, "chattering nonstop all the way to Mrs. Poppy's house, so she seemed good."

Finn's spoonful of peas halted over the bowl, eyelids tapering a hair. "All day?"

"Yes, although she wasn't as chatty on the way to town, but I think that was just because she was disappointed not to see Mrs. Poppy."

Another growl rumbled from Aiden's lips, and Maeve huffed out a sigh. "Really, Aiden, a grunt is not a conversation, so just speak your mind."

Aiden took some roast beef from the platter and handed it off to Blaze. "All right, I will," he said, aiming his fork in Finn's direction. "I know this is your house, Finn, and we're mighty beholden to you for your hospitality, but the main reason we're here is to shake some sense into my mule-headed daughter, so when are you going to do it, dad-gum-it?"

"For heaven's sake, Aiden, coarse language has no place at the table, nor does your temper." The ruffles on Maeve's shirtwaist rose and fell as she huffed out a sigh. She placed a hand on her husband's arm while she lanced Finn with a look far more threatening than Aiden's temper. "What Aiden is trying to say, Finn, is that he and I have exhausted both our words and our patience with that stubborn daughter of ours. She refuses to listen to either of us, so our hands are tied." She cocked her head, lips pursed all the more. "But *yours* are not."

Finn glanced up from the roast beef he was cutting. "And what's that supposed to mean, ma'am?" he asked, shoving a piece of beef in his mouth.

"It means, Mr. McShane, that you have to steep your tea while the water's hot."

"But Uncle Finn doesn't drink tea, Mrs. O'Shea," Shaylee said with a pucker in her brow. "He says it's for women and weak-minded boys and that real men only drink coffee."

Aiden drilled Finn with a heated gaze as hot as the cup of tea steaming in his hands. "If that's the case, then I suggest you have Angus brew you a strong pot, McShane, because you're going to need it."

Blaze nodded his head toward the basket of rolls in front of Shaylee. "Hey, Short Stuff, pass the rolls this way please."

"Sure thing, Blaze," Shaylee said, promptly firing a couple of rolls over the table.

"Shaylee Ann Donovan," Finn said with a heft of his chin, "dinner is not a ballgame, young lady, so I suggest you mind your manners and pass the basket next time."

"Yeah, Squirt," Dash said with a grin while an entire biscuit rolled around in his mouth, "anybody would think you've been raised in a barn."

Finn grilled Dash with a feigned glare that spurred a titter of laughter around the table. "And you should know, Dashiell Robert, talking with food in your mouth."

Blaze chuckled as he reached over Sheridan to grab the butter. "Yeah, he makes a cow chewing its cud look downright mannerly."

"You should talk." Dash aimed a pea at Blaze, eyes in a squint as if looking through the sight of a rifle. "I would have taken a bite out of your arm if you reached over me like you did Sher."

The pea bounced off Blaze's nose, and he didn't miss a beat flinging it right back with a grin. "And I would have kicked your kie—"

"Brendan Zachery Donovan!" Finn's look could have fried the potatoes—*again*. "I'm hard-pressed to say who wins the prize for the most offensive manners—Dash or you."

"Wait—there's a prize?" Dash grinned and tossed the pea in the air, catching it with his teeth.

Cauterizing his nephews with a silent warning, Finn returned his attention to Maeve as he sipped his coffee. "Libby is not a child, Maeve, no matter how much she acts like it."

Maeve's mouth took a twist as she spooned sugar into

her tea, slipping both Blaze and Dash a knowing smile. "Neither are your nephews, Finn, but you seem to keep them in line just fine."

It was Finn's turn to grunt. "I lost her the first time by trying to 'keep her in line,' Maeve, remember?" He stabbed at his beef, torn in two over what he should do to win the blasted woman back. She was out of control, and if her parents couldn't rein her in, how could he?

"Maeve's right," Aiden said, buttering a roll, "it's your house, and she's your guest whether she wants to be or not, so you need to march up there and tell her how it's gonna be."

"Yeah, and you saw how well that worked for me last time." Mouth tight, Finn sawed at his meat, just as tired of tiptoeing around Libby as the rest of them. Dash it all, this was his house and his wife, confound it, and he'd have walloped Blaze or Dash if they ever disrespected him like this.

"Uh, I don't know if this will be of any help or not," Maggie said with a nervous grate of her lip, "but Aunt Libby was Mama's best friend and even Mama would get aggravated with her stubbornness from time to time, Finn. In fact, I remember more than once hearing Mama say that what Libby needed was a strong man to stand up to her because nobody else ever would, even Mama."

Finn stared, his mouth curving into a slow smile at Maggie's words. "Not even her fiancé?"

Maggie put a hand to her mouth to stifle a giggle. "Goodness, Finn, *especially* not Professor Pipp, at least according to Mama. She claimed the only reason Aunt Libby liked him in the first place was because he would do whatever she wanted."

Finn's smile bloomed into a grin. "Your mama sounds like she was a very wise woman, Maggie, because that's the same feeling I've always had about your Aunt Libby." His brows angled low as he studied her, lines fanning on either side of his eyes. "Why didn't your mother stand up to her?

You know, tell her the truth?"

"Believe me, she tried—over and over again, but, well ..." She gave a small lift of her shoulders. "You know Aunt Libby."

Finn's smile went flat. Yes, he knew Aunt Libby. *All too well.*

"And to be honest, Finn"—Maggie's face softened in sympathy—"I think Mama was too afraid Aunt Libby would leave and never come back."

"I know the feeling," Finn muttered, staring at his half-eaten food while his gaze trailed into a hard stare. "I haven't pushed because I hoped with time she'd come to her senses."

"Humph." Aiden drained his cup of tea. "That presupposes one has sense in the first place."

"Oh, for heaven's sake, Aiden. One does not rise to the ranks of teacher at an institution like Vassar if they have no sense, even *with* the influence of her father." Maeve brushed a biscuit crumb from her husband's moustache with her napkin.

Aiden slapped his wife's hand away. "Thunderation, woman, don't coddle me like you coddled our daughter. And I'm not talking about noggin sense; I'm talking about the heart kind. Libby is as bright as a shiny new penny, but the girl never did have a lick of sense when it comes to truly giving of herself."

"What on earth are you talking about?" Maeve's hand—now holding a fork laden with potatoes—dropped back to her plate. "Why, Libby gives of herself tirelessly on behalf of her orphans at St. Patrick's, her students at Vassar, and her volunteer work on behalf of women, with a heart as big as her father's is stubborn."

Aiden's jaw rose. "Of course she does, Maeve, but it's not the size of the heart in question here, it's the sense of it. Between your coddling and pushing her into women's rights—"

Maeve arched a dangerous brow.

"And me bullying her and trying to push her into what I wanted, the girl never learned to give her heart to the most important things first."

"Such as ...?" Maeve's jaw was now even with her husband's.

Aiden blinked, all bluster fading as he cupped a gentle hand to her face. "Such as family, Mrs. O'Shea—her parents, her spouse, her friends ..." His Adam's apple hitched in his throat. "Her God."

Maeve stared back, her shock crumpling into a sheen of moisture. "Oh, Aiden, she hasn't, has she?" she whispered, eyelids squeezing closed as she pressed her hand over his on her cheek.

Finn watched as the hardest, gruffest man he'd ever known wrapped tender arms around his wife. "Libby loves us, Maeve, of that I have no doubt, but I'm afraid we've done her a grave disservice when it comes to priorities. Because as my heart attack taught me all too well, the deepest, purest love thrives in the soil of faith. And not just any faith, mind you, but that which is nourished by trust and respect. First for God, then for family, and finally for whatever cause or calling the Lord so ordains."

Maeve sniffed. "Oh, Aiden, what are we going to do?" she whispered, blotting her eyes with her napkin.

Aiden's husky chuckle broke the gloom of silence that had hovered over the table. "Other than pray, my dear, we're not going to do a single thing." He turned to deliver a resolute smile in Finn's direction, raising his water glass in a confident toast. "Finn is."

CHAPTER TWENTY-SIX

"SO, WHAT'S IT GONNA BE—THE best lemon meringue pie you ever et or"—Gert coughed with a fist to her mouth—"plain ol' cobbler?" She propped the swinging kitchen door open with a bony hip, her drab gray calico dress hanging on her frame like a scarecrow and complemented by dusty cowhide boots as wrinkled as the frown on her face.

"It's not 'plain ol' cobbler.'" Angus pushed past her with several bowls of cobbler in his hands, the smell taunting Finn's stomach. "It's cinnamon apple, missy, and I done told you before—my family loves cobbler."

"And mine loves lemon meringue, old man, so why don't we just let them decide?" The two of them stared each other down before eyeing everyone at the table, daring them to pick the other's dessert.

Finn huffed out a sigh, about as tired of Angus and Gert battling in the kitchen as he was of Libby hiding away in her room. "One of each for me, please, but I'm warning you two right now—this is the last night for two desserts, you hear? Gert—you can make dessert on Monday, Wednesday, and Friday, and Angus—you get Tuesday, Thursday, and Saturday, no arguments. The other ladies will cook and bake on Sunday as usual to give you two a day off, understood?"

"Yes'um, Boss." Angus set the two cobblers down in front of the O'Shea's with a smirk and headed back to the kitchen about the time Gert let the swinging door fly. It goosed Angus in the backside but good, and Finn had to stifle a smile.

With a smug look on her face, Gert began to collect Libby's unused plate and utensils. "Pie coming right—"

"Leave it," Finn ordered with a stiff smile, and Gert paused midway, squinting across the table at Finn like he was Angus. He crooked a smile to show her he wasn't. "Libby will be down shortly, Gert, so she'll need her plate and utensils."

"Well, it's about bloomin' time." Aiden pushed his empty plate away and glanced at Gert. "But I'm finished, so you can take my plate away." His eyes narrowed. "And where the devil is your uniform?" he snapped, touching on a sore subject for Gert according to Maeve—the "Frenchie" black and white uniform Aiden insisted she wear.

Gert turned her death stare on him, mumbling something under her breath that made Sheridan and Shaylee giggle. "Flapping on the wash line," she said, snatching up Maggie's and Blaze's empty plates, her barely audible mutter obviously not meant for Aiden. "Where you should be." She all but stomped over to Aiden's side of the table to snatch his plate, pert near nipping his nose in the process.

Shaking his head, Finn rose and tugged the sleeves of his pinstripe shirt down, then adjusted his tan leather vest. "A fresh pot of coffee, if you don't mind, Gert, because I do believe we're going to need it."

"Well, I'll certainly drink to that," Aiden said with a lift of his cup, "and with coffee this time, not tea."

"What if she won't come down?" Maeve offered a solemn gaze that matched the face of everyone in the room.

"Oh, she'll come." Finn's smile firmed into a straight line.

"Darn tootin' she will." Aiden lifted his tea, aiming it at Finn. "Like I always say— respect is a steel palm in a velvet glove, Finn." He upended his cup. "And I have faith in you, boy, so you bet she'll come down."

"But what if she doesn't, Uncle Finn?" Shaylee asked, a crimp in her brow that was probably dirt. "You can't send her to her room like you do with us because she's already there."

"She'll be down, Shay, guaranteed." He pushed in his chair and gave her a mysterious smile. "I have a secret weapon."

"Oh, do tell, Uncle Finn—what is it?" Sheridan asked, a gleam in her eyes as she propped elbows on the table and chin in her hands.

"Sorry, Sher, it's only a secret weapon if it stays a secret." He tossed her a wink on his way into the foyer. "Wish me luck."

"How about we pray for you instead?" Maggie called, and Finn couldn't help but grin on his way up the stairs. *Even better.*

He strode down the upstairs hallway to Libby and Maggie's room, determined that Liberty Margaret O'Shea would not only follow his rules in his house, but by gum, she would like it.

Eventually.

Pausing in front of her room, Finn sent up a quick prayer for wisdom and strength, then tapped on the door.

"Who is it?"

"Finn." Palm to the frame, he hung his head, wondering how on earth to reach a woman like Libby.

Respect is a steel palm in a velvet glove.

Finn blew out a long, withering sigh. Oddly enough, that wasn't his style, at least not anymore. He'd done a lot of changing since Libby had left—drawn closer to God, which in turn had tamed most of the temper and stubborn streak that had damaged his marriage. Without question, years of raising four children had matured and mellowed him into a man far more patient and humble than he ever believed he could be. Unfortunately, those same years appeared to have hardened Libby, souring the sweet nature and gentle heart he fell in love with. And most importantly, dimming that fire and passion he'd so loved in her eyes.

Oh, the fire was still there, no doubt about that. But now it was aimed square at him, scorching him every single chance she could get. Just like Pastor Poppy had once said.

"It's my belief, son, that when people are truly wounded, they stop growing from the point of impact, growing a hard, calloused scar over that part of their heart."

Finn issued a silent grunt. Words of wisdom from long ago that certainly rang true when it came to Libby. Which meant that for all her indifference and indignation, he had deeply wounded the woman he loved. And love her he did, whether he wanted to or not. Because for some reason, the good Lord had chosen to stoke the fire burning inside of him for the mule-headed woman on the other side of that door, making darn sure Finn had never married another.

For some reason?

He pinched the bridge of his nose with a faint smile.

And the two will become one flesh. So, they are no longer two, but one flesh. Therefore, what God has joined together, let no man separate.

Which is what Libby and he were—one flesh in God's eyes. And if Finn had his way—one flesh in Libby's eyes too, God willing. He huffed out a loud sigh. "We need to talk, Libby—now."

"I'm sorry, Finn, but I don't feel well, and I'm in bed." Her tone was lethargic at best.

A tic flickered in his jaw. "Well, then, you best get out, darlin', because we *are* going to talk—face-to-face."

"For the love of decency, Finn," she said loudly, not sounding a bit under the weather, "I'm not even dressed!"

Smile twitching, Finn shifted, convinced that Aiden was right. Respect with a woman like Libby would only be won with a steel palm in a velvet glove. Because she would never love him if she didn't respect him. *And as God is my witness, this woman* will *respect me, if nothing else.* His smile went flat. "Decent or indecent, we're going to talk, Libby, so either you open up or I'm coming in."

He heard the bed squeal as she mumbled, then grinned when the closet door slammed. Bare feet stomping across the room, she lashed the door open, pinching her lavender wraparound satin robe closed at the hollow of her neck. "All right, Finn. You wanted to talk? Talk."

"Not in the hallway," he said, pushing past to enter.

"Good heavens—have you no modesty? I told you I'm *not* dressed." She glared, one hand safeguarding her robe while the other gripped the doorknob like a weapon.

His eyes roamed from the wild russet hair tumbling over her shoulders, down the tightly cinched robe that showcased a body far more endowed than he remembered. Trailing back up, he delivered the lazy smile she'd once told him drove her crazy. One side of his mouth kicked up. *Good*. Now they were even.

"Well, that's an easy fix, *Mrs. McShane*," he said, nodding toward a sliver of scarlet plaid skirt peeking out above her bare feet. "Just take off your robe."

"Oh, you are impossible!" she said with a jerk of her robe, her face as red as her skirt. She tossed the wrapper onto the bed and crossed her arms over a lace-trimmed shirtwaist. "All right, I'm listening."

Leisurely reaching for a spindle-back chair at the desk, he turned it around and straddled it with hands loose over the back. He gave a short nod toward the door. "Uh, you may want to close it, Libby," he said with a patient smile, "unless you want everybody knowing our business."

"We have no business, Mr. McShane," she said, her voice a testy whisper, "we have incarceration! And if you'll remember, the *last* time the door was closed, you pinned me to the bed."

He ducked his head to idly scratch the back of his neck, a grin stealing over his lips. "Yeah, pretty hard to forget that," he said, meeting her fiery gaze with a chuckle, "although

I seem to remember a moan or two of pleasure from that will of yours, if I'm not mistaken."

"Oh, you are incorrigible, Finn McShane!" A pretty shade of rose flooded her cheeks.

"That may be, darlin', but I'm also your husband and this is my ranch, so I have a few house rules for you to abide by."

"Such as?" Her chin lashed up.

"Well, for starters, not only will you eat dinner with the family every night and join in on parlour games after, but while you're here, the only time you're to be in your room is for bedtime, a short nap, or if you're sick."

"I am sick!" she shouted.

"Yes, I know, Libby, sick of me, but that doesn't count. I don't want any complaining or long faces when you're around me or the family, is that clear? Act like you like us for pity's sake."

"That I can do," she said with a stiff smile, "with them. It's *you* I have a problem with."

He pierced her with a pointed look. "Then-*fake*-it, Libby," he bit out, determined her sour attitude would end right here, right now. "I would rather have kind fabrication than nasty reality." She opened her mouth to speak, but he didn't give her the chance. "On Sundays, you will not only go to church with either your parents at St. Mary's or with us at First Presbyterian, but you will set aside time to tutor Shaylee and Sheridan. May as well share some of those fancy things you learned in that finishing school you went to and make yourself useful while you're here."

"Fair enough." Eyes averted, she fixed her gaze out the window. "Is that all?"

Expelling a weary sigh, he studied her intently, hands loosely clasped. "No, that's not all. This is a happy home, Libby, and you will do your part to continue that, including helping to cook and bake dinner every Sunday with the rest of the ladies."

"What?" Her gaze shot to his in a full-fledged gape. "But I don't cook!"

"High time you learn, then, darlin', because everybody on this ranch carries part of the load, understood?"

"But—"

"Finally," he said, cutting her off with a firm tone that matched the determined look in his eyes, "you will—no ifs, ands, or buts—spend time alone with me every Saturday night beginning this Saturday.

"What?!"

He silenced her with a palm in the air. "Be it dinner at The Gold Hill Hotel, a picnic supper by the river, or either dancing or seeing a show at Piper's Opera House. Lillie Langtry maybe, or John Philip Sousa, whatever. But you and I are going to spend time together, Libby, whether you like it or not, so you may as well make the best of it, understood?"

"And if I refuse?" She steeled her shoulders for battle, employing the stubborn press of her jaw and that I-dare-you tilt of her head he remembered so very well.

"You won't," he said in a nonchalant tone, rising to return the chair to the desk. He casually moved toward the door, tamping down a smile when she took several steps back. "Because if you do, there will be consequences, Libby, mark my words."

She slapped her palms to her hips. "Ha! My father already doled out the worst consequences, Finn McShane, forcing me to stay here. So, I doubt there's any threat left."

He stepped right into her space, his very presence forcing her to stumble against the open door. "Wanna bet?" A slow smile inched across his lips as she backed away, affording him the opportunity to cage her in with palms to the wall. "If you get my drift."

"I'll scream," she rasped, palms and body pasted to the wallpaper.

"Go right ahead, Libs. You're my wife and I guarantee

there's a whole houseful of people downstairs rooting for me." His gaze drifted to her mouth and held. "Besides, darlin'," he said in a husky voice meant to underscore his intent, "I'd just love the opportunity to silence any screams, defiance, and nasty comments or looks on your part in *any* way, so please, Libby"—he pinned her with a faint smile—"go ahead, darlin', answer my prayers."

Throat bobbing, she charred him with a look that singed his pride but not his humor. Her mouth instantly clamped shut as if to restrain any response that might trigger her worst nightmare.

And my dream come true. He grinned. "Good, I'm glad we've reached an understanding. And in case you think that silence qualifies as compliance, Mrs. McShane, think again." He hovered close enough for the scent of lilacs to trigger his pulse, making him wish she'd retaliate just once. "You will converse not only with the family but with me in a manner that is both warm and willing whether others are present or not, is that clear?"

She gave a short nod.

His grin grew as he leaned in.

"*Yes*, it's clear!" she said in a rush, her breathing harsh as she slammed palms to his chest.

"Yes, it's clear, *Finn*," he emphasized with a calm smile.

She swallowed again and lifted her chin. "Yes … it's clear … Finn."

"Good." He stepped away and offered his arm. "The family is waiting on us for dessert, Libby, so shall we go?"

He could have sworn her body was trembling—with fury, no doubt—when he escorted her from the room. But taming of one's temper was a good thing, he decided, especially for someone like Libby. Heaven knows she'd not learned to restrain it herself.

"You hungry?" he asked.

"Yes, Finn." She stared straight ahead, smile stiff.

His mouth crooked. "You know, Libby, when I said fake

it, what I really meant was the more you act like you're enjoying yourself, the more you will. Which means, yes, I want smiles and sweet tones, but you're free to speak your mind or the truth as long as it's not too nasty, all right?"

"Yes, Finn."

"So, now that we have that out of the way and you've been freed from your room, what do you want to do after dinner?" he asked, ushering her down the stairs. "Play charades, backgammon, or checkers inside? Or maybe a game of badminton or horseshoes out on the lawn? Just name your pleasure."

"Mmm … while all of those things sound lovely," she said with a tilt of her head, apparently giving it some thought, "what I'd really love to do after dinner, Finn …" She turned to flash the first genuine smile she'd awarded him all week, along with a once-familiar spark in those twinkling green eyes. She fluttered her lashes. "Is target practice."

CHAPTER TWENTY-SEVEN

"YOU KNOW, BIG BROTHER," DASH said, hands perched on top of his pool cue at the Ponderosa Saloon, "Rachel's been pumping me for information as to why you haven't been around." Taking a quick swig from his mug of beer, he set it back down at the end of the long, polished wood bar where a bartender poured drinks for a noisy crowd of cowboys, miners, lumberjacks, and gamblers. He wiped his mouth with the side of his sleeve and glanced at the clock on the wall, his game of pool about to end with the start of his shift. "And I gotta tell you—it's getting harder and harder to put her off."

Bent over the table, Blaze glanced up from the shot he was about to make, pulse catching as he stared at his brother through a haze of cigarette smoke. "You didn't tell her about Maggie, did you?"

"Nope." Dash pushed off from the edge and circled the table, finally leaning a hip against the far corner, cue straight up in his hands. "Figured it was your place, not mine. But you need to tell her soon because it's not fair to Rachel." His pale blue eyes, usually glinting with humor, tended toward somber gray as he pierced Blaze with a calculated look.

"I know. Four ball, far right." Blaze executed a shot that should have put a smile on his face as a loud crack sent his last two solids swishing into the far pocket. But all he could do was scowl, the tinny sound of piano music suddenly getting on his nerves as much as Dash's conversation. "Look, I'm just trying to be hospitable like Uncle Finn asked, that's all."

"Sure you are." Dash eased onto the corner with cue in hand, one leg dangling.

Blaze chalked his cue, his scowl growing. "What the devil is that supposed to mean?" He glared, wishing Dash had opted for their usual game of Faro before work rather than a friendly game of pool, where the conversation seemed anything but "friendly."

"It means you're spending all your time with Maggie when Rachel is supposed to be your girl." It was one of the rare times his brother didn't sport a smile.

"Oh, you're loco," Blaze said, the pinch of his brows planting the seed of a headache. He leaned back over the table, positioning his cue. "Uncle Finn charged me with teaching her how to drive the stupid wagon, that's all. Side left pocket." With expert aim, he promptly buried the eight ball. *Like I wish I could do to this conversation.*

"To and from the hospital, Blaze, but not every single night, taking her on private fishing outings, picnics, playing checkers, or what-not."

Strolling around the table, Blaze emptied the pockets and set up once again, rolling the balls until the cluster was nice and tight. Like his jaw. "Maggie and I are just friends, Dash."

"Is that so?" Perched on the corner of the table, Dash folded his arms, cue tucked in the crook of his elbow.

Annoyance itched hot beneath Blaze's wingtip collar, forcing him to loosen his four-in- hand tie, making him wish he hadn't worn it. But he liked the feel of being clean and well-dressed after a grueling day on the ranch, so he always dressed for town. *And* for Rachel. "Yeah, that's so, *Hash,*" he said, emphasizing the nickname he'd given his brother during fistfights as boys, when Blaze threatened to parse him down to size, like Angus's hash.

"Yeah, well no man spends that much time with a friend, especially one of the female persuasion … *Hot-shot*."

Hot-shot. Hunkered over the table with cue firmly in hand, Blaze winced at the nickname his uncle's friend Sir Alec Bentley had coined when Finn gave Blaze his first gun at sixteen. He'd nearly blown Dash's toe off in a taunt one day. Heat braised the back of Blaze's neck even now at the Brit's definition of a nickname Blaze now despised: "a reckless person and trouble-maker, overeager to fire a gun." From that moment on, Blaze had taken great precaution and care, not only with his weapons, but with his words and his actions. His eyes shuttered closed.

Till now.

Sucking in a harsh breath, Blaze bowed his head, suddenly aware Dash was right. He was being reckless with Maggie—that had been more than obvious when he'd all but forced her to slide down the front of his body in slow motion, igniting feelings—and desire—he'd tried so hard to deny. Heat flashed at the memory, and he quickly fumbled with the buttons of his scarlet brocade vest, desperate to allow him and his once crisp white shirt to breathe.

"You know I'm right, don't you?" Dash said quietly.

Blaze huffed out a noisy sigh. "Yeah, I know you're right, but even so, Maggie and I have already established that we are nothing more than friends." He bent over the table once more, sliding the cue between his fingers while he squinted at the triangle of balls. He shot, and an explosion of cracks erupted, balls ricocheting everywhere except into the pockets.

Foolish shot.

And foolish friendship?

Dash moseyed over to take his turn, bending low to blast the triangle of balls and bury two in the pockets. "Maggie may feel that way, maybe," he said, straightening to his full height, which matched Blaze's six foot two to an inch. He peered at Blaze beneath thick dark brows bunched low.

"But I see how you look at her sometimes, Blaze, like you're dying of starvation and Maggie's a holiday feast."

He ignored the fire that torched both his guilt and his body. "Oh, you're crazy as a loon, Dash. Maggie and I have a lot in common, and we make each other laugh, so what's wrong with that?"

Dash burned him with a silent gaze for several seconds. "Nothing," he finally said in a tone as sober as Blaze after three mugs of root beer, "long as you don't break Rachel's heart."

Blaze studied his younger brother, wondering for the hundredth time if Dash had romantic feelings for Rachel other than friendship. He always denied it vehemently, of course, but the two of them were as close as foam on beer. Not just because they worked together night after night, but because Rachel's Uncle Clyde owned the Ponderosa, the very bar Dash hoped to buy one day.

From the moment Rachel had arrived in Virginia City two years ago penniless and alone, somehow Dash had taken on the unlikely role of guardian over Clyde's niece. His fierce protectiveness had even pitted brother against brother when Blaze laid claim to Rachel's affections, resulting in a fistfight that had required Uncle Finn's intervention.

Upending his sarsaparilla, Blaze clunked the mug down. "Don't plan to, Little Brother."

"Then act like it, confound it," Dash bit out, detonating a cluster of balls so hard, all but one found a pocket, neatly confirming that Blaze wasn't the only cowboy who could whip hide in a pool game. Eyes fixed on his brother, Dash rounded the table to take his last shot. "She acts like it doesn't bother her, Blaze, but I can tell she's hurting inside, and I'm telling you right now, I don't like it."

His gaze suddenly flicked over Blaze's shoulder, and Blaze knew Rachel had entered the room for her shift. Both brothers watched as she mingled with the crowd, hair the color of winter wheat piled high while one silky curl trailed a knee-length scarlet dress trimmed with black lace.

Easily the most popular girl at the Ponderosa, Rachel clearly earned her wages. She entertained with singing, sometimes with the other girls, sometimes alone, but either way, she was always a rousing success. Even so, most of the profits came from dancing with customers—as many as fifty men a night—who gladly paid a dollar for a ticket to hold her in their arms, Blaze included.

The bartender handed her a tumbler of whiskey that Blaze knew was only tea, and she thanked him with a generous smile, laughing and teasing with every man on her way to where the Donovan brothers stood. Several cowboys halted her with a loop of her waist, trying their darnedest to win her affection, but Blaze never worried. He downed the rest of his sarsaparilla as she approached, well aware she'd be all his by the end of the evening.

"You're on the clock, Donovan," she said as she plucked the pool cue from Dash's hand, turning to give Blaze a smile that warmed as much as if he'd downed a keg of real beer. "*Both* of you." She perched on the corner of the pool table with cue in hand, black lace stockings accentuating the casual cross of long, shapely legs. Her blue eyes homed in on Blaze with a sultry look that won the envy of every man in the room. "Especially you, Blaze Donovan, since you owe me a rematch from your last thrashing in pool."

Dash hooked an arm to Rachel's waist and pressed a kiss to her head, his dangerously direct gaze at Blaze a clear signal. "You'll be happy to know I just delivered a thrashing to him, sugar pie, and I'll gladly mete out another if he even comes close to thrashing you again."

"Oh, I think I can hold my own with your brother, Dash," she said with a glance behind the bar where her uncle was, no doubt, eyeing them both. She held out her hand to Blaze. "You up to the challenge, Mr. Donovan?

Because Clyde is waiting for the money to hit my palm whether it's dancing or playing pool, and I'd much rather spare my feet."

Pulling a couple of silver dollars out of his pocket, Blaze slapped them into Rachel's palm with a half-lidded smile. "Better your feet than your pride, ma'am."

"Gotta go to work." Dash grabbed his beer from the bar and emptied the mug, sidling past Rachel with a casual air that didn't quite match the intensity in his eyes. "Burn him, darlin'," he said with a wink before slapping his brother on the back, the warning in his face more of a challenge than Rachel was likely to be. "Before he burns you."

CHAPTER TWENTY-EIGHT

"IT SURE IS A BEAUTIFUL night," Rachel whispered from the front seat of Blaze's wagon, parked in front of their favorite lake for moonlight picnics, talks, or otherwise. Her profile glowed in the moonlight as she stared up at stars that glittered more than the sequins on her dress. Burrowing into his hold, she rested her head on his chest while she circled a lazy finger on his vest. The ripples of heat shuddering through him rivaled those of the ribbon of moonlight shimmering over the water when her hand dropped to his thigh. "Or it could be."

Blaze released a silent sigh, not all that sure that bringing Rachel to their favorite sparkin' place was a good idea, at least not tonight. He hadn't seen her for almost two weeks now, and the citrus scent of her bergamot perfume was driving him crazy, along with the heat of her hand resting on his leg. But she'd pleaded, and he'd given in, guilt eating him raw that he'd caused her any pain.

"She acts like it doesn't bother her, Blaze, but I can tell she's hurting inside."

Blaze could, too, by the neediness of her manner, and it made him feel like a low-down skunk. Of course, Dash's overly protective attitude didn't help, acting like Blaze didn't care about Rachel when he and everybody else knew that he did. Blue blazes, she was the only woman he did care about, the only one he wanted to spend time with, and the only one who raced his pulse.

Maggie's face flashed through his mind and Blaze immediately scowled, determined to spend more time with Rachel in the weeks ahead. He closed his eyes to enjoy the closeness they shared, a connection that suited them both like a well-worn saddle. For pity's sake, Rachel was the only woman he'd ever thought about over the last two years, the only one he ever craved to kiss, and the only one he wanted to talk to about his day. Almost like a marriage without the license or the bedroom, he decided, an arrangement that had truly served them both well.

Of course, right from the start, he'd made sure Rachel understood he wasn't a marrying man, leastways not for a good long while, and she always told him over and over that it didn't matter. He'd even assured both Clyde and Dash he had no intention of taking advantage of Rachel in the Biblical sense. No designs on taking her to bed. Not only because he didn't want to hurt her, Clyde, or Dash, but because he respected Uncle Finn too much. His uncle had pert near pounded morality into his and Dash's heads, promising a horsewhipping if they even thought about bedding a woman without the benefit of marriage.

But dad-burn-it, Rachel sure didn't make it easy, luring him a number of times into the bed of the wagon for some pretty heated sparkin'.

Just like she was trying to do right now.

"Come here, darlin'," he said, suddenly more interested in giving her the attention she seemed to need rather than satisfying his own desires. He lifted her chin with a gentle finger, gut clenching at the look of love in her eyes. "I've missed you, Rachel," he whispered, chastened when he realized just how true it was. He grazed his mouth against hers with a tender kiss that felt almost reverent, skimming his fingers down the silky curve of her face. "I've missed talking to you, laughing with you, and holding you like this, sweetheart, and I plan to make it up to you with dinner at The Gold Hill Sunday night, all right?" He deposited a kiss to her nose. "Forgive me for staying away?"

"Of course I forgive you, Blaze." She cupped his face in return, thumb rasping against the scruff of his jaw. "But I will admit, I'm a bit worried as to the reason why." A lump dipped in the creamy column of her graceful neck. "Especially since hear tell one of the young nurses from St. Mary Louise is living at Silver Lining Ranch along with the O'Shea's."

Blaze sucked in a harsh swallow of air, well aware there were no secrets in a town like Virginia City. *Particularly* when it came to the household of one of its most respected citizens, a citizen expected to run for mayor like Uncle Finn was planning to do.

He bundled Rachel in his arms once again, tangling his fingers in the silk of her hair while he tucked her head to his chest. "No reason to worry, darlin'. Uncle Finn asked me to drive Maggie—she's the nurse you mentioned—to and from the hospital every day and teach her how to drive the wagon on her own, so I've just been busy with that."

"Is she"—she swallowed hard, and he felt it clear to his gut—"pretty?"

His eyes weighted closed, shame thickening the walls of his throat. He did a little swallowing of his own. "Not as pretty as you, Miss Dixon, guaranteed, and definitely not my type."

She lifted her head to search his face, her vulnerable look so at odds with the confident and carefree woman she seemed to be at the Ponderosa. "What exactly is your type?" she whispered.

"You already know, darlin'." He absently fondled the lobe of her ear. "You're my type—beautiful, smart, a woman I care for and enjoy being around, and one who's looking for the same thing as me." He caressed the tip of her chin with the pad of his thumb. "A way to chase our loneliness away without tying each other down."

His stomach cramped at a sudden sheen in her eyes, and

he quickly cradled her face in his hands, voice husky with concern. "Rachel darlin', when we started all of this, you told me that was what you wanted too," he whispered, alarmed that her feelings might be deeper than his.

"And it still is, Blaze." Any moisture he thought he'd seen was gone in the blink of an eye, chased away by a smoky look that accompanied the touch of her hand on his leg. Rising up, she gave him a kiss that lured a groan from his throat while she slowly tugged him down on the seat. "For now."

CHAPTER TWENTY-NINE

"SOOO ..." ABIGAIL GRACE MITCHELL leaned in, voice rife with gossip as she finished her stew in a nook of the hospital kitchen, where the nurses ate their lunch. "How is it living under the same roof as Virginia City's number one heartthrob?" She wiggled her dark brows for good measure, a twinkle dancing in eyes as black as the cup of coffee steaming next to her bowl. "Running low on smelling salts, are you, with all the swooning?"

Maggie rolled her eyes to deflect the warmth that invaded her cheeks, blowing on her spoonful of hot stew Ida Mae had just dished up. "No smelling salts, I assure you, Miss Mitchell, just a brain chock-full of common sense, unlike you and half the women in this town."

"Half? Ha!" Andrea Jo Stephens cut loose with a low chuckle, her brown, almond-shaped eyes sparkling as much as Abigail Grace's over the rim of her cup. "Try 'all' except the ones buried in the graveyard at St. Mary of the Mountains and *you*, Miss Mullaney, which frankly, I'm finding rather hard to believe. Especially since said heartthrob drove you to and from work every single day for weeks."

"Well, believe it," Maggie said dryly, her smile sliding off-center. "Blaze Donovan and I are friends and *only* friends. And for your information, he only drove me the first week in case you haven't noticed the rig parked behind the hospital."

Abigail Grace pushed her empty dish away and bent in,

crossing her arms on the table. "Aw, come on, Maggie—admit it. Blaze Donovan is every girls' dream come true, and every woman in this hospital is just waiting for you to wake up and realize it."

"Not Sister Fred," Maggie said with a heft of her chin, grateful she had at least one ally in her quest to stay as romantically far from Blaze Donovan as she possibly could. "Besides, Blaze has made it perfectly clear he's sweet on some girl named Rachel at the Ponderosa Saloon. Who is, and I quote—his 'special girl,' and the 'only lady' to whom he's 'committed.'"

Ida Mae grunted at the sink where she was peeling carrots for the dinner meal, apron haphazardly tied around her barrel waist. "'Committed,' maybe, but not to marriage, I can tell ya that. Men don't marry women like that."

Maggie glanced at Ida Mae, brows pinched in a frown. "But Blaze says the Ponderosa Saloon isn't like most of the saloons in Virginia City where girls are expected to"—Maggie's cheeks throbbed with heat, hotter than the blasted stew—"well, *you know*. According to Blaze, the girls who work for Rachel's uncle only sing and dance with customers, nothing more."

"Except with Blaze Donovan, I'll wager," Andrea Jo said with a wink, her prim and proper bun belying the flirtatious nature that always appeared whenever Blaze Donovan was in the building. She plunked her elbow on the table with chin in hand, the bodice of her pinafore uniform rising and falling in a wistful sigh. "Lucky dog."

Maggie gaped at the young woman who'd become one of her best friends. "Andrea Jo Stephens, I'm tempted to wash your mouth out with soap! There is nothing 'lucky' about a woman giving into a man's advances, no matter how handsome he is."

Properly chastened, Andrea Jo actually blushed. "Oh, I know, Maggie, don't worry. But even so, I can't help but be a wee bit jealous of any girl who catches the eye of Blaze

Donovan even *if* she does work in a saloon. At least it's the Ponderosa Saloon and not The Silver Pistol or Naked Lady, where you have to make the sign of the Cross if you even walk by across the street, for heaven's sake! In fact, I heard from Millicent Gilroy, who heard from a teller at the bank whose neighbor frequents the Ponderosa, that Clyde is a stickler about his girls' reputations as far as ..." Two blotches of pink actually dusted Andrea Jo's cheeks, relieving Maggie that at least she had *some* moral compunction. Her young friend nibbled the edge of her smile. "Well, you know."

"One can only hope." Abigail Grace sighed and took a sip of her coffee.

"And pray," Maggie emphasized, grateful that at least Rachel wasn't that type of girl.

I hope.

Maggie tore off a piece of her bread and dipped it into her stew, striving for nonchalance. "So ... what is this Rachel like anyway?" she asked in a casual tone, blowing on another spoonful.

"Gorgeous, of course," Andrea Jo said with a wry smile, "and a favorite at the Ponderosa according to Millicent." Her mouth took a hard slant. "Especially with you know who."

Abigail Grace finished off the rest of her roll, licking the crumbs from her fingers. "I heard she does the bookkeeping for her uncle as well as being his most popular dance girl, so she has to be smart."

"Not necessarily," Ida Mae said with another grunt.

"Hey, Maggie ..." Andrea Jo's smile suddenly veered serious, but that couldn't hide the wicked gleam in her eye. "Maybe you ought to go down to the Ponderosa Saloon sometime and tell Rachel all about God like you always do with us." She fluttered her lashes before giving her friend a wink. "Knowing Blaze Donovan's reputation, I bet she sure could use it."

"*You*," Maggie said with a teasing stab of her finger, "are a little brat, Andrea Jo Stephens, and I am going to say extra prayers for you tonight." She rose and pushed in her chair before picking up her tray, returning Andrea Jo's wink with a saucy one of her own. "Which could take all night."

"Maggie Mullaney!" Andrea Jo feigned mock offense. "*Now* who's the brat?"

"You are," Ida Mae said in her no-nonsense tone, not even bothering to glance up as she dumped a bowl of carrots into a boiling pot of water. A barely perceptible lift of her lips was the only indication she was teasing.

"Why, thank you, Ida Mae." Maggie delivered her tray to the sink and washed her dishes before pressing a kiss to the old woman's wrinkled cheek. She tossed a sassy grin over her shoulder on her way out the door. "Take your time, ladies. Heaven knows I do most of the work anyway."

Humming on her way down the hall, Maggie poked her head into Sister Fred's office. "I'm finished with the sponge baths, Sister Fred. I was planning to head up to collect lunch trays unless you have something else you'd like me to do."

Sister Fred glanced up from an intimidating stack of papers with a heavy sigh, her triple chins sagging so much, they multiplied to four. She waved Maggie in. "How did Mr. Gristle do today, my dear—any problems?"

Maggie bit back a smile. "Not since I put ice into his sponge-bath water like you suggested, Sister, assuring him only cooperative patients deserved hot water."

"Ah, yes," Sister Fred said with a loud squeak of her chair as she sank back with a weary groan. "Threats do work rather nicely with some of the element in this town, unfortunately. But regrettably, it always costs me a trip to Father Daly for absolution, I'm afraid. But oh well." Snatching her pen, she sat up straight and tall to tackle her papers once again, her smile suddenly as bright as the sun streaming into her window. "Hopefully the good Lord will see it as a fair trade, mmm?" She scrawled her signature across the bottom of her top page before giving Maggie an audacious wink. "A small smudge of dirt on one's soul for the sake of a clean body."

CHAPTER THIRTY

"UH … EXCUSE ME, S-SISTER Fred?"

Maggie turned to see sweet Sister Elma wringing her hands in the doorway with saucer eyes, ridges crisscrossing her brow. Her normally rosy cheeks were white as the bib of her habit, where a Crucifix quivered on her chest. "Please p-pardon the interruption, Sister Fred, but oh my goodness—there was a brawl at one of the saloons. We have a number of casualties, but I can't find Dr. Murray."

"Ah, yes, just another day in Virginia City," Sister Fred said with a wry smile, lumbering up from her chair with a groan. "Calm down, Sister Elma, Dr. Murray is on lunch break, but we can handle this till he returns. Please round up several of the senior nurses, and we'll get the process started. Come along, Maggie," she said with a firm hook of Maggie's arm, "and you can help."

Even before Sister Fred marched into the waiting room like an army of one, you could hear a loud ruckus, as if whoever awaited had brought their noisy brawl along. Swear words sizzled the air along with threats and shouting, braising Maggie's cheeks.

Shreeeeeeeeeeet!

Maggie froze on Sister Fred's heels at the entrance of the waiting room, the sound of the nun's deafening two-fingered whistle shocking Maggie as much as it did the motley group who gaped back. "*This* is a hospital, gentlemen," she said in a tone of authority that brooked no argument, chins high and voice low. "*Not* your favorite saloon." She aimed a steel finger at the hospital entrance with all the impact of a Colt 45, cocking the imaginary trigger with a steel press of her jaw. "So, I suggest anyone who would like to be treated sit down quietly *now,* or I'll be tempted to add to your injuries by tossing you out that door." Her dark brows beetled low as she burned each and every one of six men with a warning glare that immediately put their butts in a chair. "Thank you." One hand clasped over the other on her formidable stomach, she assessed their injuries like a general assessing his troops while Maggie trailed behind.

As far as Maggie could see, she hoped the injuries looked worse than they were. She winced at one man whose nose was obviously broken and shaped like a swollen comma. There was so much blood from a gash in the middle, he was striped from nostril to chin. Another's eye was swollen completely shut with purple bruises above and below while Sister Fred questioned a third bloody man who groaned as he cradled his arm.

Three senior nurses arrived to usher some of the men to rooms for treatment just as the hospital door flew open with a loud crack to the wall. "So help me, JR, you and Murdock will pay every red cent for damages to my saloon, you hear?" The tall, barrel-chested man with stormy gray eyes ushered a woman to a seat on the far side of the room before Sister Fred could even turn around. Settling the injured woman into her chair, the man descended on one of the brawlers, a bloody man with a red scraggly moustache. "Or so help me, I will make sure you can't show your ugly mug in any saloon in this city."

"Oh, pipe down, Bruner, you know we'll cover the bill."

"You're darn tootin' you will, or I'll see your sorry carcasses thrown in jail."

"Ahem." Meaty arms crossed, Sister Fred loomed over the red-haired man and the newcomer like a pending sandstorm, her gritty gaze actually forcing the newcomer back. "One more threatening word out of you, Mr. Bruner, and I'll see *your* 'sorry carcass' tossed out on its ear, understood?"

With a duck of his Adam's apple, Mr. Bruner took a step back and his Stetson off, intimidation thick in his tone. "My apologies, Sister Fred, but my place looks like a stampede hit it with broken chairs, tables, and glass, and I aim to see JR and Murdock make it right."

"And I'm sure that will happen, Mr. Bruner, but not before I get these men patched up. Then you can take them apart all over again if you like, but not in my hospital, is that clear?"

"Yes, ma'am." Bruner fiddled with his hat in hand, eyes flitting to the woman sitting in the far corner. "And if you wouldn't mind looking at my girl, either, I'd be most obliged."

"Nurse Mullaney," Sister said with an impatient flick of fingers, motioning Maggie forward. "Please see to the young woman while I attend to the ruffians."

"Yes, ma'am." Without another word, Maggie hurried over to the girl who was hunched in her chair, head in her hand. "Pardon me, miss," Maggie said in a gentle voice, "are you hurt?"

Without a word, the girl slowly raised her head, and Maggie tried to restrain a gasp, mortified at the damage done to this poor creature's face. One eye completely disappeared into a pulpy balloon of shiny purple like an overripe plum, and the other held a nearly vacant stare as if she were in shock. A trickle of dried blood trailed at the edge of her mouth while a crimson scratch jagged over greenish-black bruises that mottled her skin from hairline to chin.

Moisture stinging the back of her lids, Maggie squatted before the girl and took her limp hand in hers, covering it with her own. "I am so sorry, miss," she whispered. "Are you in pain?"

The girl didn't speak, but the sudden sheen of tears in her eyes did.

Maggie rose and gently helped her up, wrapping an arm to her waist as she led her to a vacant room down the hall. "I'm Nurse Mullaney," she said softly while she guided the girl to a chair, stooping once again to look her in the eye. "And I'm going to do everything I can to ease both your pain and the swelling. But first, can you tell me your name?"

The girl merely stared at the floor for several moments before her gaze lifted to Maggie's. "I'm so tired." Her voice was no more than a whisper, as frail as the poor girl appeared to be. "So very tired."

"Here," Maggie said, coaxing her to lie down on the bed, "put your feet up and rest while I fetch a cold compress and antiseptics to clean up any scrapes. Do you have a headache, miss?" She placed a hand to the girl's forehead, grateful her skin was cool.

"No way out ..." The girl's desolate tone was as lost as the faraway look in her eyes.

Maggie gave her hand a light squeeze. "Oh, sweetheart, there's always a way out with God," she whispered, thumb grazing the girl's wrist.

The girl shook her head, saltwater spilling down her bruised cheek. "I wish I could believe that, ma'am, but it's too late."

"It's never too late," Maggie said softly. "And after we clean you up, I'm going to tell you why, all right?"

For the very first time the girl's gaze connected with Maggie's, and a thrill coursed through Maggie's veins when she saw the faintest glimmer of hope flicker in the young woman's eyes. She gave a slow nod.

"Good." Maggie patted her hand and hurried to the door, turning to offer her most assuring smile. "Everything's going to be all right, you'll see, Miss—" She paused and tipped her head, hand to her chest in apology. "Goodness, I didn't even get your name."

The seed of a smile shadowed the girl's lips as a lump dipped several times in her throat. It's Dixon, ma'am," she said in a voice almost too soft to hear, "Rachel Dixon."

CHAPTER THIRTY-ONE

"HERE YOU GO, GIRL." BLAZE pulled an apple from his pocket and fed it to Minx, loosening her girth after he put her in the paddock. "A quick snack before we head back out," he said, absently running his hands down the mare's legs to feel for cuts, bumps, or rubs from his boots. He stroked her mane and huffed out a sigh, his mind far more tired than his body after seeing Rachel.

He unbuckled the holster and gun he only wore on the range or in town at night and hooked it on Minx's wall before tugging his string tie off. Shoving it into his pocket, he unbuttoned his collar, making his way to the house where the sound of laughter carried on a breeze along with the smell of fried chicken. A faint smile lifted the edges of his mouth as he remembered how much Rachel had enjoyed the dinner plate he'd asked Angus to fix for them, a private picnic in her bedroom at the Ponderosa. The smile dissolved when he thought of just why she was holing up in her room, too embarrassed to show her face in public until the bruises faded.

Which'd be a *whole* lot sooner than Murdock's would, that's for darn sure.

Undoing a few buttons of his silk vest, Blaze grunted as he trudged up the porch steps, absently touching his sore lip. At least Murdock would suffer more than Blaze tonight after the battering he'd given him. Accident or no, Murdock had hurt Rachel with a punch meant for JR when she'd tried to break up a fight. Blaze's jaw ground tight. The last punch he'd ever throw at the Ponderosa.

Before the screen door squealed, Scout was waiting for him, tail wagging while Frannie merely hissed like the silly thing did whenever anybody entered the room. "Already took one weasel down tonight, rodent," he muttered to the ferret, scowling at Frannie while he gave Scout a good scrub of her snout. "Don't make it two."

"*Noooo* … not the whipping post!" someone moaned, and Blaze smiled his first honest smile all night. Recognizing Maggie's mournful cry from the parlour, he surmised a game ofThe Mansion of Happiness was in progress, a board game where Sabbath-breakers were sent to the whipping post. He quietly moved to the wide beamed doorway of the log parlour, where Uncle Finn concentrated on chess with Aiden on one side of the massive stone hearth. On the other side, Blaze's sisters, Maeve, Aunt Libby, Gert, and Maggie played a rather noisy game of Mansion of Happiness. Blaze grinned straight-out when Maggie—in true Mullaney fashion—dropped her head in her hands with great drama, her lingering groan reminding him how badly she hated to lose. "But I was *so* close …"

"Uh-oh," Shaylee said with a wiggle of brows, "maybe you should have gone to *our* church on Sunday instead of that Catholic one with Aunt Libby and her parents."

"Shaylee Donovan," Uncle Finn called from his chess game, focusing on the board while his tone veered toward dry. "Might I remind you that God is no respecter of persons? *Nor* churches for that matter."

Gert cut loose with a healthy grunt. "Nor age, evidently."

"Unfortunately." Maeve sighed as she studied the board.

"Sorry," Shaylee said in a distracted tone, rubbing her hands together for what Blaze could only presume was a wish for good luck. Eyes squeezed tight, she spun the teetotum as hard as she could, finally emitting a loud whoop when she was able to move her marker to the "Humility" square, which in turn, sent her to the Mansion of Happiness. "Holy bug bones!" she shouted, "I won, I won!"

Blaze grinned when Maggie's face went pale, another groan trailing from her lips.

"Blaze, you're home!" Shaylee shouted as he ambled into the room. "Guess what? I landed on the "Humility" square and beat the boots off everybody!" she announced with far more pride, he was certain, than the "Humility" square allowed.

Aiden chuckled. "Ah, an apt expression for what I'm doing to your uncle as well," he said, his next move making Finn groan.

Blaze laughed as he sidled over to massage Shaylee's shoulders. "So, are you telling me the ladies at this table are shoeless?"

"Literally," his Aunt Libby said with a subtle hike of her stockinged foot, "for which I am *most* grateful since *someone* forced me to walk all over God's creation today." She cast an evil look in Finn's direction, which made Sheridan and Shaylee giggle while Maggie and Maeve grinned.

"I heard that," Finn said without a glance. "Told you to wear decent shoes."

"I *did* wear decent shoes," she shot back, "for a civilized walk, not traipsing through fields of cow biscuits and cactus for your idea of a 'little fresh air.'" She wrinkled her nose while she leaned in to slide Shaylee and Sheridan a wink, her voice barely a whisper. "Fresh air, my boot! Not sure what smelled more—the cows or your uncle."

"Heard that too, Liberty Bell," Finn said with a casual move of his rook, causing his nieces to giggle again, "and you need to know that I'm keeping score, darlin', so you owe me one."

It was Libby's turn to go pale as she glanced over her shoulder, and Blaze laughed out loud when she stuck out her tongue, thinking that sometimes his aunt and Shaylee had a *whole* lot in common.

"Two," Finn said without turning around, the humor in his tone evidence of just how much he thoroughly enjoyed teasing Aunt Libby. He finally shifted in his chair to stare her down. "Because sure as the sun is in the sky, Miss Bell, I'm betting you stuck your tongue out at me, didn't she, Shay?"

Libby's eyes expanded as she silently pleaded with Shay via a little shake of her head.

"Uhhhh ..." Shaylee chewed on her lip in a stall.

Blaze saved Libby with a quick tweak of his sister's shoulders. "You do realize, Shay," Blaze said with a wink at his aunt, "that your win makes tonight's riding lesson with Maggie all the worse since she tends to get crabby when she loses."

"Ha! Wrong again, cowboy," Maggie said with a smile as thin as the look she gave Blaze before offering Shaylee a handshake. "Congratulations on the win, sweetheart." Her gaze returned to Blaze with a definite glare. "And what riding lesson? Dash said you'd be at the Ponderosa tonight."

"Nope, Rachel's under the weather," he said, shooting a quick glance out the window where enough daylight remained for a quick lesson. "Although I might be, too," he said with a wince, leaning to loudly whisper to Sheridan with a hand to his mouth, "after Miss Cranky gets done with me."

"Which one?" Finn teased, tossing a grin at Aunt Libby.

"*This* one," Maggie said in a clipped tone Blaze hoped was just for show, rising so abruptly, he actually took a step back. "Ladies, forgive my departure, but the sooner I learn to ride a horse, the sooner I can be free of your bossy brother."

"I beg your pardon, but I am *not* 'bossy,' Miss Nightingale. I've just learned one has to be firm when dealing with so-called 'independent women.'"

"Which one?" Finn said again.

Aiden laughed as he moved a pawn. "I'd say it's a bloomin'

epidemic, my boy, in this very room alone."

"One can only hope," Libby muttered.

Blaze headed for the door. "Well, let's get a move on, Miss Mullaney, daylight's burnin'."

"How's Rachel?" Maggie asked as she followed Blaze down the porch steps, her voice considerably softer.

He halted midway and turned. "You know Rachel?"

"I *treated* Rachel," she said with an edge, bypassing Blaze altogether to march to the barn in a fast clip as if propelled by anger. "I was mortified when I saw what happened to her."

He caught up, his tone bordering on a hiss that would have made Frannie proud. "Yeah, well, I 'treated' Murdock—the one who started the fight and clipped Rachel by accident—and I guarantee *he'll* be 'mortified' when he looks in the mirror."

Maggie slowed as they entered the barn, her sideways glance pinched with sympathy. "Is that how you got the split lip?" She reached to lightly skim the crevice beneath his eye. "And it looks like you have the start of a shiner as well."

"Yeah," he said as he entered Snowflake's stall, patting her mane before leading her out. "Had dinner with Rachel, then dessert at Murdock's, giving him a licking he won't soon forget." He grabbed the grooming brush from the hook on the wall and handed it to her, satisfied when she proceeded to groom Snowflake in the methodical manner he'd taught her last week.

"I sure hope the owner of the Ponderosa won't allow him back." Maggie finished grooming Snowflake and replaced the brush, then headed for the tack wall to retrieve the Western saddle she'd been using.

Blaze fought the urge to help her as she lugged it over, finally hefting it over the horse's back with a grunt. But she needed to know how to do everything herself if she was going to ride, and he'd learned all too well that Maggie was nothing if not fiercely independent. "He won't," he said as he cocked a hip to the stall, arms in a casual cross while he watched her go through the paces. "Murdock has been banned from the premises, and JR has been given a warning since he was actually trying to defend Rachel from Murdock's advances."

She cinched up the saddle just like he'd shown her, making sure the girth was good and snug. He then held Snowflake's head while Maggie took both reins in her left hand and gathered them with a tuft of mane, hooking a boot into the stirrup. He grinned when the woman hopped up into the saddle so efficiently, Blaze actually felt a surge of pride. Maggie Mullaney was not only a quick study for someone who'd once had a fear of horses, but she looked like she'd been born to ride from the start.

"I should have worn Sheridan's split leather skirt," she mumbled while she tugged on her dress to cover beautiful legs Blaze had enjoyed glimpsing now and then during their lessons. She arched a dark brow as she settled in, huffing out a sigh. "But *someone* failed to mention we'd have a lesson this evening."

"Sorry about that." He strode out of the barn, leaving Maggie to follow while he headed for the paddock to saddle up, tightening Minx's girth before he mounted. "But it's Rachel's night off, and I promised to take her to dinner." His tone turned acidic. "Only I sure didn't expect to be dining in her room 'cause Murdock bruised her up. It was all I could do not to storm right out and hunt him down after we ate, but she wanted me to stay till she fell asleep, which wasn't long with the awful day she'd had." He nodded toward the front gate. "I think you're ready for a ride outside the ranch to experience different terrains."

They trotted to the front gravel drive where they broke into a gallop. Maggie's chestnut hair instantly fell from its pins to stream behind as wild and free as Snowflake's mane. Approaching the gate, they slowed to a canter on the packed dirt road that led into town, finally easing the horses into a natural walk.

Silent for a good, long mile, a peaceful calm surrounded them along with graceful ponderosas and yellow pines flanking the dusty road like a verdant wall, helping to still Blaze's anxious soul. He closed his eyes and drew in a deep breath, the scent of butterscotch or vanilla drifting in the air like Sheridan had just baked a fresh batch of cookies.

"Goodness, what's that wonderful smell?" Maggie breathed in deeply, lips pressed tightly as she took in a full breath, nose in the air like a deer on the scent.

"Yellow-belly ponderosa pines," he explained."

She glanced over, two ridges digging in at the bridge of her nose. "What?"

He smiled, the lazy rhythm of his horse lulling him into a strange contentment that had a whole lot to do with the lady beside him. "When a ponderosa pine reaches 110 to 120 years old, which is about Sheridan or Shaylee's age for a tree, it begins to shed its black bark to reveal an inner bark of yellow, which is why the locals call it the yellow-belly phase. Believe it or not, if you stick your nose into a crevice of the bark during this phase and take a big sniff, it smells like someone's baking cookies."

"Oh my goodness, it does!" she exclaimed, the little-girl glow on her face making him smile. "It smells like cinnamon or coconut, maybe."

"Or butterscotch or vanilla like it does to me." He nodded toward a break in the trees at a wildflower meadow, where the late-day sun glimmered gold on a faraway fishing pond he and Dash had frequented as boys. "How 'bout we take a rest over by that pond, and I'll let you sniff one firsthand."

Her hazel eyes lit up, pert near the color of fire in the shaft of sunlight that washed over her face. "Really?"

"Yes, *really*, Miss Mullaney. That is"—a slow smile slid across his lips—"as long as you can keep up with me."

Shortening the reins, he gave her a wink before squeezing Minx's flanks in a forward lean. "*Yah!*"

Minx flew like the wind through the meadow, her hooves pounding in rhythm with Blaze's hammering heart while adrenaline coursed through both his and the mare's veins. Sweet mother of mercy, how he loved spending time with Maggie! The thought was rudely interrupted by Rachel's face, battered and bruised, and his good mood suddenly slowed to a halt, along with Minx's stride as they neared the edge of the pond.

He glanced over his shoulder, pulse sprinting at the sight of Maggie wild and free, as graceful and magnificent as the animal she rode. He grinned at her stern concentration as she bent low over Snowflake's neck with a nasty scowl, and was pretty sure he was in a heap of trouble because he'd challenged and stolen a lead. Even so, she and Snowflake were flying, their speed blowing Maggie's skirt clear up to her thighs. A dangerous heat kindled low in his gut, reminding him once again she was only a friend. He swallowed hard. But friend or no—he had a sinking feeling that either way …

He was in a whole heap of trouble.

CHAPTER THIRTY-TWO

MAGGIE WAS PANTING AS HARD as Snowflake by the time they reached Blaze. He was lying against one of those yellow-belly ponderosa pines, hands propped behind his neck and Stetson low over his eyes, as if taking a nap. Long legs sprawled out with boots crossed, he slowly nudged his hat up with a lazy smile. "Blue blazes, Miss Nightengale, what took you so long? I'm about done with my nap."

"You're done all right," Maggie said with a mock glare, sliding off Snowflake so fast, her skirt billowed up. "Soon as I get my hands on you!" Marching over, she slapped two palms to her hips and glared him down.

His grin took a tilt as he peered up, hand shading his eyes. "Is that a promise, Nurse Flo? Because I do believe I *am* feeling somewhat poorly." He put a palm to his forehead, the cocky grin skewing into a pained look.

"You haven't *seen* 'poorly,'" she threatened, voice cracking when she tried to suppress a chuckle. Plucking his Stetson off his head, she began whacking him with it. "You are not only a cocky cowboy, Blaze Donovan, you're a cocky cheat!"

Jumping up, he tried to fend her off, but he was laughing so hard, she whopped him all the more. "And you're a poor loser, ma'am," he teased, snatching the hat back before bolting to the other side of the tree. "Although I will admit, a mighty cute one when you're all riled up."

Hands latched to the tree, he taunted her with a white flash of teeth.

She jerked one way then quickly the other, but he was too fast, dodging her for several turns. "Look, you want to smell the bloomin' tree or not?" he finally asked, tunneling fingers through disheveled curls before reseating his Stetson with a firm tap.

Finger aimed his way, she scorched him with another glare for good measure. "Yes, but if you ever cheat on a challenge again, mister, it's two bags of butterscotch candies whether you win or not, understood?"

"Yes, ma'am," he said with a brisk salute. "Come on over here, Miss Prickly."

Smile pursed, she marched to his side of the tree with arms crossed. "What?"

Leaning one palm to the tree, he gave a nod toward the trunk where snaky lines of dark gray bark flanked a patch of golden-red swirls that looked like The Judge's burlwood desk. "Go on, take a sniff."

Eyes closed, she bent forward and breathed in, instantly transported back to better times with the scent of her mother's homemade Christmas cookies. Tears instantly brimmed in her eyes.

"So, what's it smell like to you—butterscotch and vanilla or cinnamon and coconut?" Blaze asked, still casually propped against the tree.

Blinking to clear the wetness, she looked up at him, somehow managing a tremulous smile. "It smells like home," she whispered, feeling a bit silly as she swiped at the moisture in her eyes.

He immediately stood up tall. "You're crying . . ." Concern laced his voice as he reached to graze a gentle finger to her cheek, halting the trail of her mourning. The tenderness of his touch unleashed a grief she'd fought so hard to resist.

"I guess I miss my mother," she whispered, totally

stunned at the sob that broke from her lips, almost as if it belonged to someone else.

"Aw, Maggie …" She was totally unprepared for the warmth of his body as he bundled her in his arms, surrounding her with caring and comfort and that musky citrus scent that never failed to flutter her stomach. The warmth of his breath caressed the skin of her neck as he bent his head close to hers, and like a floodgate that had been opened, she wept uncontrollably against his chest. "That's okay, darlin'," he said quietly with a gentle massage of her back, "you go right ahead and get it all out."

And she did. All the grief over missing her mother, all the pain that David and The Judge had inflicted, all the worry over Aunt Libby's apparent unhappiness. It all came gushing out against the blue silk of Blaze's vest, the firm warmth of his body providing yet one more reason for her angst …

The swirl of heat deep in her belly.

The tingling sensation that weakened her knees.

The dryness in a mouth that suddenly ached to be kissed.

Breathless, she jolted from his arms, her words stuttering as quickly as her pulse. "G-Goodness, all this over the b-bark of a s-silly tree," she said, tempted to fan her face for all the heat steaming her cheeks. "You must think me a perfect goose." She whirled around, intent on escaping to the edge of the pond.

He stayed her with a gentle hand. "You got the 'perfect' part right, Maggie," he said quietly, gently tugging her to face him once again. She swallowed a hard knot when he lifted her chin with a finger, completely unsettled by the tender look in his eyes.

Taking a step back, she hugged her waist against the onslaught of feelings he stirred, pinning her gaze to his boots rather than his face. "Thank you, Blaze, for your kind concern." Her eyes rose to meet the deep blue in his, and the intensity she saw unleashed a scatter of goose bumps all over her body. "You're a good *friend*," she emphasized, determined not to give in to impossible feelings for a man of no faith.

Especially one with a girlfriend.

She held his gaze with a lift of her chin. "At least Rachel is a lucky girl in that respect, if none other."

The tenderness in his eyes dimmed with a squint. "What's that supposed to mean?"

Maggie turned and walked to the edge of the pond, arms still crossed in a barricade, both against the emotions he evoked and the anger suddenly simmering over his relationship with Rachel. "I mean, yes, she's lucky to have you as a friend, Blaze, but I think her luck ends at the door of the Ponderosa Saloon, where girls who work there are constantly exposed to danger."

He joined her at the shore, his gaze lost on the scarlet-gold shimmers of dusk as they rippled over the water. "Not really. What happened to Rachel was a fluke, Maggie. Clyde takes good care of his girls. Gives 'em a place to stay, food, security, and a paycheck."

"Yes, but at what cost?" She stared at his hard-sculpted profile, some of her anger bleeding into her tone.

His jaw compressed as he snatched up a pebble, hurling it across the water with enough force to skip it four times before plunking into the water. "Before Clyde took her in, Rachel and every other girl there fled from true danger, be it abuse at the hand of a relative, husband, or beau, or even just plain starving on the streets. Trust me, Maggie, until Clyde, none of them felt they had a life worth living."

"And they do now?" Her harsh tone drew his gaze.

"Yes, as a matter of fact they do, Miss Mullaney." He scooped up another stone and pelted it even farther before scowling at her out of the corner of his eye. "Because despite the fact these girls work in a saloon, Clyde's is one of the few in Virginia City that requires them to entertain customers with singing or dancing rather than other less desirable pursuits. Unless they choose to do so."

Heat scorched Maggie's cheeks, suddenly incensed over the unfairness of it all—men defiling and using women for their own pleasure. "Oh, and I suppose Rachel 'chooses to do so,'" she said in a tight tone, "at least with you."

It was his turn to blush as he turned to gape, blood gorging his cheeks. "That's none of your blasted business, Maggie," he hissed, "so butt out." He hurtled a stone across the water with a grunt, singeing her with a look of warning. "You can just button down your dad-burned morality because regardless of what you think, lady, I care about Rachel a great deal."

"Enough to marry her?"

He twisted so fast, she faltered back, the blaze of wildfire in his eyes true to his name. "I already told Rachel from the start and now I'm telling you—*again*. Don't plan to marry anybody—*ever!* Rachel knows I care about her and she's happy just the way we are, so leave it alone."

"Oh, sure she is," she returned with enough fire in her eyes to go nose to nose with his, "but only because you haven't given her any other choice."

"We need to go." He stormed toward the horses, and she knew she should let it go. But the image of Rachel's battered face haunted her mind, and there was no way she could turn her back on one of her own.

"So, you're basically saying you'd be happy if Sheridan or Shaylee had a relationship like that," she said, hot on his heels, "is that it?"

"What the devil are you talking about?" He grabbed Minx's reins and mounted, glaring down at her like she was a snake in his path. "They're my sisters, for pity's sake, and I'd kill any man who so much as touched them."

"And yet," she said in a voice that tapered off to a whisper, "you refuse the same courtesy to Rachel, disrespecting her like you'd never allow any man to do to Sheridan or Shaylee."

Never in all the time they'd spent together had she seen Blaze Donovan lose his temper like the day they'd first met at the hospital. But she saw it now in all its blazing glory as he leveled a blunt finger with a look harder than the granite in the mountains behind. "This is none of your blasted business, so I suggest you either drop *it* or our friendship, Maggie—take your pick."

She stared up, sorrow suddenly siphoning the anger from her body. "All right, Blaze," she said quietly, I'll drop it." Reaching for Snowflake's rein, she slipped a boot in the stirrup and climbed into the saddle, shoulders back as she pierced him with a disappointed look, "but at least you gave *me* a choice."

CHAPTER THIRTY-THREE

"CARSON CITY?" LIBBY'S FACE SUDDENLY matched the white silk shirtwaist tucked into her bustled skirt, her navy jacket making the contrast all the starker.

Finn fitted his hands firmly to her small waist, taking his sweet time in lifting her out of the buckboard. "Yes, ma'am. I told you we were going to dinner on Saturday night, Mrs. McShane, remember?"

When he put her down, she wobbled, and he gladly steadied her with a brace of palms, marveling for the hundredth time what a little mite of a thing she was. Hooking his arm through hers, he proceeded to lead her to the V&T Truckee train to Carson City.

Her blue velvet heels dug into the powdered dirt of the street in front of the station, halting their progress. "Yes, dinner," she rasped, "but in *another city*?" Her voice cracked.

Finn squelched a grin. *Especially the city where we'd taken our official honeymoon for three glorious days.* "Hear tell there's a new chef from Paris at the Ormsby House Hotel, so I've been wanting to go."

If possible, the woman paled even more, and it was all Finn could do to keep a straight face as he coaxed her toward the train, pert near dragging her all the way.

"Finn, I don't really think this is a good idea …"

He tugged her forward, chuckling when her heels left grooves in the dust. Dear Lord, if the woman were a mule, she'd be braying! "Sure it is, Libs. It'll be fun. That's where we spent our honeymoon, remember?"

No response.

Finn couldn't fight it any longer—he laughed outright, literally swooping her up in his arms as he boarded the train, which promptly elicited a squeal from her lips. "I even requested the same room," he said in a nonchalant tone that was anything but. "You know, the one with the double bathtub where we—"

"I remember," she said in a rush, her voice hoarse and somewhat garbled as he mounted the final step to the passenger car. Wiggling to get down, she suddenly froze as if she just realized the implication of a rented room, her body stiffer than long johns on a wash line in a winter storm. "Wait—y-you r-requested a *r-room*??"

Jerking free, she all but vaulted out of his arms, green sparks shooting from those remarkable eyes as she teetered in the corridor with a hand to her chest. "Of all the low, despicable, sneaky"—she literally gasped for air, all the blood that had deserted her face before now rushing back with a vengeance—"If you think I'm going to share a bed with you, Finn McShane, you are sadly mistaken," she shouted, a tossup over which shot more fire—the flash of her eyes or the toss of her auburn hair. She tried to push past to disembark the train.

"Uh, Libs?" Finn lowered his voice as he halted her retreat, giving a sympathetic nod over her shoulder. "You might want to keep it down, darlin'."

She spun around just as the whistle blew, and Finn braced her when she swayed like a drunken miner. A harsh breath escaped her lips while a carload of passengers silently gaped. Eyelids flickering, she fainted dead out before the exit door slammed shut, and with a conciliatory smile to those in the car, he quickly scooped her up.

"*Ahem.*" Someone cleared his throat, and Finn turned to an impeccably attired porter in a crisp blue uniform agleam with gold buttons. Giving a short bow, the porter delivered an awkward smile while two spots of color promptly stained his mustached face. "Welcome back, Director Finn," he said with a nod of respect, utilizing the title Finn once owned as Director of the V&T Truckee Railroad years ago. "I'll escort you and the lady to the private coach, sir."

Carefully sidling past Finn, he led them through the crowded car to the next section, a private parlour car with cherry-wood booths and dark-green tufted velvet seating. An exquisitely carved varnished bar at the back boasted bottles of wine and crystal decanters of whiskey that glimmered along with a crystal chandelier. Green velvet curtains with gold sashes offered a cozy frame for large viewing windows where shafts of sunlight streamed across an Oriental rug. Attired in a starched white uniform with gold buttons, an attendant delivered snifter of brandies to several booths of well-dressed gentlemen and ladies while the porter led Finn to the most private and luxurious parlour seating in the back.

"Thank you, Mason," Finn said, gently setting Libby down on a plush gold brocade love seat before slipping a five-dollar bill into the man's hand. Smile warm, Finn slapped the porter on the back. "It's good to see you again, my friend. Give Alma my love."

"Will do, sir," the porter said with a click of his heels, signaling the attendant with an authoritative nod in Finn's direction on his way back to the passenger car.

Finn turned to attend to Libby who was just coming to, eyes groggy as she slowly sat up. He laid a gentle hand on her shoulder. "Are you all right? Can I get you something to drink?"

In a wild flutter of lashes, she shot up in panic mode, gaze darting out the window of the moving train before she sank back into the seat with a low groan, head in her hands.

Finn squatted next to the loveseat. "Libby, we're not spending the night in Carson City, sweetheart," he said quietly, tone tender. "I requested the room as a courtesy in case you wanted to freshen up after arrival and before departure."

She peeked out between two fingers. "We're not spending the night together?"

"No, ma'am," he said with a hint of a smile. "Not unless, of course, you'd like to …"

She whopped him with her reticule, but he detected the barest thread of humor in her scold despite the dusting of rose in her cheeks. "Finn McShane, you haven't changed one solitary bit since high school. You are still the same incorrigible tease who always drove me crazy."

The crinkles of laughter around his eyes softened along with the tenor of his tone, which suddenly faded to husky. "That used to be a good thing," he said, gaze locked on hers before it flicked to her lips and back, "leastways since that night at the Poppy's."

The rose in her face bloomed to crimson while she swiftly focused on the scenery outside. "I imagine Carson City has changed quite a bit since then," she said, voice breathless as she casually tucked herself as far back in the corner of the loveseat as possible. Fingers shaking, she set the offensive reticule on the seat beside her and clasped her hands on the oval linen-clad table, a sweet scent drifting in the air from a crystal vase of fresh flowers.

"Quite a bit," he said with a glance at his pocket watch. He moved to his loveseat across the table, gaze connecting with the attendant's before he settled in with an arm over the back of his chair. "But underneath the modern trappings, it still retains its original charm and appeal." He paused for effect. "Like you, Libby, for me."

She turned from the window just as the waiter arrived to take their drink orders. "I'd love a glass of port if you have it," she said to the man, worry lines bunching her brow as she looked over at Finn. "Is that all right?"

"Certainly." Finn gave a nod to the waiter. "And I'll have a cup of coffee, black, please."

"Very good, sir." The waiter left, and Finn studied Libby with a curious air. "You didn't used to drink."

"Not usually, but I'm hoping it'll help me to relax." She nervously buffed her arms as she gazed out the window, the pink in her cheeks kicking up a tad. "Well, not ever, actually, but …" She faced him square-on for the first time all night, those luscious lips edging up. "I'm not sure, but I think the threat of your snoring scared the living daylights out of me if you must know, so I have to do something to settle my nerves."

He grinned, then nodded his thanks to the attendant when he delivered the wine and coffee. "Really? I thought it might be my singing in the bathtub."

She laughed, and the sound was a balm to his soul. "Well, that, too." She took a slow sip of her wine, then leaned back to assess him through shuttered eyes, gaze cautious. "Why are you doing this, Finn? You didn't make a move for seventeen years and suddenly I'm the love of your life."

"You've always been the love of my life," he said quietly, forearms on the table as he absently grazed the sides of his cup with his thumbs. "From the day you walked into our classroom at the age of twelve until this very moment." He pinned her with a potent look. "I loved you then, Libby, and I love you now, so help me, God. But, just for your information, darlin'"—he lifted the cup to take a slow sip, his eyes burning hot over the rim—"I wrote you dozens of letters, but your father made good and sure you never saw a single one."

CHAPTER THIRTY-FOUR

"WHAT?" SHE SAT STRAIGHT UP. "I never received any letters!"

"Of course, you didn't," Finn said with a hard set of his jaw, his anger at Aiden kindled all over again. "Your father told me recently that he issued strict orders for your aunt to throw them away. Nor would *she* respond to any of my telegrams except the first one, where she wired that not only didn't you want to see me again, but that you no longer resided with her."

Libby's jaw dropped. "*What?* I lived with her for a good six months before Vassar hired me on with room and board."

"Ah, yes, Vassar," he continued with a dry slant of his mouth. "Yet another ruse by your father to throw me off-track. Apparently he spread the rumor that you were a teacher at The Convent of the Sacred Heart, which by the way, threatened to contact the police if I didn't stop sending letters for you to their school."

Mouth hanging open, Libby quickly guzzled some wine before sagging back in her chair, Finn's revelations obviously stealing the wind from her sails.

"So, you see, Libby, I *did* try to find you."

She was silent for several moments as she stared aimlessly into her glass. "But you didn't come after me," she whispered, her voice barely audible.

"I *did* come after you," he insisted, "even risking my job

at the V&T to travel to New York months later, to talk to both your aunt and The Convent of the Sacred Heart, all to no avail."

She looked up with moisture brimming in her eyes. "But not after I left that day." Her look of hurt hollowed him out. "You let me walk out that door, Finn, without a single attempt at compromise like you promised before we got married. You let me sob myself to sleep every single night for three days, aching inside that I'd married a man who wanted to control and bully me just like my father, no matter how much you swore you wouldn't."

Heat circled his collar, well aware that she was right, despite the fact he hadn't thought so at the time. "Dash it all, Libby, we were kids, the both of us. Stupid about marriage, stupid about each other." He reached to take her hand, the taste of regret bitter on his tongue. "And I'll admit I was angry, darlin', enough to stay away, hoping you'd come to your senses and come on home."

Moisture glazed her eyes with the same sorrow that cramped in his chest. "Then it seems we were at cross purposes," she said quietly, "which makes me very sad."

He grazed her palm with his thumb. "I know, me too, Libby, sick over all the time that we've lost." He leaned in, hope surging like a rush of adrenalin. "But that doesn't mean we have to lose our future, darlin'."

She blinked several times before easing her hand from his, quickly gulping more wine before setting it down with quivering fingers. "I'm heartsick about this too, Finn, more than I can say, but …"—there was a despair in her eyes he'd felt all too often himself after she'd left—"it's too late for us," she whispered.

"Why?" His gaze bore into hers with a passion that belonged only to her.

The silence was deafening as she stared into her half-empty glass, her body suddenly trembling along with it.

"*Why* is it too late?" he asked again, working hard to

keep the frustration from his tone.

She idly skimmed a finger along the rim of her glass, avoiding his eyes. "Because I'm engaged."

"No, Libby, you're *not* engaged—you're *married* to me." The tension in his body leaked into his tone.

"Only because of an oversight on my part and my father's, Finn, nothing more."

"An oversight on your father's part, certainly, but I refuse to believe it on yours." He sat back with arms folded over his chest. "You know what I think? I think you failed to sign those papers on purpose, because you still loved me."

A heavy sigh parted from her lips as she leaned back to rest her head, brows sloped in sympathy. "Whether that's true or not doesn't matter now because I promised Harold I'd marry him and it's *his* ring on my finger, Finn, not yours."

"Do you love him?" he snapped, tempted to rip that stupid ring off her finger and toss it out the blasted window.

Her chin inched up. "As a matter of fact, I do. Harold doesn't rouse my temper like *some* people I know."

"I'll bet," Finn said with a hard smile, downright incensed some moron named Harold thought he could claim her for his own. "Nor anything else, I'll wager."

Her face whooshed scarlet as she threw back the rest of her wine, glass straight up. Her hand was trembling along with the glass when she set it back down. "I *am* going to marry Harold, Finn, so if we're going to be civil to one another the rest of this evening, I suggest you change course immediately."

Tears brimming, she turned to stare out the window with a stone face, and Finn suddenly remembered just how difficult it had always been to rein in his temper with his wife. But rein it in he would, because he was no longer that immature selfish husband she'd once known, but a man of prayer and patience who thrived on a challenge.

And if ever there were a challenge, her name was Libby

McShane.

Blasting out a noisy sigh, he gulped down the rest of his cold coffee, thinking Libby had never been more wrong. There *was* something he could do about it whether she liked it or not. Signaling the waiter for more coffee, he studied her steely profile with a look just as tenacious, more than willing to "change course." A slow smile wended its way across his face. Like changing course on his original decision to win back his wife fair and square.

Without those powerful kisses that had always melted her resolve.

And his.

The waiter returned to refill his cup, and Finn thanked him while he lifted the steaming brew to his lips, hoping to brew a little steam of his own. After all, it had been said that all was fair in love and war, and this was one adage Finn was definitely looking forward to proving true, civil or no. He savored the rich aroma of his coffee as he watched Libby work so hard to ignore him, the thrust of her chin easing his smile into an out-and-out grin. And sweet Song of Solomon, when he did …

It'd be *anything* but "civil."

CHAPTER THIRTY-FIVE

PING!

"Whoo-eee, Clint, I do believe we just taught these girls a valuable lesson in horseshoes," Jake Sullivan crowed on the front lawn of the Silver Lining Ranch after dinner. He shot Sheridan and Maggie a wink before tipping his Stetson to Aiden and Maeve, who applauded from the front porch while they sipped lemonade in their rockers.

Shaylee lay on her stomach beside them, legs crossed while she tried to keep Frannie and Scout from swiping at her pet tarantula, Annabelle. The smell of cinnamon and apples drifted in the air from pies cooling on the wide split-log railing while Gert and Angus glared nose to nose in a game of stud poker.

Jake hitched his thumbs in the pockets of his blue jeans and attempted a cocky grin that Maggie knew was all for show. As Blaze's best friend since childhood, sweet Jake Sullivan didn't have a cocky bone in his body.

Unlike his best friend. One side of Maggie's mouth hooked as she retrieved the three horseshoes Jake and Clint had neatly looped around the post. *God bless his cocky cowboy soul.*

"Ha! Is that so?" Hands on the hips of her fringed leather riding skirt, Sheridan sashayed over to stare up at Jake, her petite five-foot-two totally dwarfed by Jake's brawny six-foot-one. "Set up a chessboard, Sullivan, and we'll see who gets the applause."

"Doubt that, Half-Pint." Teeth flashing white against bronzed skin, Jake had the nerve to tug on one of Sheridan's loose blonde curls like she was the pesky little sister he'd always believed her to be. But Maggie knew better.

After almost a month living at the Silver Lining Ranch, she quickly learned there was nothing sisterly about Sheridan's crush on Jake Sullivan. At seventeen—almost eighteen as Sheridan was quick to point out—Blaze's little sister was determined to prove she was a woman to her brother's best friend. Unfortunately for Sheridan, Jake Sullivan seemed just as determined to ignore the fact completely.

Bending to retrieve the last stray horseshoe, Maggie hid a secret grin when Sheridan slapped Jake's hand away, pretty sure Jake was either blind or blessedly oblivious. Because for all the snug dresses and shirtwaists that highlighted Sheridan was no longer a little girl, they may as well have been pinafores and pigtails for all that Jake noticed.

"One more game of horseshoes, and winner takes all," Sheridan challenged the two men, and Maggie shook her head as she moseyed over to join them. Well aware Sheridan had been rigorously practicing horseshoes during the day while the ranch hands were occupied elsewhere, Maggie also knew the little stinker purposely lost their first two games, plotting to win the third with a bet attached.

"Uh … I'm not sure plotting is the best way to win a man's heart," Maggie had said to Sheridan after dinner when the seventeen-year-old had shared her plan to "innocently" suggest she could whip Jake's hide in horseshoes.

The poor thing had nearly chewed the skin off her lower lip, so nervous was she that Maggie might not go along. "But, Maggie, how else am I supposed to get him to notice me?" she'd whispered back, gaze darting at the barn where Jake was laughing with the other ranch hands.

Sucking air through a gritted smile, Maggie couldn't help but feel a wee bit responsible since Sheridan needed a woman's opinion, clearly looking to Maggie as a big sister. "I don't know, Sher—to trick him into taking you to the rodeo dance?" Maggie shook her head, wishing Aunt Libby were home to help dissuade Sheridan rather than at dinner with Finn in Carson City. "There must be an easier way to get Jake to notice you, sweetheart."

Sheridan had merely grunted in the grand fashion of her uncle and older brothers. "A gun would be easier," she said with a wry bent of her lips that quickly melted into a lovesick smile. "Only I'd really like him alive and well when he finally realizes I'm the girl of his dreams."

Glancing at Sheridan now while she fluttered her lashes at Clint to lure him in, too, Maggie had little doubt Sheridan was up to the task. Despite her innocence from a sheltered life at the hand of her Uncle Finn and older brothers, the young girl had the grit and determination to make her dreams come true. Maggie shot a grin at poor, sweet, unsuspecting Jake. And maybe those of a lovable and easy-going cowhand, as well, if Sheridan got her way.

"So, what do you say?" Sheridan said with an impatient tap of her boot, dangling the bait both she and Maggie knew would easily hook both men. "You win, and Maggie and I will march right into that kitchen and bake you a fresh batch of my famous chocolate chunk cookies."

Maggie bit back a grin when Jake's Adam's apple actually bobbed several times, his mouth watering, no doubt, for what he always claimed was his favorite dessert and demise.

Which in this particular case, certainly would be.

"And in the extremely remote possibility that you *do* win," Clint said with a wink at Maggie as he folded muscular arms, "what do *you* ladies get?"

A shot of color bruised Sheridan's cheeks over and above the hint of beet juice she rubbed on her cheeks and lips when her Uncle Finn wasn't around. "Wellllllll," she dragged out with a squint of blue eyes that spelled nothing but trouble, "I have been dying to learn how to become a sharpshooter like Annie Oakley ... and Jake *did* promise to teach me when I was old enough …"

Jake offered a patient smile. "Sorry, Half-Pint, but seventeen doesn't qualify as 'old enough' in my book."

"Annie Oakley was only fifteen when she won that shooting match against Frank E. Butler," Sheridan defended, "and Lillian Smith *just* joined Buffalo Bill's Wild West show this year as a trick shooter at age fifteen."

"What about you, Miss Mullaney?" Clint sidetracked, homing in on Maggie with that crooked smile he always seemed to reserve just for her. "What do you win?"

"Oh, Maggie needs an escort to the rodeo," Sheridan announced happily, obviously thrilled that Clint had diverted all attention away from her.

"*What?*" Maggie's mouth slacked open. "Sheridan Marie Donovan!" Her cheeks burned as if she herself were wearing a whole pot of Sheridan's silly beet juice.

"Is that a fact?" Clint said with a broad smile.

"*No*, it isn't a fact—*ouch!*" Maggie rubbed her arm where Sheridan pinched her, tempted to ignore the plea in the little brat's eyes.

Clint tipped his hat. "Well, either way, I do believe that's a challenge we'd like to take on, don't you, Sully?"

Thumbs hooked in his back pockets, Jake shifted his stance with a slow shake of his head, his smile calm even if the leery squint of his eyes was not. "I don't know, Clint," he said with an idle scratch at the back of his neck, "I'm not comfortable with teaching Half-Pint to shoot—"

"Then I'll think of something else, I promise," Sheridan begged in a giddy rush, hands clasped to her lips in hope.

"Come on, Sully." Clint elbowed Jake before looping an arm over his shoulder. His voice lowered to a tease. "We both know the chances of them winning are as likely as a blizzard in July."

"You're on!" Sheridan squealed, not even giving Jake a chance to object as she dragged Maggie back to their side of the lawn. "And we'll even give you the first toss," she called over her shoulder.

"Sheridan Marie, what on earth were you thinking?" Maggie's voice was close to a hiss as she marched alongside Sheridan, finally hooking her around to stare her down. "You are in big trouble, young lady!"

"Not me," the imp said with a wiggle of brows, nibbling her lip as she shot a furtive glance Jake's way. "It's that stubborn man down there who's in trouble if I win." She put a hand to her mouth to stifle a giggle. "Oh, and you, of course, Miss Mullaney, since Clint Keller *is* known to be a lady-killer."

Maggie groaned and slapped a hand to her eyes, parting two fingers to give Sheridan a stern look that could've curdled beet juice. "So help me, I have a mind to throw this game."

"Oh, Maggie, please don't," Sheridan pleaded. "I turn eighteen this year, so this is the best present you could ever give me! Besides"—she tossed a glance over her shoulder to where Clint stood, all strapping six-foot-three of him with the bluest eyes Maggie had ever seen—"Clint Keller is the cutest cowboy on this ranch besides Jake and my brothers, so what are you complaining about?"

Maggie blew out a blast of air that ruffled wisps of gold around Sheridan's heart-shaped face, remembering Blaze's warning that Clint was not only "sweet" on her, but had a "reputation" as well. "So help me, Sher, if Clint Keller so much as gives me an iota of trouble—"

"He won't," Sheridan assured with saucer eyes that revealed the naive little girl inside. "Because Uncle Finn and my brothers won't let any of us out of their sight, I swear."

"Let's get this game started," Clint called. "Sully's hankerin' for some chocolate chunk cookies."

Unfortunately, the only thing poor Sully appeared to be "hankerin'" for twenty minutes later was a stiff drink as Sheridan took careful aim with her second to last horseshoe. Maggie held her breath as the shoe appeared to sail through the air in slow motion, the loud ping of which merged perfectly with Jake's and Clint's groans when she tied the game up.

"*Eeeeeeekkkkk!*" Maggie couldn't help it, she grabbed Sheridan up by the waist and spun her around and around, the both of them dizzy when they finally wobbled to a stop. "Great balls of fire, girl," she shouted, her drive to win completely obliterating all prior objections, "I swear you are on fir —!"

Hard hoofbeats interrupted, drawing her and everyone else's attention to the stallion and rider racing toward them in a cloud of dust. "Talk about on fire," Maggie said with a chuckle. Only she didn't realize just how close to the truth it was until Minx skidded to a stop in front of their game, veritable sparks shooting from Blaze's eyes. His face was etched in stone as he cauterized Maggie with a glare. "You, me—in the barn, Miss Mullaney—*now*!"

"For heaven's sake, Blaze," Sheridan said with a crease in her brow, "we're just about to win the game, so Maggie will be there when we're done."

Not bothering to respond, Blaze slapped the reins in a fury, stabbing his heels into Minx's flanks like his glare stabbed into Maggie's mind, driving Minx toward the barn without a glance back.

"Good heavens, what on earth has gotten into him?" Sheridan stared after her brother, her jaw as gaping as Maggie's. "I've never seen Blaze so angry before."

"I don't know," Maggie whispered, a niggle of guilt confirming that just maybe she did. "All I can say is, let's get this game won, because from that red-hot glare on your brother's face?" She almost welcomed the cold chill that skittered her spine given the blistering heat she'd seen in his eyes. "Gotta feeling I may be needing some of Clint's so-called 'blizzard in July.'"

CHAPTER THIRTY-SIX

"SO HELP ME, MINX, IF she wasn't a woman ..." Blaze jerked the bridle off his horse and all but hurled it onto the tack wall before wiping it down with a rag. He snatched a wet sponge from a bucket to cool Minx down, thinking he could use some cooling down as much as the mare.

Temper seething, he rubbed her down with brisk motion, checking for rubs or chafing from the bridle or other tack out of pure habit. He was barely aware as he ran his hands down her legs to feel for cuts, bumps, or rubs from riding her so hard. His jaw calcified. But one thing was for dead sure: Minx wasn't the only mare he intended to ride hard today.

Yes, Maggie had her quirks that sometimes annoyed, no question, but mostly she was a good friend whose company he enjoyed. A nerve pulsed in his jaw. Despite the blasted attraction that hovered beneath the surface. He ripped the grooming brush from its hook. But this time she'd really done it, gone and fired him up but good. His teeth ground till he thought they might crack.

And he fully intended to return the favor.

"Blaze?"

He stiffened, as taut as the brush in his hand.

"Are you ... all right?"

No, Miss Mullaney, I'm not. And when I'm done, you won't be either.

Completely ignoring her, he continued to groom Minx with carefully controlled strokes, the tic in his temple keeping time with the movement.

"I'm … not exactly sure why you are so angry with me, but I"—she stood so close, he actually heard her gulp—"might have a vague idea …"

"Vague?" He spun around, causing her to stumble back when he slammed the grooming brush back onto its hook. "The only 'vague' thing here, lady," he ground out, "is our so-called friendship, which I plan to redefine quite clearly in a moment." Shoving past, he led Minx to the paddock before returning to the barn, the fire in his eyes matching that in his gut.

"Blaze, please—let me explain …"

He shoved his hat up hard and slacked a knee, hands welded to his thighs as he glared her down. "No, let *me* explain how it's going to be between you and me from now on, Maggie."

"Hey, Boss, when are we—" One of the cowhands barreled into the barn and stopped dead in his tracks, the scowl on Blaze's face apparently threatening enough to flare his eyes.

"Get out, Dawson," Blaze ordered in a deadly tone, eyes locked on Maggie without a blink.

"Uh … yes, sir." Dawson was gone in one violent clip of Blaze's heart, quietly closing the door behind until the stream of daylight at the entrance was cut off.

Kind of like this friendship is about to be …

"Blaze, listen to me, please—" She stood like a statue in the shadows of the barn, arms wrapped so tightly to her waist, she could have been a tree shivering in the wind.

"No, Maggie, you listen to me, and you listen good." He took a step in, fist curled white while he stabbed a finger just inches from her face. "I told you to butt out of my life, but no, you couldn't leave it alone. You had to peddle your Christianity hogwash to Rachel, and now you've ruined what we had."

"Better than ruining *her*!" Maggie shouted, the sparks in his eyes obviously igniting hers.

He re-aimed his finger straight down, drilling toward the dirt floor like he planned to do with Miss Busybody, hopefully to keep her out of his bloomin' life from now on. "*This*, right here, lady, is exactly why I have no stomach for judgmental, hypocritical, so-called holier than thou women like you, not content to let people live and let live. Oh, no," he shouted, throwing his hands in the air, "you gotta stick your stuck-up little nose in where it doesn't belong and peddle your confounded morality where it's not wanted—"

She cut him off with a rigid finger of her own, thumping it hard against his chest while she thumped *him* with a scowl rivaling Gert's on a bad day. "Oh, it's wanted, all right, you ... you ... cocky cowboy! Just not by the likes of you, a rogue more concerned with his own pleasure than the safety and care of the woman he supposedly loves."

"I *do* love her," he bellowed, "you meddlin' morality monger!" His voice rose in an uproar that startled the horses, causing several to neigh and buck against their stalls.

"Then prove it!" she screamed, pushing him back with the heel of her hand.

Never would Blaze raise a hand to a woman, but sweet mother of patience, *never* had he been tempted more. Emitting a frustrated growl, he hurled his hat against the stall.

"For the love of decency, marry her!" she shouted, fisting his paisley vest with both hands and jerking it hard before shoving him away. "And make an honest woman out of her!"

In knee-jerk reaction, his palms snapped onto her arms like a prison padlock, holding her at bay so stiffly, her boots nearly dangled over the floor. She literally stopped breathing when he backed her toward a stall, expanding her eyes like a mare who'd just been spooked. "Seems to me you already did that, Miss Pure and Pious, when you turned Rachel away from me, convincing her that any sparkin' between us is straight from the devil."

He leaned in till his face was mere inches away, voice lowering to a dangerous level. "Well, you made an honest woman out of her, all right, Maggie, so how 'bout I do the same for you? Because if you're going to steal something from me, Miss Mullaney, I'm sure in the devil gonna steal something from you."

Ignoring the sharp catch of her breath, he butted her to the wall and molded his mouth to hers, his intent fueled by both fire and fury. Her open-mouthed gasp allowed access to explore with a passion he'd only dreamed about, liberating haunted thoughts of Maggie late at night while he lay in his bed.

He had wanted to make her pay, to steal the kisses from her that she'd stolen from him with Rachel. But he'd *never* expected this—a fire licking through him hotter than anything he'd ever known, white shivers of heat that near singed his very soul. In the space of one hoarse groan, he clutched her close and took it deeper, the want so strong, it produced an ache in his gut that shot clear to his throat. The mere taste of her threatened an addiction for which he had no cure, and the very notion turned his body to stone.

God help me—I'm falling in love with her!

Needles of sleet shot through his veins, and he pushed her back so abruptly, she thudded against the stall, lips swollen pink and breathing as ragged as his. Chest heaving, he slashed a shaky hand through his hair, the desire coursing through his veins coagulating into strangled panic he'd never experienced before. *No!* He would *not* sell his soul to any woman *or* to her god.

No matter how much he wanted her.

A white-hot rage stoked in his gut, and aiming a stiff finger, he scorched her with a look that brought a sheen of tears to her eyes. "This friendship is o-ver, *Miss* Mullaney, you got that?" He bludgeoned a palm to the stall that made her jump, then jerked his hat up and yanked it back on before searing her with a final glare. "Stay away from me, Maggie," he warned, his voice hoarse from both anger and attraction. Stalking to the front entrance, he hurtled the door open with a hard slam to the wall before he flung one last threat over his shoulder. "And stay out of my life!"

Or else.

CHAPTER THIRTY-SEVEN

G*OODNESS—WHEN WAS THE LAST TIME I felt this relaxed?* Libby rested her head against the back of the blue velvet chair in the intimate restaurant at the Ormsby House Hotel, leisurely twirling the stem of her wine glass. A smile tickled her lips.

Uh … never?

Grateful Finn had excused himself to visit the privy, she breathed in the lingering scent of apple cinnamon tarts, a dessert both she and Finn had thoroughly enjoyed. Lashes lowering to savor the memory, she whetted her lips to envision the taste, only to have her eyes pop right open with a quick catch of her breath. Because suddenly it wasn't the tarts she was tasting at all, but Finn McShane's lips.

Each and every night he'd made love to her in a room upstairs.

She quickly threw back more wine.

"Another glass, miss?"

She jolted, face whooshing hot as she blinked up at the waiter, then down at her near-empty goblet.

Yes!

No!

She chewed on the edge of her lip. *I really shouldn't …*

Peeking around the waiter to make sure Finn wasn't on his way back, she gave the man a wobbly smile. "Uh, that would be lovely, yes, and quickly, if you don't mind."

"Yes, miss."

The waiter was gone in a flash, and Libby plopped her head against the back of her chair with a groan. "Now why did I do that?" she whispered, regretting her decision already. But she'd never been this nervous around Finn before, at least not in the last seventeen years. She'd always had her anger to keep him at bay, but since he'd put his foot down about her behavior after she'd arrived, something had changed. She was starting to respect him again, laugh with him again, enjoy his company again.

And fall in love again?

She bolted the last of her wine, the very thought scaring her silly.

Because heaven knows that wasn't what she wanted.

She swallowed hard. *Was it?*

"Your wine, miss." Placing a fresh glass of wine before her, the waiter removed the other, and Libby thanked him with a grateful smile, well aware Finn would not be happy. He hadn't objected to wine on the train because he knew she was upset, and he couldn't very well deny her wine with dinner, although it was clear he didn't approve. But he'd be fit to be tied to see her drink another when she was already tipsy as a top. A smile sneaked in as she nipped at her lower lip with her teeth.

Oh, what a glorious shame!

A hiccup sneaked out, and she slapped a hand to her mouth, carefully looking around to make sure no one had heard. A wispy sigh drifted out as she set her glass down, regretting she had to resort to alcohol to help cope. But Finn was wearing her resistance thin with dinners out, concerts at Piper's Opera House, or evening rides and picnics, treating her with such kindness and respect, she was starting to care all over again.

She grunted and upended her wine. Who was she kidding? She'd never stopped caring, and that had become abundantly clear when she'd learned they were returning to the scene of the crime: The Ormsby House Hotel.

Where'd they spent three nights of wedded bliss, barely leaving their room.

Over the years, her volatile Irish temper had convinced her she'd escaped a bully who didn't really care. But in light of the facts he'd professed on the train, she found her resolve wavering, and she couldn't afford that. Not when his mere presence could still flutter her stomach, woefully confirming he still controlled a piece of her heart. Her hand shook as she hurriedly took another deep swig.

But she could never allow him to control a piece of her life.

He entered the room, and her bones immediately went to jelly, stomach quivering more than the tomato aspic they'd had at dinner. Of course, he'd always had that effect on her from the start, but she'd managed to tuck it away over the years. Out of sight, out of mind. But heaven help her, he was dead center *in* sight at the moment *and* in her mind, sorely tempting her to fan herself with the napkin.

Mercy, but he was a good-looking man, and unfortunately that assessment had only improved with age. He stopped briefly to talk to the maître d', and she took full advantage, scanning from thick dark hair templed with gray to a handsome and hard-sculpted face weathered by hard work and time. Once tall and lean, Finn now sported massive shoulders far broader and a hard-muscled body that seemed thicker—and more powerful—than before, causing her pulse to stumble all over itself. Hands suddenly moist, she threw back another gulp, heart teetering as much as the glass when she set it back down.

Shaking hands with the maître d', Finn turned his focus on her, hazel eyes burning right through her as he approached with that infuriating smile that confirmed everything was under control.

She guzzled more liquid courage.

Including me, if I'm not careful!

"Miss me?" He took his seat and reached for his glass

of water, gaze flicking to her near-empty goblet of wine before resettling on her with a humorous smile.

Another hiccup slipped out, followed by a giggle. "The last five minutes, yes. The last seventeen years?" She raised her glass in a toast, reverting to the easy camaraderie they'd obtained over dinner. "Nope." Delivering a wink as uncharacteristic as drinking wine, she sank back into her chair with a contented sigh.

"Well, that's progress, I suppose," he said with a dry smile, retrieving his wallet to lay several bills on the table. Glancing at his pocket watch, he rose and pushed in his chair. "Ready to go? You have just enough time to freshen up before we head to the station."

"Mmm …" Libby laid her head back once again, suddenly too relaxed to do anything but close her eyes. The moment she did, however, the room started to spin, and she jerked straight up, head as dizzy as her heart when Finn squatted to study her with a tender look.

"Are you all right, sweetheart?" The graze of his thumb on her hand might have tumbled her insides if her stomach wasn't already awhirl, threatening to dislodge her dinner.

"Uh … I … I'm not sure," she managed in a shaky voice, knuckles curling white on her napkin as she gripped his arm. "I … I think I m-might be sick—"

Napkin and hand flew to her mouth just as Finn swept her up, striding out of the room and up the stairs while the contents of her stomach started to rise.

"Open your eyes!" he commanded in a tone that would have set her temper afire if she wasn't so blasted sick. Her lids snapped up, and the awful spinning abated somewhat. "Hold on, darlin'," he said softly as he jangled a key in a door, "just a few moments more …"

Which, unfortunately, wasn't quite long enough. Feeling like death, Libby spewed her dinner on the floor of the water closet before Finn held her steady over the bowl, sicker than she'd ever been. Crumpling to her knees when she was through, she vowed to never drink again.

"Here, sweetheart," he whispered, and she felt a wet washcloth against her lips and face before he gently prodded a glass of water to her dry lips. "Swish and spit."

She did as she was told and tasted peppermint in the rinse, well aware Finn always carried the leaves in his pocket, a habit since she'd known him. He patted her lips with the cloth again before refilling the glass and handing it to her with more peppermint-scented water. Taking a long, long sip, she finally pushed it away, her voice as dry and raspy as her throat. "Thank you," she whispered.

"Always, Libby." His words were no more than a wisp of warmth in her ear, but it calmed her far more than any wine or tea could ever do. Eyelids suddenly heavy, she felt languid and limp, as if she were slowly sinking away. A breeze cooled her face when he whisked her up once again, her body and her brain utterly weightless while he quietly carried her to the bed. The heat of his chest against her cheek lulled her to a heavenly place she'd only been one time before.

"Please don't let go …" Her voice was a worried rasp when he tried to lay her down, panic rising at the prospect of his glorious warmth fading away.

"Never." His husky response carried a promise that set her free to curl against him when he lay down on the bed. He drew her close, strong arms cocooning her in a heavenly warmth that soothed her into the peace and safety of sleep, taking her to a place she hadn't been in a very long time.

Home.

CHAPTER THIRTY-EIGHT

HE WAS TIRED, HE WAS hungry, and he probably smelled like vomit. But Finn McShane hadn't been this happy in a blue moon.

Seventeen years of "blue moon" to be exact, but holding his wife in the same bed in which he'd once made love to her made a puke-permeated hotel room seem like the gates of heaven.

His mouth hooked. Or a mite further south when Libby woke up, discovering she'd just spent the night in his bed.

Again.

He chuckled softly as the light of dawn streamed through the window, helpless to wipe the smile from his face. Because for all her protests and temper, he was pretty darn sure Libby O'Shea McShane still loved him—enough to get stinkin' drunk when he knew she never indulged. And enough to cling all night long like a second skin. His smile bloomed into a grin.

And heaven knows he loved her. How else could he explain cleaning her up—and himself—when the sight and smell of vomit had always made him sick? Then traipsing down to the train station to hire Mason as a messenger to inform Aiden and Maeve their daughter had taken ill, necessitating an overnight stay in Carson City. He shook his head, hardly able to believe he had hand-washed her shirt and his in the tub without throwing up himself.

The bluish pallor of her skin and lips had alarmed him,

knowing full well the effects of too much alcohol. She'd been like a piece of ice, curled into a ball, so he'd done the only thing he'd known to do. He slipped into the bed to hold her—her in just a chemise and him in trousers and no shirt—worried sick. He relinquished a grunt. He was sick all right—lovesick to the core—and he'd be hog-tied and hung up to dry if he'd ever let her go again.

"Don't let go," she'd whispered before she'd faded into a deep and peaceful sleep, and whether it had been intoxication or revelation that had loosed that plea from her lips, Finn had no intention of doing anything else but holding on.

Forever.

"Mmm ..." Arm tucked around his bare chest, Libby released a soft moan before rolling over with an adorable little grunt, legs tucked.

Turning on his side, he cuddled from behind like he used to, arms wrapped around her waist while he breathed in the scent of her hair. Obviously fallen loose in her sleep, the touch of it felt like silk against his skin.

Unable to resist, he carefully lifted it aside to gently graze his lips against the nape of her neck. His body instantly reacted with a flood of heat that all but swallowed him whole, leaving him powerless to do anything but mold closer and skim his mouth once again.

He knew the exact moment she awakened because she went completely stiff in his arms. Then with a harsh gasp, she shot up from the bed like a bottle rocket on the Fourth of July, her voice a startled stutter. "W-What on earth are y-you d-doing?" she rasped, ripping the sheet from beneath the blanket to cover her chemise.

With a sheepish cuff of his neck, Finn sat up, delivering the boyish smile that had always worked wonders before. "You asked me to hold you last night, Libby, so I did."

"All *night*?" she said in a near-shriek, "in my—" she glanced down at the sheet she'd haphazardly wrapped around her body and jerked it higher, her face suddenly as white as the linen in her hands. "My *chemise?*"

Finn rose from the bed with an awkward scuff of his chest. "You threw up, Libby, all over your dress and my shirt, so I had to wash them both in the tub." He retrieved the laundered items from the wash room, smile fading as he cautiously laid her blouse on the bed. "I was worried about you," he said quietly. "You were like ice, and too much alcohol can cause body heat to plummet dangerously low."

She avoided his eyes as she reached for her blouse, fingers quivering while she clutched it to her chest. "And my skirt?"

"Right here." He retrieved her skirt from where he'd neatly draped it over the back of a chair along with her jacket. "I figured sleeping in your chemise would be a lot more comfortable, so I hope you don't mind."

Mind? That she'd just spent the night with her estranged husband in a bed where he'd been nibbling her neck? Heat blasted through her body like a radiator gone awry, making it difficult for her to breathe, much less speak. Feeling faint, she put a shaky hand to her throbbing temple while the most handsome man she'd ever known—or kissed—stood there shirtless, muscles cording his arms and dark hair matting his chest.

"You were pretty sick, darlin'," he said softly, "and asked me to hold you, so I did."

Her breathing stopped as a knot ducked in her throat. "Merciful Providence, we didn't …?" She couldn't even finish the sentence, mouth suddenly drier than dust.

"No, ma'am." He held up a firm palm as if to reassure, but it wasn't working. "I just held you, Libby, you have my word." The off-kilter smile was back as he gave a shrug of those ridiculously broad shoulders. "Well, that and a few innocent kisses on the back of your neck."

"Innocent!" Her voice was a croak. "For the love of all that's decent and holy, Finn, we just slept together in the same bed!"

He casually scratched the back of his neck with a smoky look she remembered all too well in this very room alone. "Yes, but I guarantee you, darlin', a lot less happened than the last time we did." His mouth took a tilt. "Which is a darn shame to my way of thinkin'."

"Finn McShane!" She stomped her bare foot, the effect totally lost against a thick-pile rug. "We are *not* married," she said in a croak, motioning him to turn around with a slash of her blouse in the air. "And the least you can do is look the other way so I can get dressed!"

A muscle flickered in his cheek while his smile tightened a hair, the steel edge of his jaw all the more ominous with a dark shadow of beard. "Actually, we *are* married, Libby, and to be honest I'd been well within my legal rights to make love to you every hour on the hour if I wanted. So maybe you best say 'thank you', darlin', and go ahead and get dressed."

Blood gorged her cheeks till she thought she might faint. "Turn around!" she ordered with a thrust of her chin.

"Nope." He took his time buttoning his own shirt while he stared her down with a mulish look. "I'm perfectly entitled to see whatever is under that sheet, darlin', so I suggest you dress quickly before I decide to take advantage."

"You wouldn't," she whispered, the pounding of her heart far louder than the frail rasp that escaped her lips.

"Probably not." He retied his string tie while he fixed her with a pointed stare. "But I seem to remember you owe me some kisses, Mrs. McShane, and I surely aim to collect." Gaze never wavering from hers, he lifted his suit coat off the chair and slid it on, the kick of his smile issuing a clear warning. "Just up to you whether it's sooner or later, darlin'."

All moisture fled from her mouth while her hands grew moist, and spinning on her heel too quickly, she groaned with a hand to her eyes. But she had no one to blame but herself for the awful throbbing in her head. Expelling a wavering sigh, she dropped the sheet in a puddle and put on her blouse, startling when Finn offered her skirt from behind.

"Thank you," she said quietly, the words scratching raw from her throat."

"You're welcome." His footsteps receded as he walked to the door, the turn of the knob unloosing a strange reluctance to let him go. "I'll let you freshen up alone, then meet you in the dining room for breakfast when you're done, all right?"

She nodded, heart thumping as much as the pain in her head. "Finn …?"—she swallowed hard, desperate to dispel the awful pride that clogged in her throat—"I'm sorry," she whispered, shocked when a sheen of tears blurred in her eyes. "For … *all* of this."

Both he and her breathing painfully paused before he finally spoke, his voice gentle and low. "Don't be, Libby—I'm not." His statement was punctuated by the soft click of the door.

She stood there frozen for several seconds before a sob finally broke free, the skirt she pressed to her mouth clutched tightly in hand. Against all reason and resistance, a flashflood of revelation spilled along with her tears, prying her heart open when it became abundantly clear …

Neither was she.

CHAPTER THIRTY-NINE

"GOODNESS, I NEVER THOUGHT I'D say this," Maggie whispered to the ladies sitting at her end of the table, "but thank God for corsets!"

Leaning back in her spindle-back chair on Finn's back porch, she fanned herself with a cloth napkin while she offered Mrs. Poppy—Finn's special guest for the evening—and Maeve a limp smile, praying her stays wouldn't bust.

The heat of the day joined forces with the bountiful barbecue she'd just consumed to make her feel like a melted lump of lard. She attempted a heavy sigh despite the tight pinch of her corset, quite sure vanity was not worth the loss of air. "Although I fear my figure will be lost forever, corset or no, if Angus and Gert continue battling it out in the kitchen."

"What's a corset?" Shaylee asked, more barbecue splotches on her face than on the napkin tucked around her neck.

"An implement of torture," Aunt Libby said with a wry smile, slipping Shaylee a wink. Her gaze traveled to Finn at the other end of the table where the men were discussing the upcoming state rodeo. "Designed, no doubt, by men such as your uncle to keep all women restrained."

Mrs. Poppy chuckled as she patted a blue-veined hand to Libby's own, her snow-white topknot as crooked as her elfin smile. "As much as you'd like to saddle poor Finn with every grievance against women over the ages, Libby dear, I doubt he had any control centuries ago."

Libby's lips took a swerve as she eyed Finn over the rim of her cup. "Maybe not, Mrs. Poppy, but he certainly *acts* like he does." The dryness of her tone belied the twinkle in her eyes that Maggie had noticed since she and Finn spent the night in Carson City three weeks ago.

Grinning, Maggie shook her head as she dipped her napkin in her water glass, proceeding to wipe barbecue sauce off of Shaylee's chin and nose. "A corset is an undergarment that's pulled tight with lacing to flatter a woman's figure, Shaylee," she explained to the sweet tomboy who'd stolen her heart over the last month and a half. "But I'm not sure you'll find too many women who think corsets are worth it."

"Well, I have it on good authority that they're not." Sheridan flipped a pickle in her mouth. "Which is why I never intend to wear one."

"*Excuse m-me?*" Poor Aunt Libby sputtered as if she were choking, hand to her chest while she grappled for her tea cup to take a healthy swig. "Good heavens, Sheridan, every well-bred woman wears a corset, darling."

"I don't understand why." Sheridan filched an uneaten pickle from her sister's plate. "Because men sure don't like them."

Libby spewed her tea, eyes bugging wide while she quickly swabbed her mouth with a napkin. "Great day in the morning, Sheridan Marie, it's the proper thing to do, sweetheart, that's why. And how on earth would you possibly know a man's opinion on such things?"

Sheridan gave a small lift of her shoulders, shooting a gaze of longing toward the corral where Jake, Clint, and the rest of the hands were practicing for the rodeo. "Because I overheard Jake, Dash, and Blaze talking about it one day when they didn't know I was around, that's how."

She issued a sigh pert near bigger than her as she plunked her chin in her hand. Her eyes trained on Jake while he perched on the fence with Clint and the others to wait their turns at busting a bronc. "Both Blaze and Dash were saying how they preferred the women at the Ponderosa because they were soft and womanly like a woman should be, not all trussed up in whalebone and glue."

Maggie blinked, pretty sure her whalebone was expanding as hot tea pooled in her mouth, heating her cheeks as well.

Libby frantically blotted the back of her neck with her napkin. "Trust me, young lady, what men *say* they prefer and what they marry are two different things," she said with a blush that, no doubt, mirrored Maggie's to a shade. "Isn't that so, Mrs. Poppy?"

All eyes instantly lighted on the elderly woman hailed as the Matriarch of Virginia City. A notorious matchmaker, Mrs. Poppy was the reason Pastor Poppy had unexpectedly married Libby and Finn in the parsonage so many years ago. A legend to the town and beloved by all, Mrs. Poppy's innocent overuse of poppy seeds in her prized cake, tea, and ice cream had drugged everyone's mind that night, according to her aunt, seducing Libby and Finn into a marriage never meant to be. But noting the humor that twinkled in the old woman's rheumy blue eyes, somehow Maggie doubted both Mrs. Poppy's innocence in the affair *and* Libby's assertion she and Finn were never meant to be.

Mrs. Poppy delivered a pixie wink to Aunt Libby that brought a grin to Maggie's face. "Well, you should know, my dear," she teased. "After all, Finn always swore he'd never marry an irrepressible woman."

"What's ir-re-press-ible mean?" Shaylee wanted to know, tossing a piece of corn fritter into the air and snapping it with her teeth.

"Pig-headed," Finn called from the other end of the table, hand cupped to his mouth as he lounged back in his chair with a lazy smile, gaze trained on Libby.

"Better than mule-brained," Libby said with a proud lift

of her chin, gaze challenging Finn's until Maggie could have sworn an electric charge sizzled the air.

Mrs. Poppy's laughter floated over the table. "Truly a match made in heaven," she said with a wink in Finn's direction, "during a celestial lightning storm, no doubt." Taking a sip of her tea, she set the cup down and patted her mouth with her napkin while she offered Sheridan a mischievous smile. "Actually, young lady, I'm of the opinion that restraint is an admirable thing, whether one is referring to corsets *or* the gentlemen who don't prefer them."

"Speaking of which …" Libby nodded to where Jake and Clint were waving their hats wildly, hollering for Dash and Blaze to join in on the practice rodeo contest. "It would appear all 'restraint' will now be directed to the broncs, thank goodness."

As if on cue, the men rose as one, pushing their chairs in while Aiden lit his pipe.

Finn strolled over to Mrs. Poppy and offered his arm. "Ladies, I believe the contest is about to begin, so shall we mosey on over to the grandstand to cheer our hands on?"

"Holy snake snot, you bet!" Shaylee jumped up so fast, her chair wobbled as much as the table when she bumped it in her haste to get to the corral.

"Whoa, girl," Finn said with a hitch of her overalls, ricocheting the little stinker against his chest with a squirm of a smile. "First of all, young lady, snake snot is *not* holy and secondly, secretions of any kind—human or otherwise—are not appropriate terms for anyone, much less a thirteen-year-old girl, all right?"

Shaylee huffed out a sigh that sagged along with her shoulders. "Yes, sir."

"Come on, Shay," Maggie said with a tug of the young girl's hand, hooking Sheridan's arm on the way, "if we hurry, we'll get the top bench on the grandstand."

"Holy frog spi—" Shaylee stopped short, brown eyes peeking up at Finn, who only shook his head with an affectionate smile. "Sorry, Uncle Finn—I meant yeah, Maggie, let's go!"

Mrs. Poppy and Maeve chuckled while Finn tweaked the back of Shaylee's neck. "Go cheer your brother on, Shay—he's been a bit of a crab lately."

"Oh really? Which one?" Sheridan said with a roll of her eyes, snatching the last of Shaylee's corn fritter before rising to join Maggie and her sister. "Since Rachel gave Blaze the boot, he's been grumpier than a bear without a cave."

Maggie snuck a peek to where Blaze shuffled toward the corral with his brother, Stetson low and hands deep in his pockets, painfully aware she was the cause for his grumpy moods over the last three weeks. He'd steered clear of her with nary a word or a look, spending most of his evenings at the Ponderosa even though she knew Rachel had quit and moved out.

"All the reason to give the bear a little honey, darling," Mrs. Poppy said with a chuckle, allowing Finn to support her arm as she rose from the chair. "To help spread a little joy."

Ah, yes—joy, indeed! Maggie smiled as her thoughts shifted to Rachel, the girl with whom she'd forged a friendship founded on God. Maggie had been ecstatic when Rachel broke it off with Blaze and moved into Mrs. Cleary's Boardinghouse. All it had taken was for Sister Fred to learn that Rachel wanted to leave the saloon, and the dynamo nun had worked her magic to secure a room in Mrs. Cleary's attic in exchange for housecleaning and serving.

Both Rachel and Maggie had been downright weepy with gratitude. Then utterly beside themselves when Sister suggested Saturday evening parlour piano recitals where Rachel entertained and Mrs. Cleary sold tea and dessert. That brilliant suggestion earned Rachel a small weekly paycheck that would now help put her on the path to a new life. Maggie released a grateful sigh. A true blessing from God for everyone involved.

Except Blaze.

"Aiden, shall we escort these lovely ladies to the festivities?" Finn offered his other arm to Libby while Aiden followed suit with Maeve.

Maggie was as bubbly as Sheridan and Shaylee as they scrambled onto the double-slatted grandstand Finn had asked Jake to build for optimum viewing. *Until* the girls plopped down by their brothers, forcing Maggie to sit right beside Blaze. One by one her bubbles of excitement popped when he silently rose and moved to sit on Dash's other side, leaving a gaping hole.

Both on the bench and in Maggie's heart.

Thank goodness the air was abuzz with men's laughter and shouts, helping to dispel Maggie's melancholy over Blaze's rejection. No less than twenty cowhands straddled or leaned on the corral fence, preparing to compete, placing bets, or just jawing, their excitement fairly shimmering in the air.

After seating Mrs. Poppy and Libby on the end of the first row, Finn put two fingers to his mouth and blew a shrill whistle that immediately settled the crowd. Grabbing a cow horn, he addressed everyone with enthusiasm as palpable as the smell of hay and horses in the air, all tinged with the fading scent of barbecue and cowhands eager to perform.

"Okay, everyone, listen up!" he shouted. "This isn't the first practice run we've ever had over the years for the statewide rodeo bronc-busting contest, but it's certainly the best with the presence of some very special ladies. That said, save any drinkin', swearin', and chawin' for later, understood?"

A few murmurs rumbled while Finn glanced over at Jake. "Everybody signed up, Jake?"

Jake tipped his hat, stopwatch in hand and hip cocked to a post. "Yes, sir, everybody rides but you, Mr. O'Shea, and

Angus."

"Humph." Lips gummed tight, Angus scowled from where he sat next to Gert on the second bench, shuffling a well-worn deck of cards obviously meant for another game of poker. "I can outride every one of those young whippersnappers if you just let me, and you know it," he muttered, slashing cards toward Gert in a deal that didn't bode well for the O'Shea's cook.

Finn shot a conciliatory smile. "I know you can, Angus, and everyone else knows you can too, my friend, but when it comes to ensuring sustenance for the Silver Lining Ranch, I'd much rather feed our stomachs than your pride, eh?"

"Hear-hear!" Dash and several cowhands called.

"What pride?" Gert said with a wicked smile, fanning her cards out with a gleam of trouble in her eyes. "When I'm done with this hand, he ain't gonna have any."

Laughter filtered through the crowd as Finn turned his attention to the cowhands. "As usual, Jake, Dash, and Blaze will ride last so they can man the bucking shoot. They'll be the final word on verifying all boots make contact above the horse's shoulders before front legs hit the ground. Eight-second rides are required, and those that manage to hang on will be judged by Angus, Aiden, and myself. Three best scores represent the Silver Lining Ranch in the statewide rodeo bronc-busting contest in September at the Bar J Ranch. Highest score walks away with a nice bonus. Second place receives two silver dollars, and third place receives one. Any questions?"

Finn glanced around and nodded to Jake when no one spoke up. "Good. Then may the best cowboy win. Jake—first rider up."

Checking the first name off his list, Jake looked up at Clint with a grin. "That would be Lady-killer Keller," he said with a chuckle, "and let's hope he's as lucky with horses as he is with women."

"No hopin' about it, Sully." Clint swaggered over to where Maggie sat, a crooked smile on his lips while he tucked his thumbs in the pockets of his dusty jeans. "Sure would appreciate a ribbon for good luck, though, ma'am."

Heat all but swallowed Maggie whole as she peeked up at the cowboy who'd been dogging her heels since she arrived at the ranch, reluctant to admit the man possessed an easy charm that could sway a girl's thinking.

Sheridan nudged her. "Give him your ribbon, Maggie—it's tradition."

Clint swept his Stetson to his chest with flair, offering a slight bow. "Yes, Maggie, please, because win or lose, I'll be riding high if I'm wearing your colors."

Somebody cut loose with a sarcastic grunt, and Maggie was pretty sure it was Blaze, who'd made it perfectly clear he didn't approve of any association she had with 'Lady-Killer Keller.' In one timid beat of her heart, all the frustration she'd tamped down over Blaze's behavior boiled up inside, spilling over in a less-than-righteous resolve to pay the mule back.

Without another thought, she snatched the blue ribbon that bound her curls to the back of her head and handed it to Clint, unconcerned when chestnut tresses rippled over her shoulders. "Good luck, Clint." Managing a tight smile, she felt the singe of Blaze's stare.

"Oh, I won't be needing that, ma'am," he said with a smoky smile accompanied by the hoots and hollers of several of the cowhands. Tying the ribbon around his neck, he promptly tucked it inside the loosened collar of a well-sculpted chambray shirt, where a hint of dark hair matted a bronzed muscled chest. He gave her a wink. "At least … not now."

Maggie fought a gulp as he strolled toward the chute in his chaps with all the poise and confidence of a champion rider. No, when it came to women and winning, she suspected Clint Keller didn't need a whole lotta luck. He tipped his hat with an easy smile, and she twisted a strand of her hair in a nervous spiral that matched the one in her gut. Because she had a sneaking suspicion about somebody who just might.

Me.

CHAPTER FORTY

"READY TO DO SOME BUSTIN'?" Dash peered up at Blaze, eyes in a squint as he and Jake latched hard to restrain the meanest horse on the ranch.

You have no idea. Blaze gave a curt nod as he positioned his heels above Nightmare's shoulders to mark the animal out, the ornery quarter horse few of the ranch's cowhands had mastered. He glimpsed Maggie out of the corner of his eye laughing with Clint, and his fist gripped the rein till his knuckles felt ready to crack.

First the bronc, then Keller's pretty face.

One of the cowhands opened the chute, and Nightmare lunged forward with a wild leap that would have unseated most men. But Blaze held on, calibrating both his breathing and his movement with that of the horse. Arm in the air, he spurred the animal from shoulders to saddle in a rhythmic motion that correlated with Nightmare's violent thrusts like a fine-tuned machine. Power crackled through Blaze like fire to kindling with every powerful thrust of the mare's body, and although the force of their wills were polar opposite, horse and rider may as well been one.

Like Maggie and me.

The thought jolted as much as Nightmare's thrusting when Jake's whistle pierced the air. Teeth gritted, Blaze forged on beyond the eight seconds out of pure stubbornness, finally jumping off as smoothly as he had ridden. He dodged the mare's hooves with as much practice as he dodged any woman who threatened his peace of mind.

Like Maggie.

"Whoo-eee, boy, that was one dandy of a show." Stopwatch in hand, Jake slapped him on the back as Blaze returned to the chute while cowhands cheered and whistled. Acknowledging them with a listless wave, he unbuckled his chaps with a clamp of his jaw, his clean ride doing little to improve his state of mind.

"Yeah, Hotshot," Dash said with a wide grin, "riding after the whistle just to put the other contender in his place. If I didn't know better, I'd think you're trying to impress the ladies."

"Not trying to impress anybody," he muttered, the notion suddenly souring his mood all the more when he realized Dash might be right. Since he'd ended his friendship with Maggie, he'd been downright miserable having to live under the same roof and not able to speak to her, laugh with her, or savor her company like he had before.

And her kisses?

He stifled a grunt as he cast a lidded look to where Clint flirted his fool head with the woman. Yeah, that, too. Oh, he was still hotter than a jalapeno in a flamin' frypan over what she did, but what riled him more than even the breakup with Rachel was the red-hot fire Maggie had sparked in his soul.

"You sure?" Dash said softly, his gaze following Blaze's to where Maggie was smiling at Clint.

Blaze slid his brother a scowl. "Yeah, I'm sure. Just wasn't about to let Keller steal my thunder, that's all."

Dash chuckled. "Doubt that could happen. You've been a raging thunderstorm since Rachel left the Ponderosa."

Blaze unloaded a grunt as he draped the chaps over the fence. *No, Little Brother, since I kissed Maggie in the barn*. And that's exactly what he'd told her when she'd hounded him to get their friendship back on track last week, waylaying him in the barn for the fifth blasted time.

"No!" he'd shouted with a crack of his hand to the wall, "it won't work, Maggie. Not just because you stuck your nose in my business and riled me to no end. But because of that infernal kiss in the barn, confound it." He leveled a stiff finger, jaw hard as flint. "So, help me, I'm warning you right now to steer clear, woman, because I want nothing to do with that *or* with you ever again." Even now the memory of her tortured look twisted his gut, but it had been the only way to save face.

And heart.

Finn's two-fingered whistle drew everyone's attention as he waved Jake's list in the air, using the cow horn to announce the results. "That was some great riding, boys, and I'm proud of each and every one of you."

"Except Murrell," somebody shouted, and laughter circled the corral where cowhands were perched on the railing. They always ribbed the newest member of the group, especially a spindly kid like Murrell who'd been one of the orphans Blaze trained a few years back.

Finn chuckled. "Don't you pay them no mind, Murrell—every last one of these upstarts hit the dust in the beginning—"

"Some still do," one of the older hands called out, and more laughter ensued.

"True enough." Finn shook his head with a patient smile before continuing. "Since the Silver Lining Ranch has taken home the prize for the best bronc buster six years running, we'll be fixin' to send today's winners into that corral come September. And as usual, the two runners-up will receive a smaller monetary prize and step up if the winner breaks a leg."

A few chuckles circled the crowd.

"Now for the sake of the ladies who may not know how the scores are tabulated, judges score both the horse's bucking action and the cowboy's control of the horse and spurring action. That said, I'm pleased to announce third place goes to Chester Walton."

Cowhands whooped up a storm while Chester—one of the oldest hands—limped up to receive his silver dollar from Finn. "Good job, Chester," Finn said with a clap on the man's back before continuing on. "Second place is mighty important because there's been many a time the rider gets tossed on the first turn and can't finish the second and third rides, so I'm proud to say that honor goes to Blaze Donovan."

More cheers and hollers thundered through the corral as Blaze raised his hat in thanks, the smile on his lips as stony as the mountains on the horizon since this meant Clint likely beat him out.

"And finally, the winner of today's practice rodeo—halting Blaze's winning streak of three years running, I might add—is Clint Keller."

The crowd erupted in cheers while Finn shook Clint's hand. After he awarded the prize money, Finn announced there'd be ice cream on the back porch. Pandemonium broke out as a horde of hands charged the ranch house, where Gert and Angus waited next to several churns of ice cream lined up.

After offering a handshake to Clint, Blaze scowled when the cowhand presented his arm to Maggie to escort her to the ice cream social. Temper taut, he stormed past them both to stride toward the barn with a granite jaw.

"Hey, you don't want ice cream?" Dash called as he and Jake ushered Shaylee and Sheridan toward to the house.

"Nope, not hungry." With an offhanded wave, he strode toward the barn with head bowed, suddenly wishing Maggie Mullaney had never come to Virginia City. He tossed a glance over his shoulder to see her laughing with Clint, and the bitter taste of jealousy tainted his tongue, chilling him more than a churn full of ice cream.

"Only four months to go," he muttered as he entered Minx's stall, determined to get as far away from Maggie

Mullaney as he possibly could. He didn't want to see anymore of her sunny smiles. Hear anymore of her musical laughter. Feel anymore of her dad-burned gentleness when she tried to approach him like he was some skittish bronc.

Oh sure, she'd tried to apologize plenty over the last three weeks, obviously missing his friendship as much as he missed hers, but he'd always just walked away, too blasted afraid she'd breech his defenses and make him care more than he already did. He paused at Minx's stall with a hand to the railing, eyelids weighting closed with the painful reality that he cared for her far too much as it was. Ice prickled his spine.

He was already halfway in love with her now.

Minx nickered and nuzzled his hand, and Blaze unleashed a weary sigh, grazing the mare's neck with a gentle rub. Who was he kidding? He was flat-out moony over the woman, and the very thought iced the blood in his veins.

"What am I gonna do, Minx?" He scrubbed the horse's snout in a manner as listless as the malaise that had lingered from the moment his lips had touched Maggie's. "I want her, girl," he whispered to the mare, gaze numbing into an empty stare as he fondled the horse's mane. "I want her real bad, but I don't want all the blasted trappings that come along with her."

Commitment.

Marriage.

God.

Every muscle in his body suddenly twitched with resistance, calcifying along with his resolve. *Two blasted months, and the woman has me craving her like a cool drink of water in a desert drought.* He pounded the stall with his palm, then stormed to the tack room for his saddle, slamming it over the wooden railing of Minx's stall. "Worse than a blasted bottle of rotgut," he hissed while he snatched the curry comb to remove loose hair from the mare's sleek body, "so blasted dizzy and sick I just want to puke."

"Is that why you didn't want ice cream?"

Blaze spun around, heat chasing his blood clear up his neck at the sight of Maggie standing not twenty feet away. "What are you doing here?" he snapped, turning his attention back to Minx as he combed her body a little more vigorously than usual. "Thought you'd be out there meltin' ol' Clint's ice cream." The moment the words were out of his mouth, he cursed under his breath, downright irked that she reduced him to some jealous dogie craving its mother's milk.

"I came to check on you because I was worried," she said quietly, the tenderness of her tone shooting an ache straight to his heart.

Along with a fuse to his temper.

"Well, I don't need a nursemaid, Miss Mullaney," he said, practically spitting the words, "so you can just go focus all your attention on ol' Clint 'cause I guarantee you, he wants it a whole lot more than I do."

"I don't think so." Her words were soft and tentative as she approached the stall slowly, as if he were that dad-burned horse that had spooked her when she was small. "I think you do, Blaze, just like me."

He paused to gape at her. "Are you daft? What do I have to do to prove I want nothing to do with you, lady?"

Her jaw nudged up the slightest bit as she clutched her arms to her waist. "Well, acting like a mature human being instead of a scalded mule kicking and nipping at everyone might be a good start."

He slapped the curry comb back on its hook and snatched the brush instead, all but brandishing it at her as he glared her down. "I told you once, and I'll tell you again, Maggie—stay away from me!"

She stepped in, a bit of fire kindling in those amazing golden eyes. "I *have*, Blaze, for three lonely weeks, while you freeze me out with a shoulder colder than those two churns of ice cream out on the back porch."

"Ha! Lonely?" He brushed Minx with hard strokes as rigid as his body. "Could have fooled me. And if you want a shoulder to warm you up, sweetheart, I suggest you stick with Lady-killer Keller, because I promise he'll light your fuse just fine, keepin' you plenty warm at night."

She slammed a fist to the rail, his lewd comment obviously hitting the mark. "Nobody lights my fuse like you, you … you cocky mule of a man, too blasted stubborn to admit that you need my friendship as much as I need yours."

The truth of her remark stung, and whirling to face her, he aimed the brush right in her face. "I'm telling you for the last bloomin' time, Maggie. I don't need you or your blasted friendship, so just *leave me alone*!" Stomping to Minx's hind end, he proceeded to brush her tail with a vengeance, expecting Maggie to turn tail and run like all the other times he'd turned her way.

Only she didn't.

"Maybe not, Blaze"—her voice was barely a whisper as she stood there like some little, lost orphan, picking at her nails with crocodile tears in her eyes—"but I need yours."

A low groan escaped as he dropped his head, eyes squeezed tight to shut her out.

Only he couldn't.

"I've … never had a friend like you," she said in a fragile tone that tore at his gut. "Someone that cared for me just … as I am." Her voice faltered, cramping his chest. "Or at least acted like he did."

"Maggie, stop …" His voice came out hoarse as he put his head in his hand, fighting the urge to comfort her like he wanted.

"Someone I could talk to about anything, Blaze, down to the deep, dark recesses of my soul. Oh, sure, I had a friend or two in New York, but only because I was the stepdaughter of The Judge, so-called friends hand-picked by him to spy on me."

He groaned, fingers pinched white on the brush to keep from reaching out.

"The only real friend I ever had was Aunt Libby, but only because Mama asked her to take care of me, so that doesn't count." Her voice cracked on a sob and he groaned out loud before his gaze lifted to hers. "Please don't turn me away," she whispered, the pitiful sound wrenching him to the core, "because I need you in my life, Blaze." The pain in her tone matched the tears in her eyes, shredding him into a hundred miserable pieces.

"Aw, Maggie ..." He threw the brush down and wrapped her up in his arms, burying his head into silky hair that smelled of lavender and Maggie. Her body heaved as she wept against his chest, and gently stroking her back, he shut his eyes to steel himself against the pull that she wielded. But it was no use. Maggie owned his heart whether he liked it or not, and he couldn't ignore her in her time of need.

Need.

His fingers fairly shook with a need of his own, but he silently vowed to provide the comfort of a friend and nothing more. No matter how much "more" tempted with the tentative wrap of her arms to his waist, molding her body to his.

A perfect fit.

Posing an imperfect fate.

"All right, you win," he said in a gruff voice edged with frustration, gripping her arms to hold her at bay. "I'll be your friend, Maggie, but that's as far as it goes—*ever*—understood?"

"Oh, Blaze!" She shot back into his arms, squeezing him so tightly, heat licked through his body like wildfire before she pulled away with a glow in her eyes. "Thank you! And you have nothing to worry about, I promise. This relationship will be purely platonic." She teased her lip with a scrape of teeth before she distanced herself considerably, an imp of a grin curving on her beautiful mouth. "You're the cocky cowboy type who can't abide religion, remember? And I'm one of those annoying respectable types who will only badger you into church, so friendship is undoubtedly the safest course."

Safe? His pulse kicked up as she sashayed to the door of the stall. She turned with a tilt of her chin, hands perched on the hips of a body that made his mouth go dry. "I made Gert promise she'd save you some ice cream, so you ready to cool down?"

Oh, he was ready all right. But he doubted ice cream could do it.

"Sure." Retrieving the brush, he returned it to its hook before skimming a palm down Minx's main, wondering what in the devil he was doing cozying up with the friend who haunted his dreams. *You can do this*, he told himself as he nuzzled the mare one last time. Four more months is all it will take, and the temptation would be gone when Maggie moved back to Virginia City.

He smothered a grunt as she tossed a smile over her shoulder, alarm constricting his stomach that even New York might not be far enough.

Purely platonic? The pure he could believe because after all, this was Maggie. But platonic? He tugged on the brim of his hat as he followed her out the door.

Dad-burn it all—bring on the ice cream!

CHAPTER FORTY-ONE

"MY, WHAT A BEAUTIFUL EVENING!" Mrs. Poppy leaned back in the rocking chair on Finn's porch as the sun gilded the mountains with a dusky pink. Her rocker squeaked up a storm as they sipped tea and watched Maggie and the girls play baseball with Finn and the others.

"Indeed," Libby said quietly, lounging in her own comfortable rocker—as sturdy and strong as the man who'd built it and other pieces for his house. She breathed in the sweet almond scent of white-thorn hedges lining Finn's porch, which merged amiably with the lingering smell of wood smoke from the barbecue. Taking a quick gulp of her tea, she knew she hadn't been this content in years.

Nor this nervous.

Her gaze lighted upon the source of her anxiety, and her stomach automatically flipped when he handily caught the baseball to tag Shaylee out. Swooping her up in a hug, he spun her around while his rich laughter merged with her giggles. Shirtsleeves rolled and collar loosened, Finn McShane was a man at ease with everyone he met—from babies and children, to adults and the elderly, and easily one of the most charismatic people Libby knew. Not to mention handsome, a deadly combination that had always been the problem. From high school till adulthood, the man had churned her stomach as briskly as Gert and Angus churned the ice cream in their endless contests to produce the favorite dessert. A wispy sigh feathered her lips. *A problem she wasn't sure she wanted to battle.* Because Finn McShane was a good-looking mule who would always demand his own way.

"It would seem Finn is still mighty handy with the catch," Mrs. Poppy said with a husky chuckle, gaze trained on Finn as thoroughly as Libby's own. "And not just on the baseball field, I'll wager …" The old woman's voice was suddenly soft, eyes flicking to where Libby sat stock-still with her face warming more than the cup of tea in her hands. "You still love him, don't you, Libby?" Mrs. Poppy whispered, drawing Libby's gaze with a knowing smile tinged by a touch of sadness.

The heat in Libby's cheeks pulsed to full throttle as she returned her attention to the game, Mrs. Poppy's potent stare causing her to guzzle her tea. "We're just tolerating each other until I can go home, Mrs. Poppy."

A throaty chuckle floated in the air. "I would say you're well beyond tolerance, my dear, but what I don't understand, Libby darling, is *why* are you fighting it?"

Libby's eyes drifted closed.

"It's either your silly suffrage movement, Libby, or me, so take your pick!"

"You're afraid, aren't you?" The tenderness in Mrs. Poppy's tone sparked tears in Libby's eyes as she stared at the man who could weaken her with merely a smile.

"Terrified," she admitted quietly, wishing it could work, but doubting it ever would. Moisture stung the back of her lids as a Scripture haunted her mind, the one her father had given her the day she'd walked out on Finn.

Better a dry morsel, and quietness therewith, than a house full of sacrifices with strife.

She swiped at her eyes, knowing full well that Harold may not elicit the passion that Finn did, but at least he would never deny her dreams.

"Libby dear …" Mrs. Poppy laid a gentle hand on Libby's arm, her compassion and love evident in the sheen that moistened her eyes. "Have you prayed about it?"

Libby blinked, the thought of prayer so foreign to her now that heat braised her cheeks. A lump dipped in her throat. "Uh …"

Mrs. Poppy patted her hand while a soft chuckle drifted from her lips. "No fret, darling—God already knows we're not perfect. It's certainly no surprise to Him when we falter or fail … or even forget how much He loves us." She settled back in her chair with that serene smile that had never failed to calm Libby's soul, frail hands holding her teacup in her lap as she watched the baseball game with a faraway look. "It is, in fact, *because* of our falterings, our failings, our forgetting just how much He wants to be a part of our lives that He went to the cross in the first place—to wipe the slate clean. So, none of that matters a whit to Him if we just call on His name, dear girl." Translucent lids closed as she lifted her face to the sky, her words as steady and sure as the Scripture on her lips. "You, oh Lord, are forgiving and good, abounding in love to all who call to you."

Resting her head on the back of the rocker, she refocused on Libby. Understanding glimmered in eyes that wielded a wealth of wisdom. "Because no matter what we have done, where we have gone, how we have failed, who we have hurt, who we've been hurt by, *or* how long we have strayed—the cross calls us home. *Home*," she repeated with a tender smile, "to His forgiveness, His love, His wisdom, His healing, and abundant blessings that exceed our very hope."

There was no way Libby could stop the tears that suddenly brimmed in her eyes. "Oh, Mrs. Poppy, I didn't mean to stray, I promise, but I was so hurt after I left Virginia City …" Her voice tapered off as her gaze trailed out to where Finn was at bat.

"There, there, sweet girl, no one is blaming you, least of

all God." Sadness welled in the her eyes as surely as salt-water welled in Libby's. "If anything, He aches because He knows how much pain you've endured on your own, my dear"—she paused briefly to offer a tender look laced with sympathy—"and how much He could have helped to ease it. He longed to be the One who carried you through, Libby, to the good things He planned for you based on a Father's love. Not the things you planned for yourself based on pain, anger, or fear."

Mrs. Poppy patted Libby's arm, the gentle touch unleashing a trail of moisture down Libby's cheeks. "I'm afraid it's the age-old story of man, my dear—God's will vs. our own, compliments of Eden. Most people don't realize that prayer can conquer any problem, large or small, and God's precepts can guide them through. Because the truth is, darling girl, human beings see insurmountable problems, but God sees golden opportunities to bless us, grow us, and most importantly, set us free to be the people He created us to be."

Her bodice rose and fell with a fluttery sigh as she glanced out at Finn, the affection in her face hard to miss. "And I believe He created you to be Finn's wife and he your husband, but unfortunately, humanity often gets in the way, robbing us of God's best."

"I believed I was meant to be Finn's wife, too, at one time, Mrs. Poppy," Libby said as she pushed the tears from her eyes, "until he gave me an ultimatum out of anger, demanding I make a choice between my passion for him and my passion for women's rights." Pain convulsed in her throat as she stared at the man she had married. "So I did."

Mrs. Poppy gave a slow nod of commiseration. "Ah, yes, anger can often distort the lens of wisdom, something I soon discovered in my own marriage. But you know it's a funny thing about the men that we love, Libby; they're desperate to know they're more important than anything else in our lives." Pausing to take a sip of her tea, she settled the cup back in the saucer, pinning Libby with a penetrating stare. "Because you see—that's how they measure true love. But I'm afraid they come by it honestly."

Libby tipped her head. "What do you mean?"

The softest of laughter bubbled from the old woman's lips as she slipped Libby a mischievous wink. "Why, like Father, like son, of course."

Libby blinked in confusion. "I'm not sure I understand."

A soft giggle drifted in the air as Mrs. Poppy took another drink of her tea. "I mean they're no different than the God who created them, Libby, who longs to know that *He,* too, is the most important thing in our lives. Longs to know that we love Him enough to trust Him with the desires of our heart, choosing His will over our own. But you know what the really extraordinary thing about that is?"

Libby shook her head, barely aware she was holding her breath.

A twinkle lit the old woman's eyes as she bent close to Libby's chair, her face so luminous, she could have been an angel sent straight from above. "When we make Him the most important thing in our lives, our desires become His and His ours, unleashing a fierce yearning in Him to bless us beyond measure. Because never forget, my dear, love begets love and blessing begets blessing." She sighed, the sound almost melancholy. "That was a lesson I learned the hard way in my own marriage to Pastor Poppy."

"You?" Libby asked, more than a little surprised that Mrs. Poppy had had any difficult lessons at all, as perfect as her marriage had always seemed.

The old woman nodded. "Yes, I'm afraid so. You see, when the California Gold Rush hit in '49, Horace had a fire in his belly to minister to the countless poor souls who flocked to San Francisco during its boomtown days. Oh, and a wicked place it was for sure …" Her gaze lapsed into a faraway stare as she grazed a thumb along the rim of her near-empty cup, the faintest of smiles shadowing her lips. "But Horace made a difference, and oh my, how he loved it! Never wanted to leave, he said, in fact." Her chest expanded with a weary sigh. "But somehow I had this sense, this feeling, we were needed elsewhere."

She peered skyward, her face taut with memories. "So, when I received a letter from a dear friend in Nevada, begging us to come to this lawless boomtown called Virginia City, I was certain it was God's will." A deep chuckle escaped as a glimmer of tears glazed in her eyes. "It was no more than a ramshackle town of tents and shacks that had sprung up on the heels of the Comstock Lode, but it was rife with souls in dire need of the Almighty, so it became my passion."

A soft grunt escaped as she shook her head, silver-white wisps dancing with the motion. "But it certainly wasn't Horace's, much as suffrage wasn't Finn's at the time, I suppose. But oh my, how I pleaded and begged, telling him I was certain it was what God wanted us to do, but all to no avail." One edge of her mouth tipped. "That bull-headed man flat-out said no, that he was the head of the house and his decision was final. "

"So, what did you do?" Libby chewed on her thumbnail, her body abuzz with curiosity.

She gave a short nod. "Why I stormed through the house and called him a bully, that's what, then flat-out refused to make his dinner."

Libby bit back a smile, unable to imagine sweet Mrs. Poppy causing such a stir. "But I'll bet you didn't throw a teapot," she said with a shy chew of her lip.

"Oh, good heavens, no!" the silver-haired imp said with a gleam in her eye, "I threw an iron, and a mighty hefty one at that, putting a dent in the door if not in his head."

Libby's jaw dropped a full inch, her smile sliding into a grin. "No!"

"Oh, yes, ma'am, and I surely thought that would do the trick, but that mule of a man just packed up his things and slept in the church."

"Oh my goodness, what did you do?" Libby gaped with a hand to her mouth.

Shimmying deeper in her chair, Mrs. Poppy lifted the cup to her lips with a pert thrust of her chin, a squirm of a smile teasing her mouth. "Why I called out the big guns, of course. Locked myself in the bedroom and got on my knees. Told God flat-out that if He wanted us in Virginia City, He had some mighty fancy footwork to do with one of his own."

Libby grinned outright.

"Yes, ma'am," she continued with a mock scowl that quickly slanted into an off-center smile. "Only problem was, the fancy footwork He had to do was on me, not Horace."

"What?" Libby sat straight up in her chair. "But he was bullying you, Mrs. Poppy, while all you were trying to do was the will of God!"

"Ah, yes, the will of God," she said with a chuckle, "a seemingly nebulous thing about which most of us have no earthly idea. But the truth is, God's will is as simple and succinct as a single word." Halting, her voice seemed suspended in air, right along with Libby's breathing. A sparkle lit in eyes quickly awash with moisture as she leaned close, as if to whisper a coveted secret. "God's '*Word*.'"

Head cocked, Libby studied the old woman's face with a pucker in her brow. "What do you mean?"

"I mean, my dear, that God made no bones about it—nailed my hide to the wall with His Word. Ephesians 5:22 — Wives, submit yourselves unto your husband as unto the Lord."

Libby gasped. "No!"

"Yes indeedy, but He *also* assured me in Psalm 37:4-5 that *if* I committed my way to Him and trusted Him, He would give me the desires of my heart even if Horace wouldn't!" A pixie grin eased across her weathered lips as she gave Libby a wink. "But my favorite Scripture He gave me was 1 Peter 2:15, which cinched the deal."

"And what was that?" Libby asked, her curiosity definitely piqued.

Mrs. Poppy giggled as her gaze darted to the baseball game and back, cheeks as rosy as the mountains awash in the colors of dusk. "For it is God's will that by doing good you should silence the ignorance of foolish men."

A giggle spilled from Libby's mouth that unleashed an onslaught of chuckles from both women, drawing curious looks from the men on the lawn.

"And although I wasn't sure I could do it, mind you, Hebrews 10:36 promised assurance that when I have done the will of God, I would receive what is promised. And you know what?" She sent Libby a puckish wink that set off another round of giggles. "I did! So you see, dear Libby, application of God's precepts is not to bully us; it's to bless us."

Libby glanced at Finn, ribcage constricting with doubt she could ever trust him with her passion for women's rights.

And how can I trust Finn if I don't even trust God?

"You know, Libby," Mrs. Poppy continued, almost as if she could read Libby's mind, "trust is not only a gift to those we love, my dear, it's a gift to ourselves as well. I know you're afraid to trust Finn, but he loves you and I believe he always has. And you love him."

Libby chewed on her lip. "But I don't trust him, Mrs. Poppy, and I don't know how to change that."

"No, but God does if you'll let Him. You see, my dear, love is the soil in which trust flourishes, but trust is the seed that allows love to bloom. Which means the more you realize just how much God loves you, the more you will trust Him. And the more you trust Him, dear girl, the deeper your love. It's no different with Finn, Libby. The more he loves you, the more your trust will grow, deepening your own love beyond anything you have ever dreamed."

"I don't know, Mrs. Poppy," she whispered, her heart in a cramp, "I'm just so afraid …"

"Fear will tell you it's not possible," Mrs. Poppy said softly, "but fear is one of the most potent reasons to forge on, because not only does perfect love—God's love—cast out fear, but it nourishes trust and peace and hope."

Perfect love. God's, not hers. Could she do it? Could she trust Finn? A shiver skittered through her mind as memories flashed of her father's control, stealing her freedom, thwarting her dreams. Her father loved her, she knew, but she never trusted him. Could it be different with Finn?

Shaking her anxiety off, Libby reached to clasp Mrs. Poppy's hands in her own, gratitude welling in her eyes that God had brought this amazing woman to Virginia City. "Well, the important thing is that you won, Mrs. Poppy, and so did Virginia City."

"Oh, I most certainly did! A very hard-won lesson that has served me well all the days of my life." She patted Libby's hand, fragile fingers gnarled and bent from a lifetime of righteous living. "And that is, my dear child, that one's heart's desires belong at the foot of the throne, where a Father who truly loves us can give them their flight."

CHAPTER FORTY-TWO

"WHOA, BOY." FINN SLOWED HIS prized Hooker phaeton at the corner of B and Union Streets before giving Lightning a tug in front of the brand-new Piper's Opera House. Dressed in his best three-piece suit, he hopped out and tied the reins to the post alongside a long line of other horses and buggies, all owned by patrons attending John Piper's summer ball.

"In case I haven't told you, Libby," he said as he reached up to assist her from the carriage, "you look absolutely beautiful tonight." He clasped her tiny waist before sweeping her down, reluctant to let go. She was breathtaking in a green satin dress trimmed with cream lace, the scent of lilacs teasing his senses as much as her V-necked bodice teased his body, a dangerous hint of creamy breasts he hadn't seen in far too long.

"Uh, not in the last five minutes," she said with a smile in her voice, a stray auburn curl grazing her alabaster neck like he so longed to do. "But I do thank you, Mr. McShane."

His heart sped up as he offered her his arm, wishing this ball was for a far different reason than celebrating his bid for mayor.

Like a renewal of vows.

"'Evening, 'Mayor.'" Propped against the brick archway with hands in his pocket, Finn's good friend, Milo Parks, flashed a welcoming grin as he nudged up his best Stetson. "Fashionably late for once."

Finn scowled, the idea of arriving late as uncomfortable as this confounded high-standing collar and silk necktie he was forced to wear. "Sorry about that—Shaylee took sick."

"Nothing serious, I hope." Milo's perennial smile faded.

Finn's mouth quirked. "Nothing an early night's sleep can't cure," he said, still smiling over the ladies' hysterics when they discovered Shaylee had lost her pet tarantula, Annabelle. *In the house and against Finn's orders.*

Along with Annabelle's egg sac.

"Good to hear. And sweet thunder—Libby! Why, we haven't seen you in—what's it been, Finn—ten, fifteen years?"

"Seventeen," Finn said with a slant of a smile, shaking hands with the boyhood friend who was now editor of *The Territorial Enterprise*. "Come October."

Milo grinned, affording Finn a quick nod before he tipped his hat to Libby. "Heard a rumor this old fox was keeping you holed up at the ranch, probably under lock and key since we haven't seen hide nor hair of you, ma'am."

Libby slid Finn a nervous smile before reaching to give Milo a hug, the man who had once been her employer. "The lock and key were *all* mine, I assure you, Mr. Parks," she said, the tease in those remarkable green eyes, causing Finn's rib cage to expand with pride.

And hope.

"Well, I can certainly see why, Miss O'Shea," Milo said with a sly wink at Finn.

Mrs. McShane, Finn wanted to growl as Milo held her at bay to assess head to foot a little too thoroughly. But as far as Virginia City was concerned—and his best friend—Libby and he were no longer married. That had been Libby's one stipulation when he'd driven her to the ranch that night—the botched annulment was to be kept a secret to everyone but the immediate family.

Milo slapped Finn on the back with a wicked grin. "Well, you've never looked better, Libs, so I'm pretty sure a lock and key would be most essential to keep this one away."

"You the welcoming committee, Parks?" Finn said in a dry tone, "or has Bettie finally come to her senses and thrown you out on your ear?"

"I am, as a matter of fact, Mr. Mayor, dispatched by John Piper himself to haul you in as soon as you arrived. And I assure you Bettie is waiting inside at our table, as lovesick as ever along with Jo Beth and her escort for the night."

Finn stopped short. "Jo Beth is here? What the devil for? And does her father know?" He gaped at Milo, both shocked and annoyed his opponent's daughter—and the woman he nearly courted before Libby—would be attending Finn's support function.

Smile zagging toward dry, Milo opened the intricately carved wooden door with great fanfare, pushing it wide to usher them in. "You know why she's here, Finn," Milo said with a heavy sigh. "She's still smitten, my friend, so she asked Bettie if she could come as our guest. And, no, I'll wager her father would have a fit if he knew." He shot Libby a wink. "Besides, both she and Bettie are most anxious to see Libby again after all these years."

I'll bet. Especially Jo Beth. Finn didn't miss how Libby stiffened at mention of the woman Finn had once stepped out with before her. Ushering Libby into the cozy candlelit foyer that led to the main theater, he was pretty sure Jo Beth Templeton Morrissey—now a wealthy widow—was the last person Libby had wanted to see when she came to Virginia City.

His smile took a tilt. *After me, of course.*

"Right this way, folks," Milo said with an outstretched arm. He guided them to the gilded double doors that led to a three-story theater transformed into an elegant ballroom for this evening's function. Milo opened the doors, and Finn heard Libby catch her breath. And with good reason. The magnificent theater owned by his good friend John Piper had just been rebuilt in the spring for the third time after two previous fires, and John had certainly outdone himself.

Dark walnut flooring gleamed to a shine, providing the perfect complement to walls of cream French provincial wainscoting on the proscenium and elaborate balcony boxes that circled the room. A Virginia City landmark since 1863, Piper's Opera House boasted the best entertainment money could buy, from lectures by Mark Twain and social reformer Henry Ward Beecher, to performances by Shakespearean thespians and top theatrical names such as Lily Langtry, W.F. Cody, and John Philip Sousa.

For this evening, however, theater seating gave way to linen-clad tables arrayed in flowers and china, where silver candelabras flickered and glowed as much as the guests arrayed in satins and silks. The soft strains of a string quartet drifted through the crowded room while waiters in coat and tails served soup from silver tureens.

"Oh my, I had no idea it would be so grand!" Libby whispered, her once vocal "cow town" opinion of Virginia City obviously no match for the bustling city it was today.

Finn leaned close with a smile, voice lowering for her ears alone. "'It's not New York, I know, Libby, but even 'cow towns' enjoy culture and refinement."

She had the grace to blush, and he gave her arm a playful squeeze to let her know he was teasing, remembering all too well how shocked she'd been the summer she'd graduated from Vassar to discover she loved the rustic appeal of Virginia City. No matter how much culture or refinement New York City had provided, Libby had settled into the West—and into their marriage—as if she had finally come home. And she had as far as Finn was concerned, her contentment as satisfying as the rosy glow of her cheeks or the frequent laughter that bubbled from her lips.

Till I stepped on her dream.

Well, he'd certainly learned his lesson there and had every intention of restoring that dream. But to do that, he needed to be elected Mayor of Virginia City first, his stepping stone to senator of the great state of Nevada. His ribcage tightened, stifling his air as much as the confounded collar. On a platform Libby *would not* understand.

"Trust me on this, Finn—you can*not* tell her," Aiden had warned in a private meeting with John Piper and other supporters just last week. "So, it's best to avoid talking about the election altogether until it's over."

Finn had scowled, the idea of keeping Libby in the dark until after the election not settling well. "That's just it, Aiden—trust *is* the issue with Libby. If she finds out I am on the wrong side of the suffragist movement in this election—whether inheritance rights, women voting on city issues, or even the right to be a school trustee—she'll blow like a powder keg if I don't tell her, and I'll lose her."

"And you'll lose the election if you *do* tell her, Finn, it's that simple," Aiden had emphasized, the conviction and concern in his eyes mirroring that of every man at the table. "All we're asking for is your commitment to avoid the subject with Libby until *after* the election. Templeton has already been spreading rumors that you're soft when it comes to women's rights. Claims that housing two suffragists is turning you into a radical who plans to toe the suffragist line, and you can't afford that, Finn—not in Virginia City."

Finn glanced around the table, lips compressed as he considered their argument. "I think you underestimate your daughter, Aiden. The only way I can effect positive change on behalf of women is in the legislature, and I can't get *there* touting women's rights. I think Libby will understand that. I believe she'll see forfeiture of local women's issue a necessary evil, both in this election and during my term as mayor, in order to position me for the greater good."

"Do you, now?" Aiden leaned back in his leather padded chair, palms resting on its arms as his gaze bore into Finn's. "Did you know I overhead her telling Maggie and the girls that they needed to establish a suffragist club? And that if she lived in Virginia City permanently, that's the first thing she would do?"

Finn swallowed hard, the very idea causing sweat to dampen his collar. One whisper of a rumor like that, and he'd be dead in the water.

"Look at it this way, Finn," John Piper said calmly, "the election is only a little more than two months away, so you won't have to keep quiet for long. Let's just get through this till then." He put a hand on Finn's shoulder, his fatherly manner easing some of Finn's strain. "And by all means, let Libby know that you agree with her on women's rights. But all we're asking for, son, is for you to keep a lid on your platform till *after* you're elected mayor. Then you can explain to her what you just told us—that you have every intention of pursuing the suffragist agenda in the legislature, but she'll just have to trust you till then."

Trust him.

Like she had before.

Before he let her down.

Aiden struck a match to light his pipe. "Once you're mayor, Finn, Libby can spout her suffragist spiel all she likes because your record will immunize you against it, helping to ensure an easy election in two years when you run for Senator Stewart's seat." Aiden offered a tight smile as he puffed on his pipe, sympathy clouding his gaze while smoke clouded the room. "Easy as the slide of barrel-aged whiskey, my boy."

The five men around the table mumbled and nodded their agreement.

"So, what do you say, Finn?" John Piper had said with a firm grip of his shoulder. "Do we have your word?"

Finn repressed a groan. *Yes, unfortunately.* Practically signed in blood.

More of which would be spilled if Libby found out.

"Attention, everyone—the guest of honor has arrived,"

Milo announced at the door, and the crowd broke out in applause that heated Finn's collar, burnishing the back of his neck along with Libby's face.

With a smile and a wave, Finn followed Milo to their table at the front of the stage, shoring Libby up with a hand to the small of her back. "Nervous?" he whispered in her ear.

She peeked up with a chew of her lip. "Terrified! I still can't believe I agreed to accompany you. I must have been out of my mind to say yes."

"Or tipsy," he replied with a smile, reminding her of their trip to Carson City where he'd taken full advantage of her embarrassment over her inebriated state to ask her to the ball. Not the gentlemanly thing to do, he supposed, but then he figured he was due after his gentlemanly restraint while holding Libby all night in his bed.

"Finn—welcome, my man!" John Piper rose from a scarlet brocade chair to pump Finn's hand with the same vigor with which he did everything. A shrewd businessman who rose from alderman to mayor to state senator, John now devoted his time to what was touted as one of the "most significant theaters in the West," giving it—and anything he put his hand to—his all.

Including Finn's political career.

"I can't thank you enough, John, for hosting this grand kickoff to my bid for mayor." Finn glanced around, amazed at the number of supporters who'd shown up. "I'm humbled and honored, my friend."

"And I'm humbled and honored you finally said yes. I've been harping on you for years now, young man, because you're just what this city and state needs, so I aim to do everything in my power to see it through."

"Appreciate it, John." Finn glanced at the rest of the table with a warm smile, greeting Senator Jones and his wife first, Jo Beth and her escort, then both Milo's wife and John's. "Good evening, everyone. I'd like to introduce

Libby O'Shea, who as you may know is staying at the Silver Lining Ranch with her parents and goddaughter until the O'Shea's house is rebuilt."

Turning to Libby with a slight bow, Finn motioned a hand to those at the table, introducing her—or reintroducing in Milo's, Bettie's, and Jo Beth's case—to each one, ending with John.

"Ah, Aiden's daughter, all the way here from New York, eh?" Tugging on his scruffy salt-and-pepper goatee, John surveyed Libby with warm interest, brown eyes spanning as wide as his smile. "I've heard much about you, my dear," he said, giving Libby's hand a polite squeeze, "and I must say I'm very impressed with a dutiful daughter who would put her life on hold to tend to her parents as diligently as you."

Finn bit back a smile when Libby's cheeks flamed bright red, giving the scarlet chairs a run for their money.

Libby grasped John's hand in both of hers. "It's a pleasure to meet you, John, and please—the credit all goes to Finn, I assure you," she said with a bright smile. "Why, the man practically blackmailed me, insisting on providing shelter for my parents and me." Head tipped, she peered up at Finn with a definite smirk. "Isn't that right, Finn?"

"Right on the money." He gave her a wink that bloodied her cheeks all the more.

"Doesn't surprise me in the least," John said with a slap on Finn's back. "This man will do whatever it takes to make things right, isn't that so, Finn?"

"Yes, sir, it is." Helping Libby into her seat, Finn allowed his fingers to graze the soft skin of her arms while he gently pushed her chair in, noting the pretty blush that suddenly rose in her cheeks.

Including courting my wife.

CHAPTER FORTY-THREE

"SO, TELL ME, LIBBY – did you have a good time?" Finn's voice was soft as they drove away from Piper's Opera House. The gentle whisper of the wind through mesquite trees harmonized with crickets and katydids while people still milled outside, saying their good-byes.

A good time? Libby peeked at Finn out of the corner of her eyes, stomach fluttering more than the wispy canopy of leaves overhead. *No, more like … a heavenly time.*

The food. The music. The friends.

Finn.

"I did," she said softly, wondering exactly when she'd fallen back in love with her husband. She wasn't quite sure, but somewhere over the last three and a half months, he'd breeched her defenses. She suspected it had begun in Reno when she'd awakened in his arms. Her smile tipped. Of course, Mrs. Poppy hadn't helped with her conversation a few weeks ago, urging Libby to pray about loving and trusting Finn, which she had. The loving part had definitely become easier after that, so much so Libby's pulse picked up whenever Finn returned in the evenings from overseeing branding on the south forty or full days at the mine.

But the trusting? Libby released a quiet sigh. Definitely slower although definite progress had been made through countless talks with Finn since Mrs. Poppy's conversation—and, no doubt, her prayers. Libby had been surprised to learn just how much she and Finn actually agreed on women's rights. Just not *how* to go about acquiring them for the gentler sex who were still perceived in many states as nothing more than a husband's property.

But tonight! She gave in to a contented sigh, the throaty hoot-hoot-hoot-hoooooo sound of an owl seeking its mate a gentle confirmation Finn was doing much the same. Was it the way his fingers had lingered, brushing her skin? The warmth of his palm to the small of her back? Or maybe his tender tone whenever he spoke to her, or the way he held her close when they danced, as if she were a priceless treasure he couldn't let go. Her heart had swooped at the heated look in his eyes as if she were the only woman in the room. And, oh, sweet mother of mercy, how she wanted to be!

For him.

His husky chuckle filled the starlit night—and her heart—with beautiful music that surrounded her like the warmth of his arms during a candlelight waltz. "So the evening was so good it's stolen your tongue?" he asked with laughter warm in his eyes. "Or so good that you're too worn out to talk?"

A feathery sigh wrapped around her smile as she drew her shawl closer, hugging it to her chest. "So good it reminded me how we fell in love."

His teeth flashed white in the night. "That good, huh?" he said, extending an arm to hook her in close, his warmth seeping into her side like his love was seeping into her heart. "I was proud to be with you tonight, Libby, proud that you're my wife, even if nobody in town knows it. Everybody loved you."

A soft grunt escaped her lips, a hint of jealousy edging her tone. "Not Jo Beth. If looks could singe, I'd be fried to a crisp while she brazenly fawned all over you."

His chuckle rumbled against her side. "She's just looking for another husband, and I'm the one that got away, remember? I'm pretty sure she's never forgiven you for that—or me. But you and I both know she never stood a chance after you came home from college. You're bright, beautiful, gentle and kind when you're not riled, darlin', which has always stirred me like no other woman." He gave her waist a playful pinch. "And feisty and full of fire when you are, which has always stirred my blood like nobody else."

Smiling, she leaned her head on his shoulder, remembering how no other boy or man had ever captured her like Finn either, right from the start. "Well, I was proud tonight, too, Finn, because everyone respects and admires you so. But then, people have always adored you, even when you were just a 'cocky womanizer.'" Her smile bled into her voice over her favorite taunt from years ago.

"All right, I'll give you 'cocky,' Mrs. McShane, but the only woman I ever wanted was you, Libs, and I hope by now you know that's never changed."

"I do," she said softly, rib cage expanding with pleasure as Finn pressed a kiss to her head, her trust factor expanding along with it. He continued talking about the evening, and Libby had no doubt that with his warm and winning way, he was a natural for politics. After seeing his rapport tonight with so many influential supporters, she wondered if returning to be Finn's wife wasn't what God had in mind all along.

Even now his excitement was contagious, fairly shimmering in his voice like moonlight shimmered in his eyes. She chuckled along as he shared interesting anecdotes about all the people she'd met—both political and personal. He had always been a charismatic boy, but now he'd become a charismatic man who garnered great influence with influential people. Could it be that theirs was meant to be a marriage of true passion—both Finn's and hers for each other … *and* hers for women's rights?

Finn's horse, Lightning, jostled the dirt road to turn onto

a weedy lane off of Finn's property, and Libby sat straight up on the seat, clutching Finn's arm. Her stomach surged along with the phaeton as the horse trotted through the weeds when she saw where they were going. She gulped.

True passion, indeed!

"Remember this place?" His husky tone told her that he certainly did, his thumb grazing her hip with one hand while he tugged on the reins with the other. "Whoa, boy," he said, halting the phaeton in front of a spring-fed lake where she and Finn had spent many a moonlight picnic. A saffron sash of light rippled across inky waters, swaying to the music of trees whispering in the breeze and crickets crooning their night songs. "If not, I can certainly jog your memory," he whispered against her temple, burrowing in to feather her ear.

"Finn"—her voice was little more than a rasp, pulse skyrocketing when he lifted her onto his lap and dipped her back to explore her neck with his mouth.

"Mmm?"

"What are y-you d-doing?" she said, her words stuttering along with her heart.

"Reminding you of just how good we are together, Libby." Heat coursed through her veins when he softly brushed his mouth against hers before gently tugging her lower lip with his teeth.

"I … remember all too well," she whispered breathlessly, palms to his chest to hold him at bay.

A slow grin meandered its way across his lips. "I don't think you do, Mrs. McShane, because if your memories were as potent as mine, darlin', you'd be kissing me back right about now." He captured her mouth with his own, and she had no control over the moan that slipped from her lips, tangling with his own. "Stay with me," he whispered, his voice fraught with so many things she recognized in herself—desire, desperation, devotion.

And a love that had never died.

"I want you, Libby—*forever.*" His fingers softly traced the curve of her neck to rest in the hollow of her throat where the wild beat of her pulse spoke even if she couldn't. Eyes burning into hers, he bent low, skimming her collarbone with his mouth. He pressed a tender kiss to her bare shoulder before rising to whisper warm in her ear. "Promise me, please, that you'll think about staying."

Heart ricocheting wildly, she closed her eyes, suddenly aware how very much she wanted him too. *Think about staying?* She swallowed hard, a warm shiver licking through her as he teased the shell of her ear with his tongue.

Sweet mother of mercy—as if she could think of anything else!

CHAPTER FORTY-FOUR

"SOMETHING COOL TO DRINK, MAGGIE?"

Maggie jolted, dragging her gaze from where Blaze danced with another girl to Clint's face as he whirled her in his arms at the Bar J Ranch rodeo barn dance. She blinked, barely seeing Clint much less hearing him as he held her close. "What did you say, Clint?"

All around them, couples waltzed to the banjo twang of "Clementine" in an intimate candle-lit barn aglow with lanterns strewn clear across the rafters of the vaulted ceiling. Around the perimeters, clusters of tree stumps boasted an array of beautiful oil lamps, no doubt on loan from the ladies of Virginia City. A welcome breeze drifted in from the wide double doors on both sides of the barn, ushering in the fragrant scent of honeysuckle and fresh-mown grass, a nice complement to the smell of hay and horses and men.

Her gaze wandered again, and a wavering sigh parted from her lips when Blaze's heart-melting grin was given to another girl. Eyelids sinking closed, Maggie berated herself for feeling this way about her best friend. Ever since she'd convinced him a month ago to reinstate their friendship, they'd settled back into the easy and honest relationship they'd had before—whether working, playing, laughing, or debating. Sharing their hearts and their hopes for themselves, for their families, and for their country.

But somewhere between his deep love of family and fishing expeditions with orphan boys or his endearing charm with nuns, nurses, and teachers at the hospital, orphanage, and school, she'd gone and done exactly what Sister Fred had warned her not to.

She'd fallen in love with the town's confirmed bachelor.

A rogue.

A radical angry with God.

A reliable friend who turned her insides to mush.

"Maggie?"

She blinked several times, once again caught off-guard by Clint's voice since up to now, he'd been holding her far too closely to talk face-to-face. "Pardon me?"

The slow and dangerous grin that no doubt fluttered many a girl's stomach—including hers—eased across his handsome face with reckless abandon. With masterful motion, he spun her wide, flaring her blue satin and lace dress while he grazed the small of her back with his thumb. "You look flushed, so I thought you might like a cold drink to cool down."

Against her will, her gaze flicked to where Blaze whispered into his partner's ear, eliciting a giggle before he drew her closer. Maggie's smile stiffened over the fact that her best friend—Blaze Donovan—had pert near danced with every single female tonight but her, and somehow the thought irked beyond belief. *Cool down?* She stifled a grunt. It would take more than a cold drink to do that. More like a washtub of ice in which they *kept* the jugs of cool drinks.

"Maggie?"

She caught her breath, face heating at the notion that Clint had caught her staring—*again*—at the man who had stolen the blue ribbon in the rodeo today. Remorse tented her brows as she strove to award Clint her most sincere smile. "I'm sorry, Clint—please forgive me, and yes, a cool drink would be lovely, thank you."

"All right, Maggie." He glanced over his shoulder to

where she'd been staring, and a scowl shadowed his lips just as the song ended. Grip suddenly firmer than before, he escorted her back to their table where Aunt Libby and Finn chatted amiably with Mr. and Mrs. O'Shea and Gert and Angus. Clint leaned close to Maggie's ear as he seated her between Aunt Libby and Sheridan. "I'll be right back," he whispered, palms coasting her arms with an intimacy that braised Maggie's cheeks.

"Are you having a good time, Maggie?" Aunt Libby asked with a tentative smile, voice low and a tiny crimp of concern in her brow.

"Oh, absolutely!" Maggie fibbed, flashing her godmother a bright smile as she gave her hand a quick squeeze. *Except for this stupid jealousy over Blaze dancing with everyone but her.* "But I must admit that right about now, I envy you and Finn sitting every other song out." She reached down to slip a heel off and rub her ankle. "Clint certainly enjoys dancing."

"Uh, I don't think it's the dancing he enjoys so much, do you, Aunt Libby?" Sheridan's smile bordered on mischievous. Looking way too grown-up in one of Maggie's scoop neckline silk dresses, the young girl possessed a wee bit more décolletage than a seventeen-year-old should have.

"No, I don't," Libby said with a tilt of her head, as if assessing Maggie's true state of mind. "But I do think it's a shame he's not giving the other men a chance with you, although I suppose as your escort, claiming every dance is understandable."

Sheridan unleashed a truly impressive grunt as she motioned her head to Jake, who sat on her other side laughing with Shaylee and Dash over a game of pigs in a pen. "Would you mind telling that to *my* escort?" she muttered, plopping her head in her hand. "*He's* only danced with me once tonight, holding me so far away, I could have been on the other side of the room."

Libby's brows dipped in sympathy. "Surely other boys have asked you to dance, Sheridan, haven't they?"

"Yes," Sheridan said with a pout, "but *Jake* is supposed to be my escort, and I don't want to dance with anyone but him."

"Maybe *that's* the problem." Maggie gave Sheridan's waist an affectionate squeeze. She leaned close to the young girl's ear. "Someone as pretty as you, young lady, needs to be out on that dance floor, so stop saying no and maybe a certain *someone* will notice."

Sheridan blinked, her blue eyes going wide before a slow smile curled on her lips. "Maggie Mullaney, you are a genius!" she whispered, casting a smug look over her shoulder to where Jake was teasing with Shaylee.

Genius? Maggie's gaze shot to Blaze, who was just finishing up a dance with Rachel, and her smile went flat. *Apparently not since my best friend won't give me the time of day much less a dance.*

Huffing out a sigh, she quickly diverted her attention to the cluster of cowhands leaning against the far wall, noting several whom Sheridan had already turned down. "Murrell has asked you to dance no less than three times tonight, Sher, so I think it may be time to reward the boy's courage, don't you?"

Sheridan glanced over her shoulder to where sweet Murrell Porter stood with one boot propped to the wall and arms folded, eyes fixed on Sheridan like she was one of the blue ribbons he'd tried to win for barrel racing.

A wispy sigh drifted from Sheridan as she sent a smile Murrell's way. "I suppose, although honestly, Maggie, he's so smitten now, I hate to encourage him since my heart leans toward . . ." She gave a sideways nod toward Jake, who appeared to be doing his best to avoid Sheridan completely.

Eyes tender, Maggie cupped a hand to Sheridan's jaw. "I know, Sher, but until that happens"—she ducked to stare straight into the girl's eyes—"*if* it ever happens, you need to make the most of every day, sweetheart, by reaching out and blessing others." She tossed a look over her shoulder, sympathy welling for the sweet boy who hadn't taken his eyes off Sheridan all day. "A good place to start might be with Murrell, giving him a dance that will light up his night. It's been my experience, Sher, that when one focuses on blessing others, blessings abound for them too." She tugged on one of Sheridan's golden curls. "Besides, not only will it help to get your mind off you-know-who, but you might just end up having more fun than you think."

Head cocked, Sheridan studied Maggie intently. "I can do that," she said with a smile that slowly bloomed from ear to ear. She lunged to give Maggie a hug. "Oh, Maggie, thank you so much! I wish you could stay with us forever."

"Me too, sweetheart." Maggie's eyelids sagged closed as she squeezed Sheridan back, a sharp ache in her chest. There were only two months of the six left to go until the O'Shea's—and Maggie with them—would be leaving the Silver Lining Ranch.

Jumping up, Sheridan pushed in her chair just as the band struck up the lively tune of "Buffalo Gals," delivering a pretty smile in Murrell's direction. "I'll be back." She gave Maggie a wink. "Or not."

"Hey, Hash—Rachel's looking for a dance with you, little brother." Blaze arrived back at the table, the sound of his voice annoying Maggie when it caused her stomach to flip.

"Just bidin' my time till you ran out of charm, Hot-shot." Tweaking Shaylee's neck, Dash hopped up, gaze homing in on where Rachel sat with a table of ladies down the way. He gave Maggie a wink as he shoved in his chair and slapped Blaze on the back. "Watch out for this one, Maggie—he has a reputation for charming the socks off any woman foolish enough to dance with him, so steer clear." Grinning, he tipped Blaze's Stetson off-kilter before heading Rachel's way.

"Hey!" Tugging his hat back in place, Blaze claimed Sheridan's chair as he glanced around, tone terse the moment he spotted Murrell leading his sister out on the floor. "Hey, Sully, I thought you were Sheridan's escort tonight. Why the devil is she dancing with Murrell?" he asked, a bigger scowl on his face than the one on Jake's.

"I don't know," Jake said, eyes narrowing as he watched Murrell loop an arm to Sheridan's waist. Deep ridges lining his forehead tainted his usual good-natured manner.

"Because he asked her." Maggie tipped her head to give Jake a pointed stare. "Three times, as a matter of fact, and as we all know, gentlemen—this *is* a dance."

Blaze elbowed his best friend. "Go cut in, Sully—you're supposed to be keeping an eye on her, remember?"

"No, he's playing pigs in the pen with me, aren't you, Jake?" Shaylee tapped her pencil on Jake's arm, obviously reminding him it was his turn.

"I'll play with you, Sweet Pea," Blaze said with a prod of Jake's arm, all but shoving him out of the chair. His tone lowered. "We both agreed Sher's too young to be gallivantin' with the hands, and you're her escort, so *go-cut-in*."

"Sorry, Doodle." Jake tugged on one of Shaylee's pigtails before lumbering to his feet. "But Blaze is right. I need to go rescue your sister."

"But she looks like she's having a good time," Shaylee said in a near whine, watching Sheridan smiling up at Murrell while the two of them two-stepped along with a lively crowd of dancers.

"I know." Smile suddenly compressed, Jake tugged on his vest with a threatening look in Murrell's direction. "Which is exactly why I need to rescue her." He stalked away, and Maggie grinned, not sure what dismantled Jake's perennial good mood more—Sheridan dancing with Murrell or the fact that Jake was forced to.

"All right, Sweet Pea, set 'em up." Blaze switched into Jake's chair while Shaylee focused hard on putting dots on her paper for another game of pigs in a pen, tongue peeking out the side of her mouth. Folding his arms on the table, Blaze slid Maggie a sideways look. "Speaking of escorts, Nightingale, where's yours?"

Maggie spied Clint at the refreshment table, flirting with a group of ladies while he held two glasses of lemonade in hand. She nodded his way before giving Blaze a dry smile. "Getting me a cold drink—I think."

Blaze's gaze followed hers and he frowned. "Or lukewarm by the time he tears himself away from the ladies. Look, Maggie, I told you before, Clint has a reputation as a womanizer, so just be on your guard."

You mean, like I am with you? Maggie sighed, almost wishing she liked Clint a bit more so she could eradicate these annoying feelings for Blaze.

"Blaze, you go first," Shaylee said, pushing the paper toward her brother.

Blaze connected two dots with his pencil and pushed it back, tossing Maggie a scowl over his shoulder. "Far as I'm concerned, it was downright stupid for you to say yes to a blatant womanizer in the first place."

Maggie bristled, the idea of Blaze "flirt-and-flee" Donovan calling Clint a womanizer galling her to no end. Sure, she might agree that she'd been somewhat short-sighted in saying yes to Clint in the first place, but as far as she was concerned, the only "stupid" thing she'd done was to fall in love with her best friend—the biggest flirt of them all.

"Here you go, Maggie." Clint showed up just in time to keep Maggie from telling Blaze just who she thought the true womanizer was and none too nicely. Drinks in hand, he nodded toward the barn doors while he extended his arm. "It's pretty stuffy in her, so do you want to get some fresh air and enjoy these outside?"

Her first inclination was to tell Clint no, but the warning look in Blaze's eyes tripped her temper, flipping her response along with it. "Certainly." She rose from the chair, ignoring Blaze's glare while she hooked her arm through Clint's. "All of a sudden, it *does* feel rather stuffy in here, so lead the way."

She paused when Blaze grabbed her wrist, his eyes probing hers with a silent threat. "Actually, Maggie, I was hoping you'd give me the next dance."

Hackles high, she arched a brow. "And deprive some lucky girl a chance with one of the handsomest cowboys in the room?" She pulled away and placed her hand on Clint's arm as she studied Blaze through sober eyes. "Why, I wouldn't *dare* risk the wrath of the female population, Mr. Donovan. With so few dances to spare, that would be a real travesty," she said, smile stiff as she allowed Clint to lead her away.

Like our friendship.

CHAPTER FORTY-FIVE

"BLAZE!" SHAYLEE'S VOICE BROKE THROUGH Blaze's mental tirade, jerking his gaze from the double doors at the front of the barn to where she sat beside him. Her tiny brows dug low with a flinch of freckles as she tapped her pencil on the table. "The game is right here, mister, not outside."

He scowled. *One can only hope.* Maggie and Clint had been gone for over fifteen minutes now, and that fact alone had Blaze strung as tight as a banjo wire. Everything in him wanted to stomp outside and drag her back in, but she'd made it pretty darn clear she wanted him to butt out. Blasting out a noisy sigh, he turned his attention to his sister. "Sorry, Doodle, I guess my mind is somewhere else." He boxed in a square and wrote his initial in it, making up his mind that Maggie deserved whatever she got with Keller.

Shaylee grunted loudly, the gruff sound way too big for such a little girl. "Boy, I'll say, and turtles to tadpoles, it's with Maggie."

A nerve flickered in his steeled jaw as he filled in two more boxes. *Nope, not anymore.*

"Goodness, but that was fun, wasn't it, Jake?" Sheridan plopped down in her chair while Jake grunted, the glow on her face at total odds with the rare frown on his.

"Who's winning?" Jake asked, hovering over Blaze and Shaylee like the Angel of Death.

"Me." Shaylee filled in another box with great precision, tongue peeking out once more. "Because Bren ain't concentrating."

"*Isn't* concentrating," Sheridan corrected. "And where's Maggie?" She spun around to scour the dance floor.

"Outside with Clint, which is why Bren ain'—*isn't*—concentrating." Shaylee initialed her final two boxes and pushed the paper away with a heft of her little chin, a definite gloat in her eyes. "I win."

"What?" Jake stared at Blaze, a pucker at the bridge of his nose. "You let Clint take Maggie outside?"

"She's a big girl, Sully," Blaze said in a near growl, rising with a harsh scrape of his chair. "I'm not her guardian."

"No, just mine." Sheridan huffed out a heavy sigh as the band tuned up with "Home on the Range. "Oh, I just love this song!" she said with a happy squeal, homing in on Jake with a shy flutter of lashes. "Jake—can we dance?"

Jake wasted no time stealing Blaze's chair, relief edging the apology in his tone. "Sorry, Half-Pint, but Shay needs a partner for pigs in the pen."

"But I need a partner too …" Sheridan said in a sad little-girl voice that plucked at Blaze's heart.

"Come on, Sher, I'll be your partner for this dance." Blaze held out his hand.

Sheridan's lower lip pushed into a pout. "No thanks, Bren. I'd rather sit this one out than be seen dancing with my brother."

"What?" Blaze shifted, hands on his hips while his big-brother's heart broke a little bit. "Just last year, you were begging me to dance every dance—what's different this year?"

"I am," she said with a pert lift of her nose. "I'm a woman now."

Jake's doubtful grunt braised her cheeks, and shooting to her feet, Sheridan singed the back of his head so hard, Blaze was surprised the man didn't flinch. "Well, if nobody *here* wants to dance with me—"

Blaze slid an arm to his sister's waist. "Now, hold on, darlin'—I said I would dance with you, didn't—"

"Ahem." Everyone froze at the nervous clear of Murrell Porter's throat, the kid's eyes locked on Sheridan despite the blotches of red crawling up his throat. "Miss Sheridan—may I have this dance?"

"Uh … sorry, Murrell," Blaze said with a clap of his hand on Murrell's shoulder, "but Sully here was just fixin' to dance with Sher, weren't you, Sul?"

"But Jake's playing gallows with me!" Latching onto Jake's arm, Shaylee glared her sister down.

"What's all the commotion going on over here?" Dash returned to loop an arm over Blaze's shoulder, gaze darting from face-to-face with a curious smile.

"No, *Dash* is playing gallows with you, Doodle," Blaze said, hauling Jake from the chair before pushing his brother down next to Shaylee. He slapped Murrell on the back with a sympathetic smile. "Sorry, Murrell, but Jake is Sheridan's escort tonight, so you know how that is." He leaned close, casting a look at a table of young ladies down the way. "But here tell that Bessie Monroe has been lookin' your way quite a bit tonight, so you might want to give her a dance, all right?"

"Sure, I guess." With a final look of longing at Sheridan, Murrell moseyed off while Blaze pushed Jake at his sister.

"Wear her out for pity's sake," Blaze said under his breath, breathing a slow sigh of relief that Sheridan was out of harm's way.

Least somebody was. Determined to put Maggie out of his mind, Blaze gave Shaylee's pigtail a little tug. "Shay, when you're done stringing this boy up, I'll give you some real competition, all right?" He surveyed the groups of single women throughout the barn. "There's still some ladies I haven't danced with yet."

"Blaze, I need a favor, son." Uncle Finn broke from his

conversation with Libby to pierce him with a sober look.

"Yes, sir?" Blaze bent in while his uncle gave a quiet nod toward the barn doors, voice lowering well below the chatter of the others as he leaned across the table. "Maggie's been gone a while. You mind checking on her?"

With pleasure. "Yes, sir." Smile grim, Blaze strode outside with a twitch in his temple, wanting to kick himself for not following Maggie sooner. If Uncle Finn was worried, that was confirmation of the uneasy feeling in Blaze's gut, and so help him, if Keller tried anything . . .

A mountain breeze washed away the heat of the crowded barn, filling his lungs with the clean scent of sagebrush and pine. Strains of music filtered out to where people milled about in a meadow area lit by moonlight and lanterns sporadically hung on a log fence.

Squinting hard to adjust his eyes to the dark, Blaze scanned from clusters of adults chatting here and there to packs of kids roaming the grounds playing hide and seek or midnight. With a hand shading his eyes, he peered toward several outhouses along the far tree line where lines of folks patiently waited, but Maggie wasn't among them.

"Dad-burn-it, Maggie, where the devil are you?" he muttered, snatching a lantern off a fencepost and marching to the back of the barn where several couples were entwined in shadowed corners. The moment the lantern light appeared, they pulled apart, allowing Blaze to make sure it wasn't Maggie.

The sound of female laughter jerked his head toward the woods where a well-worn path led to the creek. A group of mixed company emerged from the forest shadows, chatting and laughing as they strolled back towards the barn.

"Why, Blaze Donovan, I believe you owe me a dance," Andrea Jo Stephens said with a bat of her eyes, easily one of his favorite nurses at St. Mary Louise Hospital.

After Maggie.

"I believe I do, Miss Stephens, and I'll get right to it as

soon as I find Maggie." He nudged up the brim of his hat. "Anybody seen her?"

Several of the girls glanced over their shoulders along with Andrea Jo. "I think she's down at the creek with Clint," one of them said, "at least I *think* it was Maggie."

Andrea Jo shook her head. "Can't be—not with Clint." She sidled close to Blaze to give him a wink. "She's a bit too strait-laced for that boy, if you know what I mean."

One of the Bar J cowhands nodded to the woods. "Don't know any Maggie, but I do know Clint Keller's down there with some pretty little thing."

Blaze's jaw ground to rock. "Much obliged." With a tip of his hat, he tore for the woods.

"I'll be waiting for that dance, Mr. Donovan," Andrea Jo called after him, but Blaze was too riled to answer, slapping trees and sagebrush out of his way as he stormed for the creek.

"Maggie?" He stood at the rocky shore of the fast-running creek, straining to listen over the gurgle of the water and the trill of the tree frogs and crickets. "Maggie—where the devil are you?" he shouted, his pulse pounding in his ears.

"Blaze …"

He barely heard it, Maggie's call a good distance downstream. Breaking into a dead run, he leapt over rocks and boulders along the shore like a mule deer spooked within an inch of his life. And he *was* spooked—worried sick about the one woman who'd made him care more than any other. "Maggie—where are you?"

"Here …" She suddenly bolted through a thicket not 200 feet away, nearly stumbling several times before she shot straight into his arms. "Oh, Blaze …"

"It's all right, darlin'," he whispered, "I'm here now." Pressing a kiss to her hair, he quickly held her at bay to study her. "Are you hurt?"

She shook her head, dislodging tears from her eyes.

"Where's Clint?" he demanded, fingers gripped tightly to her arms.

"Right here, Boss." Clint pushed through the thicket, ambling forward to stop a few feet away from where Blaze held Maggie, his jaw as rock-hard as Blaze's.

"What did you do to her, Keller?" he snapped, Maggie's death grip to his waist the only thing stopping Blaze from tearing the cowhand apart, piece by piece.

Clint shrugged his shoulders. "Just a few kisses, Boss, nothing more."

"Only because I got here in time, no doubt." He tugged Maggie from his chest, heart squeezing at the frightened look in her eyes. "Is that true, Maggie?"

She managed a jerky nod, head bowed and gaze fixed on Blaze's boots.

"Keller, you ever touch this woman again, and you're out of a job—you got that?"

Clint nodded. "I'm sorry, Maggie—didn't mean no harm."

"Get out. And when we get back to the dance, you better be gone."

Without another word, Clint pushed past to disappear upstream, leaving Maggie whimpering in Blaze's arms.

"Let's go home," Blaze whispered.

Her head bobbed against his chest, and bundling her in his arms, he ushered her back up the shoreline, wanting nothing more than to make her hurt go away.

And his.

Because at the moment, he wasn't all that sure … which of them was aching more.

CHAPTER FORTY-SIX

THE RIDE HOME WAS SILENT. Nothing more than the grind of the wheels on the dusty road, Minx's occasional snort, or the lonely hoot of an owl that mirrored Maggie's mood completely.

Sadness.

Emptiness.

Longing.

Because although Clint's kisses had been hungry and probing like those of her former fiancé, they hadn't pushed her away from the idea of marriage like they had before. No, *this* time they had pushed her toward something that could do far more damage.

Blaze.

Her eyelids weighted closed as the wagon jostled up to the front porch of the Silver Lining Ranch, the darkened house only underscoring the painful void in her own life at the moment. A life in which she'd once been content with nothing more than her faith, her friends, and her newfound family at the ranch.

But Clint had changed all of that, confirming that the very kisses and love he'd sought from her tonight belonged to the one man who had stolen her heart.

The best friend who sat beside her.

"You tired?" he whispered, bringing the wagon to a halt while he held her close, the slow thud of his heart in perfect harmony with her own.

"No." She burrowed in, and a wonderful warmth purled through her at the touch of his lips to her hair, enveloping her in a cocoon of safety as surely as the strong arms that drew her near.

"Feel like talking, then?" His voice was husky and low, edged with the barest hint of hope.

She nodded, and he kissed her head again while a gray-bearded cowhand on watch slowly approached from the bunkhouse with rifle in hand. "Evenin', Boss—everything all right?"

"Fine, Shelby, just brought Miss Mullaney home a little early since she wasn't feeling all that well. You mind putting Minx and the wagon up for me?"

"No problem, Boss," the hand said, patiently waiting while Blaze helped Maggie down. He led the rig toward the barn while Blaze gingerly ushered Maggie up the steps to her usual rocker.

She halted him halfway, unwilling to lose the comfort of his arms. "Would you mind terribly if we"—she swallowed a gulp while nodding toward the porch swing on the far end of the deck—"sit together? It's getting chilly out, and I think I could use the warmth."

"Good idea," he said quietly, leading her to the shadowed niche of the wraparound porch where Finn and Libby had taken to sitting a spell every night after dinner. "I'm going to fetch a blanket for you, Maggie—you want anything else while I'm up? Water? Lemonade?"—a smile crept into his voice—"Butterscotch candy?"

You, her heart wanted to shout, but she merely shook her head, not sure what she was going to do with this wayward heart of hers. He disappeared into the house, and her thoughts began to race as furiously as her pulse. What should she do, she wondered? Being so close to Blaze everyday was only making the situation worse. She needed distance, and lots of it to try and temper this flame of love that he stoked with every lazy tip of his smile, every maddening twinkle in his eyes. Every touch of his lips to her hair.

She shivered, suddenly not so cold anymore.

"This has g-got to s-stop," she stuttered, staring up at a starlit sky while panic cooled the heat in her veins. "Please, God, I can't love him that way. He disdains marriage and he disdains You, so show me, please, what can I do?"

The stars winked overhead as if privy to a secret that God refused to share. Expelling a mournful sigh, Maggie slumped back into the swing, knowing full well what she needed to do.

She would leave.

Two months of the six left or no.

Move into town as soon as she possibly could.

"Here you go, Mags." Blaze draped a blanket around her, then sat and pulled her close, resting her head against his chest. "Feeling better?"

No. "Warmer, at least," she said softly, *which has nothing to do with the blanket …*

"Want to talk about you and Clint?"

No. I'd rather talk about you and me. Her chest rose and fell in a shaky sigh. "In hind sight, I think I may have made more of it than it was, so I apologize for reacting so badly."

His grunt reverberated in her ear. "In *hind* sight, Nurse Nightingale, I should kick your hind end for even stepping outside with the leche. Confound it, Maggie, I warned you he had a dangerous reputation, didn't I?"

She nodded. *And Sister Fred warned me you had one, too, but I failed to realize how much.*

"Why'd you do it, then?" Hurt threaded the gruffness of his tone. "Why'd you step outside with a womanizer like Clint Keller, much less traipse all the way down to some lonely creek?"

"I was mad at you," she whispered.

"Humph, no kidding. I tried to give you an escape by asking you to dance, but you just bit my head off in that sarcastic-sweet way of yours, pert near scorching my hide."

Escape. Maggie's throat muscles hitched several times. *If only.*

He pulled back to gently nudge her chin up with his thumb, his face so close, peppermint stirred her senses while his touch stirred her soul. "I'm your best friend, Maggie—why would you turn on me like that when you needed me the most?"

Because I needed you the most … "You danced with everyone but m-me," she said in a quivering tone that made her feel younger than Shaylee, embarrassed she couldn't stop the tears that sprang to her eyes.

"Aw, Maggie …" His voice trailed off as he bent to brush a kiss to her forehead, his lips lingering long enough to unleash an aching need in her belly. "I'm sorry, darlin', but I guess I was a little miffed at you, too, agreeing to go with Clint in the first place, so I just stayed away." His voice lowered to husky as his mouth skimmed over to nuzzle the erratic throb of her temple. "I don't like him sniffin' around."

"M-Me eith-er," she said, the words too breathless to suit while his lips moved to trace the shell of her ear.

"We're best friends, Maggie, and you belong to me, not him." His breath blew warm against her skin, kindling more fire in her belly when he began to suckle the lobe of her ear.

Oh, Blaze … The moan that escaped her merged with his when he mated his mouth to hers, their groans lost in the ecstasy of wonder and want and gentle exploration.

She gasped when he jerked away, painfully bereft of the taste of his lips. "Heaven help me, Maggie, I want you," he whispered, taking her mouth again with such gentle dominance, she had no will to say no.

"Then heaven help me, too, Blaze—because I feel the same." Her jagged breaths infused her confession into the cool desert night, warming the air between them like it was the full noon of day. Breaking the claim of his lips, she cradled a palm to his bristled jaw, hope winning over fear at the naked look of love in his eyes. "So, what do we do now?"

He stared like a man possessed, his breathing harsh and his eyes dark with desire. "I guess it means our relationship has changed, Maggie. Seems like our friendship has deepened into you being the only woman I want to see."

Her pulse stuttered. "See? Or spark?"

Even in the moonlight, she spied the ruddy rise of color up his neck as he gave her a sheepish smile, his broad shoulders lifting in a noncommittal shrug. "Can't it be both?" he said, bending in to feather the warmth of his words along the curve of her jaw.

"Already told Rachel and every other woman in this confounded town that I am not the marrying kind, so they best not get any ideas."

Could it be both? Reality skittered her spine, turning the warm chills of Blaze's touch as cold as the gust of mountain breeze that now fluttered her hair.

No, it couldn't.

With God's help, Rachel had garnered the courage to prove that and now Maggie needed to prove it too. Chest heaving, she pushed him away, scooting back while she pulled the blanket more firmly around her shoulders. "No, it can't, Blaze, because I'm respectable, remember? Any sparkin' that happens would have to be inside of a courtship, so are those your intentions?"

Blaze blinked, the hard duck of his Adam's apple a telling sign of where his so-called "intentions" lay. Removing his Stetson, he sucked in a deep draw of air, expelling it again with an unsteady scrub of unruly curls. "Well, I'm not exactly ready to court, Maggie," he said with a crimp of his brow.

"I understand, and that's absolutely no problem, truly." She stood to her feet, ignoring the ache in her chest as she clutched the blanket like a shield. "Because I'm not ready to spark either. Good night, Blaze."

He clamped a fist to her wrist, and she caught her breath, the sound of his shallow breathing keeping pace with hers. "Sit down, Maggie," he said in a dangerous tone that told her she'd pushed too close to his limit. "We need to talk."

"Fine." She nodded to the rocking chairs at the other end of the deck. "We'll talk over there, then, in separate chairs."

He glared, that hard-sculpted jaw grinding as he stared her down. "I thought you didn't want to be cold."

With a boost of her chin, she turned to march to the other side of the deck, tone tinged with a sarcasm she seldom employed. "Suddenly that doesn't seem like such a bad thing."

Taking his time, he finally rose, moonlight emphasizing the chiseled stone of his face as he followed, stopping to stand in front of the empty rocker next to hers. Lips clamped tight, he merely probed her with a penetrating gaze, hip cocked and eyes cool as if waiting for her to relent.

Steeling her jaw to match his, she shimmied in, blanket tucked protectively around her. *Likely to be a long wait, mister, so you may as well settle in.*

The breath whooshed from her lungs when he yanked her up fast, the blanket tumbled to the floor along with her stomach. He jerked her near, molding her so close, the heat of his body matched that in his eyes. "All right—we're courtin' then," he whispered in a ragged voice, and cupping the back of her head, he kissed her long and hard, his groan reaching deep inside to mingle with one of her own.

Near gasping for air, Maggie shoved him back. "We can't—you don't go to church."

He gaped, mouth dangling along with her hopes. "Blast it all, Maggie," he hissed, wildfire blazing in his eyes, "I'll go to church, then, confound it."

"You will?" Her heart took flight despite the adorable scowl on his face.

"I said so, didn't I?" He bent to kiss her again, and she pushed him away once more, determined to confirm his intent.

She peeked up with a nervous chew of her lip. "So, we're officially courting, yes?"

"Hang it all, Maggie, how the devil do you want it, in blood?"

She paused, her smile tentative. "That would be nice, but since the likelihood is completely remote, I just want you to say it as if you're actually happy."

Gaze averted, he mumbled something before he took a deep breath. "Yes, we're courting, Miss Mullaney," he said in a decidedly softer tone, his gaze gentling along with it. "I love you, Maggie—against my better judgment and great effort not to. But darlin', you gotta give me some time to get used to this because not one hour ago, we were just friends."

"*Best* friends," she whispered, reaching up to sway her mouth slowly against his, which we'll always be, Brendan Zachary Donovan, no matter how much you heat my blood."

He groaned and finished it off with an urgent kiss before sidetracking her with a playful nip of her earlobe. "So … I heat your blood, do I?" He carefully nuzzled the nape of her neck. "Just imagine what I'll be able to do with a ring on your finger …"

Swallowing hard, she distanced herself to peek up. "So, we're courting now as well as going to church together every single week, right?"

He huffed out a sigh, looping his arms loosely around the small of her back. "Yes, and yes," he said with a dry slant of a smile. He arched a thick brow. "Anything else?"

"Well …" Nibbling the edge of her smile, she stood on tiptoe to brush a tender kiss to his mouth. "Now that we're officially on the path to marriage …" She gave his lower lip a tiny tug with her teeth, quickly retreating before he could take over from there. "I don't mind a few kisses, Blaze, because it's downright pleasurable. But the kind of sparkin' I'm guessing you had with Rachel?" Softly bussing his cheek, she stepped out of his embrace and hurried toward the door, hand on the knob while delivering a secret smile. She blew him a kiss. "*That*, my adorably cocky cowboy, "belongs to a wife."

CHAPTER FORTY-SEVEN

"UNCLE FINN, CAN WE DO this again tomorrow night?" Shaylee vaulted up from the back of the wagon where she, Gert, Angus, Jake, and Sheridan sat in a bed of hay, a quick and comfortable fix for those who couldn't ride up front on the single bench. Blaze had been noticeably upset when Maggie had taken sick, so he plainly hadn't been thinking clearly when he'd inadvertently driven her home in the two-benched rig. The result was only four seats on the single bench for the rest of the family on the ride back to the ranch, so Finn had improvised with hay. His smile skewed sideways. *Obviously a wise decision.*

"Please, Uncle Finn?" Shaylee pleaded as the wagon rumbled through the front gate. It jostled the bed so much, she toppled over in a joyous shriek, falling right on top of Jake, who tickled her unmercifully.

"Sure, why not? I'm rather partial to hay." Finn grinned down at Libby as their shoulders bumped on the bench seat, giving her a wink that dusted her cheeks with a pretty moon glow. He bent close, his voice considerably lower. "Although I prefer it in a loft to a wagon, don't you, Mrs. McShane?" he whispered for her ears alone, reminding her of their first "official" kiss in the Poppy's barn loft that fateful night so many years ago.

"Oh, *yes,* another hayride, please!" Sheridan baptized Jake with more hay, only one of many handfuls over the course of the drive home, amid laughter and giggles and silly songs in the cool desert night. "I think that would be another wonderful family event."

Gert's grunt rose above the girls' laughter and Jake's mock threats, and Finn grinned as he glanced back at the O'Shea's crotchety maid. Arms in a tight fold, she bumped along with the others, her perennial scowl tipped with tease. "Followed by a family dunk in the river, no doubt, with a bar of lye to chase the chiggers."

"I must admit, it was a fun addition to the evening, this impromptu hayride, Finn," Maeve said in the front, head resting on Aiden's shoulder. "Made me feel young again," she said wistfully.

Gert cut loose with a cackle. "Crawl on back here, Mrs. Maeve, and the chiggers'll whittle off a few more years if you want, along with a little of your hide."

A shiver shook Maeve's shoulders as she glanced back into the bed, nose in a scrunch. "No thanks, Gert, too many nasty critters bedded in that hay to suit, and the smell tickles my nose."

"Cain't argue with you there on the critters *or* the smell," Gert replied, most likely with a scowl in Angus's direction.

Finn shook his head as Jake issued a warning to Sheridan. "Okay, Half-Pint—anymore hay in my face, and you're going to be wearing it home, understood?" Laughter edged his threat as more hay instantly flew in the air along with Sheridan's and Shaylee's giggles.

A veritable free-for-all broke loose just as Finn pulled the wagon in front of the house. He glanced back to see Jake laughing while he pinned Sheridan to the bed, and the sight pulled him up short, even with Shaylee wiggling on Jake's back like a batch of earthworms. As Blaze's and Dash's best friend, Jake was practically family, always wrestling and teasing with Finn's girls just like their brothers did. Only seeing Sheridan's burgeoning body beneath his hold now set off warning bells Finn hadn't heard before.

"Everybody out of the bed—*now!*" he said in a voice sterner than usual. "We're home, and everybody needs to clean up and go to bed."

Libby looked up with a slight pinch of brows. "Everything all right?" she whispered, and he released a heavy sigh, grateful she was considering staying because he sure couldn't mother these girls alone.

"Sure. Just worn out from the long day, I suppose." He hooked her waist when she started to follow the others out of the wagon, tugging her close to whisper in her ear. "Help me put the wagon up?"

She nodded, and he pressed a kiss to her hair as everyone else trudged up the porch steps laughing and yawning except Jake, who moved to stand on Finn's side of the wagon.

Nudging his hat up, Jake peered up at Finn, pieces of hay clinging to his shirt and hair. "Mr. McShane, I'll be happy to take care of Lightning and the wagon while you head on in, sir."

Finn's heart warmed as he looked at the boy who'd always been a best friend to his nephews and a gentle big brother to his nieces. Plus the closest thing to a son Finn knew other than Blaze and Dash. Any angst he'd felt over the image of him and Sheridan suddenly faded in the light of the respect and trust Finn held for this man. "No, Jake, I'll take care of it, but thanks. You get some sleep. We have some hard days ahead with the cattle drive."

"Yes, sir. Good night." Jake tipped his hat to Libby. "Ma'am."

"Good night, Jake," Libby called as Jake strolled to the bunkhouse.

With a light snap of Lightning's reins, Finn slowly exhaled as the wagon rumbled to the barn, Libby's head on his shoulder making him wish this night would never end. "Whoa, boy," he said when they were inside, hopping out to help Libby down. "Tired?" he asked, hands still wrapped around her tiny waist as he drew her closer.

"A little, but it's a good tired," she said with a relaxed smile.

"Too tired to talk awhile?" Grazing his thumb down the curve of her face, he slowly leaned in to nuzzle her neck.

"Mmm ..." Her eyes drifted closed as her head tipped to give him full access. "No, but why do I have the feeling talking's not *all* you want to do?"

He grinned and deposited a kiss to her nose. "Because you're clairvoyant?" He strolled over to turn up the oil lamp Shelby had left burning.

Her lashes flipped up as she gave him a pursed smile. "No, because I'm experienced with the likes of you, Griffin Alexander McShane, so I know what to expect."

"Ah, but not always," he said with a wink, relieving Lightning of the harness and saddle. "Talk to me, Libby, and tell me what your favorite thing was about tonight?"

Finn watched her mosey on over to perch on the fence partition of Lightning's stall, thinking she was the prettiest little thing he ever did see. "Well, other than my handsome escort ..." Hands braced to the railing, she gave him a shy smile. "I'd say attending a social function with my parents was like a dream come true. Papa would never take Mama to dances way back when, so it was a real joy to see them dancing and laughing together all night. And chatting with them, too, as if they finally realized I was all grown up."

A grin split Finn's face as he brushed Lightning with strong, firm strokes, tossing Libby a wink over his shoulder. "Oh, no doubt about that, ma'am, and anybody who can't see it is plum blind." He continued grooming while Libby chattered on, her excitement over the evening satisfying proof of just how far he and Libby had come in four short months. And if Finn had his way, the next two would be better yet.

With a quick check of Lightning's hooves, Finn led him into his stall and removed his halter, hanging it up on the wall before offering the horse an ample drink from a bucket. Closing the gate, he handed the palomino a piece of an apple from his pocket. "Here you go, boy," he said, nuzzling the horse for several seconds before ambling over to where Libby sat on the railing, absently kicking her legs.

His voice turned husky. "Now it's *your* turn," he said softly, caging her in on the fence with a wayward smile. Picking pieces of hay out of her hair, he gently grazed his lips against her temple while looping his arms around her waist. "You look good in hay as I recall." He nuzzled the nape of her neck before slowly skimming his mouth to hers for a leisurely kiss. "You know, Mrs. McShane, I do have a loft in this barn, and since we had our first kiss in one—"

"It was our *second* kiss," she corrected, pushing him back with two firm palms, a twinkle lighting her eyes. "Which taught me, sir, to never go into a hayloft with you unless I have a ring on my finger."

"Mmm ... is that so?" Tugging her from the fence, he pinned her with a shuttered look while he carried her to a wooden bench in the tack room.

"Finn!" She made a half-hearted attempt at wiggling free as he snatched a blanket and tossed it over the bench. "What are you doing?" she said, her whisper a near squeal.

"Just following orders, ma'am." He carefully set her down with a quick kiss to her cheek before reaching into his vest pocket and dropping to one knee. "Liberty Margaret O'Shea," he said as he held up a diamond ring that shimmered in the lamplight as much as the surprise in her eyes, "will you marry me?"

"Oh, Finn!" Hands folded to her mouth, she caught her breath, tears glazing her eyes as she gazed at the diamond. "It's absolutely beautiful!" A nervous giggle escaped as she stroked his raspy jaw. "But we're already married, Mr. McShane."

Turning his head, he kissed her palm. "Don't remind

me," he teased, bending in to trail his lips along the creamy lines of her throat, "Or I just may carry you up into that hayloft to stake my claim." He gave a playful tug of his teeth to the lobe of her ear before depositing a gentle kiss to her temple. "Seriously, Libby—I love you, and I think you love me, so let's start over, darlin', with a real wedding this time to renew our vows." He drew her to her feet, scooping her close while he studied her for some clue as to how she might answer, praying it would be the one he needed to hear. Heart thudding, he pressed his forehead to hers, his shallow breathing caressing her face. "So … what do you think?"

What do I think? Libby's breathing accelerated along with her pulse. The idea of renewing her vows with Finn rather than ending them turned her heart—and her plans for her life—completely upside down. Did she love him enough to say yes? She squeezed her eyes shut as she reveled in the gentle touch of his forehead to hers, the whisper of his breath fragrant with the peppermint leaves he so loved to chew. The woody scent of bay rum surrounded her like the strong arms that held her—sweet, safe, and so very secure.

Like my love for Finn, she suddenly realized.

The love that had begun over twenty-five years ago, which had ripened over the last four months through countless hours getting to know the man she'd never stopped loving.

"Say yes, Libby, please …" His voice was a pained rasp as he kissed her forehead, the warmth of his lips lowering to slowly brush each eyelid with such care and deliberation, the breath swirled still in her lungs. He nuzzled her temple, her cheek, the sensitive cup of her ear before straying to feather the soft flesh of her lobe, coaxing a soft moan from her throat that seemed to spur him on. "Now, more than ever—I need you," he whispered, finally meeting her mouth with his own.

And then, in the space of one chaotic heartbeat, it dawned, as swift and powerful as the wild beat of her heart—she needed him too! "Oh, Finn!" She lunged, returning his kiss with a fervent one of her own. "Yes!"

He jerked back to stare, hands gripped to her arms and hope stark in his eyes. "Yes?"

Chewing her lip, she gave a shaky nod.

"Oh, Libby," he whispered, gently cradling her face in his hands. Gaze intense, it was as if he made love to her with his eyes, heat purling through her when his mouth nuzzled hers with such tenderness, she all but melted into his arms. "You've just made my life complete. When?"

"Mmm?" Her lashes fluttered up as she expelled a contented sigh, too dizzy for her own good.

He grinned as he softly brushed a stray curl over her shoulder. "When do you want to get married, darlin'? Tomorrow? Next week? The week after?"

She blinked. "Tomorrow?" she said, her voice a squeak. "Good heavens, Finn, a wedding takes time, and then we still have to tell both your family and mine."

He grinned and sat down on the bench, tugging her into his lap. "How about after the election then?" He placed a soft kiss to her nose. "That will give you time to plan the wedding you want while I spend my time at campaign dinners and meetings." His mouth quirked. "Templeton is vowing to bury me and spending a boatload of money to do it, so I have some work to do in the next two months if you're going to be the mayor's wife.

Besides"—he tilted her back to leisurely trail her neck with kisses—"come our second honeymoon, I want to be able to focus on *you*, Mrs. McShane, not getting elected." He teased her mouth with gentle exploration before kissing her so deeply, she was little more than a rag doll draped over his lap. With a heavy sigh, he finally tugged her back up, gently sweeping her loose curls over her shoulder. "Ready to go in, darlin'?"

"Mmm ..." All Libby could do was blink, body dazed and tingling as always from one of Finn's kisses.

"Unless you'd rather stay ...?" he whispered, a bit of the devil in his tone as he slowly eased her back with a leisurely nibble of her lower lip. "Because I do believe I hear that loft calling ..."

"No!" Libby shot up in his lap, her breathing—and her desire—ramping up way too quickly for both of their safety. She swallowed hard, the smoky look in his eyes not boding well for her own self-control. "But two months?" Her voice cracked.

Burrowing in to nestle his mouth along the curve of her neck, he skimmed down her throat to place a delicate kiss in the very hollow of her collarbone, leaving a trail of fire on her skin that matched the one in his eyes. "I know," he whispered, his breathing suddenly as ragged as hers while he gave her a wink that bordered on wicked. "Tomorrow's sounding better all the time."

CHAPTER FORTY-EIGHT

"OH MY GOODNESS—A WEDDING!" SQUEALING loud enough to hurt Blaze's ears, Sheridan jumped up from the dinner table and scurried around to give Aunt Libby a hug while Uncle Finn beamed ear to ear.

Blaze pasted on a smile, unwilling to let anyone know—*especially* Maggie—that weddings made him flat-out sick to his stomach.

"Looks like the good Lord answered our prayers, eh, Maeve?" Aiden rose to slap Finn on the back while Maeve and Maggie joined Sheridan and Shaylee in squeezing Libby half to death.

Blaze guzzled his sarsaparilla, afraid his face was about to crack. Blue blazes, even Gert was flashing teeth as she took her turn dispensing a bear hug to Libby while Maeve and Maggie dabbed napkins to their eyes. Muffling a grunt with his own napkin, he rose from the table.

Yeah, weddings make me cry too.

"This calls for a superior dessert," Gert announced, slapping a palm to the swinging kitchen door as she lobbed a wink over her shoulder. "Mine."

Shaking his head over Gert's and Angus's ongoing game of dueling desserts, Blaze joined the crowd around Finn and Libby, offering his uncle a handshake with an off-center smile. "Now you've gone and done it, Uncle Finn, upsetting the natural balance of male dominance in this house."

Uncle Finn laughed, the hearty sound making Blaze grin outright. "It's time you learn, Brendan my boy, that male dominance is so much sweeter when the odds are even."

"Excuse me—*male dominance*?" Libby said, nose wrinkled as if she just smelled something bad. Her brows dipped in tease that somehow carried a threat. "I'd say that's a bit of a risky subject before the bride says 'I do,' Mr. McShane."

Chuckling, his uncle struck with a steel arm to Libby's waist, making her squeal when he reeled her in to bury his lips in the crook of her neck. "Just a façade, Libs, to keep my pride intact." He pressed a kiss to her cheek. "*Everybody* knows who wields the *real* power."

Humph. Blaze bit back another grunt, gaze flicking to where Maggie oohed and ahhhed over Libby's ring. He blasted out a noisy sigh.

I sure didn't know.

Till last night.

"But, Uncle Finn—why are you getting married again if you're already married?" Shaylee wanted to know, her smattering of freckles—or dirt—screwed up in a scrunch.

"Well, your aunt and I never had a real wedding the first time, Shay, so I thought it would be nice to give the love of my life the full-blown thing with all the bells and whistles right here on the ranch. Besides," he said with a wink at Aiden, "Mr. O'Shea will be footing the bill."

Aiden's laughter boomed through the house. "A small price to pay for my peace of mind, my boy, knowing my wayward daughter has *finally* come to her senses."

"Papa!" Libby gaped with an open-mouthed smile.

"Far sooner than her father, however, I'd like to point out," Maeve said with a rare smirk.

"Holy frog spit, are we inviting the whole town?" Shaylee shrieked, eyes near as big as her plate.

"It's holy matrimony, young lady," Finn corrected with a patient smile, giving Shay's neck a tweak, "and I guarantee you 'spit' has nothing to do with it."

Wanna bet? Blaze returned to his seat, not sure if his mouth was watering from the apple pie Angus was passing out or the urge to spit.

"And since nobody in town knows Libby and I are still married, we figured this is the perfect scenario to correct it. So in answer to your question, Shay, yes—the whole town will be invited."

"So, when is the wedding going to be?" Sheridan said, sliding back into her seat to dive into her dessert. "And more importantly"—she wiggled her brows—"am I going to be in it?"

"Of course, you're going to be in it," Libby said with a pinch of Sheridan's waist. "And Shay, and Maggie, and even Gert if she wants."

"Humph. Now that'd be a sight to see." Angus shook his head while toting his empty tray back to the kitchen. "Gert all gussied up for a wedding." He paused at the door to flash a gap-toothed grin. "With a fresh deck of cards."

"Move out of the way, old man." Gert bumped Angus aside to divvy out fresh-churned cinnamon ice cream with a wicked smile. "I'm guessin' that tasteless pie of yours needs a little help with the dad-burned best ice cream in the state, judging by our last barbecue."

With a tug of the apron towel around his waist, Angus stomped over to swipe a finger into the crock, rolling the ice cream around on his tongue with a scowl." He gummed his lips with eyes closed before scanning the table with a narrow look. "Humph—she's right, dad-gum-it." Blasting out a noisy sigh, he barreled through the swinging door, leaving Gert staring after him with a slack of her jaw.

Finn raised his coffee with a wide grin. "Looks like love is in the air all around."

"Bite your tongue," Gert muttered under her breath while she slopped ice cream onto Finn's pie.

"Uh … speaking of love in the air," Maggie began, and

Blaze's body froze colder than the ice cream on his plate. *No, she wouldn't, would she?* He stared at her across the table, the shy smile flickering on her lips a dead giveaway that *yes,* she would. Her gaze met his and the smile bloomed into a grin as she put a hand to her lips, unable to thwart the tiny giggle that slipped out. "Blaze and I are courting."

Dead silence. Blaze stopped breathing. *Dead pulse.*

Squeeeeeeeeeeal! Sheridan was up once again, and Blaze was pretty sure her shriek of excitement damaged his ear drum as his sister pulled Maggie up from her chair. Gripping hands, the two of them jumped up and down like two tree frogs pouncing on a cache of crickets.

"Oh my goodness, Maggie—just think! We'll become sisters when you're Blaze's wife!"

Wife.

The ice cream rose in Blaze's throat, freezing his vocal cords.

"I know," Maggie said with a reverence that chilled Blaze to the bone. Those innocent hazel eyes that had taken him down met his with a soft look, glowing more than the confounded candles on the blasted table. "And there's more good news ..."

More? Blaze blinked, his lungs suddenly out of air.

"More?" Sheridan said with a joyous clasp of hands. "Goodness, Maggie, not sure how you're going to top a wedding with my brother!"

Wedding? Blaze started to hack, lunging for his sarsaparilla.

Dash slapped him on the back with a chuckle. "Slow down, big brother, you'll get to the altar soon enough.

Maggie peeked around the table with a tug of her teeth to her lip, her voice literally quivering with joy. "Blaze has agreed to ..."

He started quivering too.

" ... go back to church," she finished with a soft hush that pretty much finished him off too, his eyelids slamming closed, tighter than a pitch-sealed coffin.

"Son, that's wonderful news!" Uncle Finn said, rising to give Blaze a warm hug. He slapped him on the back while Dash just sat there grinning wider than a hyena in a bowl of bunnies. His uncle circled the table to give Maggie a hug. "I've been trying to get that boy's butt in a pew for too many years now, Maggie, but obviously you have a whole lot more pull."

Pull? Blaze managed a stiff smile as he sent Maggie a taut look. *The word is "drag."*

"I say this calls for a toast," Finn said as he returned to his seat, raising his drink in the air while everyone at the table followed suit. "To Libby and Maggie—two women who have changed two die-hard bachelors for the better." He gave Dash a wink. "Two down, and one to go, eh, Dash?"

Shaking his head with a chuckle, Dash countered with one palm in the air, toasting his glass with the other. "No thank you, gentlemen—somebody in this family has to fight the good fight, so I'll gladly wear the mantle of bachelorhood forever."

"That's good, Dash," his uncle said with a wink, "because you're gonna need that mantle to keep you warm in the winter, isn't that right, Blaze?"

Blaze forced a smile as chuckles filled the room, joining in as Uncle Finn made his toast to his and Blaze's demise. *Warm?* He gulped his sarsaparilla, almost wishing it were the coffin varnish they served at the Ponderosa. He glugged it all down as if it could drown his troubles, unable to stop his tightly wrought smile from twisting into a frown.

Then why do I feel so cold?

CHAPTER FORTY-NINE

CLANG!

Hand over her eyes, Maggie peeked through her fingers, her silent groan in stark contrast to the whoops and hollers of Blaze and Finn while Aiden, Dash, Jake and Angus whistled them on from the back porch.

"I'm *so* sorry, Maggie," Libby whispered, her voice as gloomy as the dark shadows of night that crept over the mountains, the pink glow of dusk fading along with Maggie's hope.

Maggie gave her a quick hug. "It's just a silly game, Aunt Libby, so please don't worry about it, all right?" She swallowed hard. *That's my job.*

"Better luck next time, ladies," Finn called with a wink at Aunt Libby, who nervously picked at her nails while she offered Maggie a repentant look.

Maggie mustered a weak smile. She'd need a whole lot more than luck with Blaze winning their secret contest from the night before ...

"How 'bout we celebrate our two months of courtship with a moonlight picnic?" he'd whispered in her ear last night, the warmth of his lips on her neck making her wish she'd sat in the rocker instead of the swing.

"How 'bout a noonday picnic instead?" she countered, knowing full well that darkness would not serve her well in her efforts to keep Blaze from pursuing his ongoing quest for serious sparkin'.

He'd nibbled her ear, tumbling her stomach along with her willpower. "Why don't we let a game of horseshoes decide?" He deposited a kiss to her nose, as if to soften the threat of the damage his lips could do. "You've beat me the last few games after all, and you can even team up with Sheridan if you like and I'll take Finn, so what do you think?"

What did she think? *Alert! Alert! Alert!* A warning sign blinked in her mind, telling her this probably wasn't a good idea. She scooted away ... "I don't think so, Blaze—"

"Look, Mags, you and Sheridan are practically unbeatable, and if I win"—he ducked to stare in her eyes, finger tucked to her chin—"which is *highly* unlikely since you've beat me every night this week—"I'll give you anything you want."

She cocked her head, assessing him with a leery eye. "Anything?"

He placed a hand to his heart, his little-boy smile trampling her defenses. "*Anything.*"

Gnawing her lip, she considered his offer, thinking it would be sheer heaven not to have to be the strong one when he melted her bones with a kiss. And frankly, she was getting tired of being the one who took this courtship so seriously, as a pathway to a deep and abiding marriage rather than just a reason to spark. She studied his handsome face with a keen eye, knowing full well he'd buck like a thorn-saddled mule if she limited him to one goodnight kiss on the porch, but if she won with those terms, what choice did he have?

And frankly, what choice did *she* have? Since the night he agreed to courtship two months ago, he'd been so very loving and attentive. But there was no denying a subtle thread of resistance in him she couldn't quite put her finger on. All she knew was that it manifested itself in his growing persistence to push Maggie beyond her boundaries whenever they were alone. And *this* little wager might just be her answer. After all, with Sheridan on her team—who had fine-tuned her skills even more than Maggie—how could she lose?

"All right, you have a deal." She held out her hand, and he shook it with a wide grin. *Right before* he hauled her into his arms with another belly barnstorm of a kiss. Gasping for breath, she distanced him with shaky palms to his chest. "If I win, one kiss per day," she rasped, chest pumping for air, "and no outings alone, including the front and back porch."

"*What?*" He launched to his feet so fast, she bobbled on the swing. Slapping hands to his hips, he leaned in with a tic in his temple. "You can't be serious—we're courting for pity's sake, Maggie."

She shot up as well, arms barricaded to her waist. "I assure you I am, Blaze. The question is, are *you*?"

"What's that supposed to mean?"

The smile dissolved on her face. "It means I'm starting to wonder if we're courting because you love me or because you want me."

He turned away, gouging a hand through his hair. "Hang it all, Maggie, why can't it be both?"

Her heart sank a little, along with her hopes. "Because true love doesn't seek its own," she said quietly, praying he would understand the kind of love she longed for, "it surrenders it."

He scowled, looking so much like a petulant little boy, she was tempted to tousle his hair. "Blast it all, what happened to good ol' give and take?" he groused.

"Oh, it's alive and well, Blaze, I promise." She stood on tiptoe to gently brush a kiss to his cheek, her smile tender as she cupped his stubbled jaw. "And I'll prove it tomorrow when I win at horseshoes, cocky cowboy." Patting his cheek, she'd given him a smug smile. "When I 'give' the rules and you 'take' them seriously."

"Maggie?" Libby's whisper jolted her back to Blaze's

cocky smile as he shook Finn's hand across the way. "I wish Sheridan could have been your partner, sweetheart," she said with a wring of her hands, obviously upset she'd lost Maggie the game. Although Maggie hadn't told her the terms, her aunt had known how much this contest had meant between her and Blaze. Her aunt sighed as she gave Maggie another hug. "Honestly, who knew Jake was taking her and Shaylee into town to spend the night with the Edwards girls, Connie Michele and Laurie Mae?"

Maggie's eyes narrowed as she peered at Blaze over her aunt's shoulder, his and Finn's laughter a little too loud as they headed Maggie's way.

One guess.

"Good game, ladies," Blaze said with a wink at Maggie. He leaned close to her ear, the warmth of his whispered words giving her cold chills. "Just not good enough, Nightingale."

"Who wants seconds on dessert?" Gert called from the back door, and a crescendo of male assent rose to the sky as they all filed inside.

All but one.

Ushering Libby to the house, Finn turned when Blaze and Maggie didn't follow. "Aren't you two coming? I would have thought you worked up quite an appetite after three do-or-die games."

Maggie gulped. *Well, I suspect one of us did …*

"Nope," Blaze said with a loose hook of Maggie's waist, "I promised Maggie a picnic."

Finn glanced up at the darkening sky. "In the dark?"

"No sir, by lamplight and moonlight, just inside the barn by the door." Blaze gave a sheepish shrug of his shoulders. "Gert packed us a basket with dessert."

"Why, that sounds very romantic!" Libby said with a bright smile. She glanced up at Finn with a twinkle in her eye. "Maybe you can teach your uncle a thing or two."

Maggie swallowed a gulp. *Oh, no doubt about that …*

Finn's smile took a tilt. "Sure, Blaze, make me look bad, why don't you!" He shook his head as he led Libby up to the porch, turning at the top step. Eyes in a squint, he pointed a finger at his nephew. "Don't be too late, son, and make sure you're on your best behavior, understood?"

"Yes, sir," Blaze said with a sharp nod, "you have my word." With a light squeeze of Maggie's waist, he guided her in the direction of the barn.

His best behavior. Maggie sucked in a deep breath. But by whose definition?

His or mine?

CHAPTER FIFTY

"CLOSE YOUR EYES, DARLIN'," BLAZE whispered, the touch of Maggie's skin like silk as he grazed a gentle finger down her cheek. He carefully pressed her shoulders to the wall at the end of the barn while the moon kept guard, its soft light highlighting the nervous nibble of her lip. The comforting scent of horses and hay filled the air until Blaze stepped in closer, his senses suddenly heady with the clean scent of lavender and Maggie. Somewhere an owl hooted, harmonizing with the cadence of crickets and katydids to create a summer symphony he hoped would ease the worry lines in Maggie's brow.

Reaching into his pocket, he pulled out a butterscotch candy and tenderly pressed it against her lips, the catch of her breath slowly blooming into a beautiful smile as she opened her eyes.

"You've been to Mort's," she whispered, the glow of the moon dancing in her eyes. Gaze sparkling, she quickly sucked the candy from his hand, and a slow fire ignited when her mouth grazed his finger. "I've been lost for weeks since Mort's supply ran out."

"I know." He leaned in to tenderly fondle her lips with his own, the taste of butterscotch and Maggie calling him home. "And I've been lost for years and didn't know it until I met you."

Her husky giggle tickled his lips as he opened his eyes, an impish smile teasing him while she sucked on the candy.

"Excuse me, sir, but I believe it was your clothes that were lost."

Grinning, he dove for her neck with a growl, eliciting a tiny squeal as her shoulders lifted in a scrunch. "Oh, that's right," he said, suddenly lost in the clean scent of her skin as he buried tiny kisses at the nape of her neck, "you were responsible for one of the greatest humiliations of my life, Nurse Flo, so perhaps you should make amends."

Her chuckle was pure mischief as she nudged him away. "Oh no, you did that all on your own, mister, so perhaps the amends need to be made to everyone who saw you traipsing around town in that sheet …" Her neck bobbed as she swallowed the candy and held out her hand. "More, please, because I believe you owe me for the most games won this week."

He tucked another candy into her mouth with a wayward grin, finger lingering to skim her lower lip "Ah, yes, but I believe you have a debt as well, yes?"

The smile faded, and he pressed a gentle kiss to her nose. "Maggie, I love you," he whispered, cradling her face in his hands, "and I would never hurt you." He cupped the back of her neck, grazing his thumb against the nape as he searched her face with a tender gaze. "Don't you know that?"

She gave a jerky nod, but the knot that ducked in her throat told a different story, dimming his good mood. All he wanted was to spend some time alone with her, hold her …

Her stomach growled and a pretty blush dusted her cheeks as she moved to the moonlit space just outside the barn door. She turned to face him with a tentative smile, hands clasped in expectation. "So … where's our picnic?"

He strolled forward and twined his hand with hers, grinning while he led her to a ladder she'd never noticed before. "It's waiting for us up in the hayloft … *along* with a bag of butterscotch, so shall we?"

He motioned to the ladder, but she merely took a step back, arms to her waist. "Blaze, I'm … not sure this is such a great idea …"

"Maggie." He placed his hands on her shoulders with a sober look. "It's a simple picnic of dessert and lemonade and a bag of butterscotch, darlin'." He ducked to peer into her eyes with a tender look. "I just want to spend time alone with you, that's all. Is that so wrong?"

She gave him a shaky smile. "Well, no … as long as you're on your best behavior like you promised Finn …"

"Yes, ma'am." Hand over his heart, he gave her a solemn look despite the tug of a smile, thinking she was so darn cute when she was suspicious.

Her bodice rose and fell. "All right." She wagged a stern finger in his face despite the hint of a twinkle in her eye, "but if you don't, just remember it's a hard fall from the loft window to the ground."

He grinned while he guided her with a hand to her back. "Yes, ma'am."

The evening was all he hoped it would be. Maggie's gasp of a surprise when she'd seen the quilt he'd laid out by the window—complete with wild flowers in a canning jar and a shaft of moonlight—made his heart near burst with pride. The candle lantern he'd lit and placed next to the flowers flickered and danced like the merriment in her eyes as they talked and laughed while eating Gert's cobbler. He'd never gone to this much trouble for any woman, but then Maggie wasn't just any woman he'd realized over the last month—she was the one he intended to marry.

Eventually.

"More cobbler?" he asked when she'd finished her second piece, packing up the tin of remaining dessert and crock of lemonade in the basket Gert had put together.

She waved him off with a palm to her stomach, handing him her fork and plate. "Goodness, I couldn't eat another thing, Blaze, honestly."

"Now why do I find that so hard to believe?" he said with a grin, tucking her dirty dishes away before plopping a bag of butterscotch in front of her with a wicked grin.

She giggled as she fumbled with the tie on the small burlap bag. "I guess you know me a little too well."

"That I do, Nightingale." He set the basket, flowers, and lantern aside in order to scoot over and stretch out on the blanket beside her, head propped on his elbow. His tone lowered to husky as he nodded to the bag of candy, his gaze never leaving her face. "Just like I know I want to spend the rest of my life supplying you with butterscotch, Maggie, if you'll let me."

"Oh, Blaze …" A sweet smile trembled on her lips while she untied the bag the rest of the way, and digging her fingers in, she gasped as she reached for a candy. "What in the world …?" Mouth agape, she pulled out the little velvet box he'd tucked inside.

"It belonged to my grandmother." His voice was almost reverent as he reached to graze a finger across the soft green velvet of the antique jewelry box. Finn had given it to him when he'd graduated from college to keep for his future wife. "Open it," he whispered.

Her fingers shook as she lifted the lid, and instantly, another gasp popped out.

"Uncle Finn said I should give it to the woman I intended to marry one day, so I am." Carefully lifting his grandmother's silver cross and necklace from the box, he rose to kneel behind Maggie, gently brushing her silky hair aside before grazing a kiss to her nape. He clasped the jewelry around her neck.

"Oh, Blaze …" She spun around to throw her arms around him, nearly melting his heart when she burrowed into him with tears in her eyes. "It's beautiful!"

"Maybe," he said with a light skim of his thumb across her lips, "but it can't hold a candle to the woman wearing it." He bent in to nuzzle her mouth, the taste of her making him wish he could marry her tomorrow. But just as quickly, a sudden shiver cooled some of the heat flashing through him, reminding him of one very important fact.

I'm just not ready.

Jumping up, he placed several hay bales close to the window, then draped part of the quilt over them so they could sit and savor the stars. He extended a hand. "Sit with me, Maggie? I know it's getting late and we need to go in, but I'd love to just hold you for a while."

Fingering the silver cross around her neck, she nodded and settled in beside him, cuddling close when he draped an arm around her shoulder. Her wispy sigh floated between them as they studied the silver-white orb in the sky. "Why is it that moonlight calms me down, making everything seem so still and serene?" she whispered.

A chuckle rumbled from his lips as he leaned close to feather her ear, giving her lobe a gentle tug. "Funny, it does the exact opposite for me." The clean scent of lavender roused his senses as her warmth seeped into his body, and all at once, his pulse kicked up, luring his mouth to the soft skin of her throat. "Hang it all, Maggie, you smell so darn good ..."

"Blaze, maybe we should—" She turned to face him, and he claimed her mouth with a slow and tender kiss meant to convey just how much he cared, taking his time to touch and taste with a reverence he'd never felt for a woman before.

A tiny mew escaped her, and the sound made him forget all about his promise to his uncle, stoking the embers of a fire restrained far too long. A smoldering heat purled through his body he suddenly had no will to deny, and holding her face in his hands, he kissed her again, barely aware when he eased her down on the blanket.

"So help me, Maggie, I'm crazy about you," he whispered, voice hoarse as he lost himself in the silky curve of her neck, grazing her skin with the softest of kisses. "Sweet angels in heaven, I can't wait to marry you!" His breathing accelerated as he pulled her body flush, their moans colliding when he devoured her mouth once again, desperate to explore.

She broke away with chest heaving. "When?" she rasped, swollen lips emitting shallow air.

His own breathing was harsh as he stared, her question quickly dousing the fire inside. "What?"

She placed a trembling hand to his cheek, searching his face as her ragged breathing mingled with his. "I can't wait to marry you either, Blaze, so when?"

He swallowed hard, his Adam's apple hitching several times as he gently swept stray hair from her face. "Come on, Maggie, we've only been courting two months, darlin', and you already want more?"

A sheen of moisture glimmered in her eyes as she slowly sat up. "Yes, I do, Blaze, just like you, only it seems the 'more' we both want entails different things."

Blasting out his frustration, he sat up as well, slashing a hand through his hair. "Look, Maggie, I don't know what more you want from me. I go to church with you, I court you, I follow your rules—what more do you want?"

"A commitment to a wedding date would be nice," she whispered, the very lips he'd caressed before now trembling as she pleaded with her eyes. "One that tells me I matter more than your desire for kisses, Blaze, and more than your fear of marriage and God."

His laugh was harsh as he shook his head. "You want too much too soon—I'm just not ready for that.

Moisture welled in her eyes, cramping his gut. "And therein lies my greatest fear," she said, her whispered words as broken as she. "That you might never be." He watched in disbelief as she unclasped the necklace with shaky fingers, laying it on the blanket.

He gripped her wrist before she could rise to her feet, his ribcage constricting. "What the devil are you doing,

Maggie? I told you I love you and want to marry you, just not right away, so what in blazes is so wrong with that?"

"What's wrong with that?" she repeated, offering a sad smile as she motioned a hand between them. "*This* is what's wrong with that. The moonlight, the blanket, the kisses that disarm me until I want to give you all the love that I have." She shuddered as she gently removed her wrist from his hold. "I can't afford that, Blaze." She stood up, hand quivering as she dusted bits of hay from her skirt. "It's just too hard."

He jumped up to pull her into his arms. "No more lofts, then. We'll do it your way from now on, I promise."

"Oh, Blaze, how I wish that you could!" she said with a sadness that tore at his gut. "But 'my way' is *His* way, and I realize now that our commitment is not even remotely the same. 'Choose a man of deep faith,' my mother once told me, 'for a strand of three cords is not quickly broken,' and now I finally understand what she meant."

Hackles rising, he shifted, dropping his hold to prop hands low on his lips. "What in tarnation is that supposed to mean?"

"It means that both of us were right, Blaze." Her rib-cage expanded and contracted with a weary sigh while she cupped his jaw with a gentle palm, her smile as tender as her tone. "I didn't want to fall in love with you anymore than you wanted to fall in love with me, because we knew how different we were. You aren't the marrying kind, and I'm too respectable to do it any other way. But it would appear that neither of us had a whole lot of say. So," she said with another heavy exhale, "I fell so hard for you that I was bound and determined to make it work."

Her hand dropped from his face as she stepped away, chilling his skin as much as her words chilled his soul. "But over the last few months, the more that you kiss me like you do"—her eyes flickered closed as a knot ducked in her throat—"the more I want to do it your way and give you my all, and I can't help but worry that if we wait too long"—tears brimmed in her eyes as her voice lowered to a bare whisper—"I will."

"Come on, Maggie," he said quietly, "you know I would never take it that far."

"No, Blaze, I don't know that, and to be honest, I fear that until you fully commit to God, you'll never be able to fully commit to me."

His jaw dropped. "So that's what this is about then? My faith in God or lack of it?"

"I think so," she whispered. "Because although I love you and everything about the Silver Lining Ranch, sometimes love doesn't have a silver lining. Like now, when I suddenly realize I have a choice to make. Between a man I want to give everything to … and a God who's given everything to me."

Hissing a muttered curse, he turned away, fury and feelings for Maggie warring in his mind. She was giving him an ultimatum just like his mother had with his father, just like so-called Christian women did when they wanted complete control over a man. Anger surged as he spun to face her, bludgeoning a finger right in her face. "Don't do this, Maggie," he said. "You're the only woman I want and I love you, but don't force my hand like my mother did to my father."

Tears brimmed as she shook her head, spilling down a face laden with grief. "No, Blaze, I would never do that," she whispered, "because I love you too much."

Relief coursed through his veins as he took a step forward. "So, what does that mean for us, then, Maggie—are we betrothed? Friends? Lovers? What?"

She shook her head as she moved toward the ladder, stunning him when she turned to give him the saddest of smiles. "None of those, I'm afraid," she whispered, her stark look of love blurred by a sheen in her eyes. "It means we're over."

CHAPTER FIFTY-ONE

"ARE YOU NERVOUS?" LIBBY ASKED, straightening the four-in-hand silk tie she picked out for Finn's election eve debate. Adjusting the wing-tip collar of his pinstripe shirt, she stood back to admire his stylish blue sack suit, thinking if women had the vote, the man could win on looks alone.

"Naw." He deposited a kiss to her nose before surveying himself in the full-length mirror of the bride's room at St. Mary's in the Mountains Catholic Church, the venue for the mayoral debate. She smiled when he attempted to tug his collar a bit looser, thinking that after the election tomorrow, Finn McShane would just have to get used to wearing suits again. Hooking an arm to her waist, he drew her close to his side to wink at her in the mirror. "Once all the men get a gander at you, Libby, nobody'll be paying any attention to me."

She studied their image in the glass, pleased that her new red feathered hat matched Finn's tie quite well, the white lace ruffles of her best silk blouse a perfect complement to both her navy silk dress and Finn's well-tailored suit. She waggled her brows, her smile more than a little proud. "Trust me, Mr. McShane, once women get the vote, you'll never lose another election."

He scooped her up, diving for her neck with a growl. "Are you implying that I'm going to lose *this* one?"

"Ahem." Her father waltzed into the room with Senator

Jones and John Piper, one brow jagged high in jest. "There's plenty of time for that after the wedding, McShane—you have an election to win first."

Libby slipped her arm through Finn's. "Goodness, Papa, I'd say it's already won," she said with a wide smile, "and once Finn helps women get the vote, he'll never lose, isn't that right, Senator Jones?" She beamed at the man Finn had claimed was a proponent for the suffrage resolution in the Nevada senate.

As if he hadn't heard her question, the senator glanced at his pocket watch with a pinch of silver brows. "We should be going, Finn—the debate begins in ten minutes, and there's a full house."

The smile faded on Libby's face as the senator completely ignored her question, turning instead to confer with her father and John Piper. She glanced up at Finn, and her stomach immediately swooped when he avoided her gaze with another check in the mirror. "Finn?"

"Mmm?" He gave a firm tug to both of his cuffs, turning sideways to assess the lay of his coat.

Moving to stand in front of him, she forced him to look her in the eyes with a palm to his chest. "Why didn't Senator Jones answer my question?" she whispered for his ears alone, deathly afraid to hear the wrong answer.

Shooting a quick glance at the men across the room, Finn made great show of checking his watch. "He probably didn't hear you, sweetheart, with everything on his mind." He dismissed her with a gentle kiss to her forehead. "Libby, you best head on over to The Gold Hill now for dessert and tea with Maggie and your mother. Maggie said she'd park the rig in the back to wait for you, so just head down this hall the opposite way we came in and exit the back door, all right?"

Libby could feel her Irish rising, still miffed that she couldn't attend this important event in Finn's career despite his sensible rationale. "Debates tend to be overly rowdy and loud with a very unsavory element, darlin'," he'd explained patiently, "and few women ever attend. So, it's safer for you to enjoy your evening with Maggie and your mother."

She huffed out a sigh. "I suppose, but it's situations just like this, Finn, that makes me glad you're a proponent for women's rights." She lifted on tiptoe to press a kiss to his cheek. "Women need to be involved in the process, and I'm counting on you to help change that, so promise me you will."

"I promise, Libby." He caressed the side of her face, the intensity in his eyes calming her somewhat. "But you have to trust me in the process to do what I think is best, all right?"

Swallowing her concern in a hard lump, she slowly nodded, convincing herself that Finn was on her side.

"Good." He ducked to stare into her eyes with a somber look. "Never forget, darlin', that I love you, and everything I do, I do for a reason, and always with you in my mind." He brushed a gentle kiss to her mouth. "Say one for me, all right?"

"Of course." She forced a smile as she moved to the door, nodding at the other men before silently slipping into the hall. She sucked in a deep breath and started for the back door, stopping halfway when she realized she'd left her reticule behind. Backtracking to the room, she froze at the mention of her name.

"Now, you're sure Libby won't be in the auditorium?" The sound of John Piper's voice caused a sick feeling in her stomach.

But not as sick as Finn's answer ...

"I'm sure. She's on her way to dinner at The Gold Hill, so everything is under control."

Under control. Libby sank back to the wall outside the room, eyes flickering closed as her palms pressed hot against the wood paneling.

"It better be." Her father's voice was gruff. "Templeton has spent a ton of money in the last few weeks, and the race has tightened up, so the slightest slip-up can derail you completely. And rumor has it he's stirring the troops regarding the suffrage resolution in both houses, so he'll definitely be bringing that up. Libby doesn't need to be anywhere near this debate because her views *cannot* factor into this election, Finn, is that clear?"

"Perfectly. And there's nothing to worry about, Aiden. I'm in control here, not Libby, so she will be fine."

"I hope so," Senator Jones said in a tone as heavy as Libby's heart. "We need to go."

Nearly gasping for air, Libby darted into the closest room until the men passed by, their laughter echoing in the hall. She sagged against the door with a hand to her mouth, her body as shaken as the marriage she had hoped to have.

"I'm in control here, not Libby, so she will be fine," Finn had said, but he was wrong.

She would never be fine again.

CHAPTER FIFTY-TWO

MAGGIE PEEKED INTO THE CROWDED auditorium with a kink in her brow, wondering where on earth Aunt Libby was. The debate was ready to start, and the room was abuzz with activity, the laughter and salty language more like a saloon than a church basement.

Rising on tiptoe, she scanned the room more thoroughly, but other than a sprinkling of men's wives here and there and a few saloon girls standing with Dash and Blaze at the back, the room was wall-to-wall men.

Her gaze suddenly connected with Blaze's, and she immediately froze, the cold look in his eyes the same one he'd worn since she'd broken their courtship off three days ago. She attempted a feeble smile, but he only turned away to talk to one of the saloon girls, his jaw hard as rock.

Maggie sighed, the awful ache in her heart reminding her she could no longer stay at the ranch. It was just as well. The six months were up and the O'Shea's would be moving back into their new house soon, so Maggie needed to move on too. As far from Blaze Donovan as she could possibly get so she could heal her heart.

But would it be far enough?

Someone tapped her on the shoulder, and Maggie spun around, hand to her chest. "Oh my goodness, Aunt Libby, I've been looking for you everywhere! Your mother's waiting out back for us in the rig."

"You two go on, Maggie," her aunt said, the red rims

of her eyes giving Maggie pause. Libby's gaze flicked to where Finn was shaking hands with his opponent on stage. "I lost my appetite, sweetheart, so I thought I'd just stay and watch the debate."

Boom. Boom. Boom. A gavel pounded as Maggie tucked an arm to Aunt Libby's waist. "Are you all right?" she whispered, giving her aunt a light squeeze.

Her aunt offered a sideways smile that wavered a bit too much for Maggie's liking. "No, darling, but we can talk later, all right?"

Applause drew their attention back to the stage where Editor Milo Parks was welcoming everyone and introducing the two candidates. "And finally, I would like to thank Father Murray for the use of St. Mary's auditorium for what I believe is a vital event in the history of our great city." More cheers and foot-stomping resounded as Milo explained the format and rules for the debate.

"But where are you going to sit?" Maggie studied the room where every seat was taken, along with any standing room as groups of rowdy men lined the walls.

Libby nodded to a side back door. "I plan to listen in the hallway with the door cocked. I found a crate in the closet I can sit on," she said with a pat of Maggie's arm, "so you and my mother go and have a good time."

"But we can't leave you here all alone!" Maggie clutched her aunt's hand before she could get away, suddenly losing her appetite as well.

Aunt Libby smiled and waved a hand toward the crowd, but there was no joy in her face. "I'm not alone, Maggie. I'm here with hundreds of mules who only want to silence a woman's voice, but I don't intend to let them."

"Tonight's debate will be a town-hall format," Milo said from the stage, "in which the audience will have the opportunity to pose questions to the candidates following individual addresses by both. Mr. Templeton will have five minutes to speak first, followed by Mr. McShane, and we ask you to hold your applause to the end of each candidate's speech. Shall we begin?" Motioning George Templeton to the podium, Milo smiled and shook his hand.

"Yes, let's," Aunt Libby said before depositing a kiss to Maggie's cheek. "Hurry on, darling; I'll be there as soon as I'm done."

"Oh no, I'm not going anywhere without you, Aunt Libby, and I'm pretty sure Maeve will feel the same. So, you just go and set up two more crates in the hall, and we'll be there shortly."

"Maggie, please, you don't have to—"

But Maggie was already on her way, worried sick about what Aunt Libby might do. Explaining the situation to Maeve, both agreed that Libby needed company, so the three of them perched on crates in the hall with the door ajar while Finn's opponent spoke first.

Considerably older than Finn, George Templeton was a cunning and politically savvy banker who, according to Aunt Libby, was not above spreading rumors to discredit his opponents. And, apparently, he had done just that in the last week according to Finn, cutting his lead with a rumor Finn wouldn't share with her or Aunt Libby.

But it didn't take long to discover what it was.

"During the seventies," Templeton boomed, "Virginia City was heralded as the most important city between Denver and San Francisco. As one of the oldest settlements in the great state of Nevada, we were hailed as the richest city in the nation." He paused to survey the audience, his silver hair gleaming in the light like the ambition in his eyes. "But no more. In the last ten years, we've seen a decline in our prosperity, a decline in our civil importance, and a decline in our traditions. Traditions that made our city great but which some"—he cast a smug look in Finn's direction—"would now like to abandon for the sake of the minority."

Dissent rumbled through the crowd as Templeton

slammed a fist to the podium. "This great city was built on the backs of miners, railroad workers, and businessmen like myself, and I say it's time we return to that grand era. An era when real men ruled with a silver fist, silencing those who would like to steal our voice."

Most of the room shot up with thunderous whoops and whistles and stamping of feet. Maggie's cheeks grew warm, painfully aware that she, Aunt Libby, Maeve, and likely a small scattering of other females were some of the few people who didn't agree.

When Finn took the podium, all three women watched through a wide crack of the door as murmurs and mumbling still thrummed beneath the applause. The tension in the room was as tight as Finn's smile, and with a deep clear of his throat, the man whom Maggie had come to respect more than any other finally addressed the crowd.

Before Aunt Libby had made amends with her husband, she'd claimed Finn could charm fleas off a dog. Listening to the rumblings of the crowd, Maggie prayed he could do the same with men who spit chaw and had whiskey on their breath.

"It would seem my opponent here believes we should look back," Finn said with a serious scan of the crowd, "but those who are mired in the past, have no vision for the future. A future that I believe should not only embrace the heritage of our past, but seek out the benefits of a grand future in step with a great nation that is doing the same."

Clutching Libby's hand in a white-knuckled grasp, Maggie could barely breathe, the air in her throat shallow and unsteady through most of Finn's speech. But when he made his final statement, she was certain her lungs stopped altogether when both she and Libby gasped.

"And so, in summation," he said with a sober search of the room, "I want to assure the constituency of Virginia City that first and foremost, my allegiance lies with every man in this city, and that as your mayor, my voice will be governed by *your* voice in all issues critical to you and our great municipality. Thank you."

The room exploded in ovation as everyone shot to their feet, leaving Maggie, Libby, and Maeve sitting like statues in the hall. Hand still clasped in her aunt's, Aunt Libby's grip was as hard as stone and just as cold.

Not unlike, no doubt, the boulder Finn's words had sent plunging into Aunt Libby's gut. Maggie snuck a peek at her aunt out of the corner of her eye, alarmed at the pallor of Libby's skin and the iron thrust of her jaw as she stared at the stage. Never had she seen a more passionate woman on behalf of women's rights than her aunt, and she was certain the nerve quivering in Libby's jaw did not fare well for her candidate of choice.

Maggie swallowed a knot of nerves.

Or "former" candidate of choice, if the crush of Libby's hand meant what Maggie feared.

Boom. Boom. Boom. Milo settled the crowd with a warning bang of the gavel once again while the air remained as charged as the vibrations of his mallet. "A hearty thanks to both of our candidates for their eloquent words, and now we will hear from the audience. If you wish to ask a question, please raise your hand, and if you are called, please state to whom you wish to address your question or comment."

Maggie's stomach plunged when her aunt pushed through the half-open door, her hand shooting up like Milo's gavel, poised to produce an even louder noise. But her worries were unfounded when Milo bypassed Libby over and over, calling on man after man to pose their questions despite Libby waving her hand.

When Milo concluded the audience participation of the debate with a crack of his gavel, Maggie felt her chest slowly deflate in relief. It was no secret Aunt Libby had a hair-trigger temper, especially when it came to women's rights, so Finn had obviously had the foresight to have Milo monitor all questions. The last thing Finn or Libby needed was a free-for-all shouting match that could destroy both their relationship and his career. Sucking in a deep draw of air, Maggie slowly released it again …

Until Libby snatched it away with a loud voice that siphoned all blood from her face.

And Finn's.

"Excuse me, Mr. Parks," her aunt said from the back of the room, "but I have a question for Candidate McShane, if I may."

Flushing as red as Finn was pale, Milo offered a smile that was more of a grimace. "Sorry, Miss O'Shea, but we can only allow a limited number of questions, and I'm afraid our time is spent."

Templeton gave a gruff clear of his throat, obviously trying to stifle a grin with a cough to his fist. "I certainly don't mind staying a few minutes longer if Mr. McShane doesn't. After all, who better to reveal the true heart of a man than the woman he plans to marry?"

Finn's gaze collided with Maggie's as she stood beside her aunt, shouts of assent ricocheting all over the room. His eyes burned into hers as he gave a slight shake of his head, begging her intervention.

Maggie clutched a palm to Libby's arm, a plea in her voice as she leaned to whisper in her aunt's ear. "Aunt Libby, *please*, let's leave now before trouble breaks out."

"I'm afraid it already has, darling," Libby said with a stiff pat of Maggie's hand, the firm clamp of her jaw not boding well for one of the candidates on stage. Pulling her arm from Maggie's hold, she jutted her chin with a gaze as thin as the tight press of her lips. "And I'm afraid it's wearing a red hat."

CHAPTER FIFTY-THREE

BLUE BLISTERING BLAZES—I'M DEAD. IN the space of a single heartbeat, Finn was sure his collar shrank two sizes, pert near choking the air from his throat. The sight of Miss Liberty standing proud and tall in the back of the room like her namesake in New York turned his body to stone. He stared at his wife through a gaze as unblinking as any statue.

God help me.

Finn glanced from Maggie's face to the back of Milo's head, his best friend's neck so scarlet, he was evidently having breathing problems too. "I am truly sorry, Miss O'Shea," Milo said in a stern voice that had once put Libby in her place when she was in his employ years ago, "but the audience questions are—"

"Excuse me, Mr. McShane," Libby interrupted in a loud voice as she walked down the aisle, her green-eyed gaze scorching a hole in Finn's composure, "but did you or did you not promise to support women's rights?"

A hush fell over the room as all eyes drilled into Finn while he upended his glass of water, the one on the table beside him that he hadn't touched until now. Carefully setting the empty glass down, he cleared his throat with a firm square of shoulders, a sense of calm suddenly flowing into his mind like the water had flowed into his body.

All at once the years fell away, and he was seventeen-year-old Griffin McShane once again, going head-to-head with fourteen-year-old Liberty Margaret O'Shea, the prettiest and smartest darn girl in the county.

And the most stubborn.

Finn had been the bane of her existence, taunting, teasing, and besting her in every school contest they had, never letting her know just how much she scattered his pulse. It had been sweet vindication back then, disarming, diffusing, and defeating her with his easy smile, confident air, and that maddening patience that had always driven her right up the wall.

Just like she did to him.

He managed a tight smile as he casually moved toward the podium, giving Milo a nod to let him know all would be well. True, it wasn't a spelling bee or science fair they battled in tonight, but Liberty Margaret O'Shea McShane was going to lose all the same.

Posturing loosely folded arms on the podium, he met her steely gaze with a twinkling one of his own, blood pumping through his veins at the thrill of sparring with the little brat once again. He gave her a wink that blasted her cheeks with a blush pert near darker than her hat, unleashing snickers and titters all throughout the room. "Do you mind repeating the question please, Miss O'Shea? I'm not sure I heard it correctly."

Her chin lashed up another full inch while her tone could have been dipped in acid. "I said," she reiterated curtly, "did you or did you not promise me to support women's rights?"

Finn idly scratched the back of his neck, face in a scrunch as he glimpsed John Piper's and Senator Jones's ashen faces. There was no way he could win if he gave Libby an honest answer *or* if he attempted to placate her and usher her out, not from the wildfire he saw in her eyes.

So, he opted to give the rowdies in the room a show instead. "Well, you know I'm not all that sure, ma'am." He surveyed the audience with a lazy smile, slipping them a knowing wink. "A man can promise a whole lot of things in the heat of passion."

Cheers and shouts thundered to the ceiling while men whooped and stomped their feet in approval, earning Finn a vote with every snort of laughter.

Any other woman alive would storm out of the room in utter mortification, but not his Libby, and Finn had to smother a groan when she marched right up on the stage to jab a finger in his chest. "You are nothing but a lying, conniving, yellow-bellied politician, Finn McShane, and anyone with an ounce of refinement would never vote for you."

"Well, that's real good, Miss O'Shea," he said, giving the audience a sly smile as he rocked back on his heels, "because if we passed the hat right now, I doubt we'd come up with an ounce of refinement in the lot of us."

The walls shook with hilarity as men howled and slapped each other on the backs, the broad smiles on the senator's and Piper's faces small comfort in the light of Libby's fury. Although the scowl on Templeton's face sure made up for it.

"Ohhhhh ... you are the lowest of low," she hissed, trading in her finger for a fist that bludgeoned his chest.

Snatching her wrist mid-blow, he forcefully lowered it to her side, his eyes burning with intensity despite the easy smile on his face. "Go home, Libby," he whispered for her ears alone, "this is not what it looks like."

"Oh really?" She jerked her wrist free to wiggle the diamond ring off her finger, holding it up in her hand. "Well this *is* what it looks like, Finn McShame, because *we* are no longer engaged!" She flung the ring onto the podium where it spun and wobbled like a top.

At least a hundred pair of eyes blinked, waiting to see what Finn would do. And when Libby spun on her heel to march off the stage and out of his life, he knew he had no choice. Making a scene was one thing, but leaving him high and dry in front of a room of rough-and-tumble men was political suicide. It would not only damage his career and his pride, but it was an assault on his manhood that would bludgeon his heart as well.

Plucking the ring from the podium he pocketed it with a hard smile to the men in the room while retrieving his Stetson from his chair. "Pardon my sudden departure, gentlemen," he said as he put his hat on, "but I'm a man of action who likes to tackle problems head-on, which is exactly what I would do for our great city if fortunate enough to be granted your vote." With a nod first to the audience and then one to Milo, Finn strode from the stage in time to halt Libby at the door. She gasped when he whirled her around.

"How dare you manhandle me, you brow-beating barbarian! You're not a man; you're a bald-faced bully!" Raising her tiny fist, she whacked him but good, leaving Finn only one option to save his sorry campaign.

He scooped her up and tossed her over his shoulder.

"No, ma'am, I'm a man," he said with a salute to the cheering crowd, then promptly carried her kicking and screaming right out of the deafening hall.

CHAPTER FIFTY-FOUR

OH, SWEET MOTHER OF MERCY! Hand to her mouth, Maggie gaped as Finn charged out of the auditorium with her godmother slung over his shoulder. Pandemonium erupted with men's raucous laughter, hearty slaps on the back, and Libby's salty shouts that only made the hilarity louder.

Near trembling, Maggie had been utterly stunned when Finn had hauled Libby out like a bobcat in a bag, but as she quickly led Maeve from the building, something happened that astonished her even more.

She giggled. Hand to her mouth at first. And then full-out belly laughs as loud as the men, truly wishing her mother were here to see this. After years of gently trying to rein Aunt Libby in, it would appear her godmother had finally met her match. The crowd surged around them, each and every man obviously anxious to view Libby and Finn's catfight out in the street. Spilling out of the church like ants going to a picnic, the man in the moon obliged by spotlighting the action, and Maggie wasn't all that sure that he wasn't laughing too.

Weaving through the crowd outside, Maggie slipped an arm to Maeve's waist, biting her lip to stifle her laughter. But when she saw the twinkle in Libby's mother's gaze, the two of them broke out into giggles that brought tears to their eyes. "If ever a man was intended for my headstrong daughter, it would be that one," Maeve said in Maggie's ear, and Maggie could do nothing but agree.

Libby may have been her mother's best friend, but even Mama had butt heads with her, praying God would lovingly curb her strong will. A will that often kept her from God's best, Mama would lament, and Maggie knew it was true. Deep down she'd sensed Aunt Libby hadn't been happy for years, no matter how much Harold succumbed to her every whim. But Finn had breathed new fire into her godmother, creating sparks that had made her come alive.

Iron sharpening iron.

One of God's tools, Mama had often said, for molding His children into the people He wanted them to be.

"You let me down this instant, you ... you ... unconscionable cretin!" Face as red as the feathered hat in her hand, Libby battered poor Finn with both hat and fist while he toted her to his phaeton, every high-pitched insult only making the crowd laugh even more.

"I'd say you won that debate, Finn, so you sure got my vote," one of the old-timers called, and shouts of assent rose in the crisp mountain air.

One arm locked around Libby's legs to keep her from kicking, Finn tipped his hat with the other. "Much obliged, Rufus, and thanks to everyone kind enough to give me your vote."

"Kind enough?" Libby shrieked, her voice going hoarse from screaming at the top of her lungs, "hare-brained enough, you mean, to vote for a lily-livered bully like you."

"Libby Margaret, you stop that caterwaulin' right now!" Aiden pushed through the crowd with Maggie and Maeve in tow, his face as red as his daughters. "You brought this down on yourself, young lady, and if Finn hadn't hauled you out of there, I would have."

"Pa-pa!" Libby's noise screeched to a stop, eyes saucer wide as she gaped at her father. "How on earth can you condone what this bully has done?"

"Because sometimes the only way to handle a bully is give him a bully, darlin', and Finn did just that when you tried to force him to do things your way."

"*What?* I am *not* a bully!" she shouted, feathers flying when she slapped her hat against Finn's back.

Aiden leaned in nose to nose, his tone softening while the barest hint of a smile twitched on his lips. "Then stop acting like one, young lady, and I have a suspicion Finn will too." He pointed a finger at the phaeton. "I suggest you park your bottom in that vehicle right now so we can take this circus home."

"My home is in New York," Libby said with a sudden swim of tears in her eyes, "so tell this cretin to put me down."

"With pleasure, Miss O'Shea," Finn said, plopping her into the carriage so hard she bounced to applause.

Scrambling back up, she tried to climb back down. "No thank you. I'll just walk to the Gold Hill."

Impeding her descent with a clamp of his steel jaw, Finn glanced over his shoulder. "Hey, Don, you got any room at the Gold Hill tonight?"

"No, siree, Finn, we're plum full up with the election and all, and hear tell Mrs. Cleary's and all the other hotels are the same."

"Thanks, Don." Finn waved to the crowd. "G'night, all—see you in the morning."

"*Ohhhhh!*" Libby ground out her frustration, plopping back down on the seat with a noisy huff of air while the male town folk slowly dwindled away. "You all belong in a cave. If I'm black and blue tomorrow, you'll know why."

"And if I have a pain in the posterior, *you'll* know why," Finn said with a tight smile, turning to lift Maeve into the back seat of the carriage before Aiden climbed in.

"Wait—my reticule!" Libby started to disembark once again. "I left it in the dressing room."

Finn's broad shoulders blocked her way. "Not a chance,

Liberty Bell," he said with a dry swerve of lips. "It took me fifteen minutes and countless bruises to get you this far. Maggie won't mind fetching it, will you, Maggie?"

"No, sir," Maggie said, hoping her stern tone deflected the smile tugging at her lips. She squeezed Libby's hand. "I'll get it, Aunt Libby—you wait right here."

"Oh, as if I have a choice," Libby groused with a fold of arms, and Maeve reached to massage her daughter's shoulder while she gave Maggie a wink.

Shaking her head, Maggie hurried back inside, grateful the crowds had almost dispersed except for a few clusters of men outside the church and in the hallway. The auditorium was completely empty except for Milo and Father Murray, who were tidying up as Maggie approached. "Excuse me, Father, but my aunt left her reticule in the bride's room, so I'm here to pick it up."

"Ah, yes," the elderly priest said with a broad smile, a definite twinkle in his rheumy blue eyes. "I suspect she forgot it in all the excitement."

Maggie nibbled her lip, unable to thwart the smile that tickled her lips. "Yes, sir, I suspect she did."

Milo's husky chuckle echoed within the room. "No question our Libby gave Finn more positive press tonight than *The Territorial Enterprise* could in a month of Sundays, although I doubt that was her intention."

"No, sir," Maggie said with a grin. "I'll just retrieve the reticule and bid you good night."

"Oh, it's not here, young lady." Father Murray straightened a row of chairs as he peered up beneath bushy silver brows. "I gave it to Blaze because he was one of the few men still hanging around."

Maggie paused. "I see. Well, he wasn't out front, so do you know where he is?"

Milo nodded toward a back door at the side of the stage. "He left with Dash and Clyde and a few others from the Ponderosa out the back door to avoid the crowd. But they were still talking when I took the trash out a few minutes ago, so you might catch him."

"Thank you," she said with a grateful smile, making her way to the door. Easing it open, she peered out in the dark, listening for the sound of conversation, but all she could hear was the chirp of crickets and the howl of a faraway wolf.

Which was suddenly broken by Blaze's familiar laugh.

Maggie smothered a groan. Merciful Providence, she almost wished he'd already gone! Shoulders firm, she had time for only one deep breath before she peeked around the corner to a sight that immediately snatched it away.

"I really wish I could, Chanel, but I need to go. But hang it all, you smell so darn good."

Maggie's body went to ice at the sound of the words Blaze had once said to her. Poised as if to leave, Blaze stood with hands on his hips while one of the saloon girls she'd seen in the auditorium slipped her arms around his waist. Pressing her body to his, she kissed him until he groaned and nudged her against the building. Palms splayed shoulder-height to the wall, he caged her in, but she appeared *anything* but caged. Hooking her arms around his neck, she nuzzled his throat, and he groaned again before jerking her close. Her fingers gouged into the unruly curls at the back of his head while he butted her to the wall, devouring her with a kiss so deep, Maggie's gasp was harsh in the cool desert night.

Blaze spun around in a blink, gun cocked and aimed.

Muffling a cry with a hand to her mouth, Maggie froze, heart in her throat.

"Blast it all, Maggie, what the devil are you doing here?" he snapped, quickly holstering his weapon. "That's a good way to get shot."

She started trembling, the awful shock of Blaze kissing another woman shattering her composure as much as the gun. "I came for Aunt Libby's reticule," she whispered, unable to stop the tears that brimmed in her eyes.

The hard planes of his face softened as he bent to pick up Libby's purse from the ground and handed it to her. "Here," he said quietly, "I planned to bring it home later when I was done here in town."

Later, yes. Maggie willed her tears not to fall. *When he was done sparkin' Chanel.*

He took a step forward, hands buried deep in his pockets. "Look, Maggie, I'm sorry," he whispered, the pain in his voice a faint echo of that which now slashed through her heart. "But you need to be careful sneaking up on people because that's a good way to get hurt."

Nodding dumbly, she took a step back with Libby's purse clutched to her chest, his image blurring as tears spilled from her eyes.

"Aw, Maggie ..."

Pushing past, she fled to the front of the church, saltwater blinding her as she ran to Finn's carriage.

A good way to get hurt.

Yes, it was. A ragged sob broke from her throat.

Just like loving you.

CHAPTER FIFTY-FIVE

MAEVE KEPT UP A RARE chatter all the way home, but to Finn, it only underscored the deafening silence as he drove the carriage back to the ranch. Not only was his wife stone-cold silent as the wheels rumbled over the moonlit road, but Maggie, who sat beside him—Libby refused—had returned with a tear-stained face, still as death.

Death. An appropriate analogy for the evening because right now, it felt like something had died between Libby and him. The fragile love, affection, and trust they had worked so hard to achieve had been damaged tonight, and for the first time since Aiden had proposed his six-month scheme, Finn wondered if it had all been a tragic mistake, resurrecting these feelings he had for Libby.

He realized now he should have told her—his plan to run for mayor before running for the senate. It was a brilliant strategy for his political future, John Piper had said. A chance to get his feet wet in politics and serve the city he loved for two years until Senator William Stewart's six-year term was up. He'd known there was no way he'd ever win in Virginia City on a platform that included suffrage no matter how much he believed in it, but neither John nor he had seen that as a problem at the time.

Until Libby arrived.

"You can*not* tell her," Aiden had warned and John had agreed, convincing him that Libby was too short-sighted and volatile when it came to women's rights. "I know my girl, Finn, and she will push and push and push to make it part of your platform, but in this town, you're done if they even *smell* a whiff of suffrage. Especially since being engaged to a known suffragette is already a liability you cannot afford. So just do your best to keep it *and her* under wraps till after the election. Because we both know when it comes to suffrage, Libby is a powder keg just waiting to blow."

A powder keg. Finn issued a silent grunt. *An understatement if ever there was.*

Which is exactly why he talked her out of attending the debate. But she'd bushwhacked him, dragging Maggie and Maeve along for good measure, and tonight she'd almost derailed his entire career. His mouth compressed as the carriage jostled through the gates of the ranch.

So he'd derailed their relationship instead.

"Whoa, boy," Finn said as they approached the front porch. "Aiden, I'm leaving for City Hall pretty early in the morning, so you can ride with Blaze and Dash later. Maeve, Maggie, I wish you both a good night. Libby"—his voice took on an edge—"you and I have a few things to discuss." He tugged on the reins to bring the phaeton to a complete stop, ready for Libby if she tried to bolt.

Which, *of course*, she did.

"No, ma'am," Finn said in a terse tone when Libby shot up. He reached behind Maggie to clamp a hand to his wife's arm before she could jump from the wagon. "You and I need to talk."

The ice in her tone could have frosted the roses Maeve had planted along the walkway. "I have nothing to say to you, Finn McShane, so I'll thank you to unhand me." Ramrod straight in the seat, she stared straight ahead with chin high while Maggie gingerly scooted by, bending to give Libby a quick hug before Aiden helped her down.

"Well, I have plenty to say to you, *Mrs.* McShane, so

you'll sit right there and listen. You said your piece tonight, so now I'll say mine. Yah!" he said with a snap of the reins, barely waiting till the others cleared the carriage.

"Where are we going?" Libby bolted up even higher, fingers gouging into the edge of the leather seat when he drove the carriage toward the gates once again.

"Far enough away that you can't disturb anyone with another ruckus."

She spun on the seat to face him, enough fire shooting from her eyes to light the way. "There wouldn't have been a ruckus if you hadn't deceived me," she shouted.

"Oh, come on, Libby, there would have been a ruckus either way, and you know it." He guided Lightning off the road onto the weedy path that led to the spring-fed lake. "I was just hoping it would be *after* I was elected mayor rather than before."

"That's all that matters to you, isn't it?" she yelled, making Finn *real* glad they weren't back at the ranch. "Gaining power so you can lord it over everyone, including me."

"You're blasted right it is!" Finn hurled the reins on the seat, shifting to face her with a temper no longer tethered by tolerance. "Because it takes *power* to get things done, Libby, *power* to change things that shouldn't be, and *power* to do the things *you* try to bully me to do."

She gasped, eyes spanning wide. "*Me?*" She splayed a hand to her chest. "Bully *you*?"

He shook his head at the look of utter shock on her face, a harsh laugh escaping his lips. "You really don't see it, do you?"

"See what?" Her chin nudged up while her lips tamped down.

"Your insatiable need to control."

"*My* need?" she said in a shriek that even cowed the crickets into silence. "I'm not the one who dragged me out of a hotel in the middle of the night in my nightgown, forcing me to do his bidding for six solid months, then deceives me in the process."

He slammed a fist on the bench, making her jump. "If you climb in the saddle, darlin', you sure in the devil better be ready for the ride."

"And what's *that* supposed to mean?"

He angled in, jaw as tight as the clench of his fist on the seat. "It *means*, Libby, if you're going to buck and spur your own way, you darn well better be ready for the consequences." He raised his head, his chin like rock. "Would you have kept your mouth shut about suffrage till after the election if I'd told you?"

"No!" she shouted with a fist slam of her own, "because a *real* man would stand up for what's right no matter the cost."

Something ominous snaked down his spine as a tic pulsed in his jaw. "No, Libby," he said in a tone as hard and cold as the reality he faced. "A *real* man would stand up to a woman who's wrong."

Her shoulders stiffened as a steely veneer settled over her features just like the one he'd seen when a teapot grazed his head years ago. "Then maybe you better take me back to the ranch," she said quietly, a glaze of wetness in her eyes.

He extended a hand to pull her close, but she only flinched and scooted away, cramping his gut when tears slipped from her eyes. "No, Libby, I'll take you *home*," he said quietly, "and we'll talk about this later."

"My home is in New York," she whispered with a hitch in her throat, "and there will be no 'later.'"

Finn just stared, her words gashing a hole in his heart. "You don't mean that."

"I do." A silver trail of tears slithered her cheek while grief doused all the fire in her eyes. "We're no good for each other, Finn," she said softly, her voice laced with regret. "Control is too important to both of us. I battle for control to protect myself and other women, and you battle to control me."

"That's not true—"

"It *is*, Finn." A sob broke from her lips, and he reached for her, but she only moved further away, putting a shaky hand to her eyes. "And whether it's my fault, your fault, both of ours or even the fault of others you know nothing about, I … I can't do this."

His blood chilled. "What do you mean, 'the fault of others' I know nothing about?"

She turned away, arms gripped tightly to her waist. "I don't want to talk about it. Please, just take me back."

"You darn well *better* talk about it," he said, an uneasy feeling singeing his temper, "after a remark like that. Our life is in the balance here, Libby, and I need to know what you meant."

Her lips quivered despite the lift of her chin. "It means too many men have tried to force their hand with me, Finn, well beyond you and my father, to control me and bully me, and I can't"—her eyes flickered as if she were having trouble getting the words out, tears streaming all the while—"I *won't* be subject to that again."

"Oh, Libby …" It was a hoarse whisper as Finn moved to take her in his arms, the ache in his chest a mix of both grief and fury.

"No, Finn, *please*—I'm asking you not to touch me!" She practically straddled the edge of the seat, palm quivering as she warded him off.

Swallowing hard, he backed away, heart cramping at the look of fear in her face, something he'd never seen in this woman before. "Libby," he whispered, "I love you with everything in me, darlin', so please—don't shut me out."

"I can't help it," she said, the words barely audible as her gaze lapsed into a dead stare. "Because I can't be the wife you need me to be."

"Why?" His voice cracked.

"Because I can't give you what you want."

"Libby, all I want is your love."

"No!" A spark of anger flickered in her eyes as she faced him again. "You want control, just like every other man I've ever known except for Harold. Always pushing, prodding, threatening"—her chin rose while her voice tapered off to a pained whisper—"*taking.*"

She shook her head, arms braced to her waist as if to shield her body. "I don't think this is going to work, Finn. The damage inside of me is too deep, and I don't know how to change that." Her body seemed to sag as she pled with her eyes before turning away, her face a porcelain profile shutting him out. "I'm so very tired," she whispered, "so will you take me back now? Please?"

His gaze burned into her for several excruciating seconds, mind racing as he struggled to know what to say or do. He finally relented with a long and weary sigh. "All right, Libby, I'll take you home. But this isn't over, darlin', because tomorrow we talk." Lifting the reins, he clicked his tongue to spur Lightning on, a sick feeling seeping in his gut like sludge.

She was leaving. Again. Reopening the wound she'd inflicted before. But this time Finn wasn't going to let her go quite so easily, determined to discuss this tomorrow when cooler heads prevailed. And he would do everything in his power to change her mind.

Problem was, it was her "power" that stood in the way.

His jaw tamped down as he steered the carriage up the drive. And if she wouldn't listen? Then he would just get on with his life. Throw himself into politics with a vengeance and eventually marry somebody else. He halted the carriage in front of the house, and Libby bolted without a word, closing the door behind. He snapped the reins with a little too much force, convincing himself he'd be fine either way. And he had no doubt that he would.

Once the bleeding stopped.

And the gash in his heart went away.

CHAPTER FIFTY-SIX

SOBBING INTO HER PILLOW, MAGGIE figured she deserved this. She'd known better than to get involved with Blaze Donovan, but her heart had betrayed her.

Right along with his.

"You're the only woman I want," he'd told her. She sniffed and dabbed her handkerchief to her eyes.

But apparently not.

Lumbering onto her back, she stared at the ceiling, her body limp and her emotions spent. She would leave tomorrow—she had no choice. Living in the same house as Blaze, a mere bedroom away, would kill her. It was bad enough hearing him come home late the last three nights, knowing he'd been at the Ponderosa flirting with women. Her eyelids quivered closed, leaking more tears while she smothered another sob. But seeing him kiss some other girl with such passion, her body pressed hard against his, had ripped Maggie wide open, and she feared nothing could staunch the flow but distance and time.

Lots and lots of time.

Mr. and Mrs. O'Shea's new house wasn't quite ready, so she couldn't move there. And she'd checked with Mrs. Cleary a while back about renting a room in her boardinghouse after Aunt Libby and Finn got married—*if* they got married, which was yet another ache in Maggie's heart. She patted her eyes. Well, if Mrs. Cleary still didn't have a room to let tomorrow, Maggie would just move in with

Andrea Jo for a while. Her friend from work lived with her grandmother just outside of town and had offered Maggie lodging if she'd ever needed it.

And heaven knows she did.

Now.

Of course, Aunt Libby wouldn't like it, but she would certainly understand needing distance when a man broke your heart. *Wouldn't she?* Thoughts of her aunt prompted a prayer that God would heal the rift between her and Finn because Maggie had never seen two people that needed each other more.

Like you and Blaze? The taunt in her mind stabbed, but not as much as the idea of Blaze never making amends with God. The night in the loft had jolted her, opening her eyes to the danger of loving a man who lacked faith. The painful realization had been a two-edged sword that pierced Maggie's heart, not only severing their relationship, but possibly any hope for Blaze's soul.

The doorknob creaked, and Maggie quickly blotted her face, her concerns immediately turning to her aunt. "Aunt Libby, are you all right?" Lamplight from the hall shafted into the room, silhouetting the defeated posture of the woman who suddenly seemed so very frail.

"No." Her aunt's hoarse whisper quivered in the air, and Maggie hurried to give her a tight hug, gently leading her to the bed they both shared. "Finn and I ..." her aunt continued with a broken heave, "we're through."

Maggie's heart stopped for several beats when Libby slumped into her arms with a sob, the sound of her aunt's sorrow shredding her heart all the more. "No, Aunt Libby, it's just one quarrel, that's all. You and Finn love each other." She clung to her with all of her might, desperate to absorb some of her pain.

"It d-doesn't m-matter," Libby whispered, her tone nasal with fluid and grief, "we're no good for each other, Maggie. It didn't work before and it won't work now. I have to go."

Maggie retrieved a fresh handkerchief from her nightstand drawer, rubbing Libby's back while her aunt wiped at her eyes. "Back to New York? But you don't have a job anymore, Aunt Libby, and you broke it off with Harold, so what's there to go back to?"

Libby sniffed. "Susan B. Anthony told me last year that if I was ever willing to leave Vassar, she would find a job for me at the National Woman Suffrage Association." Her shoulders slumped as she lagged into a distant stare. "It doesn't pay near as much as I was making at Vassar, but it's someplace I'd want to be."

Maggie blinked at the moisture welling in her eyes, the notion of Aunt Libby leaving sinking in for the very first time. She thrust her soggy handkerchief to her mouth to thwart a rising sob, but it was no use. The tide of heartache over Blaze broke it loose on a string of wobbly heaves.

"Maggie?" Libby gripped her arms, bending to peer into her eyes. "Darling, what is it? I know we'll miss each other, but we'll write and visit a number of times a year, I promise." She skimmed a gentle hand down Maggie's hair, searching her face. "I was so angry at Finn, I didn't notice anything else, but did something happen tonight?"

Giving a shaky nod, Maggie took another clean handkerchief out of the drawer and mopped at her tears. "I saw Blaze and he … he"—her body shuddered at the memory—"was kissing another girl."

"Oh, sweetheart …" Libby swallowed her up in a voracious hug, soothing her with gentle rocking as she stroked her hair. "My heart aches for you, Maggie," she whispered with fresh tears, "and oh, how I wish there was something I could do."

Maggie rested her head on her aunt's shoulder, a sudden hiccup turning into a pitiful smile. "Just look at us, Aunt Libby. Two heartbroken suffragists wounded by men. It's enough to make me go back and volunteer with you."

Libby jerked away, fingers still gripped to Maggie's arms. "Well, then, here's a crazy thought—why don't you?" she said with a hush in her voice, as if she could barely believe it could really happen.

Maggie blinked, then blinked again, Aunt Libby's crazy idea suddenly not so crazy anymore. Her mind raced with memories of Sister Fred and all the other nurses and nuns she would miss, and the family she'd found in Sheridan and Shay, Dash and Jake, the O'Sheas and even Angus and ol' crabby Gert. A dull ache settled in at leaving them all until Blaze's image suddenly appeared with a slash of pain so potent, she knew she had her answer.

"Yes," she whispered, then said it again with more conviction, feeling God's pull to lead her back home.

"Yes?" Libby said with a hopeful arch of brows, "you'll go with me?"

She nodded, and water welled in her aunt's eyes before she lunged into Maggie's arms.

"Oh, Maggie," she whispered, clinging as if she would never let go, "knowing we'll be together during a time like this just helps somehow, doesn't it?"

"It does." Maggie held onto her aunt with a ferocious hug, so very grateful neither of them would have to go through this alone.

Libby pulled away, the tiniest glimmer of hope in her eyes. "I'll wire my aunt tomorrow that we're coming back, and I know it will be a blessing to her as well." Dashing a tear from her face, she managed a wobbly smile. "The poor thing is so very lonely and writes all the time that she misses us terribly, so it will be good to see her again. Oh, and I'm friends with several of the ladies at the National Woman Suffrage Association who are married to surgeons and hospital administrators, so we won't have any trouble finding you a job." She gave Maggie another hug, a hint of excitement threading her tone. "And you can even volunteer with me if you want." She paused. "But there is one thing I'd like to ask if I may?"

Maggie grasped her aunt's arm, lips trembling into a grateful smile. "Anything, Aunt Libby, absolutely anything."

Libby dipped her head to peek up into Maggie's face with a fragile look, revealing a vulnerability Maggie seldom saw in her aunt. "Your mother was the only true friend I've ever had, Maggie, and the only person I trusted enough to unburden my soul, and I miss her terribly." Expelling a wispy sigh, she swiped at her eyes with a ragged sniff. "When she died, I was heartbroken, thinking I would never trust anyone like that again. But living here with you, darling, sharing a room for six months …" Libby cupped a wavering hand to Maggie's face, a gesture that brought more tears to both of their eyes. "I almost feel like I'm with her again, you know? And my heart so longs for another friend like that ..."

Her aunt's voice broke on a frail heave, and Maggie swallowed her up in a weepy embrace. "Oh, Aunt Libby, me too! Mama was everything to me, but when I'm with you, I can't help but feel like she's here, too, nudging us together to be good friends."

Libby nodded, sniffing and blotting her face with the handkerchief. "I know," she said with a shaky smile, reaching to take Maggie's hand in her own. "That's how I feel, too." She pushed a lock of Maggie's hair over her shoulder, the love and closeness between them filling Maggie with a beautiful calm. "Don't get me wrong—I love being your godmother and aunt, sweetheart, but to be honest, more than anything right now, I could sure use another friend like your sweet mother, and I think maybe you feel the same. So if this doesn't sound so very silly to you, could you … would you …"—her chin quivered as more saltwater coated her cheeks—"be my best friend?"

"Oh, Aunt Libby!" It was Maggie's turn to launch into her godmother's arms, tears falling freely as she squeezed with all of her might. "Don't you know?" Her voice was thick with emotion as she pulled away, in awe of the special ways God sometimes healed a broken heart. "You're the best friend I've ever had."

CHAPTER FIFTY-SEVEN

"CAN WE GO HOME NOW—*PLEASE?*" Shaylee's look of pain mirrored Finn's stomach exactly.

Glancing at his watch, he released a weary sigh as he scanned the ballroom of Piper's Opera House, barely seeing the crowd of people celebrating his success. It was a rare mix of cowhands and town folk dressed in their Sunday best, laughing and chatting with his wealthier supporters, each and every one a vital vote. Waiters in tie and tails passed hors d'oevres on silver trays and refilled goblets of soda water and champagne while a string quartet provided background music. It was Finn's victory celebration, but celebrating was the last thing on his mind. And judging from the looks of gloom on his nieces' and nephews' faces around their banquet table, along with the O'Shea's, it appeared he wasn't alone.

Correction: He *was* alone.

Because just as the votes had been counted early this evening deeming Finn Mayor of Virginia City, he'd learned that Libby and Maggie had left on the 2:10 to Reno. And based on the time on his watch—well after eight—*they* were *well* on their way to a city that seemed like the other end of the earth.

He was still more than a little numb because deep down, he hadn't really thought she would go. Somehow, he had foolishly believed his election as mayor would change her mind, especially when he explained just how this win could lead to a senate seat, where he could actually *do* something about women's rights. For him, winning both Libby back and the mayorship should have been a win-win.

Instead, it was a loss-win that felt way more like a loss, leaving him sitting here with a starched smile on his face and a hole in his heart, lamenting the one thing he hadn't counted on losing.

Libby.

Hand on the back of his empty chair, he upended his sparkling soda water, wondering if anyone would notice if he left. His mouth crooked as he smiled and nodded at something John Piper was saying to him and several others, a bit guilty that he was only half listening. John would notice, that was for dead sure. For pity's sake, his closest political consultant and now good friend was happier about the outcome than anyone, as if he'd run for political office instead of Finn. The edge of Finn's lips kicked up.

Then maybe John should stay and play host while I leave.

Chuckling at all the appropriate places while John told a joke, Finn set his empty glass on the table where his family quietly chatted and looked like he'd lost the election. Giving Shaylee a wink that did nothing for her scowl, Finn laughed on cue when a burst of men's laughter punctuated John's punchline.

All at once John rose up on his heels to scour the room, two tiny ridges forming above his nose that produced the first frown Finn had seen on his face all day. "Speaking of our better halves, where is Libby, Finn?"

Finn froze along with his smile.

Uh, Salt Lake City?

Giving a gruff clear of his throat, he slapped an arm over John's shoulder to lean close enough that the others couldn't hear. "Libby's gone, John. Left this morning for New York."

John's eyes expanded as his mouth fell open. Grasping Finn's arm, he led him away from the group of men, silver brows crumpling in concern. "Because of last night?" he said in a low voice, incredulity edging his tone.

"Yeah." Finn buried his hands deep in the pockets of his dress trousers, rocking back on his heels as if everyone in the room could see his shame over the broken engagement. With a shrug of his shoulders, he attempted to deflect some of his pain with a sheepish smile. "Won the election, but lost the girl, I guess."

"Finn, I am so very sorry." John hooked an arm around Finn's shoulder, the genuine regret in his eyes tightening Finn's throat. "Is there anything I can do?"

"As a matter of fact, John, there is." Finn nodded to his table where Shaylee's moping had reached new heights with her head buried in her arms on the table, either sleeping or crying her eyes out.

Finn would have opted for the second.

"My family's pretty upset over Libby's and Maggie's departures, so it's taken a bit of the wind out of our sails, if you know what I mean. I was thinking we might call it a night and head on home if you don't mind."

"Absolutely," John said with a firm nod of his head, "and I will make sure everyone knows you left out of concern for your family, worn out from the long day and all."

A silent sigh of relief seeped from Finn's mouth. "John, I can't thank you enough. Not only for hosting this celebration tonight, but for all of your critical support throughout the campaign. I would not be here if not for you, my friend, and truth be told?" He shook John's hand. "Our friendship is the best thing that's come out of this entire run."

"I feel the same way, Finn—it's been my pleasure, I assure you." He nodded to Finn's family, a smile quirking his lips. "Now go on and head out before Shaylee falls asleep on the table, if she hasn't already."

"Thanks, John. I'll see you tomorrow at the planning meeting." Slapping him on the back, Finn turned to lean both palms on the table, scanning the tired faces of his family. "Uh, I don't suppose anyone here would like to go home?"

"Oh my goodness, *YES!*" Shaylee shouted, jumping up from the table like she'd risen from the dead, almost knocking Finn down when she hugged him at the waist. She peered up with a downcast pinch in her brow as the others rose and pushed in their chairs. "I'm proud of you, Uncle Finn, but I'm too sad to celebrate tonight."

"Me, too, Doodle," he whispered, emotion suddenly clogging his throat as he bent to press a kiss to her head. "Let's go home."

The ride home wasn't much better than the evening. The O'Shea's sat silent in the back seat of his phaeton while Sheridan and Shaylee moped in the front, all escorted by Blaze and Dash, who rode ahead on their horses. The ranch was quiet as he pulled the carriage up to the house. Darkness prevailed except for the light in the barn where Dash and Blaze tended their horses, and then the bunkhouse where a few hands had volunteered to stay behind with Angus and Gert—for a poker tournament, no doubt.

Expelling a weary sigh, Finn helped his nieces down from the carriage, halting them both as they trudged toward the steps along with Aiden and Maeve. "I'd like a word with everyone before we all turn in for the night, if I may. So, Shay and Sheridan, I'd be much obliged if you turned on all the lights in the parlour and fetched some lemonade for us all."

"Yes, sir," they said in unison, mounting the steps with a sag of their shoulders while the O'Shea's followed behind.

"Uncle Finn," I'll put up the carriage and take care of Lightning," Blaze said as he approached from the barn.

Finn cuffed his nephew's shoulder, well aware his ache over Maggie's departure probably matched Finn's own over Libby's. "Thanks, Blaze—I appreciate it. Then if you and Dash will join us in the parlour, I'd like to discuss a few things."

Offering a sober nod, Blaze led Lightning and the carriage away.

"But I don't understand, Uncle Finn," Sheridan said when the family convened in the parlour moments later, "you and Aunt Libby seemed so happy and you're still married after all, so how can she leave?"

Good question. Finn cleared his throat as he studied the somber faces around the room. "Well, Sher, your aunt and I had a bit of a disagreement last night—"

Aiden grunted.

"And we all know your aunt has a bit of a temper—"

It was Maeve's turn to grunt, a completely rare occurrence. "A bloomin' time bomb even if she *is* my daughter," she muttered, shifting in one of two leather wing chairs in front of the fireplace while Aiden reached for her hand.

"Doesn't she love us anymore, Uncle Finn?" Shaylee asked, a sheen of moisture in her eyes while she hugged the old tattered bear he'd given her so many years ago.

The one she seldom carried around anymore.

Finn's heart squeezed. "Of course she does, sweetheart. Sheridan said she told you so this morning before she and Maggie left, didn't she? That she had to leave for a while because the wedding was off, but she'd be back for plenty of visits?"

"Sayin' ain't doin'," Shaylee said with a quiver of her lip.

Pushing away from the wall where he leaned with arms folded, Blaze silently moved to sit next to his sister on the love seat, pulling her close to press a kiss to her hair.

"But I don't understand why Maggie had to leave too," Sheridan said, arms folded in a pout while she stared at the tray of lemonade on the table nobody had touched.

"Well, maybe Blaze can explain it to you." Dash got up from the chair he'd occupied to amble over and pour himself a lemonade, holding the glass out to offer it to anyone who wanted it. No takers. He sat down next to Sheridan, boot crossed over his knee and took a long draw.

"What's that supposed to mean?" Finn said, gaze flicking to where Blaze tucked Shaylee close, his head bowed over hers.

"You want to tell him big brother, or should I?" Dash stared at Blaze over the rim of his glass, eyes as cool as the lemonade in his glass.

Blaze peered up beneath shuttered lids, the mope on his face turning into a scowl. "Maggie and I broke it off three days ago, so what?"

"So, what?" Finn blinked, shocked he'd been too busy to notice any rift between Maggie and Blaze. "Thunderation, Blaze, you two were courting! What in blue blazes happened?"

Blaze released a noisy exhale and rested his head on the back of the love seat, eyes closed. "Let's just say we weren't suited, Uncle Finn." His eyes opened a sliver as he delivered a sullen look. "Like you and Aunt Libby, I guess."

Finn sagged back into his chair, his spirits sinking along with him. He kneaded the bridge of his nose, wondering what in the world he could do to alleviate his family's pain.

And his.

"Can't you go after them, Uncle Finn?" Sheridan scooted to the edge of her seat, a flicker of hope in her expression. "You know, talk them into coming back?"

Finn managed a faint smile. "Sure, I can, darlin', and I fully intend to, but you have to understand, sweetheart, that's no guarantee they'll agree."

"Can you leave tomorrow?" Shaylee asked.

Finn's mouth tipped off-center. "As much as I'd like to, Shay—and as much as you'd obviously like me to—I have at least two weeks' worth of transitional meetings before I can even think about going anywhere. And then it's close to a week's travel to New York by train, so it won't be anytime soon."

"But—" Shaylee sat up.

"*But* …," Finn interrupted with a firm lift of his chin, "I know your aunt, and she'll need time to cool down anyway, Doodle, in addition to a little distance to realize just how much she misses you."

And me, God willing.

Shaylee flopped back against Blaze's side with a pout. "I guess."

"But there is something you can do in the meantime, sweetheart, that will make you feel a whole lot better. You can pray." He paused, scanning every face in the room with a flicker of hope that suddenly eased the ache in his chest. "We can all pray that God's will be done."

Tears welled in Maeve's eyes as she reached to squeeze Aiden's hand, a fragile smile trembling on her lips. "Oh, Finn, that so fills me with hope because I've always believed it *was* God's will for you and Libby to be together."

"It just wasn't mine," Aiden said with a press of Maeve's hand, his mouth tamped into a sad smile. "But God has a way of pulling our feet from the fire," he said with a low chuckle, "so if he can do it for me, he can do it for my daughter."

Finn smiled. "That's my hope, Aiden." His gaze lighted on Blaze who lay with his head back and eyes closed as he held Shaylee cocooned in his arms. "Blaze, you're welcome to go with me to New York when I go if you like."

His nephew's eyelids lifted halfway. "No thanks, Uncle Finn. Even if I wanted to—which I don't—Maggie made it pretty clear she had no room for me in her life, so I need to move on." His lashes lowered once again, and Finn sensed a hopelessness he'd never seen in Blaze before. As if Maggie's departure had totally depleted him. There was no question Libby's departure had depleted Finn, too, but at least Finn had something to fill him back up again that Blaze didn't. He released a quiet sigh.

Faith.

CHAPTER FIFTY-EIGHT

"WHY DON'T YOU CALL IT a night, Blaze?" Dash wiped off the counter of the bar at the Ponderosa, his tone casual, but the concern in his eyes as potent as the rotgut Blaze had been pouring down his throat the last two weeks.

Upending his drink, Blaze slammed the empty glass back down and slid it toward his brother, the bartender on duty for the night. "One for the road," he slurred, wondering why he'd avoided drinking all these years when it felt so good to forget.

Dash took the dirty glass and dropped it into the wash bucket under the counter with a thin smile. "One for the coffin, you mean." Pouring a cup of coffee from the pot he always brewed late to help his regulars sober up for the ride home, he eased it Blaze's way. "And I thought the last one was the 'one for the road.'"

Blaze laughed. "It was, but now it seems I need one more because apparently my little brother is trying to tell me how to run my life." He shoved the coffee back, giving a slow blink of glassy eyes when it sloshed all over Dash's clean counter to make a real mess.

Just like my life.

"Somebody has to," Dash muttered, nudging the coffee forward again before re-wiping the bar. He tossed the dirty rag into the bucket and then leaned in, palms splayed on the counter. "Look, Blaze, I'm worried about you. Since

Maggie left, you've been depressed, drinking every night, and fooling around with women you have no business fooling around with. You can't keep this up."

"Why not?" Blaze pushed the coffee back, making another mess but not giving a rat's tail because Dash was out of line. This was Blaze's life, not his. Scowling, he pivoted on the stool to scan the room for Chanel Monroe, his girl of choice since Rachel had left him high and dry. His scowl tipped into a grin when she gave him a wink from across the room. Well, maybe not *dry* ...

"Because, big brother," he said quietly, "you're gonna end up like Pa."

Dash's statement had been spoken low, almost a whisper, but the repercussions in Blaze's mind were deafening. His brother may as well have tossed scalding coffee into Blaze's face because it singed all the same, searing his mind and gut with a dangerous reality. A reality that up until now, had kept him from alcohol all these years. Eyes wild, he spun around and slammed his arm to the bar, hurling the coffee onto the floor with a crash while he angled in, voice deadly. "You ever say that again, little brother, and I'll whoop you within an inch of your sorry life, you got that?"

Dash slowly rose to his full height, his jaw as stony as Blaze's. "Yeah, I got it, but just in case you're too soused to remember, *big brother*, I'm not the one with the 'sorry life.'" Turning his back on Blaze, Dash stooped to pick up the broken pieces of the cup before mopping up the mess and moving to the other end of the bar.

Dropping his head in his hand, Blaze kneaded his temples with forefinger and thumb, not sure if his hand was shaking from anger or from booze.

"Mmm ... looks like somebody could use a little attention right now, cowboy." Chanel's husky voice blew warm in his ear as she slid on the stool next to his. "Clyde said I could leave early tonight, so how 'bout I love on you a little bit?"

Blaze stared through watery eyes, Chanel's words barely penetrating the stupor he'd drunk himself into. Without question, Chanel Monroe was one of the prettiest gals in Virginia City. But tonight, the thought of those same kisses that had helped him forget Maggie over the last two weeks suddenly roiled his gut, causing its contents to rise. Pushing her hand away, he slid off the stool, grabbing the bar when his legs wobbled too much. "Sorry, Chanel, but I'm feeling poorly right now, so I think I best just head on—"

His stomach suddenly turned, and pushing her away, he staggered into the street just in time, spewing his supper along with a half bottle of whiskey. Stumbling over to the water trough, Blaze threw his Stetson aside and dropped to his knees before submerging his head, scrubbing his mouth with his sleeve after he came back up. Water dripped from his face and hair as he slumped against the trough, legs limp and eyes closed. Chest pumping with ragged heaves, he heard someone squat before him and finally looked up through hazy slits.

"You know, big brother," Dash said with a patient smile, arms draped over his knees, "Uncle Finn will string you up till you're high and dry if you go home right now. And you'd probably fall off Minx as well, and she'd leave you high and dry too."

A silly grin stretched across Blaze's face. "Prob-ly."

"So," Dash said as he hooked his brother under the arms to haul him to his feet. His nose wrinkled as he nodded to the pile of puke next to the trough, "how 'bout a fresh pot of coffee and some solid food to replace what you lost?"

What I lost. Blaze's eyes closed, the bad taste in his mouth having nothing to do with vomit.

Maggie.

Not waiting for Blaze to answer, Dash picked up Blaze's Stetson and plopped it on his brother's head before latching an arm to his waist. Heaving a noisy sigh, he ushered him across the street to Hattie's Diner, a landmark in Virginia City that stayed open as late as the bars. Hattie always did a brisk business in the late evenings for those who needed a little something more than whiskey in their belly before they went home to the little woman.

Like Blaze. Only he didn't have a little woman.

Leastways, not anymore …

He grunted when Dash plopped him into a chair at the nearest booth, waving somebody over. Crossing his arms on the table, Blaze dropped his head on top, thinking Dash was right.

I can't keep this up …

He jumped when somebody clunked a mug of steaming coffee on the table, hand to his throbbing temple as he glared at Dash through eyes as raw as his mood. "What the devil …?"

"Nope," Dash said with a wry twist of lips, slacking a leg as he studied Blaze with hands on his hips. "You left the devil across the street, big brother, and Hattie doesn't allow any of his—or your—shenanigans over here, so you best behave. I ordered you a big breakfast and told Hattie to keep the coffee coming till you could stand without falling down."

He nodded toward the Ponderosa. "Clyde let me take a quick break to haul your carcass out of the street, but I gotta get back, so I'm leaving you in good hands, all right?" He pushed the mug of coffee in front of his brother. "Drink it," he ordered, "or I'll personally toss you back into the horse trough, understood?" Dash slapped him on the back and started to leave.

Blaze halted him with a shaky hand, avoiding his brother's gaze. "Thanks, Hash." His voice was a hoarse whisper as he picked up the mug, eyes closing while he took a long drink. He swallowed hard. "I guess you're not too bad for a little brother."

He could almost feel Dash's trademark grin. "And I

guess you're not too bad for a big one either, Hot-Shot." He paused to grip Blaze's shoulder, the humor in his tone far more solemn than before. "At least when you're sober." He flicked the back brim of Blaze's hat up with a chuckle, strolling away as it tipped low into Blaze's eyes.

Grateful for the shade it provided from the glare of the diner lamps, Blaze just stared aimlessly into his coffee, too limp to even jolt when the waitress thudded a tray on his table. She shoved a steaming plate of food under his nose before refilling his cup, and his dry mouth actually watered. The smell of fried eggs and bacon rumbled his stomach instead of roiling it, so Blaze considered that a good sign. "Thanks, Hattie," he said, hoping he'd finally purged himself at the trough of all the guilt and shame weighting him down since Maggie left. He nudged his hat up to offer a weak smile while taking a slow sip of his coffee, pert near spewing it all over his plate at the sober look on the waitress's face.

Then again, maybe not.

CHAPTER FIFTY-NINE

RACHEL SLID INTO HIS BOOTH on the other side without missing a beat, her sweet smile like a kick in the gut. "Hello, Blaze," she said in that soft voice he remembered all too well, an almost breathy, little-girl quality that had always carried an innocence despite the tight dresses and heavy rouge that she wore. But tonight, the low-cut dress and makeup were nowhere in sight. Instead, it was replaced by a modest blue calico with one of Hattie's aprons and a fresh-scrubbed face that was now as innocent as it was pretty.

"Rachel …" He bolted up in his seat, the motion sending a streak of pain through his skull. "What are you doing here? I thought you worked for room and board at Mrs. Cleary's."

She unloaded the rest of the tray with a shy smile, nudging a second plate with biscuits and gravy and fried potatoes his way. "I did for a month or so, but now between waitressing here five nights a week and performing at Mrs. Cleary's Saturday evening parlour piano recitals, I'm able to pay my own room and board now."

She folded her hands on the table as her chin edged up almost imperceptibly, a definite hint of pride sparkling in her eyes. "Which now frees my days up to"—her cheeks took on a rosy glow as she chewed on the edge of her lip—"attend Fourth Ward School to get my high school diploma and hopefully be a teacher someday."

Blaze's jaw dropped—along with his fork—as he blinked at the woman who'd once served up both drinks and kisses to him not so many months ago. He swallowed hard, suddenly aware that the tables had turned. Once she'd been the lowly saloon girl and he the college-educated foreman of one of the largest cattle ranches in Nevada. Now she was a respectable young woman aspiring to be a teacher and paying her own way.

Heat snaked up the back of his neck when he glanced down at his wet and rumpled white shirt and silk vest, both soiled with vomit and dirty water from the trough. There had been a time when she'd once looked up to him with stars in her eyes, but now all he saw was a look of tender sympathy that scalded his cheeks along with his neck.

Avoiding her gaze, he took a quick swig of his coffee, hand shaking as he set it back down. "I …" He peered up beneath heavy lids, hands gripped to his mug while he tried to find the right words to say how proud of her he was. "I can't tell you how I admire you for bettering your circumstances like this, Rachel, aspiring to something so noble."

The blush deepened on her face. "Thank you, Blaze, but all the credit goes to Maggie because she literally changed my life."

His headache kicked up a notch as he stabbed at his eggs with his fork. *Yeah, mine too.*

Just not for the better.

"Not only did she arrange for room and board at Miss Cleary's" —she averted her gaze while she picked at her nails—"but she gave me spiritual counsel that saved both my life *and* my soul, keeping me from making a tragic mistake."

"You mean like marrying me?" he said with a harsh laugh, avoiding her gaze while he shoveled food in his mouth.

"No, because you never would have married me, Blaze,"

she said softly, "and we both know it. But I cared about you so much that it was getting to the point where marriage didn't matter anymore because I just wanted to give you my love."

He paused over his plate, eyelids sagging shut at how close he'd come to stealing her virtue and possibly ruining her life.

God help me.

He froze, an eerie feeling purling through him that God had done just that.

"So, no matter how much I thought I loved you," she continued, "Maggie saved both of us from a horrible mistake because she taught me that love without commitment really isn't love at all."

His Adam's apple jogged in his throat as he just stared at his half-eaten eggs. Shame twisted his gut over how selfish he'd been, committing to himself rather than to Maggie—the woman he vehemently claimed to love.

God, forgive me.

"Blaze." He startled at the touch of Rachel's hand, his appetite for food suddenly as dead as his relationship with the one woman he longed for. "I know you love Maggie, and I know she loves you because she and I spent a lot of time together during her lunch hour, studying Scripture." She paused to give his hand a light squeeze. "And when we prayed, *you* were always at the top of her list, begging God to set you free from the pain of your past."

His eyelids sank closed once again, Rachel's words piercing his heart as emotion stung in his nose.

"And I know He will, Blaze, because that's what He did for me—through Maggie." He heard her shift in the booth as if to get comfortable, finally folding her hands on the table once again. "To be honest, I didn't think it was possible to be set free—at least not for someone like me, a woman with a past, chained to a present that all but guaranteed a lifetime of imprisonment." A soft sigh escaped her lips as she settled back in the booth. "But Maggie taught me that with God, not only are all things possible, but that Jesus came to set the captives free, Blaze. And it doesn't matter a whit if that's the captivity of a saloon girl destined to spend her days plying liquor …" She hesitated ever so briefly, as if concerned her words might offend. "Or the captivity of one's mind, where bitterness enslaves one's life as surely as it enslaves one's soul, robbing them of the journey—and the blessings—that God intended."

The blessings God intended. Blaze swallowed the emotion clogging his throat.

Like Maggie.

"You see, Blaze, through Maggie and God's Word, I learned that sin—be it bitterness, anger, unforgiveness, whatever—is a detour that never gets you to the right destination. My father believed in God, but that didn't stop him from beating me, using me, or branding me as a soiled dove"—her voice faltered the slightest bit—"when it was Pa himself who soiled me."

Blaze's head shot up, shock flaring his gaze. "You don't mean—"

Water welled as she nodded, lifting her apron to dab at her eyes. "I left after I miscarried his baby," she whispered, "finally begging Uncle Clyde for a job when no one would even speak to me for miles around."

"Oh, Rachel …" Blaze reached to gently touch her hand, the nausea thick in his throat having nothing to do with the liquor he'd consumed. "I … never knew, darlin', and I can't tell you how sorry I am …"

"Me too, Blaze." She sniffed, and he immediately handed her his napkin, which she promptly blotted to her face. "Thankyou." She expelled a heavy sigh. "So, when Uncle Clyde gave me a job, I thought I would finally be free, no longer controlled by a so-called God-fearing father. Only I ended up being controlled by something far worse. Held captive by something that darkened my soul as well as my life."

"And what's that, darlin'?" Blaze stared, suddenly deprived of all air.

She looked up then, and he had a sense that the grief in her eyes was as much for him as for herself. "Sin," she whispered, the soft touch of her fingers burning his hand along with his conscience. "I think you know as well as I do, Blaze, that when it comes to control, there's no harsher taskmaster than sin, and no darker prison for the soul. I didn't want to forgive my father, much as I imagine you don't want to forgive your parents for abandoning you like they did. But true freedom lies in a clean heart, my friend, and a clean heart lies in the hand of God, where blessings abound and light illuminates one's soul."

She gave his hand a light squeeze before settling back in her seat once again, the truth of her words breeching his long-held defenses. "I know you're hurting right now, so *please*—let me help you like Maggie helped me. Let me teach you how to let the hurt of your past go like she taught me—through forgiveness and prayer. We're slow right now, and Hattie told me to take all the time that I need, so we can drink coffee and talk all night if you want." She gave him a tender smile, the love and compassion in her face dismantling all denial. "Because I know in my heart, Blaze, that God aches to not only show you how much He cares ... but how much He longs to set you free."

A muscle convulsed in his throat while he pushed his plate away, his throat too swollen with emotion to utter a single word as he gave a silent nod.

He just did.

CHAPTER SIXTY

"IT IS NEVER TOO LATE to try what we may do." The words of Mrs. Elizabeth Cady Stanton rang through the crowded parlour of noted suffragist Dr. Clemence Lozier with all the authority and assurance of the woman herself.

But for the first time in her life, Libby wasn't in agreement with her esteemed mentor and champion of women's rights. *Never too late.* She nodded politely on the outside along with the others, but inside her heart was breaking.

Because sometimes it is.

Speaking in honor of her seventieth birthday celebration hosted by Dr. Lozier, Mrs. Stanton continued addressing some fifty women in the room, her face aglow with a passion that truly belied her seventy years. "But if our senses are not so keen as in youth, our spiritual eyes behold the unfolding of many glories we never saw before …"

Libby swallowed hard, reflecting on the "glories" she'd never truly seen before.

The joy of Finn's company.

The strength of his character.

The thrill of his affection.

Closing her eyes, she lifted her peppermint tea to her lips to savor both it and Mrs. Stanton's words, but the only thing she saw and heard was Finn's words the night she turned him away.

No, Libby, a *real* man would stand up to a woman who's

wrong."

A woman who's wrong. The tea trickled past the emotion that clotted in her throat.

Just like she was for Finn.

Wrong because she couldn't control her temper. Wrong because she couldn't trust him. And wrong because she would only continue to hurt him over and over again.

"My home is in New York, and there will be no 'later.'"

"And so, in summation, let me just say … we see visions and dream dreams of celestial harmony and happiness of the complete fulfillment of all our earth-born plans and purposes, begun in youth, in doubt and weakness, but finished at last in faith and victory."

Faith and victory.

Libby rose to applaud with Maggie and the others, but her heart constricted when she realized that she had neither. Not the strong, stalwart faith of Finn, Maggie, or Mrs. Poppy, nor the victory that very faith had brought into their lives. Victory where, unlike her, they'd chosen God's way instead of their own. Her eyelids flickered shut as reality struck hard.

Such as Finn's patience when she'd challenged his temper.

Or Maggie's willingness to forgive both her stepfather and Blaze.

Or even sweet Mrs. Poppy, always full of joy despite the early loss of her husband.

Libby slowly sank into her chair while all the others rushed to speak with Mrs. Stanton and Susan B. Anthony, two heroes in their midst who sought to better the lives of women.

But today, there was only one hero Libby wanted to speak to, one woman who had already bettered Libby's life as goddaughter and niece, and now the best friend she'd ever had.

"Oh my, wasn't that wonderful, Aunt Libby?" Maggie

reclaimed her seat with a contented sigh, reaching to give Libby's hand a quick squeeze.

Libby's lips twitched as she angled a brow, offering a smile that helped chase some of her melancholy away.

Maggie grinned. "I *mean* … wasn't that wonderful, *Libby*?" she said again, obviously having trouble dropping the formality as Libby had requested on the train.

"Yes, but I must admit"—Libby sagged back into her seat with a withering sigh far less content than Maggie's—"I'm not sure I completely agree with Mrs. Stanton that it's 'never too late to try what we may do.'"

Her gaze trailed off into a sober stare as she thought about her propensity to always choose her own will over that of those whom she loved. Her parents, Maggie's mother, Finn, Finn's family, and even Maggie at times—and she doubted that at the ripe, old age of thirty-nine, she could ever hope to change.

"Ah, but God's mercies are new every morning …" Maggie said softly, her whisper surrounding Libby like a hug, "and great is His faithfulness. Which means, Libby, it's never too late to do the right thing."

"The right thing …" Libby repeated, a quiver of despair threading her tone, "if one can actually do it. But what if they can't?" She searched Maggie's face for an answer she'd never been able to find on her own.

Maggie grasped her hand. "But that's just it, Libby—you *can* because 'you can do all things through Christ who strengthens you'!" She leaned in, her tender smile glazed with moisture. "Be not conformed to this world: but be ye transformed by the renewing of your mind, that ye may prove what is the good and acceptable and perfect will of God."

The good and acceptable and perfect will of God. Tears stung the back of Libby's eyes.

If only …

"What are you afraid of, Libby?" Maggie whispered.

A muscle convulsed in Libby's throat as she fought to keep the saltwater at bay, grateful their seats were in the back row of the room where no one could hear. She bolstered her courage with a deep swell of air, ashamed to admit that her own godchild had more faith than her.

"You know, Maggie," she whispered, "your mother was the most loving and patient friend I ever had." She patted Maggie's leg with a misty smile. "Until you." She turned to face her goddaughter, gratitude flooding that Maggie—like her mother—loved Libby just as she was.

Like Finn, she suddenly realized, and a lonely ache splintered her heart.

And God?

"Your mother would always say, 'Libby, God is just waiting for you to get out of your own way.'" A tiny smile flickered on her lips as a memory surfaced that pricked at the back of her lids. "Whenever she and I went on an outing, Alfred would drive us in the carriage, of course, and it drove your mother to distraction that I always insisted on sitting up front with her driver. 'Why can't you just sit back here and relax with me?' she would say, but somehow I just couldn't."

The smile faded on Libby's lips as her gaze lagged into a faraway stare. "Sitting up front gave me an element of control, I think, where I could see where I was going and make sure Alfred didn't run off the road. 'You'll never get where God wants you to go, Libby,' she said, 'unless you sit in the back seat.'"

Libby smiled and dashed a hand to her eyes. "But, of course, I never did." She expelled a heavy sigh while she patted Maggie's hand. "You asked what I'm afraid of, Maggie." Her smile was sad. "I'm afraid to trust men."

"What men?" Maggie stared, the innocence of her eyes comforting Libby somewhat that this sweet girl would never have to experience what Libby had.

Libby sat back, arms folded to her waist in protective

mode, feeling even now, the fury of what a powerful man had done to her. "All men," she whispered, knowing it wasn't fair, but she didn't know how to change. It was as if her heart had been stunted from the point of impact, and there was no way to heal the damage. "Including my father, Finn, and even …" She closed her eyes, not wanting to say it out loud for fear she would lose her soul.

"God?" Maggie whispered.

There was no way to stop the flow of water, and Libby shot to her feet to go, terrified someone would read her awful secret in the tears on her face.

Rising along with her, Maggie glanced at the groups of women throughout the room. "Why don't we step outside for some fresh air?" she said quietly as she grabbed her and Libby's wraps before leading her toward the front door. Carefully closing it behind them, they both put on their coats before settling into a wide, padded swing on the porch. Maggie offered a tender smile. "That way no one can see us except the One who can see the pain in our souls."

The pain in our souls. Begun years ago for Libby, courtesy of a good friend of her father's. A man of power and prestige who paved the way for her father's success.

And his daughter's demise.

Squeezing her eyes shut, Libby clutched her arms to her waist, her voice frail when she finally spoke. "He … tried to … rape me," she whispered, her shallow breathing making her light-headed as she began to tremble. The memory boiled both fear and fury within her that even now, sealed her vow that no man would ever control her again.

"What?" It was a rasp of shock, uttered from the lips of the most innocent woman Libby knew.

"Senator Lawton McAllister," Libby said, the very name causing bile to rise. "He was a friend of my father's back in New York, who came to visit after we moved to Virginia City." Her jaw hardened to rock. "But he was no friend to me at the age of fourteen."

Maggie stared with saucer eyes that glistened with tears. "He … he defiled you?"

"He tried, but something happened … so all he defiled was my soul."

"Oh, Libby!" Maggie clutched her tightly. "I am so very sorry."

Libby laid her head on Maggie's shoulder, the horrific memory somehow more tolerable with Maggie in her arms. "He was my parent's guest for the weekend and came to my room in the night. I would have screamed, but he pinned me to the bed with his body and silenced me with his hand while he …" She swallowed hard, the memory of his groping beneath her nightgown thinning her air. "I was completely helpless, Maggie, and he was in complete control, telling me if I screamed or ever told anyone, he'd make sure my father would lose his job and never find another."

"Oh, Libby." Maggie swallowed hard. "How … how did you … stop him?"

The hardest of smiles curled on Libby's lips as she remembered the stunned look on his face. "With my dinner," she said with no little pride, "all over his beard."

Maggie gasped, horror hitching in her throat. "You … threw up on him?"

"Liver and onions, with a side of creamed spinach."

Maggie put a hand to her mouth, the tears in her eyes a stark contrast to the bitter twist of Libby's mouth. "Oh, Libby … I am sick to hear this and so very sorry," she whispered, wrapping Libby in a tight hug.

"Don't be." Libby inhaled deeply, suddenly aware that the horror and hate she'd carried around all these years had lost some teeth in the telling. "I've never told this to another soul, so somehow telling you sets me free, Maggie, which means now you really and truly are my deepest and dearest friend."

Maggie clasped her hand. "I'm glad." A shadow flickered across her eyes as she quietly studied Libby for a moment. "But it's been my experience that true freedom is found in forgiveness." She paused. "Have you … forgiven him, Libby?"

"Him?" A chill pebbled Libby's skin as she sagged back in the swing, wiping the wetness on her face like she wished she could wipe the hate from her soul. "You mean 'them'?"

"*Them?*" Maggie blinked, the shock in her voice underscoring the disbelief in her eyes. "You mean there were more than one?"

A harsh laugh erupted from Libby's throat. "Oh, yes, several suitors who made it perfectly clear it wasn't marriage on their minds. Which is why I stayed as far from men as possible and why I put poor Harold off for over ten years. But it was a lesson learned the hard way, I'm afraid."

"How?" Maggie's voice was soft and low, but the thread of fear in it was loud and clear.

Libby's ribcage expanded, her exhale suddenly as wobbly as her limbs. "A man I met my first year teaching at Vassar—the brother of the Dean. His name was Peter, and he was very nice, very handsome, and I was smitten. We shared a love of literature, especially Shakespeare and Mark Twain. After a number of lovely outings, I was halfway in love, or so I thought."

Libby involuntarily shivered, more from the tainted memory than the chill of the brisk November air seasoned with wood smoke. "Several months into the relationship, Peter took me out to lunch followed by a lovely buggy ride. Only it wasn't so lovely when he brought me back to my room at Vassar," she whispered, swabbing at more tears in her eyes. "I was a corridor teacher, you see—those who lived on and oversaw a particular floor of the dormitories, but it was summer break, so most of the students were gone. Those who stayed behind were out for the afternoon, attending a play with my roommate, Amelia, and other corridor teachers, so the dormitory was fairly empty."

Libby's breathing accelerated as her eyes lagged into a glazed stare, remembering the gentle kiss Peter had given her at the door of her room. "I'd love to see your signed copy of *The Adventures of Tom Sawyer*, if I may," he'd said, wondering if he could come in for just a moment.

You see, I had boasted about the copy Mama had given me for Christmas signed by Mr. Twain himself, a former resident of Virginia City, so I was excited to share it with him. It was against the rules, of course, having a man in one's room, so I wasn't entirely comfortable with it, but one more kiss melted my resolve, and since there was no one on the floor, I said yes."

Libby squeezed her eyes shut to thwart the rise of more tears. "I should have known when he locked the door that he bore no good will, but I was so infatuated that I never clearly saw his true nature until that day—when he forced himself on me ..."

"Oh, Libby, no!" Maggie laid a gentle hand on Libby's arm, shock lacing her tone. "He didn't—"

Libby shook her head hard, spilling more saltwater, which she pushed away with a quivering hand. "No, although I have no doubt that was his intention because he muffled my mouth while he pleaded and claimed to love me, pretending to calm me down as he grappled with my clothes." Satisfaction stiffened her jaw. "But once again, Providence stepped in."

Maggie's eyes grew. "You threw up on him?"

A harsh laugh broke from Libby's lips. "No, but vomit was definitely involved. You see, Amelia came back sick, and when she unlocked the door and saw Peter on top of me, she literally lost her lunch." The hard smile returned. "All over Peter's jacket, which he'd haphazardly thrown on the floor."

Maggie smothered a gasp with her hand. "Oh, thank

God! And God bless Amelia! What happened then?"

Expelling a heavy sigh, Libby burrowed deeper into her coat to ward off a sudden chill. "He threatened both of us, warning if we mentioned the incident to anyone, we would not only lose our jobs, but my reputation would ruined when he told his brother I had lured him in."

"Oh, Libby, what a horrible man! What on earth did you do?"

Libby's mouth compressed when she recalled the control Peter had wielded over her. Not only the fear of his retaliation, but the fury of seeing him ooze his deadly charm over other women on campus while he stayed with the dean and his family that summer. "I avoided him like the devil, of course, until Providence intervened once more. A student pressed charges for a similar incident, thank God, and I never saw him on campus again."

"Thank God is right, Libby, because that's twice that God delivered you from an awful fate."

Head tipped in thought, Libby offered a sad smile. "He did, didn't He? Although the damage those two incidents alone have done to my trust in men is irreparable, I'm afraid."

Maggie paused, her smile sad as she peered into her friend's face. "Not irreparable," she whispered, "redeemable, Libby. Through both God's grace and forgiveness and yo—"

"No, I can't!" Libby was shaking her head before Maggie could even finish, her revulsion for both Peter and the senator roiling in her stomach so much, it felt like she would throw up all over again. "I just want to forget everything about them."

Maggie's next pause was even longer, causing Libby to meet her tender gaze. "The problem is"—she gently rubbed the side of Libby's arm—"you never *will* forget nor ever be truly free until you let them go."

"I *am* letting them go—" Libby began.

"From your anger and hate." Maggie's voice was barely a whisper, but the plea in her eyes spoke volumes as it seared Libby's very soul.

"I can't," Libby repeated. Her gaze dropped to her lap, her anger resident so long, it had become an iron shield for her heart, protecting her from any man who would try to control her again.

Like Finn.

"They don't deserve it, Maggie—either my forgiveness or to be let off scot-free."

"No, they don't, that's true," Maggie whispered, "but you do."

Libby glanced up. "What do you mean?"

"I mean your forgiveness sets *you* free, Libby, not them. And you're right. You can't do it, but God can. And more than can, He *wants* to, my sweet friend, because He loves you and calls you to be one of His own. And the really wonderful thing?" Her lips curved in a gentle smile. "Whomever He calls, He equips."

Libby squinted. "So, let me get this straight. You're telling me that even though I don't *feel* like I can forgive those monsters, I can with God's help?"

Maggie nodded.

"How?" Libby folded her arms, the idea of trusting God as foreign as trusting her father or Finn.

A secret smile stole over Maggie's beautiful features. "First you pray for God to help you forgive them, and then you pray for God to bless them."

"Pardon me?" Certain she'd misheard, Libby sat up with a pucker in her brow. "Did you say *pray* for them?"

"I did," Maggie said with a firm nod, "but only because God said it first. 'But I say unto you, love your enemies, bless them that curse you, do good to them that hate you, and pray for them which despitefully use you.'"

Libby gave a grunt worthy of Gert. "Whatever happened to an eye for an eye?"

Maggie grinned. "I know it sounds crazy, but it works, Libby, truly it does. Why do you think I agreed so readily to come to New York with you?"

Mouth tipping off-center, Libby offered a dry smile edged with sympathy. "Because of a certain cowboy who shall remain nameless?"

"Well, yes," Maggie said with an emphatic nod, but even so, I never would have come back to the same city The Judge lives in if I hadn't forgiven him and my roving fiancé."

"I will admit, I was surprised by that." Libby cocked her head, studying Maggie with new respect. "So, it really and truly works?"

"Yes, ma'am, it does. Even with Blaze, whom I've been praying for since we left the ranch." Her chin nudged up with resolve. "And even though it still hurts, every day it's a little bit better."

Libby sighed as her gaze wandered toward the street, thinking of Finn. "Wish I could say the same ..."

"You can, because that's the beauty of forgiveness—it purges the pain to make room for the joy." Maggie touched Libby's shoulder, drawing her gaze once more. "Finn loves you, Libby," she said softly, "and you need to forgive him. Not just to purge the pain, mind you, but to welcome the joy of a love I believe your unforgiveness has denied you far too long." She ducked her head to peek into Libby's face, the truth of her words evident by the affection in her gaze. "Because you love him, Libby, and he's your husband for better or for worse."

A muscle convulsed in Libby's throat as a groundswell of tears blurred in her eyes. "But what if I *am* the worse?" she whispered, wondering if she could ever learn to trust Finn enough to be the wife he deserved. "What if I just keep hurting him with all temper and no trust?"

Maggie skimmed a gentle palm to Libby's hair, her smile like the sun after a gray and cloudy day. "You won't, because this time you'll be doing it God's way, and when God's in control of our lives, obedience is the key that unlocks the desires of our heart. So, first you pray to forgive Finn, and then you pray to trust him, and *then* you do the hardest thing of all."

Libby tipped her head in question, face in a scrunch. "And what's that?"

A slow grin eased across Maggie's face as she gave Libby a voracious hug, finally pulling away to deliver a sassy wink. "You hop in the back seat."

CHAPTER SIXTY-ONE

"WHAT IF HE DOESN'T WANT to see me?" Libby whispered, palms damp as she and Maggie jostled in the back seat of her aunt's carriage, bumping along the cobblestone street en route to the Grand Central Depot.

Maggie smiled, pretty sure that Finn McShane would dispel that notion rather quickly once Libby surprised him by showing up for Thanksgiving with the family. "I promise you, Libby, this is going to be Finn's *most* thankful Thanksgiving." She patted Libby's hand. "And yours."

"And … yours?" Libby slid her a sideways look, the nervous chew of her lip a telling indicator she knew just how difficult this visit would be for Maggie.

Maggie managed a lame smile before she turned away to stare out the window, the smile quickly fading along with the passing cityscape. Yes, she was truly happy to see Blaze's family again, and Libby's too, but Blaze?

No, not even a little.

Because the truth was, her heartache over Blaze was still too fresh. Since they'd left Virginia City over two weeks ago, she'd prayed for him relentlessly, making definite progress in easing some of her hurt. Between her closer relationship with Libby and a nursing position she'd acquired through the good graces of Dr. Lozier, she'd made great strides at putting her heartache behind. But seeing Blaze again and spending time with him and his family would be like ripping a scab off a scar that had just begun to heal, and the very notion put a pall over her mood.

Libby's gentle touch drew her gaze back to the best friend who was now becoming as close as a sister. "It could be Blaze's best Thanksgiving too," Libby said quietly, but Maggie just offered a melancholy smile, well aware that neither she nor Blaze would be 'thankful' to see one another again. Because no matter the attraction or any commitments Blaze might be willing to make, Maggie had vowed to finally heed her mother's words no matter the cost.

"Choose a man of deep faith, Maggie, for a strand of three cords is not quickly broken."

"Maybe," Maggie said, patting Libby's hand, "but it won't be because of me."

"Why not? I truly believe he loves you, just like you insisted that Finn loves me, so maybe your absence has made him see the error of his ways."

One side of Maggie's lip crooked in a wary smile. "I doubt that. But even so, I made a vow on the train, remember? To embrace my mother's advice and only marry a man of faith, and trust me, Libby, that isn't Blaze. But hopefully his anger has waned enough that Thanksgiving won't be completely awkward."

Libby grunted and sat back in the seat. "Could be pretty awkward all the way around if Finn's decided I'm not worth the trouble." She rested her head on the back of the carriage with a heavy sigh. "He's a man of faith, but I certainly haven't been the woman of faith that he needs."

"But you are now," Maggie said with a proud smile, tucking one of Libby's stray auburn curls beneath her feathered red velvet hat. "My mother would be so proud, Libby, at how your faith has grown in a mere two weeks."

A twinkle lit Libby's eyes as she gave a playful smirk. "I do believe I heard a chorus of angels singing when I opened the Bible you lent me, led by your mother as she shouted, 'it's about time!'"

Maggie giggled, the humor helping to bolster her spirits. "You know, I think I may have heard that, too, along with applause from St. Peter and the like."

Libby's grin softened into a smile as she stroked Maggie's face with misty eyes. "And all because her daughter is a very good teacher, whom I am also blessed to call my very best friend." Her manner suddenly shifted as she stared out the carriage window, expelling another worrisome sigh. "I just hope it's not too little, too late. After all, I haven't heard a peep from him via telephone, telegram, or letter." Her mouth quirked. "And he certainly didn't follow me to New York to try and change my mind."

"I'm sure the election has kept him very busy," Maggie reassured, "especially since your mother wired that Finn had won."

"I suppose ..."

"Grand Central Depot shortly, ma'am," Alfred called from the front seat, and Maggie and Libby quickly secured their reticules. Both glanced out the window while the horse and carriage clip-clopped down 42nd Street toward the porte-cochère front entrance.

Built by railroad magnate Cornelius Vanderbilt, Grand Central Depot was truly a sight to see for both locals like Maggie and visitors alike. Maggie's chest swelled with pride as she craned her neck to admire the mammoth brick, marble, and granite structure that presided over twenty-one acres in the heart of New York City.

The carriage stopped, and Alfred hopped out to help both of the ladies down. "Miss Libby, if you and Miss Maggie will proceed to the waiting room, I will park and deliver your luggage to the appropriate baggage room, then bring your tickets prior to boarding."

"Thank you, Alfred," Libby said with a warm smile, hooking her arm with Maggie's as the two wove through the milling crowd into the massive depot.

The smell of coal and steam filled Maggie's nostrils as she

peered up at the massive arched ceiling of iron and glass, a 100-foot high canopy over the largest train shed in the country. "Which train is ours, I wonder?" Maggie asked, the two of them studying row after row of steam engines lined up on tracks beyond an ornate wrought-iron gate.

Libby sighed. "I don't know, which is why I'm so grateful that Alfred is here." Nodding toward a huge section of wooden pews, she tugged Maggie toward the waiting area, carefully threading through the bustling crowd. "Goodness, this is a madhouse, isn't it, though—*OH!"* Libby teetered on her heels when a group of six young boys darted past, one of them bumping her so hard, she landed right on her bustle in the middle of the dirty floor.

"Oh my goodness, are you all right?" Maggie bent down, hovering close while the crowd swarmed around them like so many ants, the ruffians long since disappeared into the noisy throng. She extended her hand. "Here, let me help you up—"

"OH!" Libby gasped along with Maggie when a tall gentleman hooked Libby from behind and swooped her to her feet.

Right before whirling her around and kissing her soundly on the lips.

CHAPTER SIXTY-TWO

SOMEBODY PINCH ME, PLEASE! LIBBY was too dizzy to care that Finn was kissing her senseless in the middle of a busy terminal.

"How 'bout I kiss you instead?" he whispered in her ear, and more heat blasted Libby's cheeks as well as her body. *Oh goodness—did I really say that aloud?*

Chest heaving, she pushed him away. "What on earth are you doing here?" she said, hardly able to believe Finn was holding her in his arms.

"Showing my wife how much I missed her." He slid her a wayward smile, disarming her with another kiss that stole any strength her legs may have had. She was limp as a noodle when he finally let her come up for air, his husky chuckle punctuated with a soft brush of lips to the shell of her ear. "Wasn't sure how you'd react, Libby," he said, "but something tells me I'm safe." His mouth skimmed over to hers, luring a weak moan from her throat.

"But … but …" Breathing ragged, she jerked away, her eyes round sockets of shock. "How did you know I'd be here at the depot?" she said, squinting up in confusion.

"I didn't." He pressed a kiss to her nose. "As soon as I finished up with City Hall business, I hopped on a train to come get you. Just arrived and was planning to take a hack to your aunt's when I saw you and Maggie in the crowd." Grinning, he tweaked the tall feather that swayed above her red hat. "I'd know that hat anywhere, Mrs. McShane."

"Oh, Finn!" She stroked his face, emotion stinging at the back of her eyes. "I love you and I'm so very sorry. I pray you'll consider giving me another chance."

His throaty chuckle melted into her mouth when he kissed her again, his strong arms jerking her flush for a fit that was simply …

Perfect.

"Does that answer your question, Mrs. McShane? I hope so, because I plan to take full advantage of that name as soon as humanly possible." The dangerous gleam in his eyes softened into a tender look that thickened her throat. "I aim to stake my claim, Libby, so you won't ever leave me again, so please tell me that's what you want too."

Unable to speak, she lunged to kiss him instead, hardly able to believe he was actually here.

His chuckle was warm against her mouth. "I'll take that as a yes, which is good because every mayor needs a wife."

Libby pulled back to peer up. "I am so proud of you, Finn, and *so* very sorry I almost ruined the election."

He cradled her face. "Actually, darlin', you helped the election," he said with a sheepish smile that quickly faded away, "but you ruined my life, Libby, by leaving like you did. I love you, sweetheart, and you have my word—I will never mislead you again."

Libby stood on tiptoe to sway her lips against his. "And you have my word that I will do everything in my power to rein in my temper, discussing things calmly like a dutiful wife should."

Finn paused, brows dipping low. "Is this a trick to pay me back?"

Giggling, Libby turned to nod at Maggie over her shoulder, who stood glossy-eyed, watching Finn's and her reunion with a trembling hand to her smile. "No, it's not a trick, but I do believe you owe a debt of thanks to this young lady right here who is responsible for a change of heart—and soul—for your very hot-headed wife."

Arm still firmly anchored to Libby's waist, Finn extended a hand to Maggie, his smile stretching ear to ear. "I knew I liked you, Maggie Mullaney, the moment your jaw dropped after learning Libby and I were still married."

Maggie's smile was shy. "I will admit it was a bit of a shock, Finn, but a good one."

"Like this one, I hope?" Finn asked Libby with an arch of his brow, warming her with that teasing look of affection that had always made her feel so loved.

Libby answered with a soft kiss to his cheek. "More like an answer to prayer, Mayor McShane." She wrapped her arms around his waist and squeezed hard, her head on his chest. "Oh, Finn, I have so much to tell you! Things I only just discovered in the last two weeks talking with Maggie."

He kissed the top of her head. "Well, we've got a week-long train ride in which to do it, darlin', so let's go buy you and Maggie a ticket."

"But we already have tickets," Libby said with a lift of her head, near breathless with excitement. "We were just on our way to surprise you for Thanksgiving."

"No kidding?" He grinned and lifted her up to kiss her, feet dangling as he pinned her to his waist. "So, you might say I won again, then, didn't I?" he said with a devilish glint in his eyes, teasing her like all the times he'd bested her in school, "because looks like my surprise trumped yours."

Her smile fell open as he let her down. "Finn McShane, you are—"

He silenced her with another hungry kiss, taming the fire of her temper with the fire of his kiss as only he could."

"Ahem."

Both Libby and Finn whirled to blink at Alfred, who stood not two feet away, cheeks pink and tickets in hand. "I beg your pardon, Miss Libby, but your luggage is aboard the 2:15 to Reno, and this is your and Miss Maggie's ticket for your sleeping car."

"Thank you, my good man," Finn said with a snatch of the ticket, sliding Libby a wink that toasted her cheeks. "We'll need to hurry, then, if we're going to secure a second sleeping car for me and my wife."

"Oh, no, please," Maggie said with a step back, offering a tentative smile. "You take our ticket, Finn, for you and Libby, and I'll just stay here in New York for Thanksgiving with Libby's aunt and her family."

"Oh, no you don't." Libby whirled around, determined that Maggie would not stay behind. She clasped her friend's hands in hers. "You're coming with us, Maggie, and I won't take no for answer."

Finn gave Libby's neck a playful pinch. "I'd trust her on that one, Maggie."

Maggie sighed. "But I was only going in the first place to keep Libby company," she explained with a pleading slope of brows, "but now she doesn't need me if you take her home, Finn."

"*Except* ..." Finn buttoned Maggie with that no-nonsense gaze Libby had bucked many a time. "I was given express orders to bring you *both* home for Thanksgiving, Miss Mullaney, and I aim to do just that."

"By whom?" Maggie wanted to know, arms in a stubborn fold she'd learned from Libby, no doubt.

Finn's chin nudged up, obviously more than experienced in dealing with obstinate women. "The entire family, if you must know, from Sheridan threatening to toss horseshoes"—he lowered his head to pin her with a potent gaze—"and I don't mean in a game, to Shaylee making noises about bringing Annabelle to the table if you don't come."

Libby let out a squeal at the very thought, hurrying to loop an arm around Maggie's waist. "Come on, Maggie—the family misses you, and I will, too, if you're not there."

"I don't know," Maggie hedged, grating her bottom lip as she looked up at Finn. "Blaze was pretty angry when I left, so I don't think it's a good thing for either of us to see the other again, at least not right now." Her bodice rose with a heavy sigh as she gave Libby a pitiful look out of the corner of her eyes. "Maybe Christmas?"

"Nope." Slacking a hip, Finn folded his arms, smile calm, but jaw tight. "Family's expecting both of you for Thanksgiving, Maggie, and I don't plan to disappoint. Besides, Blaze is just fine. In fact, you might say he's a new man, and he wants you to come."

Maggie's smile slid off-center as she tipped her head to give Finn a patient look. "Thanks for trying to make me feel better, Finn, but I'm pretty sure he didn't say that."

"No?" Finn cocked a brow and hooked his thumbs onto his front pockets. "Well, don't take my word for it, darlin'," he said with a lazy grin. He shot her a wink before his gaze veered over her shoulder with a definite nod. "Ask *him*."

CHAPTER SIXTY-THREE

MAGGIE FROZE TO THE FLOOR, her body a block of ice.

"Wait—you're here too?" Libby released Maggie to throw her arms around Blaze's neck, giving him a squealy hug before pulling him to face Maggie. "Oh my goodness, Maggie, isn't this wonderful?"

Maggie had stopped breathing, so she wasn't exactly sure.

"Hi, Maggie," he said in that husky drawl that always melted her like a block of ice on a cook-iron stove. "It's good to see you."

Good? Maybe, if she hadn't lost her words the same time she lost her air when he leaned in to give her a hug.

"You look good," he said quietly, and she supposed he did too, or at least his boots did, given the fact that's where her gaze was glued.

Finn cleared his throat. "Blaze, Maggie ... Libby and I are going to the ticket office to book two more sleeping cars if we can, so you two go to the waiting room and don't move."

Don't move? No problem!

"You know, Maggie," Blaze said softly, "you're going to have to look at me sometime because we need to talk, darlin'."

"No, I don't," she said with a squeeze of lashes, refusing to lose two weeks of perfectly good distance just to be undone by a pair of blue eyes. "You can talk just fine while

I stare at your shoes."

His low chuckle did as much damage as the gentle twine of his fingers as he tugged her toward the waiting area. "Well, as polished as my new boots are, I think you need to see my face when I tell you how sorry I am."

She tried to pull free from his hold while he led her to an empty spot at the end of a wooden pew, wondering if the need to throttle ruled out all the forgiving she'd done. "Oh, you're sorry all right, cowboy," she said with a rare pout in her tone, "one of the sorriest men I know."

Thumping down on the bench with a firm fold of arms, she scooted several inches away when he reached for her hand. "What do you want, Blaze?" She whirled to face him with fire in her eyes, completely shocked at all the hurt she thought had gone away. "Besides Chanel and a good time?"

"I want you," he whispered, locking her hand in his to keep her from moving when he inched closer. "I want your forgiveness, Maggie, I want your friendship, and I especially want your love." He cupped a gentle palm to her face, nudging her gaze to his. "But more than anything else, Miss Mullaney, I want a marriage with you that will last a lifetime."

Tender blue eyes swam before her as water obstructed her gaze, grief lancing her heart with the words she had once longed to hear.

"Marry me," he said with a gentle trace of his thumb to her lips, "and I promise to keep you well-stocked in lots of kisses, butterscotch, and love."

"Oh, Blaze …" Tears slipped down her cheeks as she stared at the cocky cowboy she had never wanted to love, knowing he was everything she'd ever wanted …

Except the one thing she needed most.

"Choose a man of deep faith, Maggie, for a strand of three cords is not quickly broken."

"I can't …" Her whisper was laced with pain as she

slowly shook her head.

He stilled her with gentle hands that cradled her face, the intensity she saw in his eyes bleeding into his voice. "Do you love me, Maggie?"

A single tear glazed her cheek as she memorized every line of his hard-sculpted face, every blink of blue eyes that haunted. "You know I do, Blaze, but—"

"Do you want me?" His words were both gentle and gruff, followed by a kiss so achingly tender, it almost felt like a prayer. "Because I want you more than I've ever wanted anything in my life. And I know you want me, too, because every touch of your lips tells me you do."

"Blaze—"

Reaching into his pocket, he slid onto one knee with a ring in his hand. "Any day of your choosing, darlin', and you'll turn the sorriest of cowboys into one of the most blessed."

"Oh, Blaze, how I wish that I could ..." The diamond glimmered along with the tears in her eyes as she started to shake her head and then stopped. "Wait—did you say"—a gulp bobbed in her throat—*"'blessed'??"*

A slow grin eased across his lips as he gave her a wink. "Of course, I'm no expert, but Uncle Finn assures me that's the correct term for a man who's made his peace with God."

Maggie's heart stopped cold before it took off in a wild sprint. "You did?"

"I did," he said, tilting in to nuzzle her throat before breathing a warm chuckle deep in her ear. "Does that earn me a yes?"

She slapped two shaky palms to his chest, eyes wide and air shallow. "How? When? I want facts, Blaze Donovan, and I want them now!"

Chuckling, he shifted to a squat, the ring dangling over his knees. "Pure, unadulterated thievery, Miss Mullaney, of the most insidious kind."

"What?" Maggie squinted, waiting for him to continue.

The light in his eyes dimmed considerably. "You see, it would seem that when a certain 'respectable' nurse left town, she took my heart with her. And not just my heart, mind you—my peace, my joy"—a grunt broke from his lips—"my sobriety."

Maggie's eyes circled wide as she put a hand to her chest. "You started *drinking?*"

His lips twisted. "'Drownin' might be a better term. Two of the worst weeks of my life, Maggie, that I want to blot out forever." He paused as he searched her face with a look of wonder that fluttered her stomach. "All except one night, that is, when Dash hauled my sorry soul over to Hattie's Café to sober me up in more ways than one. He bought me food, coffee, and a full serving of faith, personally delivered by none other than Rachel, who," he said with a deep inhale, expelling it in one long, wavering sigh, "literally saved my sorry soul from a fate worse than death." His Adam's apple hitched as he skimmed his thumb down the curve of her jaw. "A life without you, Maggie," he whispered, "and a life without God."

Maggie caught her breath, the sound of it as telling as the moisture that burned hot in her eyes.

"I know," Blaze said while he scuffed the back of his neck with a sheepish smile. "Believe me, I was just as dumbfounded as you, that anything could get through this hard head of mine, in addition to a heart of stone as cold as the Sierras."

His rugged features softened as he bowed his head, voice laden with a humility she'd never heard in him before. "All Rachel did was tell me the same things you told her, the same things you told me, but it took two weeks at the bottom of a bottle, Maggie"—he peered up beneath lowered lids, gaze repentant as he took her hand—"two weeks aching over the only woman who has stirred me heart and soul, for me to finally 'hear' the truth of both your words and Uncle Finn's."

He lifted her hand to his lips, eyes drifting closed as he placed a soft kiss to her palm before meeting her gaze once again. "So you see, Maggie, I'm a man of faith now," he said with a faint smile, the stark love in his eyes wringing more tears from her own, "and it's all because of you."

A man of faith! Saltwater brimming, Maggie put a trembling hand to her mouth, a sob breaking free that quickly bubbled into a giggle. "Oh, Blaze," she whispered, snatching the ring with a squeal before she launched into his arms to land them both on the floor, "why didn't you just say so?"

EPILOGUE

"I CALL THE BIG END OF the wishbone!" Sheridan shrieked, acting more like seven than seventeen as she and Shaylee raced into the O'Shea's brand-new dining room when Gert announced dinner.

Almost twice as large as Uncle Finn's supper room, the O'Shea's elegant dining room was an "extravagance" Aiden claimed to need for his growing family. The statement had promptly burnished his daughter's cheeks when he gave her and Finn a telling wink, but Blaze couldn't agree more. Taking Maggie's hand, he grinned as he ushered her to their Thanksgiving dinner behind Uncle Finn, Aunt Libby, and the O'Shea's, his heart full over the gift of faith and family. Because once he and Maggie got married the day after Christmas, he hoped to add a few dinner plates to the table as well.

"Hey, why do you get the big end of the wishbone?" Shaylee asked, freckles in a squint as she plopped into an upholstered, high-backed chair at a linen-clad table set with crystal and china. A fire crackled in a blazing hearth while snowflakes drifted outside a huge bay window, giving the room a cozy air despite its large size.

"Because Aunt Libby and Maggie don't need any more luck, but *I* do," Sheridan said with a smile aimed in Jake's direction, who'd been smart enough to take a seat on the other side of the table. Dash and he had laughed and ribbed Jake without mercy over Sheridan's obvious crush since she was six, but suddenly with their little sister growing up, it wasn't so funny anymore. At least not to Jake, who now took his suppers mostly in the dining hall rather than dinners with the family like he used to.

It hadn't been too long ago that Sheridan had worn pigtails instead of a shapely calico dress, a revolting development that made both her brothers—*and Jake*—more than a little uncomfortable. Blaze seated Maggie with a quick squeeze of her shoulder, thankful his little sisters now had two strong females to help them be the women they needed to be. His mouth crooked into a grateful smile.

Respectable.

"As far as luck," Aiden said with a wink at Libby, "I suspect Finn could do with a bit of that too." He seated Maeve, then beamed while taking his place at the head of the table, a new affability spurred on, no doubt, by his daughter's "official" wedding on Saturday and the occupation of his new home.

"Papa!" Feigning shock, Libby delivered a mock scowl that Uncle Finn quickly waylaid with a kiss, promptly earning a groan from Shaylee that seemed to trail on forever.

"Uncle Finn, *stop!*" the scamp said with both hands over her eyes, "I'm too young to see all this sparkin' going on."

"Get used to it, Shay," Blaze said with a tweak of her pigtail before he buried a kiss in Maggie's neck. Both girls' squeals punctuated the laughter circling the table as Gert and Angus delivered bowls mounded with mashed potatoes and cornbread dressing.

Sheridan released a long, lovesick sigh. "I can't wait to be kissed," she said with a dreamy look, absently spooning mashed potatoes onto her plate while Gert and Angus dispensed yet more steaming bowls of food.

"Yes, you *can,"* Uncle Finn, Dash, and Blaze said in unison, the warning in their tones as blatant as the ruddy rash crawling up the back of Jake's neck.

Uncle Finn gave her the eye tempered with a hint of a smile. "As well as waiting for prayer, young lady, before you start digging in."

"Make room for the bird," Gert announced in a robust voice, holding the door while Angus toted a golden-brown turkey and placed it on the table. "Both of 'em," she muttered with a smirk at Angus while slapping the carving knife down next to Aiden's plate.

Gingerly moving the knife away from where Gert stood in the French uniform he forced her to wear, Aiden nodded to two empty chairs at the far end of the table. "Gert and Angus, if everything's on the table, you're welcome to take your seats while our former host says grace." He glanced up at Finn with a smile. "Mr. McShane, will you do me the honor of blessing this mouthwatering feast?"

"With pleasure, sir," Finn said, bowing his head while the others followed suit, his reverent prayer of thanksgiving to God a reflection of Blaze's own heart. His uncle's husky voice filled the room with thanksgiving while gratitude filled Blaze's soul. He reached for Maggie's hand and emotion thickened the walls of his throat at how much God had changed his life for the better. Unable to resist a sideways peek at his fiancée, he felt the sting of moisture over just how close he'd come to missing out on the blessings of God.

The blessings of God.

Maggie.

And a Savior who had redeemed his life from the pit.

When Finn finished his prayer, Aiden stood and picked up fork and knife, rendering a happy sigh of contentment Blaze had never heard out of the man before. "Maeve," he said to his wife with a smile as bright as the flames flickering in the silver candlesticks, "while I carve this turkey, I think we should go around the table and toast to something for which we are most grateful." He bent to press a kiss to her cheek. "You can start us off, darling, and since the people we love are a given, let's pick something else, shall we?" Positioning the knife at the ridge of the breastbone, he gave everyone a wink. "But only one thing, so choose wisely, and make it fun."

Maeve leaned forward with a crease in her brow. "Aiden, have you been into the sherry again?"

His laughter boomed through the room as he sliced through the turkey. "No, my dear, this is Thanksgiving, so by thunder, we're going to give thanks!"

"I couldn't agree more," Blaze said, looping his arm around Maggie.

"Well, all right, then." Maeve lifted her glass to Finn. "I am eternally grateful for good neighbors who aren't afraid of fire." She tipped her head to give her daughter a tender look before giving Finn a rare wink, "In *any* form."

"Mo-ther!" Libby's smile remained intact despite the drop of her jaw.

Maeve smiled. "Now, darling, fire can be a good thing—just look what it did for us!"

"I'll drink to that," Finn said with a lift of his water glass, tugging Libby close. "And I should know. All right, Shay, you're up."

Squinting in thought, Shay peered around the table with an impish grin before snatching a piece of turkey from Aiden's platter. "Turkey!" she shouted, flipping the piece into her mouth.

"Oh, thank goodness!" Maggie said with an exaggerated shiver, grinning as she bumped Shaylee's shoulder. "I thought for sure you'd say Annabelle."

"Nope." Shaylee's brown eyes sparkled with mischief as she filched another piece of turkey. "Because Annabelle likes turkey too." Tossing most of the meat in her mouth, she tucked a remaining shred into the bib pocket of her overalls, looking inside with a sly grin. "Don't you, girl?"

Maggie vaulted into Blaze's lap with a squeal, arms pasted tightly to his neck while everyone's laughter ricocheted off the walls. Chuckling, he deposited a kiss to her head as he gave Shaylee a wink. "Much as I prefer this seating for Thanksgiving dinner, darlin', I'm a little worried I may drop gravy on your dress."

Libby shot Maggie a grin as she reached to swipe a piece of turkey of her own. "Goodness, Maggie, I haven't seen you jump that high since Annabelle had babies in the house! But I think you can take your seat now because Shay doesn't really have Annabelle in her pocket, do you, Shay?"

"Naw," the little stinker said with a grin, "I just like to watch Maggie jump." Scooting her chair back, she made a great show of peering under the table. "Annabelle prefers the floor."

It was Libby's turn to squeal as she sprang out of her chair like a horseshoe gone off course, hand to her chest while she scoured beneath the table.

"Ahem." Arching a brow at his youngest niece, Finn reached for Libby's hand with a patient smile. "Libs, Annabelle's been left at home, in a cage in the barn, I might add, where she's banned since your mother found her in the piano two weeks ago and fainted dead out."

A shudder rippled through Maeve as she grabbed Aiden's hand. "Goodness, it was enough to ruin music forever."

"*And* up our move-in date by a full week," Aiden said with a chuckle as he sawed off a drumstick.

Finn's smile took a slant as he tugged Libby back into her chair. "Although I have to admit, darlin', that I am somewhat offended you chose to bolt away rather than jumping in my lap like Maggie did with Blaze."

Scrambling from Blaze's lap to return to her chair, Maggie gave Shaylee a playful pinch of her neck while she huffed out a sigh of relief. "Although I am utterly and completely grateful for all bans on spiders," she began with a wink at Shaylee, "what I'm most grateful for"—she slid Blaze a shy smile that put a swell in his chest—"is a dear friend named Rachel."

"I'll second that," Dash said, leaning in to raise his drink with a grateful smile at Maggie, "and to the nurse who changed her life, for whom *I* am most grateful."

Blaze skimmed a gentle thumb along the curve of Maggie's jaw. "I'd say that's one of the givens around this table tonight," he said softly. "But"—he hoisted his glass of sarsaparilla with a wayward gleam in his eyes—"I also am grateful for butterscotch kisses." He laughed when Maggie turned eight shades of red.

"Blaze, you're embarrassing me," she whispered as she batted him away.

Sheridan expelled a sigh of longing while she lifted her lemonade. "Goodness, he's *inspiring* me, Maggie, which is why the one thing I'm most grateful for is"—her teeth tugged at the edge of her smile—"I turn eighteen next month, so I'll finally be all grown up."

"Sorry, Half-Pint," Jake said from across the table, his patient smile dusting Sheridan's cheeks with a pretty blush, "but it takes more than a birthday to do that."

"I know." Sheridan's chin edged up with the rare hint of the rebel. "Like a man who's willing to notice."

Finn gave a loud clear of his throat as he leaned in to peer at Angus and Gert at the end of the table. "I'm guessing you two might be toasting to having your kitchens back?"

"Oh, you betcha," Angus said, sliding Gert a humorous wink. "That and winnin' at poker."

"Ha!" Gert stuck her nose in the air while she hoisted her drink, a flicker of a smile twitching on her lips. "Gotta win more than once in a blue moon to be grateful, old-timer, so *I'm* grateful you don't."

Everyone laughed as Finn began loading Aiden's turkey on plates and passing them around. "Jake my boy, you're next, so give it your best shot, son."

Jake fisted his mug of sarsaparilla up high, flashing a grin at Angus at the end of the table. "Right now, I'd have to say

I'm grateful ol' Angus is back bunkin' in the house instead of the cot beside me. Because take my word for it, ladies and gentlemen, his food smells a whole lot better than his feet."

Whoops and chuckles sounded as all eyes focused on Finn. He slapped Jake on the back, resting one arm over Jake's shoulder while he scooped Libby close with the other. "I'd like to say that the one thing I am most grateful for tonight is the strength and joy of family. Be it nieces and nephews, cooks, adopted hands, or in-laws, or even two sassy suffragists who have only served to make us better."

Lifting his glass of water in the air, Finn managed a smile despite the sheen of emotion Blaze saw in his eyes as he took time to scan every face in the room. "You," he said with a hint of hoarseness, "are the real silver lining of this ranch, enriching me with a true treasure like no other."

"Oh, Finn!" Libby threw her arms around him while everyone shouted their agreement with applause and loud thumps on the table. "I couldn't agree more, darling." She kissed his cheek, then quickly reached for the bowl of potatoes to hand it over to her father. "And I'm most grateful Papa is finally done carving the turkey, because I'm pretty sure all of us are starving."

"Hear, hear!" Aiden said in a boisterous tone, plopping an ample portion of potatoes on his plate before passing them on. "I'll certainly agree to that."

Blaze bumped his shoulder to Maggie's, leaning close to whisper in her ear. "And you said love didn't have a silver lining, Miss Mullaney, but it looks to me like you were dead wrong."

"Oh, I don't think so." Maggie plucked a roll and handed the basket over to Blaze with a secret smile. "Because from where I'm sitting, Mr. Donovan," she said with a sweet brush of her lips that shifted his appetite well beyond turkey, "it's golden."

A NOTE TO MY READERS

THANK YOU SO VERY MUCH for reading Maggie and Blaze's story, along with the continuation of Libby and Finn's—I hope you enjoyed reading it as much as I enjoyed writing it!

I promise you that Finn and Libby will stay married this time, but no guarantees that Libby won't give Finn the ride of his life as a suffragist wife. Nor that Jake will escape Sheridan's attentions in the next book, *Love's Silver Bullet.*

For those of you who love paperback books, I'm happy to say you can now purchase *For Love of Liberty* in paperback form, along with *Love's Silver Lining.*

Thank you again for reading my books!

Hugs!

Julie

ABOUT THE AUTHOR

JULIE LESSMAN IS AN AWARD-WINNING author whose tagline of "Passion with a Purpose" underscores her intense passion for both God and romance. A lover of all things Irish, she enjoys writing close-knit Irish family sagas that evolve into 3-D love stories: the hero, the heroine, and the God that brings them together.

Author of The Daughters of Boston, Winds of Change, and Heart of San Francisco series, Julie Lessman was named American Christian Fiction Writers 2009 Debut Author of the Year and has garnered 18 Romance Writers of America and other awards. Voted #1 Romance Author of the year in *Family Fiction* magazine's 2012 and 2011 Readers' Choice Awards, Julie was also named on *Booklist*'s 2010 Top 10 Inspirational Fiction and Borders Best Fiction list.

Julie's first contemporary novel, *Isle of Hope,* was voted on *Family Fiction* magazine's "Top Fifteen Novels of 2015" list, and her historical novel, *Surprised by Love,* appeared on *Family Fiction* magazine's list of "Top Ten Novels of 2014." Her independent novel *A Light in the Window* is an International Digital Awards winner, a 2013 Readers' Crown Award winner, and a 2013 Book Buyers Best Award winner. Julie has also written a self-help workbook for writers entitled *Romance-ology 101: Writing Romantic Tension for the Sweet and Inspirational Markets.* You can contact Julie through her website and read excerpts from each of her books at **www.julielessman.com.**

OTHER BOOKS BY JULIE LESSMAN

FOLLOWING ARE JULIE'S NOVELS, NOVELLAS, and a writer's workbook. All are available in both e-book and paperback except for the novellas, which are available in e-book only.

The Daughters of Boston Series
Book 1: *A Passion Most Pure*
Book 2: *A Passion Redeemed*
Book 3: *A Passion Denied*

The Winds of Change Series
Book 1: *A Hope Undaunted*
Book 2: *A Heart Revealed*
Book 3: *A Love Surrendered*

Prequel to The Daughters of Boston and Winds of Change Series
A Light in the Window: An Irish Love Story

O'Connor Christmas Novellas
A Whisper of Hope
(formerly part of *Hope for the Holidays* anthology)

The Best Gift of All
(formerly part of *Home for Christmas* anthology)

The Heart of San Francisco Series

Book 1: *Love at Any Cost*
Book 2: *Dare to Love Again*
Book 3: *Surprised by Love*
Blake McClare Novella: *Grace Like Rain*
(formerly part of *With This Kiss* anthology)

Isle of Hope Series

Prequel Novella (*FREE DOWNLOAD!*): *A Glimmer of Hope*
Book 1: *Isle of Hope—Unfailing Love*
Book 2: *Love Everlasting*
Book 3: *His Steadfast Love*

Silver Lining Ranch Series

Prequel Novel: *For Love of Liberty*
Book 1: Love's Silver Lining
Book 2: Love's Silver Bullet
(Coming in 2019)

Other Novellas

The Gift of Grace (formerly part of *Cowboy Christmas Homecoming* anthology)

Romance-ology 101 Writer's Workbook

Romance-ology 101: Writing Romantic Tension for the Inspirational and Sweet Markets

Made in the USA
Monee, IL
28 May 2024